Aris & Phillips His

ÂNGELA DE AZEVEDO

El muerto disimulado

Presumed Dead

Edition by **Valerie Hegstrom**

Translation by **Catherine Larson**

Critical Introduction and Notes by

Valerie Hegstrom and **Catherine Larson**

LIVERPOOL UNIVERSITY PRESS

First published 2018 by
Liverpool University Press
4 Cambridge Street
Liverpool
L69 7ZU

www.liverpooluniversitypress.co.uk

Copyright © 2018 Valerie Hegstrom and Catherine Larson

The right of Valerie Hegstrom and Catherine Larson to be identified as the authors of this book has been asserted by them in accordance with the Copyright, Designs and Patents Act 1988.

All rights reserved. No part of this book may be reproduced, stored in a retrieval system, or transmitted, in any form or by any means, electronic, mechanical, photocopying, recording, or otherwise, without the prior written permission of the publisher.

British Library Cataloguing-in-Publication data
A British Library CIP record is available

ISBN 978-1-78694-071-1 cased
ISBN 978-1-78694-072-8 paperback

Typeset by Tara Evans
Printed and bound in Poland by BooksFactory.co.uk

Cover image: Bartolomé Esteban Murillo, *Two Women at a Window*, courtesy of the National Gallery of Art, Washington, DC. Used by permission.

For Rian: fiercely unique and amazing

For Dale: "... polvo enamorado"

CONTENTS

Acknowledgments vii

Introduction 1

Theater in Early Modern Spain 1

Women Writing Plays in Spanish in the Early Modern Period 3

Azevedo: Her Life, Times, and Works 10

El muerto disimulado / Presumed Dead 23

Honor, Virginity, and Constancy 23

Characters – An Ensemble Cast 25

Shifting Identities and the Tension between Appearance and Reality 28

Structure of the Play: *Cuadros* 38

Staging *El muerto disimulado / Presumed Dead* 40

Settings and Stage Sets 41

Movement on Stage 42

Stage Properties 44

Contemporary Performances 46

El muerto disimulado in Performance 46

Presumed Dead in Performance 51

Metrical Scheme 57

Editor's Note 62

Translator's Note 71

Bibliography 79

El muerto disimulado / Presumed Dead 89

Jornada Primera / Act 1 92

Jornada Segunda / Act 2 166

Jornada Tercera / Act 3 238

ACKNOWLEDGMENTS

Our sincere thanks to those who have encouraged us in the creation of this edition and translation and who have offered suggestions and support. Numbering among that group are Clancy Clements, Cristina Cowley, Charles Ganelin, Andrea Warren Hamos, Leah Hamos, Patty Klingenberg, James Krause, Donald R. Larson, Consuelo López-Morillas, Christopher Lund, Rex P. Nielson, David Pasto, Darlene Sadlier, Jeffrey Turley, Jonathan Wade, Frederick G. Williams, and Amy R. Williamsen. Additionally, we express gratitude to our mentor, William R. Blue, who encouraged our love for *Comedia* studies.

We also acknowledge the support of our home departments of Spanish and Portuguese at Indiana University and Brigham Young University, especially the BYU College of Humanities, which supported research grants that allowed Valerie to work with source documents before they were available online. In addition, we are grateful for our many enthusiastic students at Brigham Young, Indiana, and the University of New Mexico, who participated actively in courses focused on performance and women's writing, including Ângela de Azevedo's play. We note in particular the BYU Spanish Golden Age Theater project students who staged *El muerto disimulado* in the spring of 2004 and brought the play to life for the first time, at least since the early modern period. Special thanks go to Jason Yancey, the show's director, and to the talented cast and crew members.

We are especially grateful to the WSC Avant Bard performing arts organization of Arlington, Virginia, which has staged *Presumed Dead*, as well as our previous co-created work, *Friendship Betrayed*, and which, in the process, has taught us a great deal about the theater. We appreciate in particular the work of W. Thompson Prewitt, Avant Bard's artistic and executive director; Maegan Clearwood, director of audience engagement; and Kari Ginsberg, who directed both well-received productions.

We further express our gratutude to the National Gallery of Art, Washington, DC, for permission to use a reproduction of Murillo's *Two Women at a Window* as the book's cover image.

Finally, this project could not have been completed without the support of our families, who cheerfully took the time we spent in stride, and sometimes texted encouraging notes, photos, and videos. To Rian, Dale, Joseph, William, Jesse, Sam, Kris, Amelia, Gabriel, Thomas, JJ, and Baeleon: *¡Mil gracias!*

INTRODUCTION

Theater in Early Modern Spain

Early modern (or Golden Age) theater played a fundamental role in the culture of the Spanish Empire during the sixteenth and seventeenth centuries. Drama had long been a means of teaching the faith in the Catholic Church, and as secular theater began to grow, street theater and staged imitations of classical texts became so popular that in the 1580s, the *corrales de comedias* (public playhouses) emerged as places where virtually all members of society could enjoy performances. Indeed, although religious and court drama continued throughout the period, the rise of a national theater in the *corrales* represented a new direction that would define Spanish theater for years to come. The *corrales* were outdoor theaters constructed in the patios between houses. Women spectators were segregated in the back, wealthier viewers of both genders watched from the balconies of nearby homes, men sometimes sat on benches on the sides, and rowdy male *mosqueteros* (groundlings) stood in front of the raised platform stage, often expressing their opinions with loud comments or food lobbed at the actors. Theater companies were led by mostly male, but occasionally female, *autores de comedias* (stage managers/producers/directors), and the actors performed in the newly constructed playhouses in cities like Madrid, Seville, or Valencia, or took their plays on the road. Unlike the situation existing in the theaters of England at the time, and despite the attacks of the moralists who considered the practice immoral, Spanish women played female roles on stage.

As the seventeenth century dawned, one popular dramatist, Lope de Vega, wrote a treatise, the 1609 *Arte nuevo de escribir comedias* (*New Art of Writing Plays*), which described what he had been practicing for years in the *corrales* and which influenced the dramatic poets of that century. Lope detailed the characteristics of the kind of play that had brought him so much fame, the *Comedia*; he insisted that the theater should be targeted at the *vulgo* (masses), and that rather than having playwrights follow the precepts of classical dramatists, the goal should be to entertain all members of society instead of the erudite few. The *Arte nuevo* described the types of characters one might expect to see: noble *galanes* and *damas* (leading men and ladies), an old man (often a father), comic servants or *graciosos*, and depending on the kind of play, kings, queens, and other types. The characters' language and costumes reflected their place in society. The *Comedia* was written in verse, in three acts of approximately 1000 lines per act, each with a variety of forms that matched their function in the play (*romances* or ballads, for example, were often used to narrate, while sonnets might call attention to key moments). When staged, the plays often began with an introductory playlet or prologue, the *loa*, praising benefactors, and the entire theatrical spectacle included dances or farces between the *jornadas* or acts and a final celebration or *fin de fiesta* at the end. The *comedias* covered topics that might be of interest to the masses, such as history, mythology, saints' lives, religion, etc. Popular sub-categories included the *comedias de capa y espada* and *comedias de enredo*, in which plot twists and intrigues ruled, but it has often been stated that the *Comedia* almost always treats at least one of the following themes: faith, love, and honor. Early modern Spanish plays were most often comedies or tragicomedies, and the type of tragedy that was then popular in Elizabethan England did not develop in Spain. Nonetheless, Spain had its own version of tragedy in the sub-genre of the honor plays, which foregrounded how even the suspicion of impurity or dishonor on the part of a man's wife or sister, for whom he was responsible, could lead not only to her banishment to a convent, but to her murder. Whatever the type, plays frequently ended with marriage (or at least the promise of marriage) by most characters, as well as an appeal to the illustrious senate – the audience – for its applause.

Lope, an astonishingly prolific playwright, figuratively set the stage for what would follow in the remainder of the seventeenth century. The dramatic poet who succeeded him as court dramatist (and thereby received the patronage of royals such as Felipe IV and his wife, Isabel de Borbón) was Pedro Calderón de la Barca. The two schools of Golden Age drama were that of Lope and his followers, which included Tirso de Molina, and that of Calderón and those who imitated his more polished, baroque style. And as the century progressed, *comedias* were often performed in the royal palace before moving on to the *corrales*. Palace theater was spectacular, as the small artificial lake in the middle of what is now Madrid's Retiro Park became the scene of a theatrical naval battle, or set designers brought in from Italy created lavish productions. The tradition of religious theater also remained strong, and *autos sacramentales* (Eucharistic plays), performed on carts in the streets, celebrated Corpus Christi. Brief dramatic texts, such as one-act *entremeses* or farces, continued to be written and performed. Yet it is fair to state that the end of the seventeenth century did not produce as many great dramatists as at its beginning, and royal deaths, which led to the closing of the theaters for long periods of mourning, as well as ongoing concerns about the moral appropriateness of the theater, meant that ultimately Spain's prominence as a leader in world theater would begin to fade. Still, the traditions of early modern drama had played an extremely significant role in Spain for more than 100 years, and those traditions had also traveled to other parts of the Spanish Empire around the globe, as well as to countries such as France and to its playwrights, including Molière. The drama and theater of the Golden Age well deserved the name that has characterized them for centuries.

Women Writing Plays in Spanish in the Early Modern Period

Sometime during the Spanish theater's early modern period, almost certainly in the seventeenth century, Ângela de Azevedo wrote her play *El muerto disimulado*. Although the play is set in Lisbon, Azevedo wrote it in Spanish and the text may have been printed in Spain.[1] It appeared as a *comedia suelta*,[2] a pamphlet version of the play (similar to a quarto) produced cheaply to be sold inexpensively to even the most humble of theater fans. The National Library in Madrid and the British Library in London own copies of the pamphlet, and the Berlin State Library had a copy that went missing during World War II. For this edition of the play, the copy owned by the Spanish library served as the source text. Although the *suelta* was not the most auspicious format that Azevedo's play might have enjoyed, it was unusual that a play written by a woman in that time and place made it into print.[3]

1 Damião de Frois Perim, *Theatro Heroino: Abecedario historico, e catálogo das mulheres illustres em armas, letras, accoens heroicas, e artes liberaes* (Lisbon: Academia Real, 1740), vol. 2, p. 493. Damião de Frois Perim is the pseudonym of Frei João de São Pedro. Spelling and accentuation have shifted over the centuries; in the past, Frei João's pseudonym was sometimes spelled Damiaõ de Froes Perym. For the sake of consistency and to help guide readers to pertinent information, we have chosen to modernize spellings of proper names and the titles of unpublished plays both in Portuguese and Spanish throughout our introduction and bibliography. We have maintained original spelling, accent marks, and punctuation in titles of cited books and quoted material.

2 The title printed on the first page of the *suelta* reads, 'COMEDIA / FAMOSA, / EL MVERTO DISSIMVLADO / *Por Doña Angela de Azeuedo.*'

3 The Spanish language plays of only four other women playwrights found their way into print in the seventeenth century: Feliciana Enríquez de Guzmán, Ana Caro, Sor Juana Inés de la Cruz, and Joana Teodora de Sousa. Nearly two dozen other sixteenth- and seventeenth-century women playwrights never published their plays, which remained in manuscript until the twentieth century or have been lost.

Azevedo forms part of a relatively small but significant group of female playwrights on the Iberian Peninsula. Over the past quarter century, several of these women writers have received critical attention, while others have remained virtually unknown. In the following pages, we provide a brief overview of the names and accomplishments of the early modern women who wrote for the stage in Spain and its empire. A substantial number of these dramatists were Portuguese writers who composed their plays in Spanish. By the time Azevedo wrote her *comedias*, the success of Lope de Vega's theatrical formula had established Spanish as the language of the theater in both nations. But even decades before Lope de Vega was born, strong ties existed between the Portuguese and Spanish courts, and Gil Vicente (*c.* 1465–*c.* 1536), the 'Father of Portuguese drama', composed some of his plays in Portuguese and others in Spanish. Intriguingly, several seventeenth- and eighteenth-century writers list Vicente's daughter Paula as the author of various plays in manuscript, and suggest that she helped her father compose his works.[4]

Another factor that influenced the use of Spanish by Portuguese writers resulted from issues of succession in Portugal. The first was the ill-fated 'Battle of the Three Kings' (Battle of Alcácer Quibir), fought in northern Morocco on August 4, 1578, in which the young and childless Portuguese king Sebastião I and the two Moroccan sultans who were also involved died. Sebastião's uncle Henrique then assumed the throne for two years, but he, a Catholic cardinal, also died without succession. In the conflict that followed, Felipe II of Spain (Sebastião's cousin) became Felipe I of Portugal as well, and the Portuguese Philippine dynasty – with three consecutive Spanish kings also ruling as kings of Portugal – lasted 60 years (1580–1640). The Portuguese War of Restoration, also known as the Acclamation War, dragged on for another 28 years, until the Treaty of Lisbon was signed in 1668. The linguistic implications for the Castilian presence in Portugal were, therefore, significant. For almost a century following the treaty, many Portuguese authors continued to write some of their works in Spanish.[5]

---

4 See Francisco da Natividade, *Lenitivos da Dor I propostos ao augusto, e poderoso monarcha el rey D. Pedro II nosso senhor* (Lisbon: Miguel Deslandes, 1700), p. 310; Diogo Barbosa Machado, *Bibliotheca Lusitana historica, critica e cronologica* (Lisbon: Officina de Ignacio Rodrigues, 1747), vol. 3, p. 516; and Leandro Fernández de Moratín, *Orígenes del teatro español* (Paris: Librería Europea de Baudry, 1838), p. 47.

5 See Domingo de Garcia Peres, *Catálogo razonado biográfico y bibliográfico de los autores portugueses que escribieron en castellano* (Madrid: Imprenta del Colegio Nacional de Sordomudos y de Ciegos, 1890) to gain an appreciation of the vast number of Portuguese

Theater was so popular in Spain and Portugal during all these decades that beyond the *corral* playhouses, performances flourished in churches, plazas, private homes, and even within the walls of cloistered convents. Sometimes a convent would contract a theater company to perform for one of their celebrations or another convent might commission a play from a local playwright and the nuns would perform it. In several convents (in Valladolid, Madrid, and Lisbon, for example) the nuns themselves wrote plays and staged them for each other and sometimes for guests.[6] Two biological sisters from the highly educated Sobrino Morillas family, Sor María de San Alberto (1568–1640) and Sor Cecilia del Nacimiento (1570–1646), lived and worked together most of their lives in the Discalced Carmelite Convento de la Concepción in Valladolid. They wrote, composed music, created props, and directed short plays or 'fiestas' to celebrate Christmas or the profession of a sister nun.[7] Sor Marcela de San Félix (1605–1687), the daughter of Lope de Vega, and her successor, Sor Francisca de Santa Teresa (1654–1709), resided in the Discalced Trinitarian Convent of San Ildefonso in Madrid. Both of them wrote, directed, and performed in comic *loas* and light-hearted 'spiritual colloquies.' Francisca also composed a secular *entremés.*[8] In Lisbon's Franciscan Convento da Esperança, Sóror Maria do Céu and Sóror Magdalena da Glória penned plays, several of which they included in published anthologies along with allegorical novels and poetry. We have no record of the performance of their plays, but the Esperança, a

authors who composed works in the Spanish language.

6 For a study of the theatrical elements employed by nun-playwrights, see Valerie Hegstrom, 'El convento como espacio escénico y la monja como actriz: montajes teatrales en tres conventos de Valladolid, Madrid y Lisboa', in N. Baranda Leturio and M. C. Marín Pina (eds), *Letras en la celda: Cultura escrita de los conventos femeninos en la España moderna.* (Madrid: Iberoamericana-Vervuert, 2014) pp. 363–78.

7 Texts and translations of some of their works are available in Electa Arenal and Stacey Schlau (eds), *Untold Sisters: Hispanic Nuns in Their Own Works*, trans. A. Powell. (Albuquerque: U of New Mexico P, 1989), pp. 130–89. See also Stacey Schlau, *Viva al siglo, muerta al mundo: Selected Works by María de San Alberto (1568–1640)* (New Orleans: UP of the South, 1998), pp. 49–92 and José M. Díaz Cerón, *Cecilia del Nacimiento, O.C.D. 1570–1646: Obras completas* (Madrid: Editorial de Espiritualidad, 1971), pp. 639–53.

8 For Sor Marcela de San Félix's texts, see Electa Arenal and Georgina Sabat-Rivers (eds), *Literatura conventual femenina: Sor Marcela de San Félix, hija de Lope de Vega; Obra completa: Coloquios espirituales, loas y otros poemas* (Barcelona: PPU, 1988), as well Arenal and Schlau's *Untold Sisters*. For editions of Sor Francisca de Santa Teresa's plays, see María del Carmen Alarcón Román (ed.), *Sor Francisca de Santa Teresa: Coloquios* (Seville: ArCiBel Editores, 2007) and also Fernando Doménech Rico (ed.), *Teatro breve de mujeres (Siglos XVII–XX)* (Madrid: Asociación de Directores de Escena de España, 1996), pp. 49–65.

royal convent, certainly had the means to support such productions. Another poet from Lisbon, Sóror Violante do Céu, had already composed plays before entering the Dominican Convento da Rosa. She dedicated a *comedia* to Saint Engratia (or possibly Saint Eugenia) called *La transformación por Dios* (Transformation through God), written to commemorate the visit of King Philip III of Spain (II of Portugal) to Lisbon.[9] Perim also attributes two additional *comedias* to Violante: *El hijo, esposo y hermano* (*The Son, Husband, and Brother*) and *La victoria por la cruz* (*Victory Through the Cross*) (449–50). All three plays have been lost, and if they remained in manuscript in her convent, the 1755 earthquake and subsequent fires probably destroyed them. A *comedia* by the laywoman Joana Teodora de Sousa, who also lived in the Rosa Convent, fared more fortunately. A play about the Blessed Pedro González and his interactions with the devil, *El gran prodigio de España y lealtad de un amigo* (*Spain's Great Wonder and the Loyalty of a Friend*), published in the seventeenth or early in the eighteenth century, remains extant. The book has no date indicated, but it definitely appeared before the earthquake. We also have record that two women born in Torres Novas, Portugal, both of whom lived in a Franciscan convent, wrote *comedias*. Sóror Francisca da Coluna published *Comedia ao nascimento de Cristo* (*Play for the Birth of Christ*) and the laywoman Beatriz de Sousa y Melo wrote *La vida de Santa Elena e invención de la cruz* (*The Life of Saint Helen and the Finding of the Cross*) and *Yerros enmendados y alma arrepentida* (*Amended Errors and the Repentant Soul*).[10] Convents in the Americas also sometimes encouraged their nuns to create theater. The Guatemalan nun Sor Juana de Maldonado (1598–1666) probably prepared *Entretenimiento en obsequio de la huida a Egipto* (*An Entertainment in Honor of the Flight into Egypt*)

9 Perim states that this *comedia* treated St Eugenia (449), but Machado refers to the play as *Santa Engracia* (3.792). On one hand, St Eugenia's legend involves a transformation and includes a cross-dressed saint who becomes an abbott, heals a woman, goes on trial for adultery, and judges her father; the tale sounds like the typical plotline of an early modern Iberian *comedia.* On the other hand, St Engratia was born in Braga, Portugal and martyred in Zaragoza, Spain, so her story would make an interesting choice of topic to present to that particular king. Additionally, the church named for this saint is located in the same neighborhood where Violante's convent stood.

10 Cayetano Alberto de la Barrera y Leirado, *Catálogo bibliográfico del teatro antiguo español, desde su orígenes hasta mediados del siglo XVIII* (Madrid: Gredos, 1969), pp. 97, 387). Barrera includes Sóror Francisca da Coluna's play, *Comedia ao nascimento de Cristo*, in his catalog of Spanish theater. Because the play is not extant we cannot be sure it was written in Spanish. Sometimes Portuguese writers did give Portuguese titles to works they composed in Spanish.

as part of a cycle of Christmas plays for her convent.[11] In Mexico City, the *comedias*, *autos*, *loas*, and *villancicos* of Sor Juana Inés de la Cruz were staged in noble houses and churches to honor dignitaries and commemorate religious festivals.[12]

Beyond convent walls, several Iberian noblewomen also took up the pen to write plays in Spanish. Feliciana Enríquez de Guzmán (1569–1644), a writer from Seville, published Parts I and II of her *Tragicomedia los jardines y campos sabeos* (*Tragicomedy the Sabean Gardens and Countryside*) in Portugal in 1624 and 1627. Her lively 'Carta ejecutoria' (Letters patent) energetically defends her use of the classical dramatic form in imitation of ancient dramatists, stakes her claim to a position among the great verse playwrights, and can be read as a critical response to Lope's *Arte nuevo*.[13] Ana Caro (*c.* 1600–after 1645), author of two *comedias*, *Valor, agravio y mujer* (*Courage, Betrayal, and a Woman Scorned*) and *El conde Partinuplés* (*Count Partinuplés*), holds the record as the first known European woman to earn money as a playwright. Her *comedias* were staged and well received in Madrid, Seville, and other cities, and the town hall of Seville paid her on at least three occasions for *autos sacramentales* she wrote for their Corpus Christi festivals.[14] Ana Caro's friend María de Zayas (1590?–after 1647), famous for her best-selling novellas, also wrote a *comedia*, *La traición en la*

---

11 Juana de Maldonado, *Entretenimiento en obsequio de la huida a Egipto*, ed. I. Rossi de Fiori (Salta, Argentina: Editorial Biblioteca de Textos Universitarios, 2006). See also Lisa Vollendorf and Grady C. Wray, 'Gender in the Atlantic World: Women's Writing in Iberia and Latin America', in H. Braun and L. Vollendorf (eds), *Theorising the Ibero-American Atlantic* (Leiden: Brill, 2013), pp. 99–116.

12 See Guillermo Schmidhuber, *The Three Secular Plays of Sor Juana Inés de la Cruz: A Critical Study*, trans. S. Thacker. (Lexington: U of Kentucky P, 1997).

13 See Teresa S. Soufas (ed.), *Women's Acts: Plays by Women Dramatists of Spain's Golden Age* (Lexington: UP of Kentucky, 1997), pp. 225–71, and Louis C. Pérez (ed.), *The Dramatic Works of Feliciana Enríquez de Guzmán* (Valencia, Spain: Albatros Hispanófila Ediciones, 1988). For a book-length study of the plays, see M. Reina Ruiz, *Monstruos, mujer y teatro en el Barroco: Feliciana Enríquez de Guzmán, primera dramaturga española* (New York: Peter Lang, 2005). New biographical information is available in Piedad Bolaños Donoso, *Doña Feliciana Enríquez de Guzmán: Crónica de un fracaso vital, 1669–1644* (Seville: U de Sevilla, Secretariado de Publicaciones, 2012).

14 Rodrigo Caro, *Varones insignes en letras, naturales de la ilustrísima ciudad de Sevilla* (Seville: Real Academia Sevillana de Buenas Letras, 1915), p. 73, and José Sánchez Arjona, *El teatro en Sevilla en los siglos XVI y XVII* (Madrid: Establecimiento Tipográfica de A. Alonso, 1887), 249–50. Editions of Caro's extant plays are available in Soufas (ed.), *Women's Acts*, pp. 133–94. Several other modern editions and articles about the plays have also appeared.

amistad (*Friendship Betrayed*).[15] Leonor de la Cueva y Silva (1611–1705), a noblewoman from Medina del Campo, authored the *comedia La firmeza en la ausencia* (*Constancy in Absence*) (Soufas, *Women's Acts* 195–224). The poet Bernarda Ferreira de Lacerda (1595–1644) from Lisbon and Mariana de Carvajal, a writer of novellas from Madrid, both wrote plays that have gone missing.

During the second half of the seventeenth century and beginning of the eighteenth, several noblewomen living in Lisbon, Amsterdam,[16] and Valencia wrote *comedias*, *autos*, *loas*, and *bailes*. We have the titles of several of their plays, but their works have disappeared. The Countess of Ericeira, Joana Josefa de Menezes (1651–1709), left behind manuscripts of three *comedias* – *Divino imperio de amor* (*The Divine Empire of Love*), *Desdén de razón vencido* (*Disdain for Reason Overcome*), and *El duelo de las finezas* (*The Duel of the Love-Proofs*), two *autos sacramentales* – Parts I and II of *Contienda del amor divino* (*The Conflict of Divine Love*), as well as six *loas* and six *bailes*. When the Ericeira palace burned in the fires that followed the earthquake, all of these plays and Menezes's poems, written in Portuguese, French, and Italian, were lost. One of her long poems, *Despertador del alma* (*The Awakener of the Soul*), published under a pseudonym in 1695, remains extant (Perim 1.486–91, Barrera 251). Isabel Rebeca Correia (*c.* 1655–*c.* 1700), a Sephardic Jew living in Amsterdam, published her Spanish translation of Giovanni Battista Guarini's *Il pastor fido* (*The Faithful Shepherd*).[17] In her prologue to the 'kind

15 See Valerie Hegstrom (ed.) and Catherine Larson (trans.), *La traición en la amistad / Friendship Betrayed* (Lewisburg: Bucknell UP, 1999). Because a published English translation of this play exists, we include the English title in italics. Soufas included *La traición en la amistad* in *Women's Acts*, pp. 273–308, and other editions also exist.

16 In the early sixteenth century, the Holy Roman Emperor Charles V (Charles I of Spain) ruled the Low Countries (the Netherlands, Belgium, etc.). The Spanish Habsburg monarchs continued to control the region after the abdication and death of Charles. In 1581, the northern provinces declared independence from Spain, which continued to govern in the southern provinces ('the Spanish Netherlands') until the end of the War of Spanish Succession and the treaties of Utrecht and Rastatt (1713–1714), when the territories were ceded to the Austrian Habsburg monarchy.

17 Isabel Correia, *El pastor fido, poema de Baptista Guarino, traducido de italiano en metro español y illustrado con reflexiones* (Antwerp: Henrico y Cornelio Verdussen, 1694). During Correia's lifetime, the Dutch Republic was an independent country. Many exiled Sephardim lived in the thriving Jewish quarter of Amsterdam. The 'Portuguese' synagogue, where Correia probably worshiped and which survived World War II, was completed in 1675. Rembrandt lived in the quarter and some of Correia's friends and neighbors served as models for his paintings.

reader,' she promises to publish her own original plays on various subjects, but they never appeared in print (12). María Egual (1655–1735), the Marquise de Castellfort, hosted a literary salon and theatrical performances in her home in Valencia. Spain's National Library owns a manuscript of several poems and a novella by Egual, but many of her works were burned.[18] For example, she also penned the *comedia Los prodigios de Thesalia* (*Thessaly's Wonders*), the musical play *Triunfos de amor en el aire* (*The Triumphs of Love in the Air*), and a *loa* for a *comedia* by Salazar y Torres, *También se ama en el abismo* (*Love Also Happens in Hell*) (Mas 379–400). Isabel Senhorinha de Silva (born 1658), the twin sister of the Franciscan nun Sóror Maria do Céu, wrote several books and at least one *comedia, Los celos abren los cielos* (*Jealousy Opens the Heavens*), also called *Comedia de Santa Iria* (*Saint Irene's Play*) (Perim 2.499, Machado 926, Barrera 368). Throughout the seventeenth century, women residing behind convent walls and in the outside world in many cities on the Iberian Peninsula and in other parts of the Spanish Empire participated in the writing and production of theatrical works. Ângela de Azevedo contributed to that activity with *El muerto disimulado* and her two other plays, *La margarita del Tajo que dio nombre a Santarém* (*The Pearl*[19] *of the Tagus, who Gave Her Name to Santarem*) and *Dicha y desdicha del juego y devoción de la Virgen* (*The Fortune and Misfortune of Gambling, and Devotion to the Virgin*).[20]

The staging of woman-authored plays has proliferated in recent years. In the last two decades, several professional and university theater companies have performed some of these early modern texts in English and Spanish; representative examples follow.[21] Sor Juana's *Los empeños de una casa*

18 Pasqual Mas i Usó, *Academias valencianas del barroco: Descripción y diccionario de poetas* (Kassel: Reichenberger, 1999) p. 383. As the story goes, Egual had written a trunkful of literary texts, which, out of modesty, she asked her family to burn, but, apparently against her wishes, family members saved some of her writing.

19 Various translations are possible for the word *margarita* (pearl, daisy, marguerite, Margaret). In the context of Azevedo's play, 'pearl' resonates most closely with the meanings and images of the source text.

20 Spain's National Library owns two copies of the *suelta* version of *Dicha y desdicha* (T/21435 and T/32920), as well as a *suelta* of *La margarita del Tajo* (T/33142). Additionally, the British library has a copy of *Dicha y desdicha* (11728.a.27). Soufas included all three of Azevedo's plays in *Women's Acts*, pp. 1–132. Ângela de Azevedo, *La margarita del Tajo que dio nombre a Santarén. El muerto disimulado*, ed. F. Doménech Rico (Madrid: Asociación de Directores de Escena de España, 1999) contains two of the plays.

21 See also Valerie Hegstrom and Amy R. Williamsen, 'Early Modern *Dramaturgas*: A Contemporary Performance History', in H. Erdman and S. Paun de García (eds), *Remaking*

(*The House of Trials*) has seen multiple adaptations in at least five different countries.[22] *La traición en la amistad* (*Friendship Betrayed*) by María de Zayas has enjoyed at least seven productions in Chile, Spain, and the US, including a month-long run in Arlington, Virginia by WSC Avant Bard in September-October 2015. Ana Caro's *Valor, agravio y mujer* (*Courage, Betrayal, and a Woman Scorned*) has been staged twice in Spanish and twice in English, all in the US.[23] Erdman's translation and adaptation of Caro's *El conde Partinuplés* (*Count Partinuplés*), combined with his adaptation of Feliciana Enríquez de Guzmán's interlude, *Las gracias mohosas* (*Moldy Graces*) was performed in 2013 in *Suitors*.[24] The same interlude, in a Spanish adaptation, had been presented in multiple venues in Spain by the Compañía Teatro del Velador. In addition, at least four university groups have staged full or partial convent plays. Finally, *El muerto disimulado* (*Presumed Dead*) has to date had two productions, which we describe in detail below. Our desire to make Azevedo's play more easily available for performance in Spanish and to provide a playable version in English has led us to prepare this edition and translation of *El muerto disimulado / Presumed Dead.*

Azevedo: Her Life, Times, and Works

Quite ironically, the author of a play in which the identities of many of its characters are unknown has left little clear, documented evidence regarding her own life and identity as a writer. Until more facts come to light, it is impossible to know much of anything about Azevedo's biography for certain; we will therefore summarize the variety of unverified theories postulated

the Comedia (Woodbridge: Tamesis, 2015), pp. 83–92.

22 David Pasto (trans.), *The House of Trials: A Translation of* Los empeños de una casa *by Sor Juana Inés de la Cruz* (New York: Peter Lang, 1997) and Catherine Boyle (trans.), *House of Desires: A New Translation* (London: Oberon, 2005). See also Michael McGaha (trans.) and Susana Hernández-Araico (ed.), *Los empeños de una casa / Pawns of a House.* (Tempe: Bilingual P, 2007).

23 Williamsen translated Caro's play as *Courage, Betrayal, and a Woman Scorned*, although Pasto titled his production of the same text as *Valor, Outrage and Woman*; Williamsen and Ian Borden used the original title, *Courage, Betrayal, and a Woman Scorned*, for an intended audience of potential stagings by US companies. Hugo Medrano presented his adaptation of Williamsen's translation of the play as *Valor, agravio y mujer / Stripping Don Juan* in 2006. The Spanish performance used English surtitles.

24 Harley Erdman (trans.) and Nieves Romero Díaz and Lisa Vollendorf (eds), *Woman Playwrights of Early Modern Spain: Feliciana Enríquez de Guzmán, Ana Caro Mallén, and Sor Marcela de San Félix* (Toronto: Iter P; Tempe: Arizona Center for Medieval and Renaissance Studies, 2016).

over the centuries and comment briefly on their relevance with regard to the dating of *El muerto disimulado* and the intersection of history and literary history. At this point, we do know the following about Ângela de Azevedo: her name, the names of at least three of her plays, and the fact that she was Portuguese but wrote in Spanish. We also consider it highly likely that she wrote in the seventeenth century.

One mention of particular interest appears in an undated letter, written in Portuguese and sent from Brazil, most probably to someone in Portugal known only as *V. merce* (*Your Lordship*). The letter, signed 'Amigo, Amante, y Leal, El Capitan Belisario,' is a theatrical word game, in which the author describes the arrival of Governor Fernando Martins Mascarenhas in Rio de Janeiro and Minas (later, Minas Gerais) and an uprising in Minas; the letter writer uses the titles of a number of dramatic texts to narrate his story.[25] The two-page letter alludes to dozens of plays from early modern Spain; the letter is written in Portuguese, but the play titles appear only in Spanish, with a few spelling errors. The dramas were composed by many of the best-known playwrights of the seventeenth century: Calderón, Rojas Zorrilla, Coello, Salazar y Torres, etc. What makes the clever word play particularly valuable is the inclusion of *El muerto disimulado* in the letter:

> …veja V. merce **lo que son juizios del Cielo**, que chegou este Amaral a ver se em **La fuerça lastimosa**, e ainda assim dizem-me que se esperava **Bien puede ser El muerto dissimulado**, e elle **ver se, y tener se por muerto**, e nesta terra terem-no por **El Galan Fantasma**. (275)[26]

25 It is likely that the letter was written in 1705 or shortly thereafter, because the arrival of Fernando Martins Mascarenhas in Rio de Janeiro and the uprising in Minas occurred in that year. Mascarenhas governed from 1705–09.

26 El Capitan Belisario, 'Carta por Títulos de Comedias vinda da cidade de S. Paulo sobre o levantamento das Minas', Letter 28 of 'Documentos do Arquivo da Tôrre do Tombo copiados pela Dr. Emília Félix, por solicitação do Sr. José Pedro Leite Coreiro', *Revista do Instituto Histórico e Geográfico de S. Paulo* 52 (1956), pp. 271–92: '…Look Your Grace *What the Judgments of Heaven Are*, for this Amaral fellow came to find himself in *The Woeful Force*, and even so they tell me *It May Well Be* that he expected to be *Presumed Dead* and to *See Himself and Find Himself Dead*, and in this land, they took him for *The Ghostly Gallant*' (our translation). *Lo que son los juicios del cielo* was written by Juan Pérez de Montalbán, *La fuerza lastimosa* by Lope de Vega, *Verse y tenerse por muerto* by Manuel Freyle de Andrade, and *El galán fantasma* by Calderón. *Bien puede ser* may be the title of a lost *comedia* or Captain Belisario may be misremembering the title of Agustín Moreto's *No puede ser* (*It Cannot Be*).

The writer must have understood that these play titles would be familiar to his reader, which suggests that both of them knew enough about the plays to appreciate the humor and wit that mark the letter. In addition, it is useful to learn that Ângela de Azevedo and her comedy were known in the early years of the eighteenth century – and by someone in Brazil.

Although several early (eighteenth- and nineteenth-century) catalogues of Portuguese writers exist, few of them mention Azevedo. In some cases, that oversight is significant, because those texts mention other Portuguese women writers who wrote and published in Spanish. Her omission in these catalogues could indicate that 1) she was either not alive or not yet writing when the catalogue was published, 2) she was alive, but the author of the catalogue did not include any living writers, or 3) that she did not live in Portugal, or her plays were not published or performed in Portugal, so the author of the catalogue either was unaware of her work or did not consider her 'Portuguese.'

Until the late twentieth century, the few catalogues of Portuguese and Spanish writers that contain entries on Azevedo have most often mentioned the following claims about her life: she was born in Portugal early in the seventeenth century and served Queen Isabel de Borbón[27] in Madrid as a lady-in-waiting in her court; she was considered prudent, beautiful, and talented; she wrote three plays (most descriptions list the titles – and, sometimes, the fact that all three were published); she married a nobleman while in Madrid; and, after she was widowed, retired along with her daughter to a Benedictine convent, where she professed as a nun and died. To date, apart from the titles of her three plays and the fact that they were published, no substantiating documentation from the seventeenth century regarding any of those statements has been found, but from the mid-eighteenth until the early-twentieth century, the same general claims appeared in a variety of books; the most commonly cited are described below. To further complicate matters, some catalogue entries explicitly contradict others in areas of significant importance. This is a matter of consequence: much of the conflicting information on Azevedo that exists today derives from the brief entries in these catalogues and bibliographies, so issues of historical accuracy are paramount.

The first source on the life of Ângela de Azevedo[28] is Damião de Frois

27 Born in 1602, Isabel, the wife of Felipe IV, was the Queen consort of Spain from 1621 till her death in 1644, and she held the same title in Portugal from 1621 until 1640.

28 Both early and contemporary sources of information about Azevedo spell her name in a variety of ways. Ângela appears as Ángela or simply Angela in most sources, and Spanish

Perim's *Theatro Heroino: Abecedario historico, e catalogo das mulheres illustres em armas, letras, accoens heroicas e artes liberaes* (1740), which describes her as the daughter of João de Azevedo Pereira and Isabel de Oliveira, both from Lisbon. Perim states that the writer accompanied a Queen Catharina to Madrid for her marriage to Felipe I of Castile and mentions that Azevedo was married, widowed, and took the habit, along with her daughter, in the Convent of 'Saõ Bento da Villa de Madrid,' where she died in a saintly state; like other descriptions that would follow, this entry also mentions the writer's discretion, virtue, and talent as a poet. In this first account of her works, Perim notes that Azevedo wrote three plays, published in Madrid; he lists *El muerto disimulado* as the second of the three (2.493–94).[29] This entry contains information that would later be discounted by several noted cataloguers and scholars, although it would also be offered as factual by many others.

Diogo Barbosa de Machado's often-cited *Bibliotheca lusitana historica, critica e cronologica* offers several related entries in all four volumes (1741, 1747, 1752, and 1759, respectively), but they are far from consistent internally. The Volume 1 entry, which indicates that Machado had read Perim, also tells us that Ângela was born in Lisbon to the nobleman João de Azevedo Pereira and his second wife, Isabel de Oliveira; was esteemed by Queen Isabel de Borbón due to her natural discretion and rare beauty; served the Queen and was married in Madrid to someone worthy of her nobility, had a daughter, and, after her husband's death, retired to a Benedictine convent, where she professed. She excelled in the art of poetry and penned the three plays indicated by Perim. Perhaps the most intriguing element of this entry is that Machado challenges Perim for stating that Azevedo had served Queen Catharina, the wife of Felipe I (175), even though Machado himself also recants several elements of his own account in the second volume.[30]

---

catalogers and critics usually spell Azevedo with a 'c': Acevedo. We have chosen to use Portuguese spelling and accent marks when we refer to the author.

29 Perim puts *La Margarita del Tajo, que dió nombre a Santaren* as the first title, and *Dicha, y desdicha del juego, y devoción con la Virgen* [*sic*] as the third. He is the only early cataloguer who states that her plays were published in Madrid.

30 Machado argues that although Felipe married four times, none of his wives was named Catharina (175), and it is true that no other Philip of Castile was married to a Catherine. It is possible that Perim's confusion with the Queen's name might have come from the 1526 marriage of the Portuguese king, João III, to Catarina, the sister of Emperor Charles V (Carlos I of Spain); see James Maxwell Anderson, *The History of Portugal* (Westport: Greenwood P, 2000), pp. 79–80.

In Volume 2, Ângela de Azevedo is not given her own entry, but she appears in that of a relative, Dom Francisco do Rosário, in a paragraph that modifies what Machado wrote in Volume 1.[31] Machado states that although he had described Ângela de Azevedo as noted above, he now declares, 'which affirmation we retract, informed of the true information in which it is known that she is a native of the town of Paredes in the district of Pinhel in the province of Beira and [she is] the daughter of Thomé de Azevedo da Veiga, Sargeant Major and Infantry Captain in the War of Acclamation, and of Lady Maria de Almeida' (247, our translation). Machado further notes that Ângela married Francisco de Anciães de Figueiredo, but avers that they did not have any descendants; he does not mention her having served Queen Isabel as a lady-in-waiting.

The only mention of Ângela de Azevedo in Volume 3 is a brief allusion found in the entry on a woman writer Machado describes as her sister, Luísa de Azevedo. Curiously, the cataloguer both repeats the redacted information from the Volume 2 entry regarding the girls' parents and place of birth and refers the reader back to the 'incorrect' Volume 1 entry for information on Ângela. Machado further posits a potentially relevant date by stating that Luísa was born in 1655 and died in 1679 at the age of 24 (158). If Ângela and Luísa were indeed sisters and if Luísa's birthdate is correct, we then have viable parameters on when Ângela may have lived, which strongly suggest that it is unlikely that she served in the court of a Spanish queen who died in 1644. Moreover, during that time her father would have been fighting against the Spanish in the Portuguese War of Acclamation (1640–1668).

Machado's entry on Ângela de Azevedo in Volume 4 continues to cross-list the Volume 1 entry,[32] but apart from that cross reference, it ignores her writing and possible life in Madrid and includes instead the changes that appeared in Volume 2 (some of which were noted in Volume 3). The information regards her parents' names, her place of birth, husband, and lack of descendants and adds a phrase about her father's military service.[33] The inconsistencies among Machado's four volumes are striking, and they illustrate how little we know with certainty about Ângela de Azevedo's life, although they were

31 The cross-reference to this Volume 2 entry (via Ângela's relative [247]) appears for the first and only time in Volume 3 (158), in Machado's account of Luísa de Azevedo.

32 Why Machado continued to send his readers back to the Volume 1 account in the later volumes of the *Biblotheca lusitana* is unclear.

33 The Volume 4 entry states that the Sergeant Major served as a Captain in the infantry in the war 'in which the freedom of our kingdom, oppressed by the Castilian domination, was fought' (19–20, our translation), a reference to the years 1640–1668.

promulgated in a number of later catalogues and essays from the nineteenth century on. We are left with numerous questions about when and where Ângela lived, wrote, and died, whether she ever had a child, went to Spain, or served the queen, and how and where she wrote and published three plays. The questions are many, and they continue to the present day.

In the nineteenth century, Barrera y Leirado's *Catálogo bibliográfico y biográfico del teatro antiguo español* (1860), following Perim and Machado's Volume 1, also suggests that Ângela de Azevedo was born in Lisbon to the nobleman 'Juan de Acevedo Pereyra' and Lady Isabel de Oliveira, his second wife. Barrera notes Ângela's natural discretion and rare beauty, as well as the affection she received from Queen Isabel de Borbón, whom she served. He states that the writer got married in Madrid to a gentleman of illustrious birth, and that upon his death, she retired with her daughter to a Benedictine convent, where she professed and died. Barrera ends with the list of her plays (beginning with *El muerto disimulado*) and the fact that all three were published (4). Similarly, the entry on Ângela in Peres's *Catálogo razonado de los autores portugueses que escribieron en castellano* (1890) uses Barrera's account but does not mention her parents' names (7). In a separate entry, he discusses Luísa de Azevedo, who, as Machado had also suggested, was Ângela's sister, a writer and an expert in Latin and Spanish born in the town of Paredes, Obispado de Lamego, who died in 1699[34] at the age of 24 (8). Peres does not mention Ângela in this second entry, but the problems with dating the two sisters' lives (and, likely, the possible confusion regarding their places of birth) further complicate a number of key issues. Finally, at the turn of the twentieth century, Serrano y Sanz states overtly in his *Apuntes para una biblioteca de escritoras españolas* (1903) that he is using the description of Ângela de Azevedo from Barrera's *Catálogo*.[35] Once again, the discrepancies that date back to the mid-eighteenth century catalogues of Perim and Machado were passed on to future cataloguers.

The majority of twentieth- and twenty-first-century critics have tended to follow the 'Azevedo as serving Queen Isabel' narrative: some use the Perim and Machado (Volume 1) information on her family, some present

34 Machado had listed the year as 1679 (158). If Peres's 1699 date were accurate, and if Ângela and Luísa were sisters, we might expect that Ângela lived significantly later in the 17th century; even if Machado's dates for Luísa (1655–1679) were correct, they would not fit well with an early-seventeenth-century life span for Ângela.

35 Manuel de Serrano y Sanz, *Apuntes para una biblioteca de escritoras españolas* (Madrid: Biblioteca de Autores Españoles, 1903), vol. 1, p. 10.

Machado's updated material found in later volumes, some (Oliveira, for example) combine the two, and one (Urban Baños) completely rejects this most popular account of Azevedo's biography.[36] The group of critics following the majority opinion includes Soufas, Ferrer Valls, Maroto Camino, Gascón, Hegstrom, Barbeito Carneiro, Mujica, and Hormigón, to name a few.[37] Indeed, numerous scholars have accepted Soufas's idea that it is 'likely that Azevedo composed her plays during the period of her court service to Queen Isabel' (*Women's Acts* 2). Barbeito Carneiro even suggests that Azevedo most likely left for Madrid with the queen in 1619, after the recently married royals had been presented in Portugal by King Felipe III ('Mujeres peninsulares' 219). Whether or not their readings are historically accurate,

---

36 Américo Lopes de Oliveira, *Escritoras Brasileiras, Galegas e Portuguesas* (Braga: Tipografia Silva Pereira, 1983) p. 21, and Alba Urban Baños, '"La empresa más lucida y más hermosa" de Portugal: Clave histórica para la datación de *El muerto disimulado* de Ángela de Acevedo', in I. Rouane Soupault and P. Meunier (eds), *Tiempo e historia en el teatro del Siglo de Oro: Actas selectas del XVI Congreso Internacional* (Aix-en-Provence: Presses Universitaires de Provence, 2015), n. pag.

37 Soufas, *Women's Acts*, pp. 1–2; Teresa Ferrer Valls, 'Decir entre versos: Angela de Acevedo y la escritura femenina en el siglo de oro', in S. Gil-Albarellos Pérez-Pedrero and M. Rodríguez Pequeño (eds), *Ecos silenciados: La mujer en la literatura española. Siglos XII al XVIII* (Segovia: Fundación Instituto Castellano y Leonés de la Lengua, 2006), n. pag.; Teresa Ferrer Valls, 'Mujer y escritura dramática en el Siglo de Oro: Del acatamiento a la réplica de la convención teatral', in M. de los Reyes Peña (ed.), *La presencia de la mujer en el teatro barroco español. Festival Internacional de Teatro Clásico de Almagro, July 23–24, 1997* (Seville: Junta de Andalucía, Consejería de Cultura, 1998), n. pag.; Mercedes Maroto Camino, 'Transvestism, Translation and Transgression: Angela de Azevedo's *El muerto disimulado*', *Forum for Modern Language Studies* 37.3 (2001), pp. 314–25; Christopher D. Gascón, 'Female and Male Mediation in the Plays of Ángela de Azevedo', *Bulletin of the Comediantes* 57.1 (2005), pp. 125–45; Valerie Hegstrom, '*Comedia* Scholarship and Performance: *El muerto disimulado* from the Archive to the Stage', *Comedia Performance* 4.1 (2007), pp. 152–78; María Isabel Barbeito Carneiro, 'Mujeres peninsulares entre Portugal y España,' *Península: Revista de Estudos Ibéricos* 0 (2003), pp. 209–24; Barbara Mujica, 'Ángela de Azevedo: Espectros y sombras', in B. Mujica (ed.), *Women Writers of Early Modern Spain: Sophia's Daughters* (New Haven: Yale UP, 2004) pp. 232–47; Juan Antonio Hormigón (ed.), 'Acevedo, Ángela de', in *Autoras en la historia del teatro español, 1500–1994* (Madrid: Asociación de Directores de Escena de España, 1996), vol. 1, p. 403. See also the entry from the online catalogue compiled by Vanda Anastácio of the Faculdade de Letras da Universidade de Lisboa (FLUL): Letras Lisboa, *Escritoras: Women Writers in Portuguese before 1900* (http://www.escritoras-em-portugues.eu) for a contemporary perspective on what is known – and not known – about Azevedo's life. This entry impartially reports the various contradictions regarding her biography, and under 'Occupation/Charge/Post' lists only that she was Isabel de Borbón's lady-in-waiting, without further comment.

they are certainly plausible from socio-cultural perspectives. Nonetheless, as the catalogue entries described above indicate, those sources tended to pass down much of the same information – often even using the same words – although the entries were far from identical. It is virtually impossible to find substantive proof to support what many have stated is fact.[38]

A few contemporary scholars have looked in other directions for ways to document Azevedo's life and times. Barbeito Carneiro, Hormigón, and Thacker, for example, have studied the playwright's dramatic and linguistic style in a search for useful information on that topic.[39] They note the strong influence of Calderón's plots and baroque language (and, for Thacker and Doménech, those of Tirso de Molina, as well) in Azevedo's dramas, which they then use to help place the Portuguese dramatist within varying parts of the seventeenth century. Hormigón, who espouses the 'Ângela as lady-in-waiting' theory, suggests that the analysis of her undated plays indicates that they were written in the last years of the 1630s or the first years of the 1640s; he bases this in part on a reference in *La margarita del Tajo* to the lines '*que los sueños, sueños son*', easily recognizable as coming from *La vida es sueño* (1636) (403). Thacker and Doménech lean towards a later date – at least after 1640, if not 1650.[40] Urban Baños, on the other hand, argues that Azevedo could not logically have gone to Madrid with the queen in 1610 and, rather, suggests that Azevedo was in Lisbon in 1682, writing *El muerto disimulado* for a royal marriage celebration that she views as closely linked to the comedy's plot (n. pag.).[41] As if the variety of biographical information were not confounding enough, the connections between Azevedo's life, the details of the plot, her linguistic style, and the dating of her comedy make things muddier still.

38 Ferrer Valls appears to accept this position rather cautiously, as she includes a number of disclaimers in her assessment. Referring to the publication of Azevedo's three plays, she states that 'it is believed that they were all published during the life of the dramatist, although none includes a place or date of publication, and it is possible, as has been supposed, that they were performed at court' ('Decir,' n. pag., our translation).

39 Barbeito Carneiro, 'Mujeres peninsulares', p. 219; Hormigón, p. 403; and Jonathan Thacker, *A Companion to Golden Age Theatre* (Woodbridge: Tamesis, 2007), p. 90.

40 Thacker, p. 90, and Fernando Doménech Rico, Introduction, in ed. F. Doménech Rico, *La margarita del Tajo que dio nombre a Santarén. El muerto disimulado* by Ângela de Azevedo (Madrid: Asociación de Directores de Escena de España, 1999), pp. 5–31.

41 Barbeito's dating of Azevedo's departure for Madrid was actually 1619 ('Mujeres peninsulares' 219), rather than 1610, as Urban Baños cites. Nonetheless, it is still difficult to imagine Azevedo in Madrid in the early part of the century and in Lisbon, writing this play, in 1682.

At this point, we believe that the basic narrative of Ângela as a native of Lisbon who served Queen Isabel de Borbón in Madrid lacks sufficient evidence, apart from the fact that it was repeated more times than any other suggestion. We are left with difficult choices: do we side with the majority? Do we assume that Machado's 'new' information in Volumes 2, 3, and 4 of his *Bibliotheca lusitana* is more accurate than what he wrote (and cross-referenced) from Volume 1 and should therefore be trusted? Could there be more than one woman writer named Ângela de Azevedo? Could someone be using a pen name? What other issues might influence a different reading of her biography, perhaps one that implies that she lived later in the seventeenth century, and how does that affect our understanding of her and her text?

Scholars treating *El muerto disimulado* often use references in the text to the Savoy armada to help date the play, but the lack of substantiating documentation has produced wildly different responses. Azevedo's comedy is loosely based on history, but numerous historical moments, spread across centuries, could have informed her approach to the text. Soufas suggests that the allusion to the 'Armada de Saboya' refers to something that, inspired by sixteenth-century historical events, might have taken place during the first half of the seventeenth century:

> [It] probably indicates a period of time that encompassed the entire sixteenth century, when the region in northern Italy, which included the Duchy of Savoy, was contested because of its crucial position of access to northern Europe. These tensions led to military action from 1598 to 1648… It was thus reasonable to depict Portuguese and Spanish characters participating together in campaigns on Italian soil for the sake of political and economic interests of the Iberian Peninsula. (*Women's Acts* 2)

Other scholars point to later historical references and related dates of publication. Thacker asserts that all of Azevedo's plays were written 'in the second half of the seventeenth century' (90). Doménech states that *El muerto disimulado* was written after 1640 because of allusions to an expedition of the Portuguese fleet to Savoy, undertaken in order to rescue Nice, which took place during the time of the Franco-Spanish War (1636–1659) (7–8).[42]

42 See Jonathan Wade, 'Patriotism and Revolt: Uncovering the Portuguese in Ângela de Azevedo', *Bulletin of the Comediantes* 59.2 (2007), pp. 325–43. Wade critiques several elements of Doménech's thesis, adding, however, 'Whether her works precede or follow the Restoration of 1640 has little impact on the subversive quality and political import of Azevedo's plays. They either serve to affirm the Portuguese Restoration or anticipate it' (326–27).

Mujica argues that various characters in the play 'have participated in the Savoy Armada, when Spanish and Portuguese forces fought against the Duchy of Savoy in northern Italy' (232, our translation). Several other scholars, including Múzquiz-Guerreiro and Maroto Camino, also point to the armada as an indication of military intervention, asserting that the play initially suggested that Clarindo had presumably died in the war.[43] We submit that none of these assertions can be proven, based on evidence in the play, although it is fair to state that in early modern times, there were numerous naval incursions in that area involving Spain, Portugal, Savoy, France, Italy, and other countries. Ultimately, however, despite these interesting suppositions, no specific armada to (or from) Savoy would reliably allow us to date *El muerto disimulado*.

In addition to the possibility that the armada was involved in a military operation, in that time of shifting alliances, a number of fleets moved between Portugal and Savoy for quite different reasons: political alliances based on royal marriages.[44] Urban Baños reminds us that all we really know is that Clarindo left on an armada bound for Nice, and we later learn that he was most likely killed by a traitor rather than in a war. She then argues that the play was written quite late in the seventeenth century to commemorate the Portuguese armada, filled with nobles, which was sent to Savoy in 1682 to bring Víctor Amadeo II, the Duke of Savoy, to Lisbon so that he could marry his cousin, Isabel Luísa Josefa, the Princess of Portugal and presumptive heir to the Portuguese throne. Urban Baños even takes the idea one step further, adding that Azevedo must have written the play between July and November of 1682 so it could be performed during the wedding ceremony that would take place when the fleet returned to Lisbon. Unfortunately for international politics, the marriage never took place.[45]

Other interpretations are possible as well. Azevedo's play might allude to an earlier Portuguese fleet, one that also carried nobles and royals from Lisbon to Savoy for a royal wedding. For example, Barker describes the

---

43 Darlene Múzquiz-Guerreiro, 'Symbolic Inversions in Ángela de Azevedo's *El muerto disimulado*', *Bulletin of the Comediantes* 57.1 (2005), pp. 150–51, and Maroto, p. 315.

44 See John H. Elliott, 'A Europe of Composite Monarchies', *Past and Present* 137 (1992), pp. 48–71.

45 Urban Baños further speculates that 'it is more than probable that … once the union of Víctor Amadeo and Isabel Luísa Josefa was cancelled, [the play] might well have been forgotten and left in a drawer, perhaps in some convent in Lisbon, until it was published' [n. pag., our translation]; this suggestion contradicts Perim, among others, but if we assume that Perim, et al. were mistaken, Urban Baños's reading may offer a plausible alternative.

events of 1521, when the Infanta Beatriz of Portugal was escorted to join Charles III, Duke of Savoy; the chronicles describe the participants' displays of wealth and the maritime power of the Portuguese navy, all of which were intended to impress the Savoyards and the citizens of numerous cities along the way.[46] This reference to an earlier armada and royal wedding offers yet another plausible clue for dating *El muerto disimulado*, but, again, there is no solid proof that this sixteenth-century armada inspired Azevedo, nor can it provide a foundation for determining when she wrote her play. Ultimately, we cannot establish firmly whether the Savoy armada refers to events allied with war or celebration, the sixteenth or the seventeenth centuries. The ambiguities present in the play itself and the variety of possibilities based on the little information we have concerning the dramatist's biography make it impossible to substantiate the facts of her life and the historical events described in the play, which could then help us date the text. There is simply not enough evidence in the play to enable us to assert that it refers to any specific historical event. In fact, we may someday find that none of these opinions offered by the academic community is valid: perhaps Ângela de Azevedo created a dramatic fiction that combined or built loosely on historical events but did not attempt to copy any one of them. After all, she was a dramatic poet trying to create good theater, rather than a chronicler of historical events.

Although Azevedo's other *comedias*, quite different from one another and *El muerto disimulado*, are also unlikely to help us determine the facts of the playwright's life, they nevertheless do provide insights into topics that interested her. *Dicha y desdicha del juego* descends from two thirteenth-century works about the rewards of devotion to the Virgin: Alfonso X's *Cantigas de Santa Maria* (*The Songs of Holy Mary*), written in Galician-Portuguese, and Gonzalo de Berceo's *Milagros de Nuestra Señora* (*The Miracles of Our Lady*), originally composed in a Castilian dialect. In *The Songs*, *The Miracles*, and in Azevedo's play, faithful devotion to the Virgin can compensate for any sin and save the devotee from the clutches of the devil. In *Dicha y desdicha*, the orphaned but noble siblings Felisardo and María suffer poverty because of their father's addiction to gambling. On her deathbed, their mother had begged them to remain steadfast in their veneration of the Virgin Mary. Felisardo and Violante have loved each

46 Richard Barker, 'Showing the Flag in 1521: Wafting Beatriz to Savoy', a conference paper presented at *XI Reunião Internacional da História da Náutica e da Hidrografia* and *VIII Jornadas de História Ibero-Americana Conference* (Portimão, Portugal, 2 May 2002).

other since childhood, but her wealthy father, Don Nuño, seeks an equally affluent suitor for his daughter. María has no dowry so can neither afford to marry nor to enter a convent. Meanwhile, Don Fadrique returns from the Indies (the Americas) where he has earned his fortune. During a storm at sea, he had made a vow to the Virgin that he would marry the poorest, but honorable, noblewoman he could find. Upon his arrival in Oporto, he immediately crosses paths with María and falls in love, but when Don Nuño offers Violante's hand to Fadrique, he decides instead to marry the rich girl. Felisardo pleads with Don Nuño to no avail, so, desperate, he invites Fadrique to gamble with him. Initially, the games go well for Felisardo, but the tide turns and Fadrique wins everything, including María, whom Felisardo has staked as his final bet. Devastated, Felisardo leaves the city, offers his soul to the devil, and renounces God, but when the devil asks him to also renounce the Virgin, Felisardo refuses. Angry, the devil carries him away in a flight through the sky. Back in Oporto, having 'won' both women and wanting to exact revenge on Felisardo, Fadrique decides to go to Felisardo's home to find María and rape her. He finds her asleep at the base of her altar to the Virgin, and as María talks in her sleep, she reproves his wicked intentions. After the Virgin defeats the devil and saves Felisardo, he returns home to find Fadrique repentant and ready to marry María. Don Nuño relents and allows Violante and Felisardo to marry. Because of the siblings' constant devotion, the Virgin overlooks Felisardo's mistakes and saves him from the devil, protects María from Fadrique's illicit intentions, and resolves the issues that obstruct their happy endings.

One of the major subgenres of early modern Spanish theater includes the numerous plays based on the lives of saints, and Azevedo's *La margarita del Tajo* belongs to this group of plays. Spanish and Portuguese translations of Jacobus de Voragine's *Golden Legend* (1260), a collection of idealized saints' lives, were abundant and popular in the early modern period. These translations, called *Flos sanctorum* (*Flowering of the Saints*), gave rise to a large number of literary works – poems, novels, stories, convent biographies, and plays – with similar themes. In Azevedo's contribution to the subgenre, the nun Irene is celebrated by everyone in the Lusitanian city of Nabancia for her purity, discretion, and holiness. She has lived in the convent since childhood and the wise monk Remigio has served as her tutor. Britaldo, the newlywed son of the governor, sees her one day at church during a religious festival and begins to despise his bride Rosimunda and to desire Irene, which causes an illness in him that the doctors cannot cure. When Britaldo goes to the convent to woo Irene with music and poetry, Rosimunda sends her countryman Banán to follow and find out whom Britaldo is courting. An angel descends from heaven and defends Irene's honor in a swordfight with Britaldo and his men. Britaldo's passion for Irene inspires Girardian mimetic desire[47] in Remigio. Her great discretion enables Irene to talk Rosimunda out of her jealousy and Britaldo out of his inappropriate desire, but her rejection of Remigio drives him to take revenge. He prepares a potion that causes Irene to appear pregnant, bringing shame and rejection on her. Britaldo, angered that another man had what he could not, sends Banán to kill Irene. He finds her near the river, kills her off stage with his sword, and throws her body into the river to destroy the evidence. When the three men begin to feel guilty and confess all they have done, a curtain opens at the back of the stage and reveals Irene's miraculously preserved body on top of a tomb afloat on the river with angels on either side singing her praises. In a break with *Comedia* convention, the play ends when the characters announce that no marriages will take place; instead the women characters will enter a convent and the men will make a pilgrimage to the Holy Land. Britaldo gets the last word and tells the audience that the playwright does not ask for forgiveness or applause; she wrote the play not to please an audience, but out of devotion for the Portuguese saint.

Although we cannot yet verify which of the claims about Azevedo's life are accurate, we have the early printed texts of her three plays, which demonstrate the themes and issues that motivated her to write. *El muerto disimulado*, *Dicha y desdicha del juego*, and *La margarita del Tajo* illuminate Azevedo's ability to utilize as models and sources Portuguese history, Galician-Portuguese and Castilian literary texts, and the life of a Lusitanian saint, told within the conventions of the theater of her time, to create three unique *comedias*.

---

47 See René Girard, *Deceit, Desire, and the Novel: Self and Other in Literary Structure*, trans. Y. Freccero (Baltimore: Johns Hopkins UP, 1965). Girard explicated his notion that human beings and fictional characters borrow their desires from others. When a character falls in love (or admires another), that emotion is prompted because the character has recognized that his or her love object is already desired by another. Remigio, who has only ever interacted chastely with Irene, begins to desire her as a woman when he learns of Britaldo's desire. Similarly, in *El muerto disimulado*, Lisarda falls in love with Álvaro, at least in part because she believes that Jacinta loves him.

El muerto disimulado / Presumed Dead

Honor, Virginity, and Constancy

In their works, early modern playwrights returned repeatedly to the socio-cultural norms regarding honor operant in Spain and Portugal. The exploration of these ideas could support, challenge, or satirize existing beliefs, but their popularity and representation in the *Comedia* were not so much an accurate reflection of everyday life in Iberia as a recognition by playwrights that themes of honor could lay bare characters' motivations and human drama – and lend themselves to the creation of conflict and exciting plots. The idea of honor within the *Comedia* had strong connections with the nobility and hinged on both social class and gender. In many plays, male characters born into the noble classes express doubts that women or commoners can possess honor. These characters demonstrate the belief that noblemen are born with honor and it is theirs alone to lose. Some of the most dramatic scenes occur when a female character (for example, Laurencia in Lope's *Fuenteovejuna*) or a peasant (Pedro Crespo in Calderón's *El alcalde de Zalamea*) rejects these norms and stands up for her or his own honor. In the *Comedia*, honor is also tied to fame or reputation and hangs on what other nobles might think or say ('el qué dirán').

Furthermore, a man's honor can depend not only on his own actions but also on the constancy, virginity, and fidelity of the women in his family – his wife, sisters, and daughters. Suspicions regarding even the hint of sexual indiscretion on a woman's part can – at least in the drama of the time – produce duels, murder, or banishment to a convent. Dozens of honor plays (sometimes referred to as 'wife-murder' plays), including Calderón's *El médico de su honra* (The Physician of His Honor), lead ineluctably to their horrifying climax, the revelation of the dead wife's body. Azevedo herself manipulates this theme in *La margarita del Tajo* when Britaldo has the nun Irene killed, because he believes she slept with another man. The potential for violence toward women surfaces in comic plays as well. Driven by her lack of options, many a jilted *Comedia* heroine dons men's clothing to follow the man who has taken her honor and persuade or trick him into keeping his promises. To recover her honor, she must marry him or kill him, and she knows that if her male family members discover her predicament, they will try to cleanse the stain on their honor by spilling her lover's blood and possibly her own.

Many *Comedia* fathers, husbands, and lovers, even in comic plays, lament the inconstancy of women. When male characters suspect some misbehavior, they repeatedly observe that they should have expected the problem, for, they assert, all women are fickle. Azevedo inverts this convention in two of her plays. In *Dicha y desdicha del juego*, the dramatic tension depends on the inconstancy of Don Fadrique and his servant Tijera, who, motivated by flattery and financial gain, shift their affections rapidly from Doña María and Rosela to the wealthier Violante and Belisa. Tijera tells Don Fadrique that his love is the same size as his master's. Fadrique asks, 'What size is that?' To which Tijera replies, 'The size of inconstancy' (2.1473–75, our translation). Meanwhile the women characters Violante and Belisa remain constant in their love for Felisardo and the *gracioso*, Sombrero. In *La margarita del Tajo* all of the complications and violence ensue from the feelings and actions of the nobleman Britaldo, who, emotionally unfaithful to his new bride Rosimunda, lusts after the nun Irene. Britaldo blames his fickleness on Cupid: 'Love, wanting to place the portrait of Irene in my breast, pulled my wife from my heart' (2.373–76). Azevedo assigns the trait of inconstancy far more often to men than to women. Women may have a reputation for fickleness, but that does not play out in Azevedo's works; and men, to whom the *Comedia* does not generally apply the concept of constancy or inconstancy, receive Azevedo's critique.

In *El muerto disimulado*, Azevedo has created a comedy that comments on these social issues with wit and humor. The play opens with Don Rodrigo threatening his daughter, Jacinta, not because he suspects that she has lost her virginity, but because Rodrigo believes honorable children should be obedient: he wants her to marry rather than become a nun. Don Álvaro reacts in similarly violent ways when he suspects some impropriety between his sister Beatriz and their cousin Alberto, even though Alberto repeatedly offers to marry Beatriz. Álvaro rejects such a marriage on the grounds that others would also suspect some stain on his honor. Beatriz comments on her precarious position in this situation: 'I can't go home given the danger I'm in. Although my brother knows I haven't done anything to offend his honor, honor is fragile, and my life is at risk'. Álvaro's proposed solutions involve killing his cousin in a swordfight, cloistering his sister in a convent, and/or marrying his sister to his new friend 'Lisardo'. 'Lisardo', however, is actually Lisarda, who has cross-dressed not to chase a lover who has jilted her, but because her father has died and she believes her brother is also dead, leaving her alone to avenge her family's honor. In the meantime, Jacinta has befriended 'Clara', a merchant woman who tells the tale of losing her virginity because of the 'feigned words of men who deceive women'. 'Clara', who plans to kill her seducer to avenge her honor, is really Clarindo, Lisarda's presumed dead brother, and Don Álvaro is the dishonorable friend who stabbed Clarindo and left him for dead. Clarindo has donned women's clothing to gain entrance into Jacinta's home and thereby determine her constancy or lack thereof. Jacinta had promised Clarindo her constant love even if he should die, and she remains true to her vow. Near the end of the play, Clarindo calls Jacinta's fidelity 'a miracle of devotion to care so much for a dead lover'. Lisarda pleads for Álvaro's life and despite the tension that exists between the two men, Clarindo forgives Álvaro and shows himself a 'constant' friend. Finally, the female character Jacinta exemplifies constancy: she continues to love Clarindo faithfully even after she considers him dead.

Characters – An Ensemble Cast

El muerto disimulado / Presumed Dead is an ensemble piece, and determining the protagonist of the play proves difficult at best. The title character, Clarindo, seems a likely suspect, but he does not appear on stage until the beginning of the second act. Rodrigo shouts the first line of the first act but has few lines overall and plays the role of the *viejo* or *barba* (a respectable – but not necessarily wise – old nobleman), which makes him a blocking character (at least early in the play), who will get in the way of a pair of lovers who hope to marry. The play has more than one pair of lovers: in addition to Clarindo, who loves Jacinta, Álvaro also loves her and plays the roles of antagonist and murdering schemer. Alberto loves Beatriz, but his conflict develops as a minor plot twist, peripheral to the main action. Beatriz shares Alberto's subplot, but Jacinta, Clarindo's faithful lover, and Lisarda, his cross-dressing sister, could vie for leading lady. Because they are lower-class sidekicks, Dorotea and Hipólita, the maidservants of Jacinta and Beatriz, cannot compete as possible protagonists, but Lisarda's servant, the *gracioso* Papagayo, whose name means 'parrot', plays a major role in *El muerto disimulado.* He turns up in six of the 12 scenes in the play, and parrots like to talk: Papagayo speaks 521 lines or almost 14% of the dialogue and he gets the last word in the show. No other character appears in more scenes or has more lines than Papagayo, but as the *gracioso*, by definition he cannot be the protagonist. Rather than have a single leading character, Azevedo uses the entire cast, which works together to interweave the various plot intrigues and create the meanings in this brilliant comedy.

Many of the analyses of *El muerto disimulado* focus on the roles played by the three *damas*. Ferrer Valls asserts that in the creation of these noblewomen Azevedo rejects feminine stereotypes: 'The acceptance of clichéd traits attributed to women simply because they are women is answered by the creation of female characters who demonstrate that a woman can be constant like Jacinta, or valorous and warlike like Lisarda, or even fearful like Beatriz' ('Decir', n. pag., our translation). The critic describes in greater detail the female characters and what they represent:

> If Jacinta represents constancy, and with her Azevedo responds to the cliché of the inconstancy of women, and Beatriz through her 'frightened' personality shows herself more willing to accept her brother's will, even while judging it unjust, with the third of this play's protagonist-noblewomen, Lisarda, the author presents to us a woman who, disguised as a man, serves her as a tool to argue against the cliché of weakness and the lack of bravery as a quality that fits with the feminine sex. ('Decir')

From this point of view, the three female leads might function as either a combined or a fragmented female protagonist; Ferrer Valls calls them three 'protagonist-noblewomen'. Certainly, Lisarda's avenging and cross-dressing behavior links her to many a strong heroine in the *Comedia*, and Jacinta's creation of her own play-within-the-play and her positioning of herself as its director make her one of the leads within the central plotline. For Ferrer Valls (and many of the other feminist critics who have studied this text), it matters that Azevedo offers various appropriate options for female behavior in the real world, as well as alternative ways to read women characters.

In like manner, in *El muerto disimulado*'s three *galanes*, Azevedo offers three alternative constructions of masculinity. Don Álvaro's behavior most closely aligns with stereotypical masculine rashness and bravado. He responds to his problems with violence, coercion, and prevarication. He attempts to kill his friend Clarindo because of jealousy, he duels with Alberto because of a perceived stain on his honor, and he plans to force his sister into a convent or into marriage with 'Lisardo', a 'man' she has not met. In order to win Jacinta's favor, he lies about his crime against Clarindo and tries to get 'Lisardo' to take the blame.

Álvaro's cousin Alberto responds to his circumstances in a much more discreet and measured fashion. During their swordfight, Alberto tries to reason with Álvaro by explaining that he has not acted inappropriately with Beatriz and that he wants to marry her. When 'Lisardo' and Papagayo interrupt the conflict, Alberto is grateful to avoid an unfortunate outcome with his cousin and so slips away. Alberto next seeks the support of Don Rodrigo to speak on his behalf with Álvaro. Aware of 'Lisardo's' presence in his cousin's home and fearing that Álvaro may plan to marry Beatriz to this stranger, Alberto does feel jealous, but he patiently waits to see how Fortune will unfold his fate.

In Clarindo, Azevedo creates a male character who can dress and act like a woman to accomplish his goals in the play. He gains power that Álvaro does not possess because Clarindo can move and act freely within women's spaces.[48] Part of his success depends on his ability to enact femininity. In one of the conventions of the *Comedia*, female characters who cross-dress appear more refined and, therefore, more appealing than do the male characters. In Tirso de Molina's *Don Gil de las calzas verdes* (Don Gil of the Green Breeches), for example, when Doña Juana dresses as Don Gil, Doña Inés praises 'him' for his smooth face, high voice, and green breeches. The same convention plays out in *El muerto disimulado* when Dorotea delivers Jacinta's letter to Álvaro and first sees 'Lisardo'. Dorotea speaks in an aside to the audience: 'My mistress certainly doesn't lack men to choose from, and with a sparse beard making him seem even younger, this lad's charm can easily end in her desire. After all, if "jail bait" ends in "bait", it must be because he's Cupid's lure to capture hearts and souls.' Azevedo further plays with this convention and Clarindo's youthful appearance. When 'Clara' first appears on stage, Clarindo remarks in an aside that his youth will help with his disguise because he 'still lacks the signs' that would give his manhood away. In other words, he has not yet grown a beard. Dorotea, Beatriz, and Hipólita comment on 'her' beauty, and Papagayo definitely views 'Clara' as a woman with a 'gorgeous killer face.' Jacinta, Beatriz, and their servants take 'Clara' in and accept her as part of their inner circle without expressing any concern about ambiguous gender markers, even though Jacinta repeatedly remarks that 'Clara' reminds her of her beloved Clarindo. Clarindo's revelation in the final scene, his unveiling of himself as a male cross-dresser, does not affect his standing in the eyes of the other characters. Jacinta still finds him attractive, Álvaro still fears his retribution, and Rodrigo willingly and happily accepts him as a son-in-law.

---

48 For further analysis of Clarindo and women's spaces, see Hegstrom, '*Comedia* Scholarship and Performance' (165–72).

Shifting Identities and the Tension between Appearance and Reality

As a baroque comedy, *El muerto disimulado* not only treats a variety of situations that illuminate the tension between appearance and reality, but it further exaggerates them to underscore Azevedo's related goals of challenging the customs and conventions of her age – in society and in the theater – regarding the role and treatment of women. The playwright self-consciously plays with the conventions that govern identity in her female and male characters so as to examine and critique the existing state of affairs regarding power relations and social practices. She accomplishes these objectives by highlighting from a metadramatic perspective the movement between identities via word play and self-referential commentaries on linguistic and discursive shifting and disguise, and through an exploration of the connections between character and role, gender and cross-dressing, and the (in)stability of identity. Through the rupture of conventions, Azevedo's play explores the broader topic of the connections between the theatrical and socio-cultural worlds of seventeenth-century Iberia.

The *Comedia* and the idea of metadrama have long been connected, beginning with Lionel Abel's influential *Metatheatre*, which employed *Hamlet* and *La vida es sueño* to talk about dramas that underscore the idea of drama itself.[49] Scholars of early modern theater have found it a useful approach for explaining those basic metaphors of the baroque age, life is a dream and the world is a stage, precisely because theater by definition often explored the tension between illusion (or art) and reality. Richard Hornby added to the discussion by positing a typology of five categories that further helped critics speak in meaningful ways about what happens in metadramas – and why. Hornby laid out the play within a play, the ceremony within the play, role-playing within the role, literary and real-life reference, and self-reference.[50] Metadramas may highlight one, some, or all of these categories, with the goal of leading readers and spectators to 'see double,' in a conscious recognition of the fact that they are experiencing theater about theater (32). Self-conscious dramatic texts – or self-conscious performances of theater – therefore invite audiences to step back, to analyze the techniques that the dramatist uses to call attention to theatrical spectacle, break the invisible fourth wall, and invite us to question reality.[51]

49 Lionel Abel, *Metatheatre: A New View of Dramatic Form* (New York: Hill and Wang, 1963), pp. 59–72.

50 Richard Hornby, *Drama, Metadrama, and Perception* (Lewisburg: Bucknell UP, 1986), p. 32.

51 For a discussion of the connections between theorists such as Abel and Hornby and those

Due to its multiple, self-reflexive references to theater, *El muerto disimulado* offers a superb example of metadrama. Role-playing within the role emerges as central to the comedy, as illustrated by the number of characters who self-referentially call attention to donning the clothing of the opposite sex to accomplish a variety of goals, most of which involve the ability to travel with ease in society and/or seek revenge from someone who wronged them. This category connects to that of the play within the play, especially for Jacinta, who adopts the role of dramatist, director, and casting agent of an inset play intended to reveal that Don Álvaro murdered her beloved.[52] Clarindo assumes several roles within his role; he returns to Portugal with a similar goal and changes disguises (or is perceived by others as portraying a different role) frequently, and he plans to use those roles to discover if his cherished Jacinta has remained faithful to him in his absence and to deal with his 'killer'. Lisarda cross-dresses to take on a new identity that will enable her to travel freely from her hometown to Lisbon and then within the city, and she also does so in order to avenge Clarindo's murder, but unlike Jacinta, her metaplay becomes significantly less important once she meets Álvaro and begins to fall in love with him. Finally, Álvaro also tries to direct the action of his own interior play, a plot that uses 'Lisardo' to help win over Jacinta; his 'script' fails on multiple fronts, although he does eventually end up with Lisarda. All of this role-playing relates directly to larger questions of identity by reminding us of the roles that each of us plays in the dramas of our own lives and the positive and negative consequences of role-playing.[53] Williamsen states that cross-dressing 'coincides with heightened meta-theatricality', which foregrounds 'the performativity of identity and its inherent instability'.[54] In her comedy,

---

who study early modern Hispanic drama, see also Catherine Larson, 'Metatheater and the *Comedia*: Past, Present, and Future', in H. Mancing and C. Ganelin (eds), *The Golden Age Comedia: Text, Theory, and Performance* (West Lafayette: Purdue UP, 1994), pp. 204–21.

52 In reference to Jacinta's plan 'to become the "author" of an alternative plot', Gabriele suggests that this metadramatic technique grants her greater narrative authority; it ultimately helps Azevedo posit 'a critique of the dominant discourse' regarding the role of women in early modern society. See John P. Gabriele, 'Engendering Narrative Equality in Ángela de Azevedo's *El muerto disimulado*', *Bulletin of the Comediantes* 60.1 (2008), pp. 130, 137.

53 As Soufas observes, '[t]he appropriation of someone else's symbols of identity – whether of social class, political office, or gender – puts into question the stability of the political categories that the most powerful in society have every reason to want to preserve under the appearance of intrinsic and essential classifications.' Teresa Scott Soufas, *Dramas of Distinction: Study of Plays by Golden Age Women* (Lexington: UP of Kentucky, 1997), p. 109.

54 Amy R. Williamsen. 'Stages of Passing: Identity and Performance in the *Comedia*', in

Azevedo calls attention to role-playing as a means of addressing a number of serious issues: who we are, how gender is enacted, the ways in which convention and social norms govern the lives of women, etc.

In addition to using the techniques of role-playing and the assumption of theatrically oriented roles such as actor or director in interior plays within the play, Azevedo seems to delight in making direct references to her own play as theater. At the end of the first act, she lets Hipólita remind her audience of its role as an audience: 'Let's go, since here, as I understand it, is where the act ends.' In another example, Dorotea signals that the spectator is watching a play – one so complicated that it will take a while to unravel the plot: 'What is Jacinta trying to do? I'll bet that in an hour and a half no one will be able to figure out what direction this play is headed (or at least that's how I imagine it).' Papagayo connects creating art and telling lies with playwriting when he asserts, 'My God, there's no poet in the world who lies like I lie.' Moreover, at the play's end, the *gracioso* speaks to the audience in a comically contradictory observation about appearance and reality, fiction and truth:

Clarindo: And now *Presumed Dead* has its happy ending.
Papagayo: Such an affair didn't really happen, but since strange things do occur, I suppose that this one did, too.

Every example of a self-conscious reference to the theater within *El muerto disimulado* reminds readers and spectators of their engagement with fiction, which then creates greater esthetic distance between them and the text and underscores Azevedo's rather subversive response to baroque court society, which was often critiqued for over-valuing appearance.[55] Azevedo appears to enjoy playing with the conventions of theater in *El muerto disimulado*, not only in her multi-layered use of cross-dressing (physical and linguistic), but also in her characters' asides to the audience regarding the complicated plot, the fact that an act has ended, or commentary on the skill of the dramatist. The examples are many, but each offers the audience members a chance to join in the fun every time they are included in the joke:

Lisarda: Have you ever seen more unusual difficulties? In what play have you witnessed more unbelievable happenings, or a more unconscionable mess?

G. Campbell and A. Williamsen (eds), *Prismatic Reflections on Spanish Golden Age Theater: Essays in Honor of Matthew D. Stroud* (New York: Peter Lang, 2016), p. 249.

55 See especially Ferrer Valls, 'Decir' (n. pag.) and 'Mujer' (n. pag.).

Through her brilliant use of metadramatic techniques, Ângela de Azevedo answers those questions.

Self-referential discourse serves to heighten the overall metadramatic and metatheatrical stance of *El muerto disimulado.* Several characters not only switch between Spanish and Portuguese, but they occasionally also discuss language itself (including its translatability or its loss in times of emotional turmoil). Once again, self-conscious allusions – here, in metalinguistic references – add to the metatheatrical spirit of the comedy and make the audience more attuned to Azevedo's overall techniques and governing strategies. Metalanguage is, however, only one of the salient elements of Azevedo's use of language in her comedy. *El muerto disimulado* offers a typical example of seventeenth-century baroque language, but it simultaneously plays with language difference and uses discourse to foreground important elements of the plot, as well as the comedy's inherent metadramatic qualities. A number of critics have noted the ways in which Azevedo's text illustrates the influence of Pedro Calderón de la Barca and other baroque writers, which can, at times, be so overtly metadramatic that some elements of *El muerto disimulado* are easily identifiable under Hornby's category of 'literary and real-life reference.'[56] More specifically, we can observe this influence in the play's puns and word play, self-conscious allusions to language itself, and use of hyperbaton. The discourse of *El muerto disimulado* plays a key role in complementing the physical action of the play; both function as necessary elements of the text, whether the play is read or performed, yet if the point appears obvious, we must not forget that this woman writer – a dramatic poet – was emulating a remarkably complicated style of writing in a language not her own.[57]

Azevedo was certainly not the only Portuguese writer who also wrote in Spanish, which is understandable given the linguistic, political, and cultural connections between the two Iberian countries in the sixteenth and seventeenth centuries.[58] Wade emphasizes the revolutionary nature of the

---

56 It is possible to find among her three plays a few direct references; we previously noted the easily recognizable quotation from *La vida es sueño*. Hormigón points to Azevedo's 'gusto for antithesis and puns, her perfectly symmetrical lyric duets' (404, our translation).

57 Hormigón assesses the near-native quality of Azevedo's Castilian, describing her language usage as essentially correct, with the few errors that do occur no doubt due to her native language (404).

58 See Wade for a discussion of the bilingualism (in speech and print) common in Portugal at that time and the ways in which Azevedo evoked her native language and culture in her plays ('Patriotism' 325–43).

dramatist's use of code-switching in *El muerto disimulado*, which affirms 'a national identity she obviously wishes to preserve and glorify' (336). The critic emphasizes the subversive importance of Azevedo's use of the term and concept of *saudade*, which, in this play, includes a metalinguistic discussion of its role (and its untranslatability in Spanish) in capturing the spirit of the Portuguese language and culture. Moreover, this discussion of language allows her to talk to her Spanish-speaking audience and to highlight a significant discursive element of the play being performed on stage (337–39).[59]

One critic has commented negatively on Azevedo's abilities with the language of *El muerto disimulado*. Doménech complains that the extreme baroque elements of the dramatist's discursive style – the rhetorical components, parallelisms, word play, strong hyperbatons, intercalated phrases, parenthetical comments, asides, and other linguistic displays – combined with the already labyrinthine plot, can make the play difficult to decipher ('Introducción' 19). Still, although we would agree that Azevedo's text presents occasional challenges, we join those who have published analyses of the play, taught it, and seen it performed, who consider Doménech's assessment unnecessarily inflated.

In fact, we submit that Azevedo purposefully challenges the linguistic conventions of the *Comedia*. Various critics have mentioned the interrelatedness of the characters' discursive behavior, naming, and gender construction (for example, Papagayo's confusion of monks and nuns, or his discussion of a tree with two genders), while others have focused attention on the power of discourse to call attention to language itself: 'Clara' claims that 'she' has forgotten her native language but is happy speaking Castilian and underscores wordplay as in her description of '[p]urses of such value that each doubloon put inside them doubles the amount of its current value.' Papagayo emerges as the master of the double entendre ('if you're going to eat, it'll cost me half my name, for I'll prepare the *Papa* for you and I'll stick with the *Gayo* for me – those are the perks of being a parrot at Court').[60] Stoll employs the concept of liminality – in its connections to

59 For a detailed description of the large role code-switching plays in *El muerto disimulado*, see the 'Editor's Note'.

60 See also the wordplay inherent in the following exchange between Lisarda and Papagayo:

Lisarda: *To Papagayo.* Don't you see how much that person's face resembles Clarindo's? Oh, if my brother was alive and was a woman instead of a man, I'd insist she was he!

Papagayo: Not me, since that body still represents how scared I was. I'd see a lot of difference

gender, identity, metatheatrical performance, and, especially, language – to highlight Azevedo's understanding and presentation of shifting realities in the comedy.[61] As Mujica affirms, '[l]anguage itself is a fount of confusion in *El muerto disimulado*', but that language is carefully planned and constructed, allowing readers and spectators to view the confusion as part of a larger structure and a commentary on the world in which Azevedo wrote her play (238, our translation).

Azevedo exaggerates the conventions of language use in the *Comedia* to create comedy. Maroto Camino senses this when she comments on Azevedo's parody of the popular abandoned-woman complaint, delivered here by a man in drag (323). The convention of linguistic dueling between lovers finds its parallel in the single *octava real* and sonnet in which Jacinta and Clarindo, respectively, 'compose' and recite poems to illustrate their skill in defending who suffers more when lovers part: the one left behind or the person who leaves. Besides offering parallels between the characters' fictional biographies and the important themes of the comedy, Azevedo calls attention to the act of writing poetry, with the play's internal audience providing critiques of each poem. Soufas discusses the topic of self-conscious discourse as part of her larger exploration of the carnivalesque implications of *El muerto disimulado*, in which (linguistic and physical) mascarade suggests 'the instability of roles and categories' (*Dramas of Distinction* 104, 134–35). Language is therefore central to understanding the gender play associated with cross-dressing. In a text that portrays a woman dressing as a man and a man who dresses as a woman, code-switching finds its physical analogue in cross-dressing. Many of Azevedo's characters are not who they seem – and, even more, their identities constantly shift, principally as the result of cross-dressing and role-playing within those characters' roles. Physical disguise surfaces multiple times: Lisarda presents herself as 'Lisardo', and Clarindo as the street vendor 'Clara', but the comedy also highlights linguistic disguises, such as Don Álvaro de Gamboa's pseudonym, the anagram 'Urbano del Lago Amado', as Azevedo treats dissimulation from dozens of related and self-reflexive perspectives. Primary among them are

---

between this gorgeous *killer face* and that *dead face* unless what I saw before me was his walking corpse, and this Clarinda is his soul, which I say because everyone knows that the word for soul is feminine.

61 Anita K. Stoll, '"Tierra de en medio": Liminalities in Angela de Azevedo's *El muerto disimulado*', in V. Hegstrom and A. Williamsen (eds), *Engendering the Early Modern Stage: Women Playwrights in the Spanish Empire* (New Orleans: UP of the South, 1999), pp. 151–64.

references to culturally determined gender, as the dramatist explores what it means to live as a female and male in her age.

From the beginning of *El muerto disimulado*, Azevedo poses a host of gender-related questions; a large number of the critical approaches to the play from the last 20 years focus on gender and its connections to early modern society. Soufas asserts that the play problematizes controversies regarding the allocation of authority to call attention to the 'injustices residing in gender inequities and subjugation' (*Dramas of Distinction* 107). Cross-dressing allowed women on stage to underscore, and therefore critique, the limitations that society imposed upon their ability to leave the confines of the home, travel independently, and determine their own destinies. Soufas adds that in early modern dramas, cross-dressing was usually 'an honor problem that necessitates the woman's pursuit of the offender in order to confront him on terms of temporary social equality, to remain close enough to him to arrange a trick or coercion that will force fulfillment of a broken promise, or to take revenge for an as yet unpunished crime' (*Dramas of Distinction* 115); these are precisely the conditions that exist in *El muerto disimulado*. Seen from this perspective, critics such as Soufas, Mujica, Maroto Camino, Stoll, Williamsen, Vollendorf, and Ferrer Valls aver that cross-dressing in *El muerto disimulado* functions not merely as a typical early modern theatrical technique, sure to please an audience, but as a transgressive strategy that allows Azevedo to examine gender injustice.[62] Such injustice in early modern Spain includes fathers whose authority must be obeyed (Rodrigo's position in this play), and women who are portrayed as lacking in agency or unfaithful. In this female-focused comedy, Azevedo suggests a different model: her women are portrayed as strong and proactive, while many of the male characters tend to be presented as weak and ineffectual or arrogant and selfish.[63]

---

62 See Lisa Vollendorf, 'Desire Unbound: Women's Theater of Spain's Golden Age', in J. Cammarata (ed.), *Women in the Discourse of Early Modern Spain* (Gainesville: UP of Florida, 2003), pp. 275–76; Lisa Vollendorf, *The Lives of Women: A New History of Inquisitional Spain* (Nashville: Vanderbilt UP, 2005), pp. 78–79; Ferrer Valls, 'Mujer'. Regarding this, Maroto Camino explains that '[f]ollowing the theatrical tradition that a change of clothes amounts to a change of identity, [characters] do not recognize each other', although she also reminds us that several of those characters do comment on physical similarities between the cross-dressed characters and family members they know well (320–21), a strategy that further calls attention to the gender bending in the play. Maroto Camino also asserts that from the very first scene, in which the dramatist emphasizes gender expectations for both men (fathers) and women (daughters), 'Azevedo accords her play a socio-political dimension, thereby prefiguring the feminist belief that the personal and the familial are always political and public' (315).

63 See, for example, Ferrer Valls, 'Mujer' and 'Decir'.

A number of scholars writing about Azevedo and this play have also outlined the controversies of the age regarding the role of women in the theater, specifically, their participation in cross-dressing on stage; these analyses serve to illuminate the extent to which the topic was a social issue of great significance.[64] Fray José de Jesús María, for example, attacked transvestism on stage as 'prohibited and detestable by divine and human laws', adding that a woman dressed as a man provoked behavior so lascivious and dangerous in audiences that their hearts were inflamed with mortal lust.[65] In both early modern society and its theater, women's lives were scrutinized carefully, to say the least. Azevedo's subversive comedy exaggerates theatrical conventions to underscore the problems and point to the need for change.

In *El muerto disimulado*, Azevedo not only uses the more common trope of a woman dressed as a man but adds the doubly unconventional depiction of a man – and, even more, a *noble* man – dressed as a woman. Moreover, that woman, 'Clara', is initially presented not as a noblewoman like the rest of the principal characters, but as a lower-class seller of trinkets, whose movement in the streets, the public domain, leads to the implication that she might not be an honorable woman. Once 'Clara' tells her story, however, any initial doubts are replaced by the welcoming attitudes of Jacinta, Beatriz, and their servants. In the related context of identity formation, critics such as Williamsen have suggested that cross-dressing in *El muerto disimulado* relates to the idea of passing, an 'attempted transformation across lines of social identity categories', which has led critics to 'theorize the concept and its relationship to the performativity of identity' ('Stages' 243). Passing can occur in questions of race, religion, social class, and gender, with cross-gendered dressing the 'most studied type of passing found in the *Comedia*' (244). Clarindo's assumption of the role of 'Clara' is actually a double pass, since the nobleman dresses not merely as a woman of the same rank, but as a merchant woman (246–47). On multiple levels, the playwright highlights the points of contact among gender, disguise, and identity for both sexes. Gabriele summarizes Azevedo's point of view: the comedy shows an 'unambiguous female perspective achieved through cross-dressing' (128), as the dramatist challenges 'the traditional concepts of what it means to be

64 Soufas, among others, cites from Cotarelo y Mori's *Bibliografía de las controversias sobre la licitud del teatro en España* (*Dramas of Distinction*, 23–29).

65 José de Jesús María, *Memorial, Bibliografía de las controversias sobre la licitud del teatro en España*, ed. E. Cotarelo y Mori (Madrid: Revista de Archivos, Bibliotecas y Museos, 1904), p. 381, our translation.

masculine and feminine' (129).[66] Her female characters, including 'Clara', are strong and, ultimately, they turn the expectations of their age upside down to achieve their goals. The performativity inherent in cross-dressing allows Azevedo to explore her society's values and respond to them in a manner that prefigures future responses to injustice and gender identity.

The playwright illuminates this theme of challenging the traditional, negative conventions of femininity and masculinity through the brother and sister pair, Clarindo and Lisarda. Both shift and sift through multiple versions of themselves throughout the play. Often they gain power and take control of their circumstances by creating a new identity for themselves, but other times different characters assign them an uncomfortable or difficult role and they have to think and act cleverly to keep up. Sometimes trying on a new self is as easy as changing their clothes. Cross-dressing, however, is not the only method the two siblings use to forge multiple versions of themselves. For example, Clarindo also displays the instability of his identity in the various roles he plays besides 'Clara', the peddler. Papagayo calls Clarindo a 'shadow, ghost, or illusion', an alias that Clarindo uses to his advantage; he can move more freely about Lisbon and into his lover's house to gather information because the other characters do not suspect he is alive. Papagayo and Lisarda search for Clarindo's ghost, but they find 'Clara', a table maid at an inn. To further complicate matters, Clarindo is Jacinta's 'dead' lover, but 'Clara' is supposedly the jilted lover of Álvaro. This combination makes 'Clara' the lover of Clarindo's own rival in love, a man who is also the assassin of Clarindo's 'ghost'. The details of 'Clara's' fictitious biography grow even more convoluted when she invents feigned friendships between her father and Álvaro, and her father and the presumed dead man, Clarindo ('Father valued him as his own son'). Moreover, Rodrigo plans to confer another status on 'Clara'; with his financial support, she will profess as a nun. In the final scene, Clarindo forgives Álvaro and, thus, becomes his mortal enemy's friend, brother-in-law, and 'true brother'. Obviously,

66 Vollendorf also sees the comedy as a 'female-focused play' (*The Lives of Women*, 79). Mujica adds that Azevedo 'insists on the moral superiority of women (illustrated by Jacinta's constancy) and censures certain male-perpetrated injustices, for example the abuse of poor women (seen in Clarindo's role as "Clara"), materialism (personified by Álvaro's attitude towards Alberto), and despotism (evident in Rodrigo)' (237, our translation). See also Bayliss's exploration of the connections between female agency, cross-dressing, and modern views of woman-authored early modern drama. Robert Bayliss, 'The Best Man in the Play: Female Agency in a Gender-Inclusive *Comedia*', *Bulletin of the Comediantes* 59.2 (2007), pp. 303–23.

Clarindo – and 'Clara' – play or are assigned a hyperbolic number of roles throughout the play.

Similarly, Lisarda/'Lisardo' experiences analogous kinds of identity shifts, which depend on more than just cross-dressing. One factor that motivates Lisarda's enactment of masculinity is her strong identification with her roles as sister and avenger of her brother's death. Because she believes an assassin killed her brother and that the blow of that news killed her father, she sees herself as the only remaining family member who can set things right. Her sense of self becomes confused, though, when upon meeting Don Álvaro, she falls in love with him; almost immediately, however, she learns both that he loves Jacinta and that he dealt the blows that supposedly killed her brother. All at once, she becomes Jacinta's rival for the love of her brother's own assassin. To entangle the web of relationships further, Álvaro convinces 'Lisardo' to pose as Clarindo's murderer and insists that 'Lisardo' marry his sister Beatriz. This makes 'Lisardo' the killer against whom Lisarda seeks revenge, as well as the fiancé of the sister of the man whom Lisarda hopes to marry. Papagayo creates yet another identity for 'Lisardo' by describing him as his business partner and Lisarda's neighbor from Lamego. The *gracioso* also confounds the situation by mistakenly calling Lisarda a friar. He covers his mistake, 'I mean nun', explaining that friars and nuns all wear habits and live in convents.[67] Finally, when she reveals her 'true identity' in the end, Lisarda becomes the fiancée of her brother's enemy.

The ease and fluidity with which the siblings can move through and juggle their multiple roles underscore the performativity of identity. Clarindo's and Lisarda's shifting selves often cause them difficulties (Clarindo complains, 'this disguise … is too hard on a heart that knows what love is', and Lisarda protests, 'Who else besides me would experience such … strange adventures?'), but those complications ultimately empower the two characters because others do not have all the information to which the brother and sister are privy. Some characters, Alberto and Beatriz for example, lament and fret about their circumstances. Other characters – Rodrigo and Álvaro – try to take control via manipulation and coercion. Their strategies do not work as well as those of Clarindo and Lisarda, because these two characters' multiple identities have allowed them to move in more spaces and gather more information, and they can therefore see the bigger picture.

67 Papagayo's fumbling response creates a selfhood for Lisarda that corresponds to Clarindo's position as a dead man. Nuns are dead to the world – cloistered in convents, so 'Lisardo' can move about Lisbon and no one will suspect he is Lisarda.

The persistence of self-conscious allusions to the theater, language, disguise, character, and role found in *El muerto disimulado* illustrate the multiple ways in which Azevedo explores the tension between illusion and reality, as well as the (in)stability of identity, in her comedy. From myriad perspectives, the playwright focuses attention on the ways in which our own perceptions often turn out to be misconceptions. Even more, she shines a light on the conventions – theatrical and socio-cultural – of her age, especially those dealing with gender injustice, so as to enter into dialogue with the status quo.

Structure of the Play: Cuadros

As we mentioned earlier, in his *Arte nuevo*, Lope de Vega established that the *Comedia* would include three *jornadas* or acts. Early modern manuscripts and printed texts of *comedias* did not indicate scene breaks, but *Comedia* studies conceive of *cuadros* or scenes as beginning with the entrance of one group of characters and ending with the eventual exit of all the members of that group. Generally speaking, contiguous *cuadros* take place in distinct imagined spaces. *El muerto disimulado / Presumed Dead* consists of 12 such *cuadros.*

Scene	Location	Entrances & Exits
ACT 1		
1.1	Don Rodrigo's house	Jacinta enters, chased by Don Rodrigo with a dagger, and Dorotea holding him back. Rodrigo exits. Jacinta exits. Dorotea exits.
1.2	Palace Plaza / exterior and interior of Don Álvaro's house	Lisarda, cross-dressed as 'Lisardo,' and Papagayo enter. Lisarda and Papagayo exit, and Don Álvaro and Alberto enter dueling. Papagayo and Lisarda reenter to interrupt the duel. Alberto exits to escape. Papagayo exits to retrieve luggage. Álvaro exits and reenters quickly. Dorotea enters with a letter for Álvaro. Dorotea exits. Álvaro exits. Lisarda exits.
1.3	A street near Don Rodrigo's house	Beatriz and Hipólita enter. Beatriz and Hipólita exit.

ACT 2		
2.1	Outside an inn	Papagayo enters fleeing from Clarindo. Papagayo exits. Clarindo exits.
2.2	Don Rodrigo's house	Hipólita and Dorotea enter, arguing. Jacinta and Beatriz enter to intervene. Rodrigo enters. Rodrigo exits. Clarindo enters, cross-dressed as 'Clara.' Jacinta, Dorotea, and 'Clara' exit. Alberto enters. Alberto, Beatriz, and Hipólita exit.
2.3	Don Álvaro's house	Rodrigo and Álvaro enter. Rodrigo exits. Álvaro exits.
2.4	Outside an inn	'Clara' enters. 'Lisardo' and Papagayo enter. 'Clara' exits. 'Lisardo' and Papagayo exit.
2.5	Don Rodrigo's house	Rodrigo and Jacinta enter. Rodrigo and Jacinta exit.
ACT 3		
3.1	Don Rodrigo's house	Jacinta and 'Clara' enter separately. Rodrigo, Beatriz, Hipólita and Dorotea enter. Papagayo enters. The women (including 'Clara') exit. Papagayo exits. Rodrigo exits.
3.2	Don Álvaro's house	'Lisardo' enters. Álvaro enters on the opposite side of the stage. Papagayo enters. Álvaro exits. 'Lisardo' exits. Papagayo exits.
3.3	A street near Don Rodrigo's house	Alberto enters. Alberto exits.
3.4	Don Rodrigo's house	Jacinta enters. Beatriz enters without initially noticing Jacinta. Rodrigo enters and instructs Alberto to remain 'hidden' on one side of the stage. Rodrigo instructs Beatriz to 'hide' in another place on stage. Álvaro, 'Lisardo,' and Papagayo enter. 'Clara' 'hides' in a third place on stage.

3.4	Don Rodrigo's house	'Clara' enters and then exits, promising to return shortly. Dorotea enters, followed by Clarindo dressed as a man. Papagayo and 'Lisardo' exit, promising to return shortly. Hipólita enters, followed by Papagayo and Lisarda dressed as a woman. Alberto and Beatriz enter.

Staging *El muerto disimulado / Presumed Dead*

El muerto disimulado was, like virtually all drama, no doubt written with a potential performance in mind, a performance that would foreground spectacle on stage, with actors, audiences, stage properties and sets. Azevedo must have envisioned how her comedy would look if it were staged; her textual decisions, by definition, must have resulted from a great deal of thought regarding the words her characters spoke and their movement on stage. Later in this introduction we discuss the contemporary performances of *El muerto disimulado* and *Presumed Dead*; we focus attention on the choices that were made by the university-theater group and professional company that produced the texts in Spanish and English. Here, we take a performance-oriented approach to sets, movement on stage, and stage properties as we explore the decision-making that, based on her written text, Azevedo reveals.

Settings and Stage Sets

Although scenery and stage devices that allowed for elaborate special effects existed in palace theaters and public playhouses in early modern Iberia, many *comedias* relied on minimal sets and language to create the locations in which each scene of the play took place. All of the action in *El muerto disimulado / Presumed Dead* occurs in five places in Lisbon: 1) the interior of Don Rodrigo de Aguilar's house, 2) the Palace Plaza, 3) the interior of Don Álvaro de Gamboa's house, 4) the streets outside the noblemen's houses, and 5) the exterior of an inn. The characters create all of these settings verbally through their dialogue, visually through the use of small stage properties, and physically by their presence. The most obvious verbal cue that locates the action of a scene (and, in a broader sense, the whole play) occurs the first time Lisarda and Papagayo walk on stage. Papagayo declares, 'You're in Lisbon now and this is the Palace Plaza, a rich monument to the Tagus, where the deity Thetis stumbled at the river's edge'. The Palace Plaza (known today as the Praça do Comércio) lies next to the Tagus River in the Baixa district, with two hills on either side. Papagayo's speech establishes the location of the action and paints a verbal picture for any audience member who knows or has read about Lisbon. With his words, Papagayo moves himself, Lisarda, and the audience to Lisbon.

Jacinta and Beatriz, and their two servants, Dorotea and Hipólita, create the setting of Don Rodrigo's house through their dialogue and presence in the space. Jacinta positions her home on the hill to the east of the Palace Plaza, in the Alfama district of Lisbon near the Church of St Anthony, when she tells Dorotea about falling in love with Clarindo in that church. Again the mention of a landmark helps the audience imagine the location of a scene. In subsequent scenes, the presence of the four women on stage signals the domestic space of Rodrigo's house. Moreover, these characters discuss the location: Dorotea says that Jacinta should throw Beatriz and Hipólita out of the house; Beatriz tells Rodrigo that she cannot go home and needs to stay at his residence for her protection. The final scene and resolution of the play take place in this space and call for at least two simple screens behind which Beatriz, Álvaro, and Clarindo can eavesdrop before they enter the scene.

Lisarda and Papagayo locate the exterior and then interior of Don Álvaro's house through their dialogue. Lisarda tells Papagayo that she remembers that her brother's friend lives in St Paul's parish (in the neighborhood on the hill to the west of the Palace Plaza), Papagayo signals the direction they should go, and they then hear the sounds of a swordfight, talk about entering the house, and overhear Don Álvaro declare his own name from offstage. Álvaro invites 'Lisardo' and the *gracioso* to stay at his house and sends Papagayo off to the inn to collect their belongings. The suitcases he carries in a later scene become a visual cue that Papagayo encounters Clarindo's 'ghost' outside the inn. Then Papagayo verbally confirms the location of their meeting when he tells Clarindo that the inn is not Purgatory, but Hell, and asks him why his soul must wander there. In a coincidence typical of early modern comedy, Clarindo has taken a room in the same inn in which his cross-dressed sister had rented a place to stay. Ultimately, through her emphasis on the variety of settings and the movement of characters between and within them, Azevedo further draws our attention to gender-based ideas about female and male, interior and exterior space. Because the actors indicate settings through their dialogue, use of props, and presence on the stage, *El muerto disimulado* does not need elaborate stage scenery.

Movement on Stage

Azevedo was writing in a time in which the theater was exceptionally popular; playwrights such as Lope de Vega, Tirso de Molina, and Calderón de la Barca were paradigms of genius for lovers of the page and the stage in both Spain and Portugal. The conventions of the *Comedia* were firmly entrenched, and Azevedo knew the theatrical styles of her day. She emulated – and, some might say, parodied – the subgenre of the *comedia de enredo*, as well as the conventions of sword fighting and the *mujer vestida de hombre*. All of this anticipates numerous creative decisions that combine role-playing and disguise: how to have the characters move on stage so as to highlight the many plot complications, how to balance that movement with the dialogue, which was at times as complicated as the plot itself, and how to maximize the comic effect of so many cross-dressing characters. Would their movements on stage further exaggerate the relationships between role, disguise/clothing, and identity, or would they make the convention work by downplaying its difference and pretending that everybody always is someone else?

El muerto disimulado / Presumed Dead contains a great many entrances and exits, as well as key scenes filled with physical action, but it also includes a lot of talking, which suggests the need for actors to move on stage in ways that keep the overall pace rapid.[68] Complex sets are not mandatory, but a few elements stand out: the movement mostly takes place on the street and in a room in Jacinta's house, and the play uses a downstairs (street)/upstairs (home) concept, as when Lisarda, dressed as 'Lisardo,' hears the sounds of a sword fight between Don Álvaro and Alberto and decides to climb the stairs and intervene. Given the explicit and implicit stage directions in the source text and the design of the typical *corral* stage, an early modern staging of this scene likely would have played out on one level. When Lisarda and Papagayo hear a sword fight and voices off stage and exit the stage to enter Álvaro's house, they would do so through one of the two doors typically found at the back of the stage. Álvaro and Alberto would simultaneously enter through the other rear door, and the scene on stage would transform instantly from the street in front of Álvaro's house to the upstairs interior of that house. Of course, the *corral* stage had the flexibility to allow for other possibilities, and part of the scene could have occurred on the gallery-balcony above the upstage doors.

68 The actors in *Presumed Dead's* premiere in English did precisely that: the pace of the spoken dialogue was exceedingly fast, but it played well for the audience members, who seemed to enjoy keeping up with this discursive game.

The sword fight itself exemplifies a typical *Comedia* convention, but with a twist: the men prove to be rather inept, and the strongest participant by far is the cross-dressed Lisarda. Azevedo spells out the details in her explicit and implicit stage directions; for example, when 'Lisardo' steps in, the weak Alberto quickly exits, 'Lisardo' disarms Don Alvaro, and the disguised 'man' then offers his opponent another chance to duel by giving him a second sword. This stereotypical macho event is upended by the new female champion. Azevedo must have imagined not only that her dueling characters would play with the conventions of gender, but how they would do so, with moves that were choreographed to provide both action and comedy.

A similarly memorable scene occurs at the play's opening: Jacinta's father, brandishing a dagger, chases her around the stage. Don Rodrigo's action brings to life the conventionalized behavior of how a father in early modern times might attempt to 'protect' his honor and lineage by insisting that his daughter marry. In Azevedo's version, we quickly learn that the daughter is refusing to marry not because she hates all men, or because she has a lover, or even because she relishes becoming a nun, but because she had vowed never to marry anyone else if her beloved Clarindo, who had left on the Savoy armada, did not return; her reasoning becomes a female vow of honor. The scene, however, is marvelously funny, precisely because Jacinta's father, angry and armed, insists on chasing his daughter across the stage. Azevedo opens her comedy with a well-designed example of movement, one that is also fundamentally parodic.

Azevedo ends her comedy with two great reveals, as 'Clara' leaves the room only to return dressed as the male Clarindo, and 'Lisardo' corresponds by stepping off stage and reappearing in women's clothing. Both actions underscore onstage movement as the newly minted man and woman leave the confusion of the group and reenter to (re)present their true selves. The other characters then work with the two to end the comedy with the stereotypical pairing of lovers, highlighted by the onstage action of each taking the other's hand. The movement evidenced in the final scenes reminds the audience that the lines between life and art, illusion and reality, are often blurred. Azevedo's play with theatrical conventions, which begins with the father's on-stage attack on his daughter and ends with the revelation of gender, love, identity, and role, uses movement to focus our attention on the major concepts of the baroque age.

Stage properties

Early in the second act of *El muerto disimulado / Presumed Dead*, Clarindo reveals in a soliloquy to the audience that he remains very much alive. If not for this bit of dramatic irony, in which the audience learns a significant piece of information about Clarindo that eludes the rest of the characters, the play could well be read as an early modern 'whodunit'. Both Jacinta, the 'dead' man's lover, and Lisarda, the 'dead' man's sister, set themselves up as detectives who try to follow the clues to discover the identity of the murderer. One stage property, Jacinta's ring, which gets passed from character to character in the play, becomes a clue that convinces Jacinta that her suspicions are correct. The audience sees the piece of jewelry for the first time when Álvaro offers it to Dorotea as a reward for bringing him a letter from Jacinta. (At this point, no one realizes that the ring originally belonged to Jacinta, but in the play's backstory, Jacinta gave it as a parting gift to Clarindo the night before he sailed with the armada.) The bauble next appears when Hipólita (Beatriz's – and by extension her brother Álvaro's – servant) steals it from Dorotea. The two servants fight over the object, prompting Jacinta and Beatriz to intercede. As Hipólita hands the item to Dorotea, Jacinta recognizes her ring and declares in an aside: 'It looks like the one I gave Clarindo'. Jacinta correctly deduces that this evidence proves Álvaro's guilt. Later Jacinta shows the recovered treasure to 'Clara', and Clarindo tells the audience in an aside that when Álvaro wounded him and left him for dead, the villain stole Jacinta's gift from his finger, which Clarindo permitted in order to keep the would-be assassin from suspecting that he was still alive. Offering an ironically helpful red herring, 'Clara' tells Jacinta that she saw 'Urbano' with the ring; this misleading information will later support Jacinta's correct suspicions about Álvaro. At the end of the play, when 'Lisardo' claims to be Clarindo's assassin, Jacinta produces her prized possession as a smoking gun against Álvaro, who complains about the coincidence to the audience: 'Oh, how inattentive I was: without even noticing, I gave Clarindo's ring to Dorotea'. Recovering quickly, Álvaro claims that Clarindo gave him the trinket as a memento of their friendship, which elicits an aside from Clarindo, 'I can't take any more of this', and an angry response to Álvaro, 'Say you stole it'. Álvaro's prevarications about the ring become the factor that prompts Clarindo to reveal his true identity, as well as Álvaro's motives, and to solve the crime.

The first clue that had led Jacinta to suspect Álvaro's guilt was also a stage property, the letter that Álvaro sent to her to express his condolences on the death of Clarindo. Letters appear frequently in early modern Iberian theater. In Álvaro's letter, the unworthy suitor tips his hand: 'I should complain that you offered his love a magnificent welcome while mine gets nothing but scorn', which causes Jacinta to ask, 'and who might have told him that Clarindo was my lover?' Álvaro's letter indecorously goes on to suggest that with Clarindo gone, Álvaro himself might replace him in Jacinta's affections, but the grieving lover reaches a different conclusion: 'Don Álvaro was without a doubt Clarindo's murderer'. Jacinta uses her return letter to force Álvaro's hand. She will agree to marry him if he can provide the identity of Clarindo's killer. If he does not admit his guilt, he will have to give up on courting her. If he does name himself as the murderer, she vows that his crime 'will be avenged with his death'. The two letters provide information intended by their senders to manipulate the actions and decisions of their recipients; Jacinta's letter more cleverly controls the outcome of the play.

Beyond these clues (the ring and the letters), other kinds of props also visually communicate meaning in this play. The use of swords is such a common practice in the *Comedia* that the term for 'cloak and dagger' in Spanish, *capa y espada*, literally means 'cape and sword'. Rodrigo's dagger and the swords of Álvaro, Alberto, and Clarindo all signify the violent, masculine power that threatens through intimidation and coercion to resolve honor conflicts that are related to love relationships. Rodrigo might kill Jacinta if she refuses to obey him and choose someone to marry. Álvaro wants to kill his cousin Alberto for talking with his sister Beatriz in an inappropriately unsupervised manner. Clarindo readies himself to kill Álvaro, thus jeopardizing Lisarda's happy ending. Luckily, Lisarda also has a sword. She uses it to interrupt the conflict between the male cousins, thereby postponing their potentially violent acts, and she also draws her sword against her brother at the end of the play to defend Álvaro.

The small items that 'Clara' pulls out of her little basket help to define the character that Clarindo invents for his undercover persona. 'Clara' shows off gloves, mirrors, rings set with precious stones, stockings, fans, money pouches, and ribbons. This display of her wares to a group of women in the domestic space of a home links 'Clara' to other Spanish classical female characters of questionable reputation, including Fabia from Lope de Vega's *El caballero de Olmedo* and Celestina from Rojas's *Tragicomedia de Calixto y Melibea*.[69] All three merchant women enter the home of noblewomen to

69 When the sorceress Fabia enters the house of Doña Inés and Doña Leonor, she carries a little basket like 'Clara's', which contains powders and potions, soap, pills, written prayers,

facilitate the entrance of a young male lover into a forbidden space. 'Clara's' connections with Fabia and Celestina, evident in the trinkets she sells, call into question her reputation, and for this reason, Don Rodrigo imagines that he can easily send her off to a convent to keep her from getting in the way of the relationship between Don Álvaro and Jacinta. 'Clara's' wares, as well as the swords, dagger, letters, and Jacinta's ring, help with characterization, advance plot intrigues, and make *El muerto disimulado / Presumed Dead* visually stimulating.

Contemporary Performances

Due to the numerous questions that still exist regarding Azevedo's life and works, we cannot prove that *El muerto disimulado* was performed during the lifetime of the author – or, for that matter, prior to the twenty-first century. In the twenty-first century, the 2004 production by Brigham Young University described below represents the only stagings in Spanish;[70] to date there has been only one performance in English, the 2016 production based on the translation included in this volume.

El muerto disimulado *in Performance*

The BYU Spanish Golden Age Theater Project performed *El muerto disimulado* for elementary, secondary, and university student audiences throughout the southwestern United States in Spanish. Perhaps half of all audience members at every performance had little or no Spanish language skill, so the student actors developed strategies to connect with spectators in other ways. For example, the program for BYU's production of *El muerto dismulado* was 71 pages long and included short essays researched and written in English or Spanish by cast and crew members, as well as a five-page, scene-by-scene comic book version of the play's plot in English. Additionally, the actors used exaggerated movements, gestures, and facial expressions to communicate nonverbally the emotions, reactions, and ideas

---

and a letter for Doña Inés from Don Alonso, the knight from Olmedo. Fabia descends directly from the procuress Celestina, who visits the home of Alisa and her daughter Melibea ostensibly to sell the skeins of fine yarn she has spun but also to promote Melibea's seduction.

70 We also found on Vimeo what appears to be a 2015 student production: a filmed version in Spanish of a small piece of the comedy. Jacob Padilla, who describes himself as a 'student filmmaker, cinematographer, photographer, and actor', filmed and edited the first scene of *El muerto disimulado*, subtitled 'A Theater History project. Meant to look like a Spanish tella novella [*sic*].'

Emiliano Ferreira as Papagayo and Laura Pratt as 'Lisardo' in the BYU Spanish Golden Age Theater production of El muerto disimulado *(photo by Jason Yancey)*

that a large number of audience members would not understand through the Spanish dialogue. The actors frequently broke the fourth wall to involve the spectators. For instance, the show began with Rodrigo chasing Jacinta not across the stage, but through the audience, with his dagger raised above his head. The 'ghost' of Clarindo also pursued Papagayo through the audience at the beginning of the second act, and when Papagayo promised to find a priest to recite masses for Clarindo, the *gracioso* actually pulled an audience member out of his chair to hold up a cross and play the priest. The actors not only directed their asides to the audience but often left the stage to speak directly to one of the audience members, and they occasionally broke into English to converse with a spectator about something happening in the play. Additionally, actors made numerous references to US popular culture to foreground intertextualities and help bridge the gap between the early modern Iberian play and the 'horizons of expectations' that the twenty-first century, North American public brought to the performance.[71] These strategies surprised and delighted playgoers, helped them better understand the story enacted on stage, and introduced them to early modern Spanish theater in an appealing way.

The student director and set designer, Jason Yancey, imagined the play as a *commedia dell'arte* performance.[72] The concept worked well with *El muerto disimulado* because of the characters' frequently exaggerated actions and reactions. Yancey created *commedia dell'arte* masks, directed the actors to behave in parodically conventionalized, even cartoonish, ways, and included numerous instances of comic stage business in the production. Jacinta posed and moved her hips, hands, and fingers in the fashion of the *commedia innamorata* (female love interest). Holding his cane unsteadily, his shoulders stooped, her elderly father, Don Rodrigo, shuffled along, except when he was chasing his daughter and threatening to kill her. At one point, he enthusiastically laughed and jumped up and down, but his zeal ended in a coughing fit. During one particular chase scene, he and

---

71 Examples from the BYU production include the following: 1) During their sword fight, Alberto told Álvaro that he was 'not left-handed', citing Íñigo Montoya's famous line from his own duel in *The Princess Bride*. The line alludes to a person going all out to win after previously holding back and is relevant in terms of both popular culture and the plot of this comedy. 2) Clarindo sang a few bars of *West Side Story*'s 'I Feel Pretty' as he donned his flamenco dress on stage. 3) When Don Rodrigo discussed with Álvaro Jacinta's relationship with Clarindo, the father sang a line or two of *The Lion King*'s 'Can You Feel the Love Tonight?' Each of these intertextual references exemplifies Hans Robert Jauss's explanation of his notion of "the horizon of expectations". Jauss describes the set of criteria that audiences in a given historical moment bring to their readings and use to evaluate texts. In these cases, the allusions to popular culture serve simultaneously as bridges and as self-conscious reminders of the distance between the time of the play's composition and that of its performance in the twenty-first century. Hans Robert Jauss, *Toward an Aesthetic of Reception*, trans. T. Bahti (Minneapolis: U of Minnesota P, 1982).

72 An early modern Italian improvisational style of street theater in which actors wore masks, scenes involved conventional conflicts between stock characters, and comic *lazzi* or stage business added humor. The *commedia dell'arte* had a major influence on the Spanish *Comedia* and Elizabethan theater and functioned as a significant element in this theatrical engagement with Azevedo's comedy. Every year from 2002–2008, the BYU Spanish Golden Age Theater Project produced a play, each time experimenting with a different type of early modern dramatic text and the way to stage it. In addition to their venture with the *commedia dell'arte*, in other years they built a *corral* theater, created a cart that unfolded into a stage for a traveling theater troupe, performed an *auto sacramental* introduced by a Corpus Christi procession, and presented an allegorical play that experimented with the conventions of convent theater.

Jacinta ran in place, one holding a knife, the other a cane; suddenly, they turned and she began chasing him, while they both continued to run in place. Lisarda-dressed-as-Lisardo performed masculinity with a deep voice while she strutted, spat, and struggled with her sword. Álvaro behaved like a cowardly cartoon villain – all bravado and bluster with very little skill or effect on the outcome of the play. His sword fighting involved a lot of hopping and jabbing and Álvaro typically ended up undermining his own technique as a swordsman. Like the villain from a melodrama, he drummed his fingers together when planning his conquest of Jacinta, but his knees shook violently when he had to face Clarindo at the end of the play. Clarindo played a woman peddler well: he remembered to raise the timbre of his voice, showed off his wares with enthusiasm, and danced with the other women. As a 'ghost', he also modulated his voice to sound eerie, striking fear into the heart of Papagayo, who reacted by holding up a crucifix, pounding his own chest like a sinner, and trying to crawl away. The *commedia dell'arte* masks also added humor: when Álvaro and Lisarda tried to kiss at the end of the play, the noses of their masks got in the way. Papagayo also used his mask to underscore the self-consciousness of Azevedo's metadrama. When the *gracioso* complained about the playwright – 'What the devil kind of dramatic poet plotted so much nonsense?' – the actor removed his mask to speak directly, actor to audience, thus again breaking through an already fractured fourth wall.

Yancey's set design underscored the inherent metatheatricality of Azevedo's play and its movement from the page to the stage. The director, cast, and crew members created three giant (approximately 5 × 8 feet or 1.5 × 2.5 meters) books, two of which stood at either side of the back of the stage with a curtain spread between them, and one that lay on the floor center stage with its spine toward the audience. Both upright books served as entry and exit doors for the actors. The book positioned stage left was opened to the first page of Azevedo's *El muerto disimulado* as it appears in the seventeenth-century *suelta.* The title page of the play and the list of the cast of characters proved useful throughout the production. Several characters pointed out or covered up words and names as they mentioned them in their speeches. Clarindo signaled the title *El muerto disimulado* each time he talked about his own presumed death, and Papagayo called attention to Ângela de Azevedo's name when he critiqued the play's author. When Lisarda discussed her new masculine identity with Papagayo, she pulled out a strip of fabric with the name 'Lisardo' on it and used it to cover 'Lisarda' on the cast list. The book placed stage right opened up to reveal two scrapbook pages. One (which Jacinta showed to Dorotea as she described her undying love for Clarindo) displayed a portrait of Clarindo surrounded by hearts and doodles; Clarindo opened the other page to reveal a sketch of Álvaro, his would-be murderer. The third book served multiple purposes: a bench, a bed, and a platform stage. Actors sat, rested, leaned on it. Clarindo stood on the book to appear taller and more powerful than the other actors, and he re-enacted his 'death' scene there. It also functioned as a sort of treasure chest, from which actors could pull sundry helpful props and costumes, as needed: pillow, quilt, telescope, flamenco dress, hat, basket, and puppets. The giant books worked flexibly to represent the different spaces in which the characters moved.

To match the *commedia dell'arte* acting style and the large books, the crew created oversized props for the actors to wield on stage. Rodrigo's dagger looked more like an immense butcher knife. Jacinta's ring sported a 'gemstone' fashioned from a doorknob. The letters that Álvaro and Jacinta sent each other were written on large scrolls, which they unrolled before reading, and the two characters appeared on stage to recite the letter they each had written. In a comic move, Jacinta uttered completely unintelligible sounds until Álvaro realized that he held her letter upside-down. Once he righted the scroll, her words made perfect sense. Jacinta tried to decipher the clues that she followed with the aid of both an oversized magnifying glass and a telescopic spyglass, which extended five or six feet and required Papagayo's help to carry. The exaggerated and oversized stage properties repeatedly called attention to the text as theater, as spectacle, self-consciously creating humor as they simultaneously served to guide non-native speakers of Spanish in the audience.

Because they wanted to maintain the interest of their young spectators, many of whom they knew would not understand Spanish, Yancey and his actors made several cuts and other adaptations to the text, shortening and simplifying Azevedo's story. For example, they cut the Beatriz-Alberto subplot, entirely eliminating the secondary character Beatriz and reducing Alberto to a disembodied arm extended through the pages of a book to engage in a sword fight with Álvaro. This substantially reduced the performance runtime, streamlined some of the plot complications, and allowed the group to stage the comedy with fewer actors. They also dropped or abbreviated several long speeches at the end of the play. Finally, Yancey chose to have Clarindo and Lisarda remain on stage as they revealed their true identities.

Clarindo stood on the book-platform stage and pulled off his flamboyant flamenco dress in a kind of onstage striptease to expose his jerkin, breeches, and tights. Following Clarindo's disclosure, Lisarda took his place on the book to unveil her identity by covering her jerkin and breeches with the dress her brother had shed. These decisions kept the comic pace moving quickly, made it easier for monolingual spectators to follow a complicated storyline, and pleased audiences[73] at the Universities of Utah, Arizona, Arizona State, New Mexico, Brigham Young, Utah State, and BYU-Idaho, as well as several elementary and secondary schools near Provo and Salt Lake City, and in Tucson, Arizona and El Paso, Texas.

Presumed Dead *in Performance*

After the successful month-long run of Catherine Larson's translation of María de Zayas's *La traición en la amistad / Friendship Betrayed* (2015, staged by WSC Avant Bard in its venue, Theatre on the Run, in Arlington, VA), we – Hegstrom and Larson – committed to continue working on the connections between text and performance. We decided to emulate the formula that had previously proven effective by creating the combined edition in Spanish/translation in English of another Golden Age play. We were especially interested in working with a drama written by yet another early modern Iberian woman writer so as to further the additional goal of promoting the works of women, who until relatively recently had been unknown or marginalized. Our plan, we decided, was simple: to encourage interest in these often-forgotten women and their plays, we wanted to focus on a group much larger than that of traditional scholars. The first prospective audience would include readers: traditional specialists, but also intermediate and advanced students, and the book would be written to provide access to both the Spanish source text's form in verse and its translation into English prose.

The second potential audience for our project would consist of theater practitioners – and, by extension, their potential spectators – who might find such a text viable for performance. We had been fortunate to see our first translation staged by a professional acting company interested in both classical theater and women writers, so we knew our goals were possible to

73 Audience response (laughter, applause, interactions with actors during the show) was enthusiastic, but the experience did not end with the curtain calls. Following each performance, the director and actors participated in a talk-back session with audience members, who gave the cast overwhelmingly positive feedback. At elementary and secondary school performances, students asked for autographs and posed for photo-ops with actors.

achieve, and we predicted that a play with good bones might appeal to both English- and Spanish-speaking spectators. *Presumed Dead* was staged in the Spring of 2016 by the same company that had produced *Friendship Betrayed* in the Fall of 2015.[74] Fortunately for us, Avant Bard's artistic staff included us in the development of the project: they asked us to collaborate with them before and after the staged reading to promote a better understanding of the Golden Age, women writers of that era, and issues of linguistic and cultural interest. We provided information for their website, were able to enjoy the performance as it unfolded before our eyes, answered questions from the audience afterwards, and engaged directly with the actors. *Presumed Dead* was one of 12 plays selected for Avant Bard's *Scripts in Play Festival*. The company has long been interested in producing plays written by women, as well as edgy versions of contemporary and older classics, and *Scripts in Play* offered the opportunity for audiences and the producers and directors to see staged readings (virtually all with only one performance) and comment on their suitability for future, fully realized productions.

The company used an essentially bare space, and the only music employed – modern songs that reflected or parodied the themes of the comedy – set the stage, as the songs were played over loudspeakers while the audience was getting seated, before the performance began.[75] The reading of *Presumed Dead* was acted by an all-female cast, a particularly interesting decision by the director, Kari Ginsburg, as Azevedo's comedy turns on both male and female cross-dressing and the relationships between gender and power. There were no fancy costumes for the reading. The characters wore twenty-first-century street clothes, so it was difficult to link what they wore to social rank or gender, although Papagayo's outfit was brightly colored to highlight the connections between his name, personality, and comparisons with a parrot. Because this was a reading, all the characters held and read from copies of the script.

The use of the physical space was noteworthy. The stage itself was small and intimate, and it contained 11 folding chairs, arranged in a semicircle, with a stage manager/narrator seated in the middle in front of a small table and five characters on either side. For the most part, whenever characters

---

74 To date, this is the only production of Azevedo's play in English, as the translation in this bilingual book is the first-ever undertaken.

75 The playlist contained both musical compositions about 'girl power' and ballads treating longing for love; examples included Aretha Franklin's '(You Make me Feel Like) A Natural Woman' and Bobby Vinton's 'Sealed with a Kiss'.

spoke their lines, the actresses[76] playing them would leave their chairs and walk into the center space created by the semicircle, while the rest stayed seated until it was their turn to speak. On several occasions, however, the actresses left the stage and entered the audience's space, which served to call attention to the metadramas playing out on stage and emphasized the self-conscious exploration of the theater itself in Azevedo's comedy. The appearance of the *autora de comedias*/stage manager/narrator (also a woman) on stage during the entire performance further underscored the self-referential nature of the play. In early modern Iberia, most, although not all, *autores de comedias* were male, and their job as empresario and stage manager was to work off stage to make the production come together. In Avant Bard's production this onstage figure managed the sound effects and announced the beginnings and endings of acts, as well as a number of the stage directions. Mostly, however, the stage manager was in charge of the props and shared them overtly with the audience, often with a comic twist. For example, when a letter was read aloud, she would add the sound effect of rustling a piece of paper while waving it in the air. When the letter was connected to a character's bad behavior – such as Don Álvaro's clumsy attempts to woo Jacinta in writing – the *autora* also visibly expressed her disdain. The sounds of blade-on-blade swordfighting were produced with two metal serving spoons, and door slamming was accomplished by clapping two pieces of plywood together; the stage manager also produced the sound caused when one character slapped another.

In a multi-leveled and multilingual play on words, she also called attention to the most important stage property in the play, a ring, which Jacinta had given to her beloved, Clarindo, before he left on an armada bound for Savoy. Don Álvaro had stolen the ring after he thought Clarindo was dead; Don Álvaro had then given it as a gift to his servant, Dorotea, as his thanks for bringing him a letter from Jacinta; Hipólita had stolen it from Dorotea, the two had fought over it; and Jacinta and Clarindo ultimately used the ring to help reveal both Don Álvaro's malfeasance and their mutual love. Throughout the play, Avant Bard's creative use of the ring offered a series of moments that self-reflexively underscored the significance of that prop. Whenever a character mentioned the word 'ring', the stage manager would push the button on a bellhop bell that would then ring shrilly. Such code-switching wordplay between English and Spanish provided yet another level

76 So as to minimize further confusion regarding the staging of this gender-bending play and its all-female cast, we use 'actress' here, rather than the non-gendered term, 'actor'.

Dani Stoller as Don Álvaro, Jill Tighe as Papagayo, Farrell Parker as Lisarda, and Daven Rallston as Alberto in WSC Avant Bard's staged reading of Presumed Dead *(photo by Maegan Clearwood)*

of engagement for the audience members, who would pause for a moment and then laugh as they caught on to the game of words and sounds. The double meanings emphasized onstage led the audience to appreciate the issues at play in Azevedo's comedy. The dramatist, director, and actresses were united in portraying the conflict between illusion and reality, which functioned on multiple levels throughout as Avant Bard played with who was alive and who was dead, who was really male and who was female. In order to illustrate who was who, the cast even wore "Hello, my name is..." nametags in yet another anachronistic joke that brought the confusion to the audience's attention.

The artistic vision guiding this reading came from the director, Kari Ginsburg, who, just a few months earlier, had been the creative force behind Zayas's well-received *Friendship Betrayed*. We had already seen how her decision to set *Friendship Betrayed* in the Roaring Twenties in the US had led to an adaptation that really worked well on stage: Ginsburg knew that the source play was written in a very different time and place, but she understood that at its heart, Zayas's comedy highlighted independent women living in a period that was ripe for testing the limits of their society and its views on gender. Her female characters were savvy and sassy. In like manner, Ginsburg's approach to *Presumed Dead* also illuminated how female characters could successfully challenge socio-cultural norms. Azevedo's Lisarda has left her home and traveled disguised as a man to avenge her brother's supposed death, and her Jacinta refuses to marry, defying her father's wishes because of a promise made before her beloved Clarindo left on an armada bound for Savoy. Even the feigned dead man, Clarindo, pushes the limits of conventional early modern behavior for males in the *Comedia*, which in general offers few examples of noble men who disguise themselves as women. By camouflaging Clarindo as 'Clara', Azevedo encourages her audiences of readers or spectators to see how she is questioning the gender issues of her day. Kari Ginsburg accomplishes much the same thing in her staged reading with her all-women cast and use of code-switching and cross-dressing, which call attention to those same socio-cultural issues.

Ginsburg made two other key directorial decisions. Directors who stage early modern plays in the 21st century often consider the degree to which a classical play should be adapted for performance for a modern audience. Certainly, some of Ginsburg's choices (replacing early modern costumes with modern, gender-neutral clothing, a women-only cast in a play about gender, the wordplay) represent such adaptations. In addition, modern directors might choose to cut lines so as to keep an audience's attention throughout the performance. It is fair to state that cuts are not uncommon in contemporary performances of classical theater, and in early modern times, the inclusion of long monologues was more frequent than is often the case now. Several other 17th-century Iberian dramas offer examples of such speeches, including Don Gonzalo de Ulloa's description of Lisbon in Tirso's *El burlador de Sevilla*. In a society with no televisions or movie theaters, long descriptions of exotic places or exciting stories told aloud filled a cultural need; one can infer that theater audiences also tended to enjoy such intercalated narratives. *Presumed Dead* is a typical Golden Age drama, whose length (3,808 verses in the Spanish edition) might suggest that it would play better on stage if it were tightened via the introduction of several strategic cuts. Specifically, Azevedo had written some long speeches in which characters explain or recap in great detail what had already taken place and been witnessed on stage or what was happening right then. Doménech suggests that this repetition is not one of the comedy's strengths ('Introduction' 16). Ginsburg decided, however, not to remove anything in the translation for her staged reading. Rather, she focused attention on the comedy's language by foregrounding the long monologues that other directors might have cut for fear of boring the audience. When an actress engaged in reading one of those lengthy speeches on stage, the other actresses began feigning boredom by squirming in their chairs and rolling their eyes. Consequently, each time such an oration was given thereafter, the audience recognized the cue and began to laugh at this bit of stage business, thus avoiding any potential problems and creating a shared experience for the audience and actresses.

Another salient characteristic of Ginsburg's staged reading of the translation was its fast pace. Having made the decision to include the entire text, the director needed the actresses to keep things moving as they read the dialogue, and they delivered their lines at break-neck speed. The orality of the performance was thus highlighted as the audience was led to concentrate on Azevedo's words. The exaggerated pace served the comedy well, especially since the lack of costumes or sets onstage, the physical space, and the fact that the actresses were holding their scripts allowed little room for movement. It is also true, however, that each actress used the tools of her trade, her body and voice, to communicate effectively inside that relatively small semicircle. Following the lead of their director's creative interpretation and approach to performing classical theater, the professional actresses did a superb job with *Presumed Dead*.

The audience's reaction to this staged reading was enthusiastically positive, with laughter sometimes stopping the show. As the spectators began to key in to the parodic and self-conscious play with early modern theatrical conventions, their responses indicated that they enjoyed becoming part of the spectacle. At the end of the comedy, we were asked to join the director to answer audience questions about early modern Iberian theater, the creation of stage-worthy translations, and women's writing. The dialogue that ensued served as a stimulating culmination to an entertaining night of theater. This performance of *Presumed Dead* illustrated beautifully how early modern Iberian dramas can be staged successfully in the 21st century.

METRICAL SCHEME

Like other Iberian playwrights of the early modern period, Azevedo wrote her dramas in verse. In fact, when in her plays she refers to herself as a *poeta*, rather than a *dramaturga*, she uses the term that other dramatists of the period employed to refer to themselves. Each of the 3,808 lines of *El muerto disimulado* forms part of a longer stanza or poem; only the letters that Don Álvaro and Jacinta address to each other, inserted between lines 476–477 and 975–976, appear in prose. The rest of the play is made up of popular verse forms, including *romances* (ballads), *redondillas* (a kind of quatrain), *pareados* (couplets), *décimas* (a kind of decastich), *quintillas* (quintains), *sextilhas* (sestets), an *octava real* (ottava rima), and a sonnet.

As in most *comedias*, the predominant verse form in *El muerto disimulado* is the *romance*, the medieval ballad form containing an indeterminate number of eight-syllable lines with the same assonant rhyme in all the even lines. In his *Arte nuevo*, Lope suggests that the *romance* works well for narration (line 309).[77] 11 *romances* make up more than 72% of the lines in *El muerto disimulado.* On five occasions, Azevedo skips a blank verse, rhyming two lines in a row (1.922–23, 2.2157–58, 3.2915–16, 3.3038–39, 3.3765–66). It does not appear that these lines lack any information or that a line might be missing. Another 3% of the play consists of a *romance heptasílabo*, written with seven-syllable lines, which concludes the second act of the play. In this scene, Don Rodrigo confronts Jacinta about hiding her love for and relationship with Clarindo. She reveals that she believes Álvaro to be Clarindo's assassin and that she intends to make him admit it or catch him in his lie, in which case she will kill him to avenge Clarindo's death. This plan shocks Rodrigo but he agrees to arrange the confrontation. Azevedo's use of shorter poetic lines offers a unique way to represent the tension between father and daughter in this final scene of the act.

Azevedo includes two sets of *redondillas* in the first act of her play, and they comprise nearly 8.5% of the play. Lope states that *redondillas* (four-line stanzas with eight-syllable lines and the rhyme scheme abba) excel for matters of love (line 312). Azevedo uses *redondillas* to open her play. All of Rodrigo's shouting at and pleading with his daughter and her subsequent conversation with her maid Dorotea about Clarindo and Álvaro are spoken

77 Lope de Vega, *Arte nuevo de hacer comedias*, ed. E. García Santo-Tomás (Madrid: Cátedra, 2006).

in *redondillas*. Only Jacinta's narration of her encounters with Clarindo (a *romance*) and Álvaro's letter (in prose) interrupt the *redondillas.*

The two sets of *décimas* (ten-line stanzas) Azevedo includes in *El muerto disimulado* are called *espinelas*, named for the poet Vicente Espinel (1550–1624), who refined the form. *Espinelas* have eight-syllable lines and their rhyme scheme is abbaaccddc. The *Arte nuevo* says that *décimas* work well for complaints (line 307), but Lope uses the form indiscriminately throughout his plays. Azevedo, however, follows Lope's written advice and uses the *décima* for the plaintive conversations Beatriz has with her servant Hipólita and with her beloved Alberto. Beatriz and Hipólita's exchange takes place on a street near Jacinta's house, as the women have run away from their own home in fear of the wrath and violent reactions of Álvaro. Beatriz worries that her brother may have killed her beloved; Hipólita dreads their imagined entry into a convent to become nuns. In the later scene, Beatriz and Alberto meet in Jacinta's home, and they fret and bemoan their difficulties in love. When Alberto asks what they will do if Rodrigo is unable to intercede for them with Álvaro, Beatriz responds, 'Suffer, live in torment, say nothing, and lament'. In *El muerto disimulado*, the *décima espinela* becomes a type of marker that underscores the fearful personalities of Beatriz and, by extension, Hipólita and Alberto.

In the second act, Azevedo includes a set of *quintillas* (five-line stanzas) and a set of Portuguese *sextilhas* (six-line stanzas). Azevedo's *quintillas* follow a typical pattern for the form with eight-syllable lines, but she varies the rhyme scheme. Rather than ababa, her stanzas rhyme abbab. Azevedo uses this form for Dorotea and Hipólita's argument over the ring that Álvaro gave Dorotea and for the fight that ensues. The *quintillas* function as mini-*décimas*, as the servant women complain and insult each other. The penultimate stanza in this section has an extra line (abbbab). The extra line does not add any special significance in terms of meaning in the play, and it appears that Azevedo included it here accidentally.

Later in Act 2, Azevedo uses the *sextilha* form for a discussion between Don Rodrigo and Don Álvaro. Spanish *sextillas* can have varying line lengths and rhyme schemes, but they are always *versos de arte menor*, which means they contain between two and eight syllables. Azevedo's six-line stanzas do not fit within these parameters, but they do correspond to the rules of the Portuguese *sextilha,* which are much more open both in terms of rhyme scheme and line length. The lines of Azevedo's *sextilhas* alternate between seven and 11 syllables and their rhyme scheme looks almost like a shortened octave: aBaBcC. This form lends itself well to the discussion between Álvaro and Rodrigo as they try to persuade one another about the best ways to handle the issues regarding their honor and the women in their lives. Álvaro wants to send Beatriz to a convent, but Rodrigo urges him to marry her to Alberto. Rodrigo knows that Beatriz has developed a love relationship with Alberto, but Álvaro wants him to know that Jacinta has also strayed into love with a man named Clarindo. Azevedo sets her *sextilhas* up so that the first four lines (aBaB) express one or two if-clauses and the last two lines (cC) resolve the tension with a then-clause.

In the opening scene of the third act, without noticing one another, Jacinta and 'Clara' enter on opposite sides of the stage. Lost in thought, they deliver alternating and parallel lines, Jacinta to her 'sad memories' and Clarindo to his 'sweet desires'. Jacinta wishes to end her life because she has lost Clarindo; Clarindo wishes to shed his disguise because hiding from Jacinta is difficult. Azevedo chooses to have these lovers express their feelings in *pareados* (rhyming couplets). Each of Azevedo's couplets begins with a seven-syllable line and ends with an 11-syllable line. The name of the verse form in both Spanish and English matches the characters and the structure of their scene. They are a couple – *un par* – of lovers and they deliver their thoughts in tandem. In their final couplet, they decide that to solve their problems Álvaro must die.

Immediately following their pronouncement, Don Rodrigo, Beatriz, and the two women servants enter, and a conversation in the *romance* form ensues about the experience of love and separation. 'Clara' poses the question: 'in an absence, who feels the blow more strongly: the one who stays or the one who leaves?' 'Clara' and Jacinta disagree about the answer: Jacinta believes the one who stays behind suffers more, and Clarindo asserts that the one who leaves endures more pain. Their responses, of course, mirror their own experiences; Jacinta stayed behind when Clarindo left and they each feel that they have grieved more than the other. To resolve the conflict, they decide to prove their points by reciting poems in support of their position. Poetry contests and recitals in social gatherings were quite popular in early modern Iberia and the theater of the period often reflects the practice.[78] In *El muerto disimulado*, Jacinta gives weight to her position by choosing to recite an *octava real*, an eight-line stanza with 11-syllable lines that rhyme ABABABCC. The great Italian, Spanish, and Portguese writers of epic poetry

78 For example, in Lope's *La dama boba* (*The Lady Simpleton*), three suitors ask Nise to serve as judge of the sonnet Duardo has written and recites for the group.

employed the octave to tell their stories of heroic adventure.[79] Don Rodrigo, Dorotea, and Clarindo all praise Jacinta's octave. Clarindo then responds with a sonnet, the verse form with the greatest number of and strictest rules in the history of Western poetry. Clarindo's sonnet consists of two *cuartetos* (ABBA ABBA) and two *tercetos* (CDC DCD). The other characters praise his poem's beauty and elegance and 'Clara's' intelligence, discretion, and wit.

Given the verse forms Azevedo chooses to use, every line of *El muerto disimulado* should have seven, eight, or 11 syllables. At times, she employs some form of poetic license to make that happen. Synalepha (the merging of two syllables into one when a word that ends in a vowel is followed by a word that begins with a vowel) almost always occurs in Spanish verse. The letter 'y' only counts as a vowel in the word *y* (meaning 'and'). Azevedo frequently counts 'y' as a vowel in other words, for example *yo*, *ya*, *hay*, *muy*, *estoy* and *suyo*. Most of these words begin or end with a vowel in Portuguese: *eu*, *há*, *mui*, *estou* and *seu*. This may explain why Azevedo would read the 'y' in the Spanish words as a vowel in lines like 'quedase yo [eu] perdida sola' and 'pues con amor no hay [há] enemigo' (280, 1074). In Portuguese verse, the use of synalepha is optional, so hiatus (counting what could be a synalepha as two separate syllables) occurs more frequently than in Spanish. Quite a few examples of hiatus exist in *El muerto disimulado*, especially in lines containing three words that might join in a synalepha, for example the eight-syllable line 'con quien dio a otra doncella' (2120) or when a silent 'h' interrupts the synalepha, 'y si así como fue hembra' (2167). Azevedo also avails herself of dieresis, another form of poetic license in which a diphthong counts as two rather than a single syllable. In this edition, I have indicated all examples of dieresis with the diacritical mark (*crïada*, *fïar*, *dïablo*, *crüel*, etc.). Finally, Azevedo occasionally has recourse to syneresis, in which two adjacent vowels within a word would normally be spoken as two syllables but instead are counted as one. The name Beatriz has three syllables, but Azevedo always counts the name as just two syllables. Similarly, Azevedo counts the interjection *¡Ea!* (Hey!) as a single syllable. Other examples of syneresis include words such as *veamos*, *realidad*, *quedaos*, and even words with a written accent, *servíos*, *aún*, and *había*. For the few lines that do not fit within the metrical patterns or one of these forms of poetic license, I have specified the unusual line length in a footnote.

---

79 Boccaccio, Ariosto, and Tasso all used *ottava rima* in their major works. Luís Vaz de Camões composed the great Portuguese epic *Os Lusíadas* (*The Lusiads*) (1556/1572) in *oitavas*, and in Portuguese the form is sometimes called 'oitava rima camoniana' in honor of Camões.

The first table below lists all verse forms and rhyme schemes in *El muerto disimulado* and indicates the corresponding line numbers. The second table summarizes the number and percentage of lines dedicated to each poetic form.

Line Numbers	Verse Forms and Rhyme Schemes
ACT I	
1 – 192	*redondillas abba*
193 – 416	*romance (o-a)*
417 – 544	*redondillas abba*
545 – 874	*romance (a-o)*
875 – 1151	*romance (a-a)*
1152 – 1221	*décimas – abbaaccddc*
ACT II	
1222 – 1431	*romance (e-o)*
1432 – 1572	*quintillas – abbab*
1573 – 1864	*romance (i-a)*
1865 – 1954	*décimas – abbaaccddc*
1955 – 2074	*sextilha – aBaBcC*
2075 – 2237	*romance (e-a)*
2238 – 2353	*romance heptasílabo (u-a)*
ACT III	
2354 – 2527	*pareados aAbBcC...*
2528 – 2607	*romance (e-o)*
2608 – 2615	*octava real ABABABCC*
2616 – 2619	*romance (e-o)*
2620 – 2633	*soneto ABBA ABBA CDC DCD*
2634 – 2841	*romance (e-o)*
2842 – 3135	*romance (i-o)*
3136 – 3225	*romance (o-e)*
3226 – 3447	*romance (í)*
3448 – 3808	*romance (a-o)*

SUMMARY		
Verse Forms	Number of Lines	Percentage of Lines
Romances	2755	72.3%
Romances heptasílabos	116	3.0%
Redondillas	320	8.4%
Pareados	174	4.6%
Décimas	160	4.2%
Quintillas	141	3.7%
Sextilhas	120	3.2%
Soneto	14	0.4%
Octava Real	8	0.2%
Total	3808	100%

EDITOR'S NOTE

Because I want to make *El muerto disimulado* more easily available to scholars and students, as well as to directors and actors who might choose to perform the play in Spanish, this is not a 'diplomatic' edition of one of the two copies of the only source text we have of the play. Instead, I have made multiple changes to punctuation, capitalization, accentuation, and spelling to modernize the text and make it accessible to contemporary speakers of the Spanish language. I detail those changes below and include footnotes in the text to account for decisions regarding specific individual cases.

Although I have altered the Spanish in the source text in many ways, this is the first modern edition of the play that resists the 'domestication' (Hispanicization) of Azevedo's text by the dominant (Spanish) culture. I have chosen, insofar as possible, to 'foreignize' the aspects of the text that 'register the linguistic and cultural difference of the foreign [Portuguese] text.'[80] This choice should make my edition helpful to scholars who want to understand meanings in the text, because, in Schleiermacher's terms, the foreignization 'leaves the author in peace, as much as possible, and moves the reader towards [her].'[81] The tendency to domesticate Ângela de Azevedo begins with her name. As Wade points out, several nineteenth- and twentieth-century Spanish literary catalogs Hispanicize Azevedo's name as 'Angela' or 'Ángela de Acevedo' (340). As recently as 2006, 2007, and 2015, critics such as Ferrer Valls, Barbeito Carneiro, and Urban Baños have followed suit in their articles and books.[82] Curiously, Doménech's edition of the play combines the two language traditions in 'Ángela de Azevedo'. In our introduction to this edition and translation, we have made the decision to spell the author's surname as it was expressed in her age, in the *suelta*, and her native tongue.

Ângela de Azevedo wrote *El muerto disimulado* and her other plays in Spanish, but as several critics have noted, her dramatic works are all set in Portugal and the author frequently praises Portuguese culture and

80 Lawrence Venuti, *The Translator's Invisibility: A History of Translation* (London: Routledge, 1995), p. 20.

81 Friedrich Schleiermacher, 'On the Different Methods of Translating', in A. Lefevere (ed.), *Translating Literature: The German Tradition from Luther to Rosenzweig* (Assen: Van Gorcum, 1977), p. 74.

82 See Ferrer Valls, 'Decir'; María Isabel Barbeito Carneiro, *Mujeres y literatura del Siglo de Oro: Espacios profanos y conventuales* (Madrid: SAFEKAT, 2007); Urban Baños.

language. Wade calls attention to the issue by discussing Azevedo's use of code-switching in the comedy. When Lisarda and Papagayo first arrive in Lisbon from their hometown of Lamego, Papagayo uses the Portuguese word *boa* (good), rather than the Spanish word *buena*, to describe and rhyme with *Lisboa* (Lisbon). Wade observes, 'The use of "boa" stands out from the text as part of another vernacular, accentuating that literal aspect of the city name, LisBOA' (336). In another oft-cited passage, Azevedo's character Jacinta also breaks into Portuguese to describe her feelings of separation from Clarindo. She uses the words *saudoso*, *saudosa*, and *saudade*, and then defends her code-switching by stating that one can only really talk about *saudade* by using the Portuguese word (1.356–360). Again Wade comments, 'the use of the word [*saudade*] in literature should not be overlooked nor underestimated. It is one of the easiest ways to evoke Portugal' (338). Beyond her code-switching, Azevedo affirms her 'Portugueseness' by calling attention to the curious use of Spanish within her play; a Portuguese author, Azevedo, creates Portuguese characters that interact with each other in Lisbon, and they all speak to one another in Spanish. We might assume that the audience overhears in Spanish the conversation the characters carry on in Portuguese, except that the characters admit to speaking Spanish. Near the beginning of the third act when Jacinta and Clarindo talk about their disappointments, Jacinta asks 'Clara' to speak in her native tongue, adding that she (Jacinta) understands it well and will be able to follow her. This places Clarindo in a difficult position because, as 'Clara', he has claimed to hail from Savoy, and so he should speak French (or perhaps Italian) fluently. Thinking quickly, he explains that the diminishment of his happiness has caused him to forget his own tongue and for that reason he tends to use Spanish or Castilian. Jacinta remarks that 'Clara' has learned Spanish quickly, to which Clarindo replies that it is an easy language to learn (3.2412–419). By including this complicated linguistic joke in the play, Azevedo shows her awareness of and underscores her own foreignness as a Portuguese playwright working within the dominant tradition of the Spanish *Comedia*.

Our access to Azevedo, her play, and her Portugueseness is already mediated in the source text, the *suelta* version of her play, by the printer(s) who made the play available in multiple copies.[83] If the printer worked from an autograph manuscript (written down by Azevedo herself), his source[84]

83 Copyists (theater company managers and others) may have handled the text on its way to the printer. If so, they too would have modified Azevedo's text.

84 The majority of early modern printers on the Iberian Peninsula were male. However,

likely had no punctuation; that was the common practice with *Comedia* manuscripts in the period.[85] So the printer would have to make decisions about all of the punctuation throughout the play. We cannot know how many other changes he imposed on his printed version, whether, for example, Azevedo spelled her words in Spanish well and consistently throughout the play, or whether the printer corrected her Spanish, domesticating her text. It would seem an impossible task to identify the printer's interventions in the *suelta*, but he reveals his hand in at least one significant place. Near the end of the play, Alberto speaks to the audience in a soliloquy, in which he says that 'hopes and misgivings' converge or compete in his heart: 'Esperanzas y recelos / en mi corazón *concorren*' (3.3136–137). The source text spells the verb *concurren* in Spanish with a 'u' rather than in Portuguese with an 'o', but the Spanish spelling ruins the rhyme scheme. Azevedo occasionally skips a blank verse, but she never misses a rhyme in any other place in the text. The Portuguese word *concorren* fits the rhyme scheme. It forms part of a *romance*, and all of the even lines end with the assonant rhyme o-e: *concorren*, *confusiones*, *nobles*, *suponen*, *conoce*, etc. This gap in the text is a space through which we can glimpse the *suelta*'s printer correcting and thereby domesticating Azevedo's foreignness. In just such interstices we can also view Azevedo's 'linguistic and cultural difference' (Venuti 20).

On at least five occasions, Azevedo chose Portuguese words to rhyme with other words in her play and the printer did not intervene in the source text to 'correct' the Portuguese words and negatively affect the rhyme. Azevedo uses the Portuguese *requererte* rather than the Spanish *requerirte* to rhyme with *vencerte* in a *redondilla* (1.134–35). Later in the source text, the verb appears in the middle of a line in its Spanish spelling: *requerirle* (1.657). Azevedo employs the Portuguese noun *esquivança* three times in the play. The first time it rhymes assonantally with words like *ingrata*, *estaba*, and *puñaladas* (1.1015–21). The second instance occurs in a rhyming couplet with *venganza*, and the third appears mid-line (3.2502–05). Neither of the Spanish equivalents, *esquivezas* or *esquiveces*, would rhyme in these situations. In Act 2, lines 2115–16 present an interesting puzzle. In a *romance*, Clarindo

---

some women owned and supervised print shops; others made printing ink, dampened paper, collated sheets, prepared and read copy, and read and corrected proofs; a few women became skilled at working the presses. Clive Griffin, *Heresy, and the Inquisition in Sixteenth-Century Spain* (Oxford: Oxford UP, 2005), pp. 187–88.

85 Alberto Blecua, 'Sobre la (no) puntuación en los textos dramáticos del Siglo de Oro', in J. Álvarez Barrientos (ed.), *En buena compañía: Estudios en honor de Luciano García Lorenzo* (Madrid: CSIC, 2009), pp. 79–101.

says that Jacinta wants him (as 'Clara') to accompany her: 'quiere que yo / acompañándole estea'. The combination of letters in *estea* does not exist as a word in either Spanish or Portuguese, but it does rhyme with *supuesta*, *espera*, *doncella*, and other words in the *romance*. In her edition, Soufas changes the word to the Spanish subjunctive *esté*; in his, Doménech keeps *estea* and adds a footnote, 'Sic en el original' (272). In Portuguese, the third-person singular subjunctive of the verb *estar* (the form that Azevedo must have had in mind) is *esteja*, and it fits the rhyme scheme in this section of the play perfectly. Finally, during the final scene of the play, Azevedo uses the Portuguese verb *impelir* – not the Spanish verb *impeler* – to rhyme with other words that have a stressed 'i' in their final syllable: *frenesí*, *civil*, *vi*, etc. These moments in the play in which the rhyme depends on the Portuguese word give us additional opportunities to hear Azevedo speak to us in her native language.

Spelling and other aspects of the Spanish and Portuguese languages were not standardized until the eighteenth century.[86] This makes it difficult to identify some words in Azevedo's early modern play as definitively Spanish or unambiguously Portuguese. For example, *assumpto*, *carroça*, *conjecturas*, *mui*, and *prompta* (all from the source text) look more like Portuguese words, but could be read as alternative spellings in Spanish. In a few instances, though, it seems far more likely that Azevedo uses a Portuguese word that slips past the printer. For example, at the beginning of Act 2, Papagayo asks for a holy *advogado* (advocate or *abogado* in Spanish) to help him escape Clarindo's ghost (2.1230–31). Further, both Rodrigo and Beatriz describe the conflict between Álvaro and Alberto as an *abalo* (earthquake, rather than *terremoto* in Spanish) (2.1587, 3.2540). Finally, Álvaro refers to honor as a kind of fine *vidro* (glass, not *vidrio*) that cannot be repaired (2.1973–75). Covarrubias includes the Spanish words *abogado* and *vidrio* in his 1611 *Tesoro de la lengua castellana o española* (Treasury of the Castilian or Spanish Language).[87] Neither *abalo* nor *avalo* appears in Covarrubias's dictionary, in the *Diccionario de Autoridades*, or in the current *Diccionario de la Real Academia Española*.[88] The word is almost unknown in Spain

86 The eighth Marquis of Villena, Juan Manuel Fernández Pacheco, founded the Spanish Royal Academy in 1713, and the second Duke of Lafões, João Carlos de Bragança, formed the Portuguese Royal Academy of Sciences – now the Lisbon Academy of Sciences – in 1779.

87 Sebastián de Covarrubias, *Tesoro de la lengua castellana o española*, ed. M. de Riquer (Barcelona: Editorial Alta Fulia, 1998).

88 *Diccionario de Autoridades: Real Academia Española* (Madrid: Gredos, 1990) and *Diccionario de la lengua española* (Madrid: Real Academia Española, 1992). *Avalo* does appear in the online Spanish-English dictionary, *SpanishDict: English to Spanish Translation,*

and in a footnote in his edition, Doménech identifies the word *abalo* as Portuguese (253). On the Portuguese side, Bluteau includes *advogado*, *abalo*, and *vidro* in his 1712–1721 *Vocabulario portuguez e latino* (Portuguese and Latin Vocabulary), and current dictionaries continue to include and spell those words in the same way.[89] Curiously, the source text includes both the Spanish words *entretenido* (entertaining) and *entretengo* (I entertain) and the Portuguese infinitive *entreternos* (to entertain us) (3.2728–31). Azevedo also introduces a Portuguese word into the play that does not have a Spanish equivalent when Clarindo talks about the *inculcas* (suggestions or hints) he has given Jacinta (2.2088) and Don Rodrigo asks Jacinta about an *inculca* (some information) that Álvaro might give her.[90] Similarly when Dorotea and Hipólita talk to their mistresses about their *dissabores* (displeasures or annoyances) (1.428, 2.1879), the source text does not misspell the Spanish word. *Desabor* is a false cognate, and *dessabor* (insipidity, unsavoriness) also exists in Portuguese. All of these examples are spaces in the source text in which hints of Azevedo's Portuguese identity come through.

Sometimes Azevedo's characters speak to one another in a Spanish inflected or otherwise modified by Portuguese grammar. For example, they use the Portuguese personal infinitive, which does not exist in Spanish. Papagayo tells Lisarda, 'para *preguntarmos* / por un hombre amigo de otro / disparate es' (it is nonsense for us to be asking about a man who's the friend of another) (1.640–42); Dorotea asks, '¿Llamémosla para *vermos*?' (Shall we call her so we can take a look?) (2.1673); and Álvaro tells 'Lisardo', 'por eso quiero, / para *sermos* más que amigos, / que nos hagamos hermanos' (that is why, to be more than friends, I'd like us to become brothers) (3.2947–49). All of these cases of the first-person-plural form of the Portuguese personal infinitive look very much like Spanish reflexive infinitives, so in their editions, Soufas and Doménech have tended to change these verb forms to *preguntarnos* (to ask ourselves), *vernos* (to see ourselves), and *sernos* (to be ourselves). Only with Dorotea's question does Doménech recognize a different meaning in the form, so he maintains *vermos*, and adds this footnote: 'Extraña construcción del verbo *ver*, que probablemente tiene el sentido de "para que veamos"' (A strange construction of the verb *ver*, which probably

Dictionary, Translator. Curiosity Media.

89 Raphael Bluteau, *Vocabulario portuguez e latino* (Coimbra: Collegio das Artes da Companhia de Jesus, 1712–1728), vol. 1, pp. 10–11, 142 and vol. 8, pp. 482–83.

90 Spanish possesses the verb *inculcar* (to instill or inculcate), but has no noun from the same root.

has the meaning of 'so that we can see') (256). Reading these phrases as Portuguese personal infinitives (or misreading them as Spanish reflexives) will clearly affect meaning in the text.

The Portuguese equivalent of the Spanish *ir + a + infinitive* construction (to be going to do something) does not use the preposition *a*, and in several situations the Portuguese characters in *El muerto disimulado* do not include the preposition when native Spanish speakers would. For example, when Rodrigo says, 'voy buscar' (I'm going to look for), the Spanish construction would be *voy a buscar* (2.1598–99), and when Hipólita reports, 'fue del viejo el primor / hablar' (literally, the skill of the old man went to talk), the Spanish also requires *a*: *el primor del viejo fue a hablar* (2.1906–08). Spanish uses the adverb *muy* (very) to intensify adjectives and other adverbs, and the adverbs *mucho* (much) and *muchos* (many) to intensify nouns. In contrast, Portuguese has an archaic form *mui* (very), but uses *muito* and *muitos* to modify nouns, verbs, and other adjectives. This explains why Rodrigo talks about 'unas consultas mucho [*muito*] serias' (some very serious consultations) (2.1984). I have italicized Portuguese words that appear among the Spanish and included footnotes to explain moments of linguistic difference when they occur and reveal Azevedo and her characters' Portugueseness.

Throughout this edition, I have maintained contractions that are easily understandable, but no longer standard in Spanish: *désta*, *deste*, *desto*, *dese*, *della*, *dél*, *esotro*. I have imposed the following changes on the source text:

Accentuation, Capitalization, and Punctuation

The replacement of grave accents (`) with acute accents (´) for example:
acomodarà became *acomodará*, *està* > *está*, *respondì* > *respondí*, *quizà* > *quizá*, etc.

The removal of accent marks from words that do not require them:
à > a, ò > o, yò > yo, vèr > ver, viò > vio, etc.

The addition of acute accents to words that require them:
mi > mí (as an object of a preposition), este > éste (as a pronoun), como > cómo (as an interrogative), facilmente > fácilmente, gallardia > gallardía, ocasion > ocasión.

The replacement of unnecessary upper case with lower case letters at the beginning of nouns:
Religión > religión, Cristiano > cristiano, >, Esposo > esposo, Monja > monja, Historias > historias, Nación > nación, Reino > reino, Nobleza > nobleza, Caballeros > caballeros, Misa > misa, Portugués > portugués.

The replacement of lower case letters with upper case at the beginning of a sentence.

The elimination of unnecessary commas, for example 'prolija, importuna, y vana' became 'prolija, importuna y vana'.

The addition of ellipses (…) following an unfinished or interrupted sentence.

The addition of exclamation points (¡!) to mark interjections and exclamations.

The addition of inverted question marks (¿) before a question, as required by standard Spanish.

The occasional addition or shifting of question marks to clarify meaning: for example 'Luego tu amor has tenido, / pues dizes, que te dexò?' became 'Luego, ¿tú amor has tenido? / Pues ¿dices que te dejó?'

The replacement of commas with periods or semicolons to divide comma splices.

The replacement of semicolons with commas to divide dependent clauses.

The replacement of colons with periods to divide independent clauses.

The replacement of parentheses with en dashes (–) to indicate parenthetical comments, and the addition of parentheses to distinguish asides from normal dialogue.

Abbreviations

Abbreviations marked with a tilde (˜) have been spelled out:
q̃ > que, quiẽ > quien, vẽce > vence, auq̃ue > aunque, nõbra > nombra, trãsforma > transforma, impresiõ > impresión, siẽpre > siempre.

Abbreviated titles preceding a name have been spelled out:
D. > don or doña, S. > san.

Abbreviated stage directions have been spelled out:
V. > Vase, Ap. > Aparte.

Two more abbreviations have been spelled out:
D.A. de Gamb. > Don Álvaro de Gamboa, V.m. > vuestra merced.

Modernization of Printing Conventions

v > u:
mverto > muerto, dissimvlado > disimulado, segvnda > segunda, vn > un, vna > una, vña > uña, vrbanidad > urbanidad, vrdir > urdir, vltraja > ultraja.

ſ > s:
paſsion > pasión, deſeo > deseo, poderoſa > poderosa, liſonja > lisonja, ſegunda > segunda.

I > J:

Iacinta > Jacinta, Iesus > Jesús.

Modernization of Spanish Orthography

e, i:

licion > lección, recebir > recibir, condimiento > condimento.

o > u:

moriendo > muriendo, podisteis > pudisteis.

y > i:

ayrado > airado, bayna > vaina, donayre > donaire, frayle > fraile, syntoma > síntoma, traydora > traidora, traygo > traigo, embaynò > envainó, etc.

b, v:

alvedrío > albedrío, aver > haber, bayben > vaivén, bolver > volver, cavallero > caballero, dever > deber, embidia > envidia, escrivir > escribir, villete > billete, etc.

c, ç, z:

alcançar > alcanzar, azero > acero, braço > brazo, coraçon > corazón, dezir > decir, doze > doce, forçosa > forzosa, hazer > hacer, vengança > venganza, vezina > vecina, zelos > celos, etc.

c > cc:

jurisdicion > jurisdicción.

g > j:

muger > mujer, sugetar > sujetar, sugeto > sujeto, trage > traje.

m > n:

assumpto > asunto, desemboltura > desenvoltura, embidia > envidia, embuelto > envuelto, essempto > exento, presumpcion > presunción, prompta > pronta.

q > c:

consequencia > consecuencia, qual > cual, qualidad > cualidad, quando > cuando, quarto > cuarto, quatro > cuatro.

s, ss, x:

aquesso > aqueso, assi > así, assombrar > asombrar, crasso > craso, dissonar > disonar, essempto > exento, esso > eso, estraño > extraño, grossera > grosera, missa > misa, ossadia > osadía, passar > pasar, etc.

x > j:

alexar > alejar, baxar > bajar, dexar > dejar, execucion > ejecución, exemplo > ejemplo, exercito > ejército, prolixo > prolijo, quexa > queja.

Addition of an h:
aver > haber, emisferio > hemisferio, o > oh, oy > hoy.
Addition of a p:
acetar > aceptar.
Deletion of a letter:
christiano > cristiano, essempcion > exención, mentecapto > mentecato, primero > primer.

TRANSLATOR'S NOTE

The 1990s were heady times, as scholars who specialized in early modern drama began to discuss ways in which – in our classrooms and research, in print and performance – we could, as Amy Williamsen proposed, 'increase the representation of women and other underrepresented writers, not to replace the "classics" but to enrich our study of all texts as interrelated cultural discourses.'[91] We were present at the birth of new editions and theatrical productions aimed at generating greater interest in women-authored, early modern plays, and the recuperation of those texts led to the production of more translations into English. Intrigued by the challenge of such a creative project and its potential for expanding the number of people who had access to the *Comedia*, Valerie and I published a bilingual edition of Zayas's *La traición en la amistad* (the translation was titled *Friendship Betrayed*) in 1999, with the goal of introducing a superb Spanish comedy – and, we emphasized, one written by a woman – to a wider audience of students and theater aficionados, as well as general readers and scholars from a variety of disciplines. Our intention then and now has been to bring to light little-known plays by women dramatists whose works have been relegated to the margins of theater history for centuries. We remain committed to this exploration of women's cultural production with our new edition and first-ever translation of Azevedo's *El muerto disimulado / Presumed Dead.* Moreover, what we have learned by working on these comedies by Zayas and Azevedo has profoundly influenced our understanding of women's writing and our experience and interaction with the theater.

Because we had originally conceptualized the Zayas project in print format, we were frankly surprised to learn that several theater groups had decided to perform the translation, and we have since enjoyed sitting in the audience to witness the varied interpretations of the written, translated text. From my own perspective, seeing any Golden Age drama performed remains a thrill, but the power of that experience is multiplied ten-fold when directors and actors bring their own creative decisions to plays with which I have engaged intimately and whose words I know quite well. In recent years, I have begun to explore the myriad ways in which translation and adaptation have been theorized, and

91 Amy R. Williamsen, 'Charting Our Course: Gender, the Canon, and Early Modern Theater', in V. Hegstrom and A. Williamsen (eds), *Engendering the Early Modern Stage: Women Playwrights in the Spanish Empire* (New Orleans: UP of the South, 1999), p. 8.

I have thought as well about the changes in attitude and methodology that have generated contemporary approaches to the topic.[92] All translations open creative possibilities by taking into account the position that every reading of the original text, performed or not, is a unique interpretation in time and space. I no longer believe, for example, that the evaluation of a translation based on its fidelity to its source text is a particularly useful tool for measuring quality, especially when the translation is used, altered and adapted for performance by groups of theater practitioners. Translators for the stage often speak of creating a blueprint for performance, i.e., they employ language that gives actors, directors and audiences the raw material they need to take the play forward.[93] Our project intentionally combined these purposes: the overarching goal in editing and translating Azevedo's comedy was to produce a useful text for students and scholars, actors and audiences. It is fair to state that, as was the case with Zayas's *Friendship Betrayed*, my prose translation of *Presumed Dead* was influenced by the multiple audiences for whom we were writing. As a result, it tended to follow Azevedo's text relatively closely. Still, I made several conscious decisions regarding the ways I would represent Azevedo's comedy in English.

In my approach to those decisions, I employed – and outline here – a number of the elements that Michael Kidd had used in his 'Translator's Notes' for Calderón's *Life's a Dream*; I have found them useful models

92 See especially J. D. Connor, 'The Persistence of Fidelity: Adaptation Theory Today', *M/C Journal* 10.2 (2007); Linda Hutcheon, *A Theory of Adaptation* (New York: Routledge, 2012); David Johnston, 'Lope de Vega in English: The Historicized Imagination', in S. Paun de García and D. Larson (eds), *The Comedia in English: Translation and Performance* (Woodbridge: Tamesis, 2008), pp. 66–82; David Johnston, 'Sister Act: Reflection, Refraction, and Performance in the Translation of *La dama boba*', *Bulletin of the Comediantes* 67.1 (2015), pp. 79–98; David Johnston, 'Translator's Note', in D. Johnston (trans.), *The Lady Boba: A Woman of Little Sense* (London: Oberon, 2013) pp. 5–8; David Johnston, 'Translator Doubleness: The Unfaithful Original', an address presented at The *Comedia*: Translation and Performance Symposium (Theatre Royal, Bath, UK, 26 Nov. 2015), n. pag.; as well as collections of critical essays including, Harley Erdman and Susan Paun de García (eds), *Remaking the Comedia: Spanish Classical Theater in Adaptation* (Woodbridge: Tamesis, 2015); Catherine Boyle and David Johnston (eds), *The Spanish Golden Age in English: Perspectives on Performance* (London: Oberon, 2007); and Susan Paun de García and Donald R. Larson (eds), *The Comedia in English: Translation and Performance* (Woodbridge: Tamesis, 2008).

93 See Kathleen Mountjoy, 'Literal and Performance Text', in C. Boyle and D. Johnston (eds), *The Spanish Golden Age in English: Perspectives on Performance* (London: Oberon, 2007), p. 77.

for describing my own approach to the art of translation.[94] Kidd frames his textual decisions as answers to the questions and issues that translators always must face. For example, his dialect choice, 'more or less standard American English', responded to his concern that Calderón is not well known in the US, which led him to concentrate on his proposed audience of American high school and college students (41–42). In the process of reading his 'Translator's Notes', I found that many of Kidd's ideas dovetailed nicely with my own with regard to fidelity to form and content, medium of expression, wordplay, and the relationship between the translation and its audiences of readers and theatergoers.[95] Consequently, in what follows, I indicate our points of contact and divergence, but fundamentally, I echo his central motivation: to create a translation that is accurate and accessible for English-speaking audiences and avoids the 'formal stiffness of language that is little conducive to oral reception' (66).[96]

In like manner, I also found particularly useful Donald Larson's description of his recent translation of Lope's *La discreta enamorada*, which focuses on his proposed audience of theater practitioners and emphasizes their creative input in bringing the text to contemporary audiences:

> The translation is meant to be an acting version, and is for the most part not literal. I like to think, nonetheless, that it is broadly faithful to the sense of Lope's text. My intention throughout was to write in a language recognizable as modern English, although the tone is often more formal than would be common these days. I haven't avoided that elevation because I think it gives a feeling of 'foreignness' suggestive of 17th-century Spanish culture. ('Re: Translation')[97]

In translating *Presumed Dead*, I sought a balance of vocabulary and tone that could help twenty-first-century readers *and* theater audiences find relevant connections between their world and that of a classical text.[98] Like Don

---

94 Michael Kidd, 'Translator's Notes', in M. Kidd (trans.), *Life's a Dream: A Prose Translation and Critical Introduction* (Boulder: UP of Colorado, 2004), 41–70.

95 Throughout this introduction, we have discussed several of the other issues that Kidd also treats in his 'Translator's Notes'. Some, such as his approach to *La vida es sueño*'s textual history, are not directly relevant to Azevedo's play and are therefore not included in this analysis.

96 For example, Kidd emphasizes a liberal use of contractions, which he characterizes as particularly suitable for performance (66).

97 Donald Larson, 'Re: Translation', an email message to Catherine Larson, 29 March 2016.

98 This move from considering how a translation will be received by readers to one that

Larson, I have also occasionally called attention to the play's foreignness. I devoted special attention to Azevedo's only two examples of more formal poetic forms, an *octava real* and a sonnet, fashioning versions in English of those Golden Age poems to emphasize the contest between one pair of male and female leads regarding who suffers more when a lover is absent. Jacinta and Clarindo (here, dressed as 'Clara') engage in what might be called a linguistic duel; rather than swords, they use poetry:

Jacinta: I'll say what I believe, then, if only to hear you. I feel that the person who stays behind suffers more torture from absence than the one who leaves.
Clarindo: I say that person suffers less.
Jacinta: I say more, and I'll prove it in a poetic octave.
Clarindo: Show me, because if the poem comes from you, I already consider it a marvel.
Jacinta:

The mem'ry left by a good man gives vent
To cruelly torture his beloved's breast,
And the place that heart lay will not consent
To please the abandoned one so distressed;
And if that horrible pain must augment,
And the mem'ry's constancy were expressed,
The girl left behind – no doubt, for I know –
Will surely suffer the very most woe.

Jacinta recites her poem to great acclaim; Clarindo/'Clara' follows with his/'her' sonnet:

In the fortunes of love, change is unkind,
a cruel torment of worry and care,
and the torment is doubled then and there
when the change is of more than one kind.
Hostile fate follows the one reassigned:
leaving his love and his home, he'll despair;
all that remains is the good he'll forswear,
which brings relief to the one left behind.
Bidding farewell to the place where I loved
and to all the good, devotion I'd give,

takes theater audiences into account is, I would assert, indicative of the increasing interest in performance among those who study and attend early modern Hispanic theater productions across the globe.

counting as double the changes thereof,
    absent, I go not where I loved to live,
nor do I live with the one that I loved;
absent, such suff'ring cannot be outlived.

As Kidd notes and as previous translators before us have learned, translating in verse can sound stiff and artificial as a result of the vast differences between English and Spanish in rhyme, rhythm, and meter. These two poems are clearly more formal than the prose that encircles them. My decision to include the sole examples of an *octava* and a sonnet in the middle of a prose translation was intentional, to emphasize the foreignness of these verse forms within the play and offer a linguistic and contextual contrast to what surrounded them. In both form and content, the poems stand out: although far from perfect, they explain how such verbal dueling worked in the *Comedia* and give the audience a taste of early modern poetic forms and more formal language.

Kidd also states that chronological/historical differences between the seventeenth and twenty-first centuries suggest that contemporary readers and spectators will likely not respond positively to potentially discordant vocabulary choices, such as 'thou' or 'thee'. He preserved certain lexical oddities and historical and mythological references, and a representative sampling of anachronisms (44). In like manner, I sought a balance between natural-sounding discourse and occasional lexical choices that emphasized cultural difference. I kept but explained in a note the noblewoman Jacinta's reference to Latona's son Apollo, whose circuit through the 12 zodiac signs in his golden chariot alludes to the passage of a year. I also had Papagayo express himself in a much less literate register: when he tells Clarindo that his (then, cross-dressing) sister had become a monk, Papagayo covers for his mistake by saying, 'I mean nun, 'cuz this stuff with monks and nuns is all the same to me, since they all wear habits and live in monasteries;' I followed with a note explaining that the terms for 'convents' and 'monasteries' can be used interchangeably and do not specify gender in Spanish and Portuguese.

My decision-making regarding the medium of translation – verse vs. prose – also echoed that of Kidd, who reminds us that most translators of Calderón have chosen verse, which relates to their desire to be faithful to the source text's form. He argues, however, 'that authentic verse translations are impossible not only practically but also theoretically because of the vast differences in the conventions of rhyme, meter, and rhythm that exist between English and Spanish poetry' (45). For example, Spanish rhyme structures, which allow for assonant end rhyme, have no equivalent in English, and Spanish syllabic meter does not correlate to the basic unit of English meter: the foot. Moreover, Spanish poetry emphasizes power and variety in the combinations of fixed accents on specific syllables, which offers a striking contrast to the sounds of poetry written in English. Kidd concludes that the more translators try to construct faithful form, the more they risk sabotaging the creation of faithful meaning; he therefore decided that his translation would seek accuracy and accessibility via prose (50).

Kidd also devotes a section to the translation of proper names in *Life's a Dream*, indicating and analyzing the decisions that various translators of the play have made in the past. I chose not to translate any of the characters' names in *Presumed Dead*, as I believe that anglicizing 'Alberto' to 'Albert', 'Clarindo' to 'Clarenton', and 'Dorotea' to 'Dorothy', for example, may be perceived as culturally inauthentic and thereby threaten an element of the original text that is more powerful in the original Spanish. Readers will, of course, pronounce the names in ways that sound real to them; theater audiences consisting of native speakers of both English and Spanish may react well to good (or proximate) pronunciations, and they may cringe when actors don't quite carry them off. I provide a pronunciation guide for the characters' names; it is located in the List of Characters preceding Act I. Despite those issues, the decision not to translate the characters' names allowed those characters to retain a degree of foreignness that gently underscored their geographic, cultural, and linguistic otherness. In the singular case of a particularly interesting name, that of the *gracioso* Papagayo, the playtext itself and an explanatory footnote help to fill in the blanks and decipher the jokes, although it is certainly true that in a performance, textual footnotes only work when theater practitioners interpret them onstage for their audiences. Azevedo often plays self-consciously with her characters' names, including the female Lisarda and her male alter ego, 'Lisardo', and Clarindo's appearance as 'Clara'. The names point to the way the play calls attention to questions of gender and identity while slyly indicating that nothing is as it seems. As 'Clara's' new name ironically suggests, 'her' identity here is anything but clear.'

Language is central to *Presumed Dead*; it is a witty comedy, the result of punning and other types of wordplay, as well as numerous self-conscious references to discourse itself. My translation attempted to accomplish precisely what Kidd describes as his own practice: '…I have taken care to render wordplay as closely as possible to the meaning and register of the original. My aim has been to transmit the playfulness of the Spanish in a way that can be apprehended in a performance context…' (60). My own rendering of the dramatist's punning and other forms of wordplay attempts to reflect Kidd's goals and illuminate Azevedo's gift for creating comedy with language. For instance, she devotes a fair amount of attention to the face, from the connections between the eyes and love to wordplay filled with double entendres (e.g., *cara* as 'face', but also as 'expensive'), and in one instance, she has Dorotea describe the advantages that 'Clara's' face grants her: 'Clara' sells her merchandise cheaply '*porque es de caras envidia / su cara*'. I translated those lines by engaging with the same essential ideas, although with a twist to emphasize the humor: 'her products must cost very little, because her countenance counts: the beauty of her face cheapens the facades of all others. Face it.' In another example, I tried to transmit that kind of linguistic playfulness when 'Clara' describes some of the wares she is carrying in her basket. I was forced to confront the fact that much of the wordplay in Spanish, seen in double meanings of similar words (*medias*: stockings; *a medias*: halfway, *sin medida*: beyond measure), as in '*Medias de precio estimadas, / con quien las medias más finas / se llevan el lustre a medias, / que en éstas es sin medida*', did not translate elegantly into English. I therefore attempted instead to convey the sense of Azevedo's witty use of language by exaggerating the rhyme: 'Priceless stockings; they'll bring you pleasure; the finest till now are but half the treasure, for the splendor of these is beyond measure'.

I found that *El muerto disimulado* raised two issues that impacted the act of translation. The first was the playwright's decision to write in Spanish, which led to numerous examples of potential confusion between her good (although non-native) Spanish and her native Portuguese. I am grateful for Valerie's analyses of the influence of Portuguese on Azevedo's language, seen especially in the 'Editor's Note', because she was able to clarify a number of murky areas. The translation was also affected by the author's stylistic decisions, including her tendency to write sentences that run on for pages (with little guiding punctuation) and her occasional preference for incorporating lengthy reviews of plot actions. Interestingly, Azevedo's sometimes demanding artistic decisions also seemed to call attention to the confusion related to the historical context of the comedy, thereby doubling the upheaval inherent in the plot, the murder mystery that lies at the heart of the comedy's various, interwoven lines of action. That said, undertaking the translation of *El muerto disimulado* allowed me to engage in a creative experiment that encouraged me to appreciate much more fully the wit of this rarely studied woman writer. Even more, the project led me to see on a number of different levels the ways in which Azevedo understood, expressed, and parodied the conventions of the theater of her day. The dramatist delighted in playing with (and often exaggerating) the literary, theatrical, and social conventions that served as the raw material of numerous dramatic texts of her time, in particular her integration of self-conscious game-playing with the very nature of the theater and theatrical discourse.[99]

I hope that in translating *Presumed Dead* for our bilingual edition, I have helped to facilitate our goal of showcasing the cultural production of early modern Iberian women. For Valerie and me, the process of watching both Zayas's and Azevedo's comedies move from page to stage allowed us to experience the interrelatedness of the endeavors of translating for print and performance. We have been energized by the enormous possibilities offered in the creation of editions, translations, adaptations, and performances of Golden Age, women-authored plays, and we encourage others to join the ranks of those who are now participating actively in this field, which today embraces both traditional scholarship and contemporary views of it, including an increasingly emergent interest in both theatrical spectacle and the dissemination of women's writing.

99 For example, Dorotea describes the confusion created early in the play: 'I'll bet that in an hour and a half no one will be able to figure out what direction this play is headed.' In another instance, Papagayo speaks directly to the audience in an aside: 'Ladies and gentlemen… What the devil kind of dramatic poet plotted so much nonsense? It seems like something from a dream! Have you ever seen such a thing? How will this abyss of confusions end? I'll have a lot to tell if we come out on the other side of this chaos.'

BIBLIOGRAPHY

Primary Texts

Editions of El muerto disimulado

Azevedo, Ângela [Angela] de. *Comedia famosa, El muerto dissimulado.* N.p.: n.p., n.d. T/19049. Biblioteca Nacional de España, Madrid. 11728.a.28. British Library, London. Print.

Azevedo, Ângela [Angela] de. *Comedia famosa, El muerto dissimulado.* N.p.: n.p., n.d. T/19049. Biblioteca Nacional de España, Madrid. *Biblioteca Digital Hispánica*. Web. 9 Sept. 2015.

Azevedo, Ângela [Angela] de. *Comedia famosa, El mverto dissimvlado. Escritoras Españolas 1500–1900. Biblioteca Nacional de España.* Ed. María del Carmen Simón Palmer. Part 1. Libro 2. Madrid: Chadwyck-Healey España, 1992. Microfiche.

Azevedo, Ângela [Angela] de. *El muerto disimulado. Women's Acts: Plays by Women Dramatists of Spain's Golden Age*. Ed. Teresa Scott Soufas. Lexington: UP of Kentucky, 1997, 91–132. Print.

Azevedo, Ângela [Ángela] de. *La margarita del Tajo que dio nombre a Santarén. El muerto disimulado.* Ed. Fernando Doménech Rico. Serie de Literatura Dramática 44. Madrid: Asociación de Directores de Escena de España, 1999, 191–334. Print.

Editions of Azevedo's Other Plays

Azevedo, Ângela [Angela] de. *Comedia famosa, Dicha y desdicha del juego, y devoción de la Virgen.* N.p.: n.p., n.d. T/21435 and T/32920. Biblioteca Nacional de España, Madrid. 11728.a.27. British Library, London. Print.

Azevedo, Ângela [Angela] de. *Comedia famosa, Dicha y desdicha del juego, y devoción de la Virgen.* N.p.: n.p., n.d. 11728.a.27. British Library, London. *Google Libros*. Web. 12 Mar. 2017.

Azevedo, Ângela [Angela] de. *Comedia famosa, Dicha y desdicha del juego y devocion de la Virgen. Escritoras Españolas 1500–1900. Biblioteca Nacional de España.* Ed. María del Carmen Simón Palmer. Part 1. Libro 3. Madrid: Chadwyck-Healey España, 1992. Microfiche.

Azevedo, Ângela [Angela] de. *Comedia famosa, La margarita del Tajo que dio nombre a Santaren.* N.p.: n.p., n.d. T/33142. Biblioteca Nacional de España, Madrid. Print.

Azevedo, Ângela [Angela] de. *Comedia famosa, La margarita del Tajo, qve dio nombre a Santaren. Escritoras Españolas 1500–1900. Biblioteca Nacional de España.* Ed. María del Carmen Simón Palmer. Part 1. Libro 4. Madrid: Chadwyck-Healey España, 1992. Microfiche.

Azevedo, Ângela [Angela] de. *Dicha y desdicha del juego y devoción de la Virgen. Women's Acts: Plays by Women Dramatists of Spain's Golden Age*. Ed. Teresa Scott Soufas. Lexington: UP of Kentucky, 1997, 4–44. Print.

Azevedo, Ângela [Ángela] de. *La margarita del Tajo que dio nombre a Santarén. El muerto disimulado*. Ed. Fernando Doménech Rico. Serie Literatura Dramática 44. Madrid: Asociación de Directores de Escena de España, 1999, 33–189. Print.

Azevedo, Ângela [Angela] de. *La margarita del Tajo que dio nombre a Santarén. Women's Acts: Plays by Women Dramatists of Spain's Golden Age*. Ed. Teresa Scott Soufas. Lexington: UP of Kentucky, 1997, 45–90. Print.

Performances of *El muerto disimulado* and *Presumed Dead*

Azevedo, Ângela de. *El muerto disimulado*. Dir. Jason Yancey. Perf. Department of Spanish and Portuguese, Brigham Young University, Provo, UT, 2004. *AHCT Digital Video Archive. AHCT.org*. Web. 26 March 2016. Also staged at the University of New Mexico, Albuquerque; the University of Arizona, Tucson; Arizona State University, Tempe; BYU Idaho, Rexburg, ID; Utah State University, Logan, UT; and the University of Utah, Salt Lake City. Performance.

Azevedo, Ângela de. *El muerto disimulado* (staged scene from Act 1). Dir. Jacob Padilla. *Vimeo*, 2015. Web. 1 May 2016. Performance.

Azevedo, Ângela de. *Presumed Dead*. Dir. Kari Greenberg. Perf. WSC/Avant Bard, Scripts in Play Festival. Theatre on the Run, Arlington, VA, April 2016. Performance.

Secondary Texts Cited or Consulted

Abel, Lionel. *Metatheatre: A New View of Dramatic Form*. New York: Hill and Wang, 1963. Print.

Alarcón Román, María del Carmen, ed. *Sor Francisca de Santa Teresa: Coloquios*. Seville: ArCiBel Editores, 2007. Print.

[Anastácio, Vanda.] Faculdade de Letras da Universidade de Lisboa (FLUL): Letras Lisboa. *Escritoras: Women Writers in Portuguese before 1900. Fundação Calouste Gulbenkian, Associação Internacional de Lusitanistas*. 14 Dec. 2015. Web. 20 June 2016.

Anderson, James Maxwell. *The History of Portugal*. Westport: Greenwood P, 2000. Print.

Arenal, Electa and Georgina Sabat-Rivers, eds. *Literatura conventual femenina: Sor Marcela de San Félix, hija de Lope de Vega. Obra completa: Coloquios espirituales, loas y otros poemas*. Barcelona: PPU, 1988. Print.

Arenal, Electa and Stacey Schlau, eds. *Untold Sisters: Hispanic Nuns in Their Own Works*. Trans. Amanda Powell. Albuquerque: U of New Mexico P, 1989. Print.

Barbeito Carneiro, María Isabel. 'Mujeres peninsulares entre Portugal y España',

Península: Revista de Estudos Ibéricos 0 (2003): 209–24. *FLUP*. Web. 4 April 2016.

Barbeito Carneiro, María Isabel. *Mujeres y literatura del Siglo de Oro: Espacios profanos y conventuales*. Madrid: SAFEKAT, 2007. Print.

Barker, Richard. 'Showing the Flag in 1521: Wafting Beatriz to Savoy', in *XI Reunião Internacional da História da Náutica e da Hidrografia* and *VIII Jornadas de História Ibero-Americana Conference*. Portimão, Portugal. 2 May 2002. *Home.net/rabarker*. Web. 26 March 2016. Conference Paper.

Barrera y Leirado, Cayetano Alberto de la. *Catálogo bibliográfico del teatro antiguo español, desde su orígenes hasta mediados del siglo XVIII*. 1860. Madrid: Gredos, 1969. Print.

Bayliss, Robert. 'The Best Man in the Play: Female Agency in a Gender-Inclusive *Comedia*', *Bulletin of the Comediantes* 59.2 (2007): 303–23. Print.

Belisario, El Capitan. 'Carta por Títulos de Comedias vinda da cidade de S. Paulo sobre o levantamento das Minas'. Letter 28 of 'Documentos do Arquivo da Tôrre do Tombo copiados pela Dr. Emília Félix, por solicitação do Sr. José Pedro Leite Coreiro', *Revista do Instituto Histórico e Geográfico de S. Paulo* 52 (1956): 271–92. Print.

Birmingham, David. *A Concise History of Portugal*. Cambridge: Cambridge UP, 1993. Print.

Blecua, Alberto. 'Sobre la (no) puntuación en los textos dramáticos del Siglo de Oro', in *En buena compañía: Estudios en honor de Luciano García Lorenzo*. Ed. Joaquín Álvarez Barrientos et al. Madrid: CSIC, 2009, 79–101. Print.

Bluteau, Raphael. *Vocabulario portuguez e latino*. Coimbra: Collegio das Artes da Companhia de Jesus, 1712–1728. 8 vols. Print.

Bolaños Donoso, Piedad. *Doña Feliciana Enríquez de Guzmán: Crónica de un fracaso vital, 1669–1644*. Seville: U de Sevilla, Secretariado de Publicaciones, 2012. Print.

Boyle, Catherine, trans. *House of Desires: A New Translation*. London: Oberon, 2005. Print.

Boyle, Catherine and David Johnston, eds. *The Spanish Golden Age in English: Perspectives on Performance*. London: Oberon, 2007. Print.

Bravo-Villasante, Carmen. *La mujer vestida de hombre en el teatro español: Siglos XVI–XVII*. Madrid: Maya de Oro, 1988. Print.

Brown, Jonathan and John H. Elliott. *Un palacio para el rey. El Buen Retiro y la corte de Felipe IV*. Madrid: Taurus, 2003. Print.

Caro, Rodrigo. *Varones insignes en letras, naturales de la ilustrísima ciudad de Sevilla*. Seville: Real Academia Sevillana de Buenas Letras, 1915. Print.

Chambers, Donna M. 'From Within the Birdcage: Societal Relations in the Works of Angela de Azevedo'. Dissertation. Georgetown University, 2007. UMI 3302007. *ProQuest*, 2008. Web. 26 April 2016.

Clearwood, Maegan. 'Behind the Scenes at the Creation', in *Scripts in Play Festival, 26 March–23 April, 2016.* Program. Print.

Connor, J. D. 'The Persistence of Fidelity: Adaptation Theory Today', *M/C Journal* 10.2 (2007). N. pag. Web. 9 June 2014.

Correa [Correia], Isabel. *El pastor fido, poema de Baptista Guarino, traducido de italiano en metro español y illustrado con reflexiones.* Antwerp: Henrico y Cornelio Verdussen, 1694. Print.

Corrêa [Correia], Gaspar. *Crónicas de D. Manuel e de D. João III (até 1533).* Ed. José Pereira da Costa. Lisbon: Academia de Ciências de Lisboa, 1992. Print.

Cotarelo y Mori, Emilio, ed. *Bibliografía de las controversias sobre la licitud del teatro en España.* Madrid: Revista de Archivos, Bibliotecas y Museos, 1904. Print.

Covarrubias, Sebastián de. *Tesoro de la lengua castellana o española.* Ed. Martín de Riquer. Ad litteram 3. Barcelona: Editorial Alta Fulia, 1998. Print.

Delgado, María M. and David T. Gies, eds. *History of Theatre in Spain.* Cambridge: Cambridge UP, 2012. Print.

Díaz Cerón, José M. *Cecilia del Nacimiento, O.C.D. 1570–1646: Obras completas.* Madrid: Editorial de Espiritualidad, 1971. Print.

Diccionario de Autoridades: Real Academia Española. Facsimile edn. 3 vols. Madrid: Gredos, 1990. Print.

Diccionario de la lengua española. 2 vols. Madrid: Real Academia Española, 1992. Print.

Disney, Anthony R. *A History of Portugal and the Portuguese Empire.* Vol. 1: Portugal. New York: Cambridge UP, 2009. Print.

Doménech Rico, Fernando. 'Introducción'. Ed. Doménech Rico, *La margarita del Tajo*, 5–31. Print.

Doménech Rico, Fernando, ed. *La margarita del Tajo que dio nombre a Santarén. El muerto disimulado.* By Ângela de Azevedo. Serie Literatura Dramática 44. Madrid: Asociación de Directores de Escena de España, 1999. Print.

Doménech Rico, Fernando, ed. *Teatro breve de mujeres (Siglos XVII–XX).* Serie Literatura Dramática 41. Madrid: Asociación de Directores de Escena de España, 1996. Print.

Elliott, John H. 'A Europe of Composite Monarchies', *Past and Present* 137 (1992): 48–71. Print.

Erdman, Harley, trans. *Feliciana Enríquez de Guzmán, Ana Caro Mallén, and Sor Marcela de San Félix: Women Playwrights of Early Modern Spain.* Ed. Nieves Romero-Díaz and Lisa Vollendorf. The Other Voice in Early Modern Europe: The Toronto Series 49. Medieval and Renaissance Texts and Studies 501. Toronto: Iter P; Tempe: Arizona Center for Medieval and Renaissance Studies, 2016. Print.

Erdman, Harley and Susan Paun de García, eds. *Remaking the Comedia: Spanish Classical Theater in Adaptation.* Woodbridge: Tamesis, 2015. Print.

Ferrer Valls, Teresa. 'Decir entre versos: Ángela de Acevedo y la escritura femenina en el siglo de oro', in *Ecos silenciados: La mujer en la literatura española. Siglos XII al XVIII*. Ed. Susana Gil-Albarellos Pérez-Pedrero and Mercedes Rodríguez Pequeño. Segovia: Fundación Instituto Castellano y Leonés de la Lengua, 2006, 213–41. *Entresiglos.uv.es*. N.pag. Web. 4 April 2016.

Ferrer Valls, Teresa. 'Mujer y escritura dramática en el Siglo de Oro: Del acatamiento a la réplica de la convención teatral', in *La presencia de la mujer en el teatro barroco español. Festival Internacional de Teatro Clásico de Almagro, July 23–24, 1997*. Ed. Mercedes de los Reyes Peña. Seville: Junta de Andalucía, Consejería de Cultura, 1998, 9–32. *Entresiglos.uv.es*. N.pag. Web. 4 April 2016.

Francisco da Natividade. *Lenitivos da Dor I propostos ao augusto, e poderoso monarcha el rey D. Pedro II nosso senhor*. Lisbon: Miguel Deslandes, 1700. Print.

Gabriele, John P. 'Engendering Narrative Equality in Ángela de Azevedo's *El muerto disimulado*', *Bulletin of the Comediantes* 60.1 (2008): 127–38. Print.

Gascón, Christopher D. 'Female and Male Mediation in the Plays of Ángela de Azevedo', *Bulletin of the Comediantes* 57.1 (2005): 125–45. Print.

Girard, René. *Deceit, Desire, and the Novel: Self and Other in Literary Structure*. Trans. Yvonne Freccero. Baltimore: Johns Hopkins UP, 1965. Print.

Greer, Margaret R. and John E. Varey. *El teatro palaciego en Madrid: 1586–1707. Estudio y documentos. Fuentes para la Historia del Teatro en España*, 29. Madrid: Tamesis, 1997. Print.

Griffin, Clive. *Heresy and the Inquisition in Sixteenth-Century Spain*. Oxford: Oxford UP, 2005. Print.

Hegstrom, Valerie. '*Comedia* Scholarship and Performance: *El muerto disimulado* from the Archive to the Stage', *Comedia Performance* 4.1 (2007): 152–78. Print.

Hegstrom, Valerie. 'El convento como espacio escénico y la monja como actriz: montajes teatrales en tres conventos de Valladolid, Madrid y Lisboa', in *Letras en la celda: Cultura escrita de los conventos femeninos en la España moderna*. Ed. Nieves Baranda Leturio and María Carmen Marín Pina. Madrid: Iberoamericana-Vervuert, 2014, 363–78. Print.

Hegstrom, Valerie, ed. and Catherine Larson, trans. *La traición en la amistad / Friendship Betrayed*. Lewisburg: Bucknell UP, 1999. Print.

Hegstrom, Valerie and Amy R. Williamsen. 'Early Modern *Dramaturgas*: A Contemporary Performance History', in Erdman and Paun de García, 83–92. Print.

Hegstrom, Valerie and Amy R. Williamsen. 'Gendered Matters: Engaging Research on Early Modern *Dramaturgas* in the Classroom', in *Teaching Gender through Latin American, Latino and Iberian Texts and Culture*. Ed. Leila Gómez, et al. Rotterdam: Sense, 2015, 99–124. Print.

Hegstrom, Valerie and Amy R. Williamsen, eds. *Engendering the Early Modern Stage: Women Playwrights in the Spanish Empire*. New Orleans: UP of the South, 1999. Print.

Hormigón, Juan Antonio, ed. 'Acevedo, Ángela de.' *Autoras en la historia del teatro español, 1500–1994*. Vol. 1. Madrid: Asociación de Directores de Escena de España, 1996, 403–09. Print.

Hornby, Richard. *Drama, Metadrama, and Perception*. Lewisburg: Bucknell UP, 1986. Print.

Hutcheon, Linda. *A Theory of Adaptation*. 2nd edn. New York: Routledge, 2012. Print.

Jauss, Hans Robert. *Toward an Aesthetic of Reception*. Trans. Timothy Bahti. Minneapolis: U of Minnesota P, 1982. Print.

John Murray [Firm]. *A Handbook for Travellers in Portugal: A Complete Guide for Lisbon, Cintra, Mafra, the British Battle-fields, Alcobaça, Batalha, Oporto, etc*. 3rd edn. London: John Murray, 1864. Print.

Johnston, David. 'Lope de Vega in English: The Historicized Imagination', in Paun de García and D. Larson, 66–82. Print.

Johnston, David. 'Sister Act: Reflection, Refraction, and Performance in the Translation of *La dama boba*', *BCom* 67.1 (2015): 79–98. Print.

Johnston, David. 'Translator Doubleness: The Unfaithful Original', in The *Comedia*: Translation and Performance Symposium. Theatre Royal, Bath, UK. 26 Nov. 2015. Address.

Johnston, David. 'Translator's Note', in *The Lady Boba: A Woman of Little Sense*. London: Oberon, 2013, 5–8. Print.

José de Jesús María. *Memorial. Bibliografía de las controversias sobre la licitud del teatro en España*. Ed. Emilio de Cotarelo y Mori. Madrid: Revista de Archivos, Bibliotecas y Museos, 1904, 367–84. *Googlebooks*. Web. 25 Feb. 2017.

Kagan, Richard L. and Geoffrey Parker, eds. *Spain, Europe, and the Atlantic World: Essays in Honor of John H. Elliott*. Cambridge: Cambridge UP, 1995. Print.

Kidd, Michael. 'Translator's Notes', in *Life's a Dream: A Prose Translation and Critical Introduction*. By Pedro Calderón de la Barca. Boulder: UP of Colorado, 2004, 41–70. Print.

Larson, Catherine. 'Found in Translation: María de Zayas's *Friendship Betrayed* and the English-Speaking Stage', in Paun de García and Larson, *The Comedia in English*, 83–94. Print.

Larson, Catherine. 'Metatheater and the *Comedia*: Past, Present, and Future', in *The Golden Age Comedia: Text, Theory, and Performance*. Ed. Howard Mancing and Charles Ganelin. West Lafayette: Purdue UP, 1994, 204–21. Print.

Larson, Catherine. 'Translating and Adapting the Classics: Staging *La dama boba* in English', *Bulletin of the Comediantes* 67.1 (2015) 19–36. Print.

Larson, Catherine. 'Translating Hispanic Women Dramatists in the 21st Century: Are We There Yet?', in *Religious and Secular Theater in Golden Age Spain: Essays in Honor of Donald T. Dietz*. Ed. Susan Paun de García and Donald R. Larson. Ibérica Series, ed. A. Robert Lauer. New York: Peter Lang, in press. Print.

Larson, Catherine. 'Translator's Note', in Hegstrom and Larson, *La traición en la amistad / Friendship Betrayed*, 28–29. Print.

Larson, Donald. 'Re: Translation', pers. comm. to Catherine Larson. 29 March 2016. E-mail.

Lopes, Maria Antónia and Blythe Alice Raviola, eds. *Portugal e o Piemonte: A Casa Real Portuguesa e os Sabóias: Nove Séculos de Relações Dinásticas e Destinos Políticos (XII–XX)*. 2nd edn. Coimbra: U of Coimbra P, 2013. Print.

Machado, Diogo Barbosa. *Bibliotheca lusitana historica, critica e cronologica*. 4 vols. Vol. 1, Lisbon: Officina de Antonio Isidoro da Fonseca, 1741. Vol. 2, Lisbon: Officina de Ignacio Rodrigues, 1747. Vol. 3, Lisbon: Officina de Ignacio Rodrigues, 1752. Vol. 4, Lisbon: Officina Patriarcal de Francisco Luiz Ameno, 1759. Print.

Maldonado, Juana de. *Entretenimiento en obsequio de la huida a Egipto*. Ed. Iride Rossi de Fiore. Salta, Argentina: Editorial Biblioteca de Textos Universitarios, 2006. Print.

Maroto Camino, Mercedes. 'Transvestism, Translation and Transgression: Angela de Azevedo's *El muerto disimulado*', *Forum for Modern Language Studies* 37.3 (2001): 314–25. Print.

Marques, António Henrique R. de Oliveira. *Daily Life in Portugal in the Late Middle Ages*. Trans. S. S. Wyatt. Madison: U of Wisconsin P, 1981. Print.

Martín Marcos, David. 'O projeto matrimonial de Isabel Francisca Josefa de Bragança e Vítor Amadeu II de Saboia (1675–1682): Estrategias familiares e geopolítica', *Análise Social* 49.212 (2014): 598–623. Web. 29 March 2016.

Mas i Usó, Pasqual. *Academias valencianas del barroco: Descripción y diccionario de poetas*. Kassel: Reichenberger, 1999. Print.

McColl Millar, Robert. *Trask's Historical Linguistics*. 2nd edn. London: Hodder Arnold, 2007. Print.

McGaha, Michael, trans. *Los empeños de una casa / Pawns of a House*. By Juana Inés de la Cruz. Ed. Susana Hernández-Araico. Tempe: Bilingual P, 2007. Print.

McKendrick, Melveena. *Identities in Crisis: Essays on Honour, Gender and Women in the Comedia*. Kassel: Reichenberger, 2002. Print.

McKendrick, Melveena. *Woman and Society in the Spanish Drama of the Golden Age: A Study of the Mujer varonil*. New York: Cambridge UP, 1994. Print.

Miller, Jonathan. *The Afterlife of Plays*. San Diego: San Diego State UP, 1992. Print.

Moratín, Leandro Fernández de. *Orígenes del teatro español*. Paris: Librería Europea de Baudry, 1838. Print.

Mountjoy, Kathleen. 'Literal and Performance Text', in Boyle and Johnston, 75–88. Print.

Mujica, Barbara. 'Ángela de Azevedo: Espectros y sombras', in *Women Writers of Early Modern Spain: Sophia's Daughters*. Ed. Barbara Mujica. New Haven: Yale UP, 2004, 232–47. Print. Reprinted as 'Angela de Azevedo: Espejos y espejimso', in Wade, *Angela de Acevedo's*, 9–13.

Múzquiz-Guerreiro, Darlene. 'Symbolic Inversions in Ángela de Azevedo's *El muerto disimulado*', *Bulletin of the Comediantes* 57.1 (2005): 147–63. Print.

Oliveira, Américo Lopes de. *Escritoras Brasileiras, Galegas e Portuguesas*. Braga: Tipografia Silva Pereira, 1983. Print.

Oresko, Robert. 'The House of Savoy in Search for a Royal Crown in the Seventeenth Century', in *Royal and Republican Sovereignty in Early Modern Europe*. Ed. Robert Oresko, G. C. Gibbs and Hamish M. Scott. Cambridge: Cambridge UP, 1997, 272–350. Print.

Osborne, Toby. '"Nôtre grand dessein": O projecto de casamento entre o Duque Vítor Amadeu e a Infanta Isabel Luísa e a política dinástica dos Sabóias (1675–82)'. Trans. Maria Antónia Lopes. Lopes and Raviola 211–38. Print.

Pasto, David, trans. *The House of Trials: A Translation of* Los empeños de una casa *by Sor Juana Inés de la Cruz*. New York: Peter Lang, 1997. Print.

Paun de García, Susan and Donald R. Larson, eds. *The Comedia in English: Translation and Performance*. Woodbridge: Tamesis, 2008. Print.

Peres, Domingo de Garcia. *Catálogo razonado biográfico y bibliográfico de los autores portugueses que escribieron en castellano*. Madrid: Imprenta del Colegio Nacional de Sordomudos y de Ciegos, 1890. Print.

Pérez, Louis C., ed. *The Dramatic Works of Feliciana Enríquez de Guzmán*. Valencia, Spain: Albatros Hispanófila Ediciones, 1988. Print.

Perim, Damião de Frois [Damiaõ de Froes Perym, pseud. of Fr. João de São Pedro]. *Theatro Heroino: Abecedario historico, e catálogo das mulheres illustres em armas, letras, accoens heroicas, e artes liberaes*. 2 vols. Vol. 1, Lisbon: Officina da Musica de Theotonio Antunes Lima, 1736. Vol. 2, Lisbon: Academia Real, 1740. Print.

Ruiz, M. Reina. *Monstruos, mujer y teatro en el Barroco: Feliciana Enríquez de Guzmán, primera dramaturga española*. New York: Peter Lang, 2005. Print.

Samson, Alexander. 'Distinct Drama? Female Dramatists in Golden Age Spain', in *A Companion to Spanish Women's Studies*. Ed. Xon de Ros and Geraldine Hazbun. Woodbridge: Tamesis, 2011, 157–72. Print.

Sánchez Arjona, José. *El teatro en Sevilla en los siglos XVI y XVII*. Madrid: Establecimiento Tipográfica de A. Alonso, 1887. Print.

Schlau, Stacey. *Viva al siglo, muerta al mundo: Selected Works by María de San Alberto (1568–1640)*. New Orleans: UP of the South, 1998. Print.

Schleiermacher, Friedrich. 'On the Different Methods of Translating', in *Translating Literature: The German Tradition from Luther to Rosenzweig*. Ed. André Lefevere. Assen: Van Gorcum, 1977, 67–92. Print.

Schmidhuber, Guillermo. *The Three Secular Plays of Sor Juana Inés de la Cruz: A Critical Study*. Trans. Shelby C. Thacker. Studies in Romance Languages 45. Lexington: U of Kentucky P, 1997. Print.

Serrano y Sanz, Manuel de. *Apuntes para una biblioteca de escritoras españolas*. Vol. 1. Madrid: Biblioteca de Autores Españoles, 1903. Print.

Simerka, Barbara. *Knowing Subjects: Cognitive Cultural Studies and Early Modern Spanish Literature*. West Lafayette: Purdue UP, 2013. Print.

Soufas, Teresa Scott. *Dramas of Distinction: A Study of Plays by Golden Age Women*. Lexington: UP of Kentucky, 1997. Print.

Soufas, Teresa Scott, ed. and intro. *Women's Acts: Plays by Women Dramatists of Spain's Golden Age*. Lexington: UP of Kentucky, 1997. Print.

SpanishDict: English to Spanish Translation, Dictionary, Translator. Curiosity Media. Web.

Stoll, Anita K. '"Tierra de en medio": Liminalities in Angela de Azevedo's *El muerto disimulado*', in Hegstrom and Williamsen, 151–64. Print.

Stoll, Anita K. and Dawn L. Smith, eds. *Gender, Identity, and Representation in Spain's Golden Age*. Lewisburg: Bucknell UP, 2000. Print.

Stoll, Anita K. and Dawn L. Smith. *The Perception of Women in Spanish Theater of the Golden Age*. Lewisburg: Bucknell UP, 1991. Print.

Stroud, Matthew D. 'The Director's Cut: Baroque Aesthetics and Modern Stagings of the *Comedia*', *Comedia Performance* 1.1 (2004): 77–94. Print.

Thacker, Jonathan. *A Companion to Golden Age Theatre*. Woodbridge: Tamesis, 2007. Print.

Urban Baños, Alba. '"La empresa más lucida y más hermosa" de Portugal: Clave histórica para la datación de *El muerto disimulado* de Ángela de Acevedo', in *Tiempo e historia en el teatro del Siglo de Oro: Actas selectas del XVI Congreso Internacional*. Ed. Isabelle Rouane Soupault and Philippe Meunier. Aix-en-Provence: Presses Universitaires de Provence, 2015. *Openedition.org*. N. pag. Web. 30 Oct. 2015.

Vega, C[arlos] A[lberto]. *Hagiografía y literatura: La vida de San Amaro*. Madrid: El Crotalón, 1987. Print.

Vega, Lope de. *Arte nuevo de hacer comedias*. Ed. Enrique García Santo-Tomás. Madrid: Cátedra, 2006. Print.

Venuti, Lawrence. *The Translator's Invisibility: A History of Translation*. London: Routledge, 1995. Print.

Vollendorf, Lisa. 'Desire Unbound: Women's Theater of Spain's Golden Age', in *Women in the Discourse of Early Modern Spain*. Ed. Joan Cammarata. Gainesville: UP of Florida, 2003. 272–91. Print.

Vollendorf, Lisa. *The Lives of Women: A New History of Inquisitional Spain*. Nashville: Vanderbilt UP, 2005. Print.

Vollendorf, Lisa, ed. and intro. *Recovering Spain's Feminist Tradition*. New York: MLA, 2001. Print.

Vollendorf, Lisa and Grady C. Wray. 'Gender in the Atlantic World: Women's Writing in Iberia and Latin America', in *Theorising the Ibero-American Atlantic*. Ed. Harald E. Braun and Lisa Vollendorf. The Medieval and Modern Iberian World 53. Leiden: Brill, 2013, 99–116. Print.

Wade, Jonathan, ed. *Angela de Azevedo's El muerto disimulado: A BYU Golden Age Theater Production*. Provo: Brigham Young University, Department of Spanish and Portuguese, 2004. Print.

Wade, Jonathan. 'Patriotism and Revolt: Uncovering the Portuguese in Ângela de Azevedo', *Bulletin of the Comediantes* 59.2 (2007): 325–43. Print.

Williamsen, Amy R. 'Charting Our Course: Gender, the Canon, and Early Modern Theater', in Hegstrom and Williamsen, *Engendering the Early Modern Stage*, 1–16. Print.

Williamsen, Amy R. 'Stages of Passing: Identity and Performance in the *Comedia*', in *Prismatic Reflections on Spanish Golden Age Theater: Essays in Honor of Matthew D. Stroud*. Ed. Gwyn E. Campbell and Amy R. Williamsen. New York: Peter Lang, 2016, 243–53. Print.

WSC/Avant Bard. 'About'. *wscavantbard.org*. N. pag. Web. 20 April 2016.

EL MUERTO DISIMULADO

PRESUMED DEAD

COMEDIA FAMOSA,

EL MUERTO DISIMULADO

Por Doña Ângela de Azevedo

Hablan en ella las personas siguientes:

***Clarindo**, Galán*

***Don Álvaro de Gamboa**, Galán*

***Alberto**, Galán*

***Don Rodrigo de Aguilar**, Viejo*

***Papagayo**, Gracioso*

***Lisarda**, Dama*

***Doña Beatriz de Gamboa**, Dama*

***Jacinta**, Dama*

***Hipólita**, Criada*

***Dorotea**, Criada*

THE FAMOUS PLAY,

PRESUMED DEAD

By Ângela de Azevedo

The following characters speak in this play:

Clarindo (clah-REEN-doe)
nobleman [presumed dead; in disguise as 'Clara']

Don Álvaro de Gamboa (dohn ALL-va-roe day gahm-BOE-ah)
nobleman [brother of Beatriz]

Alberto (all-BEAR-toe)
nobleman [cousin of Beatriz and Álvaro]

Don Rodrigo de Aguilar (dohn roe-DREE-go day ah-guee-LAHR)
old man [father of Jacinta]

Papagayo (pah-pah-GAH-yoh)
servant [of Lisarda]

Lisarda (lee-SAHR-dah)
lady [sister of Clarindo; in disguise as 'Lisardo']

Doña Beatriz de Gamboa (DOE-n'yah bay-ah-TREESE day gahm-BOE-ah)
lady [sister of Don Álvaro]

Jacinta (hah-SEEN-tah)
lady [daughter of Don Rodrigo]

Hipólita (ee-POE-lee-tah)
servant [of Beatriz and Don Álvaro]

Dorotea (doe-roe-TAY-ah)
servant [of Jacinta]

JORNADA PRIMERA

[La acción ocurre en Lisboa.] Sale Jacinta como huyendo de Don Rodrigo, que viene con una daga en la mano, y Dorotea teniéndole.

Don Rodrigo: ¡Deja, aparta! ¡No me impidas
dar a una infame la muerte!
Dorotea: Ten, señor, el brazo fuerte
por amor de Dios.
Don Rodrigo: ¡Mil vidas,
si tantas naturaleza
le hubiera dado a mi enojo
fueran pequeño despojo!
Dorotea: Templa, señor, tu fiereza.
Don Rodrigo: ¡Suelta o mataréte a ti!
Dorotea: Pues mátame a mí y no mates…
Don Rodrigo: ¡Que así de oponerte trates
a mi cólera!
Jacinta: ¡Ay de mí!
Déjale ya, Dorotea.
No le impidas sus furores,
para que de sus rigores
ofrenda mi vida sea,
que es menos riguridad[1]
que yo a sus fieras manos muera,
que ver que tirano quiera
quitarme la libertad.
Don Rodrigo: Libertad, donde hay honor,
en los hijos no se admite.
Calla, ¿quieres que te quite…
Dorotea: …la vida? Baste, señor,
mi ama se acomodará
con tus preceptos en todo.
Jacinta: Mal con eso me acomodo.

---

1 The *Diccionario de la Real Academia Española (DRAE)* defines *riguridad* as an archaic form of *rigor* (2.1799).

ACT 1

Lisbon. Jacinta enters, fleeing from Don Rodrigo, who has a dagger in his hand, and Dorotea, who is holding him back.

Rodrigo: Leave me alone; move aside! Do *not* try to stop me from killing this vile woman!

Dorotea: Sir, for the love of God, control yourself.

Rodrigo: If Nature had given my anger a thousand lives, they wouldn't be enough!

Dorotea: Sir, temper your cruelty.

Rodrigo: Let me go, or I'll kill you!

Dorotea: Then kill *me* and don't kill…

Rodrigo: So that's how you're trying to oppose my fury!

Jacinta: Woe is me! Let him go, Dorotea. Let him boil with rage so my life will be sacrificed to his brutality. It's less harsh for me to die at his fiendish hands than to see the tyrant try to take away my freedom.

Rodrigo: When honor is involved, there's no room for freedom in one's children. Be quiet; do you want me to take your…

Dorotea: …life? Enough, sir; my mistress will conform to your wishes in all matters.

Jacinta: I don't conform to that.

Don Rodrigo: Aqueso[2] mejor le está.
(Válgame aquí mi cordura *Aparte*
y de la blandura el medio,
que a veces muestra el remedio
más que el rigor, la blandura.)
Jacinta, del corazón
única prenda querida,
de mi edad envejecida
alivio y consolación,
bien, como discreta, alcanzas
que son del padre el empleo
los hijos son su deseo
y todas sus esperanzas.
Su imaginación, su anhelo,
su importancia, su cuidado
son, su lisonja, su agrado,
su interés y su desvelo.
Y si aquesta natural
propensión se deja ver
en el que llega a tener
muchos hijos, desigual
debe de ser y diferente,[3]
pues no es amor repartido
el amor dél que ha tenido
un hijo tan solamente.
Según esto, inferir puedes,
si sola una hija tengo,
que amor a tenerte vengo,
porque[4] agradecida quedes.
Yo la gratitud que espero
hoy de tu correspondencia
es que ajustes tu obediencia
a querer lo que yo quiero.

---

2 *Aqueso* is an archaic or poetic form of *eso.* Similar forms occur throughout the play: *aquesto, aqueste, aquesta, aquese, aquesa,* etc.

3 This line contains an extra syllable, nine rather than eight.

4 Such archaic usage of *porque* here and elsewhere in the text would be expressed as *para que* in modern Spanish.

Rodrigo: She'll be better off that way. *Aside*. (May my good sense and sensitivity serve me well here, since at times tenderness, rather than harshness, can produce far better solutions.) Jacinta, beloved and unique treasure of my heart, relief and consolation of my old age, you're a sensible young woman who has realized a father's desire that his child will fulfill all his hopes and the dreams of his imagination, his wishes, his caring – everything that rewards his praise, his pleasure, his interest, and his watchful efforts. And if this natural tendency is apparent when a man has a lot of children, his love, divided among many, differs from that of a father who has only one child. You may infer from this that because I have but one daughter, I am so filled with love that you may always be grateful. Today, I hope to see your gratitude repaid when you agree to obey me by honoring my wishes. In situations

Que en esto, Jacinta, son
los padres de Dios figura,
cuando el buen hijo procura
ir tras su disposición.
Quien no sabe conformarse
con la voluntad de Dios,
aunque lo sea en la voz,
cristiano no ha de llamarse,
donde, Jacinta, colijo
que aquel hijo que disgusta
a su padre y no se ajusta
a su querer, no es buen hijo.
Argumenta tu intención
opuesta al intento mío
que es muy tuyo tu albedrío.
Digo que tienes razón:
el albedrío es exento
y no sufre violentarse,
pero debe sujetarse
para hacer merecimiento.
Podrás decirme en efecto,
que sendas mejores miras
en el estado a que aspiras,
que es estado más perfecto.
De tu opinión no disueno,
pues la religión es cierto
que es de todos mejor puerto,
mas también hay otro bueno.
Y aunque a seguir aconseja
lo mejor la perfección,
no falta a la obligación
quien por lo bueno lo deja.
Si el ser monja mejor es,
también es bueno el casar,
y así te has de acomodar
a lo bueno desta vez.
Pues no tengo quien herede

such as these, Jacinta, when a good child attempts to follow a father's orders, remember that fathers are the image of God. Those who don't abide by God's will, even if only verbally, shall not be called Christians, and a child who displeases her father and doesn't bow to his wishes is not a good child.

Your ideas run counter to mine when you contend that your will belongs to you alone. I agree that on some levels, you're right: a person's will is free of obligation and cannot be forced, but it should also strive to become worthy. Indeed, you'll tell me that from your perspective, what you're choosing is a better path, since it's a more perfect state.[1] I don't disagree with your opinion, since religion is certainly the best port of all, but there's also another good choice here. And although perfection counsels following the better path, some people are duty-bound for very good reasons to forsake perfection. Although it might be better to become a nun, it's also good to marry, and now, this time, you must follow the path of good. Since I have no one else to inherit the nobility

---

1 Rodrigo refers to Jacinta's plan to enter a convent.

de mi casa la nobleza,
hoy lo mejor tu belleza
por lo bueno dejar puede.
En todo estado sin vicio
servir a Dios bien podrás,
y quizá que en éste harás,
Jacinta, a Dios más servicio.
Yo esposo no quiero darte
de mi mano, que en la tuya,
dejo en causa tanto suya
la elección para casarte.
Privilegio no pequeño,
que muchos padres prolijos
nunca fían de los hijos
semejante desempeño.
Galanes la corte tiene
muy dignos de merecerte;
llega, pues, a resolverte,
que esto, Jacinta, conviene.
Ve, pues, a quien se aficiona
de tu persona el agrado,
que siendo noble y honrado,
yo haré rica su persona.

Dorotea: ¡Oh, buen viejo! ¡Aquesto sí,
que es tan poco escrupuloso
que deja eligir esposo!
No me hicieran esto a mí.

Don Rodrigo: ¿Qué dices? *[A Jacinta]*

Jacinta: Padre, no sé
qué diga en esta ocasión
si tanto a mi inclinación
tu gusto opuesto se ve.

Don Rodrigo: La inclinación fácilmente,
pues la prudencia la excede,
vencer la prudencia puede,
que todo vence el prudente.
Consúltalo, pues, contigo,
y haz, Jacinta, por vencerte,

of my house, you must now set aside what's best for the sake of what's good. You can serve God well in all morally correct situations and perhaps, Jacinta, you can offer Him even greater service in your status as a wife.

I don't wish to give you a husband from my own hand, since in your hand and his I will trust whatever motivates your choice of marriage partners. This is no small privilege, as many over-cautious parents never trust their children to assume similar responsibilities. The Portuguese Court[2] has many young gallants who are worthy of you; come then, Jacinta, and resolve to do as I've asked. See which man is to your liking, because if he's noble and honorable, I'll make him rich.

Dorotea: Oh, good sir! Surely it's not advisable to let her choose her own husband! They certainly didn't let me do that!

Rodrigo: *To Jacinta.* What do you say?

Jacinta: Father, I don't know what to say on this occasion if your position is the opposite of my own preference.

Rodrigo: Prudence, which can easily conquer anything, can also defeat individual choice. Think about it, Jacinta, and do what you

2 The Court to which Don Rodrigo refers is Lisbon.

que esto llego a *requererte*[5]
como padre y como amigo.

Yéndose a la criada.

Dorotea, tus razones
la dejen desengañada,
que a veces de una crïada
pueden más las persuasiones.
Dila, si quiere vivir
que mi gusto ha de observar,
que o Jacinta ha de casar
o Jacinta ha de morir. *(Vase.)*

Dorotea: ¿Sabes ya del pensamiento
de tu padre?

Jacinta: ¿Qué imagina?

Dorotea: Poco es lo que determina;
tu muerte o tu casamiento.

Jacinta: Siempre me viene a matar.

Dorotea: Muy diferente es la suerte,
señora, y muerte por muerte,
mejor es la del casar.
Cuando no es el casamiento
al gusto de la mujer,
no hay duda que viene a ser
el casar grande tormento,
mas si en su mano se deja
la elección, de aquesta suerte
es vida lo que era muerte,
lisonja lo que era queja.
¿Qué razón, señora, luego
tienes, di, para quejarte,
cuando llegas a casarte
a tu gusto?

Jacinta: ¿Gusto? Niego,
que aunque en mi padre veo
que me da la autoridad

5 This word, *requererte*, is spelled in Portuguese in the source text to rhyme with *vencerte*. In Spanish the word is *requerirte*.

can to conquer yourself, for this is what I require as your father and as your friend. *He turns to the servant.* Dorotea, perhaps your arguments can bring her back down to earth, for at times persuasion works better coming from a servant. Tell her that if she wants to live, she must accede to my wishes: either Jacinta will marry, or Jacinta will die. *He exits.*

Dorotea: Do you now grasp your father's position?

Jacinta: What is he thinking?!

Dorotea: He's only deciding one little thing: your death or your marriage.

Jacinta: Either way, he's threatening to kill me.

Dorotea: The final outcome is quite different, my lady, and of the two, death by marriage would be far better than death by murder. When a woman doesn't want to get married, there's no doubt but that matrimony can represent agony beyond words, but if the choice of whom to marry is left in her hands, she can find life where once there was death, flattery instead of complaints. So tell me, what reason do you have, my lady, to complain, when you can marry anyone you fancy?

Jacinta: Fancy? I doubt it, for although my father is granting me the

de casar con libertad,
no casaré a mi contento,[6]
que hallo por tan importuno
el casar, porque te asombre,
que en el mundo ningún hombre
me puede agradar, ninguno.

Dorotea: Tú eres la mujer primera
que sin amor he topado.

Jacinta: Después que amor me ha dejado
quedé de aquesta manera.

Dorotea: Luego, ¿tú amor has tenido?
Pues ¿dices que te dejó?

Jacinta: Amor he tenido yo,
pero dél me he despedido.

Dorotea: ¿Que de amor te despediste?

Jacinta: No me apures la paciencia,
que del alma la dolencia
agravias. ¡Ay de mí, triste!

Dorotea: Si algún mal secreto tienes,
ya tu amistad me lo diga,
señora, que de una amiga
se fían males y bienes.

Jacinta: Aunque no son para dichas
desdichas mías,[7] pues eres
mi amiga y saberlas quieres,
te contaré mis desdichas:
Una vuelta, poco más,
en su radiante carroza,
ha dado a los doce signos
el bello hijo de Latona,
después que para la empresa
más lúcida y más hermosa
que han admirado los siglos
y advertido las historias,
en que la nación insigne,

---

6 Azevedo uses assonant rhyme with the words 'contento' and 'veo.' *Redondillas,* the form she uses here, normally call for consonant rhyme.

7 Jacinta puns on the words *dichas* ('said' or 'spoken') and *desdichas* (misfortunes).

authority and freedom to choose, I still won't be happy; I find marriage so infuriating that, believe it or not, there's no man in this world who can please me. Not a single one.

Dorotea: You're the first woman I've ever run into who completely lacks love.

Jacinta: I've been this way ever since Love left me.

Dorotea: Then you mean you *have* been in love? Are you saying it left you?

Jacinta: I've been in love, but I bade it farewell. Woe is me, I'm so sad!

Dorotea: You bade farewell to Love?

Jacinta: Don't try my patience; you're insulting my soul's suffering. Woe is me, I'm so sad!

Dorotea: If you have an awful secret, you can tell me, my lady, since friends can be trusted with both good things and bad.

Jacinta: Although my misfortunes shouldn't be spoken out loud, since you're my friend and you want to know, I'll tell you why I'm so unfortunate. Latona's beautiful son Apollo has made a bit more than one circuit through the twelve Zodiac signs[3] in his golden chariot since the most magnificent and beautiful enterprise admired by time and told by history, when our

3 Latona's son was the Greek god Apollo; his journey through the Zodiac indicates that a year has passed since the events took place.

que entre las naciones todas
confunde la envidia a pasmos,
a sustos la fama asombra,
poniendo de portuguesa
en la armada de Saboya
el '*Non plus ultra*' a sus timbres
y a su primor la corona.
Concurrió de todo el reino
la nobleza más famosa
a emplear su gallardía
en ocasión tan heroica,
y entre muchos caballeros
que se hallaron de Lisboa,
en esta corte ventaja
de las cortes de la Europa,
fue Clarindo – ¡ay, cómo el alma
se aflige en esta memoria,
que las cosas que se pierden
lastiman cuando se nombran! –
Clarindo, digo, en quien puso
la naturaleza todas
las prendas que hacen amable
y querida una persona.
La gentileza, la gracia,
la discreción, que son cosas
que raras veces unidas
en un sujeto se topan,
le hicieron compuesto rico
para darle poderosa
jurisdicción de ganarle
al amor muchas victorias,
robando las libertades,
porque no es como las otras
la guerra de amor, que en ésta,
quien más vence, quien más roba.
Bien lo ha sentido la mía,[8]
que aunque exenta y cautelosa

8 'La mía' refers to Jacinta's liberty (*libertad*).

illustrious nation, which causes all other nations to combine envy with wonder and setbacks with fame, put '*Non plus ultra*'[4] as a mark of honor and skill on the Portuguese crown's Savoy Armada.[5] The best nobles of the entire kingdom gathered together to display their gallantry on this heroic occasion, and among the many noblemen from Lisbon, a court that surpasses all the rest of the courts of Europe, was Clarindo. (Oh, how my soul suffers from this memory, as what is lost wounds again every time it's said aloud!) Nature placed in Clarindo all the qualities that make a person kind and loved: charm, grace, discretion – things rarely united were combined in a single subject. They made a rich amalgam, giving him the powerful authority to win victories in love, stealing the hearts of those he conquered, because the war of love is unlike all others, since in that war, whoever conquers the most hearts, steals the most freedom. My own freedom has lamented his

---

4 Latin phrase meaning 'no more beyond' with reference to the limits of seafaring in the Mediterranean. Figuratively, it could mean 'the best example of something', and here, Jacinta is suggesting that the Portuguese Armada is the best of its kind.

5 Numerous armadas or fleets moved between Portugal and the Mediterranean ports in the southern part of the Duchy of Savoie (Savoy) in the 16th and 17th centuries, as a result of royal marriages established for political and diplomatic reasons, as well as several wars. Some fleets were described in the chronicles of the times; current historians and Hispanic literary scholars have attempted to date the composition of this play based on references to one or another of the armadas, but no study has been able to establish with certainty when *El muerto disimulado* was written, which Savoy Armada figures in the comedy, or even when in the 17th-century Ângela de Azevedo lived and died, since the experts offer a wide variety of possibilities.

de amor contra las saetas,
fue siempre constante roca.
A los ojos de Clarindo
con resistencia tan poca
se halló que quedó cautiva.
El cómo fue, oye agora:
De San Antonio en la Iglesia,
adonde, por su devota
y quedar de nuestra casa
tan vecina, voy a solas
casi siempre a oír misa,
vile, y viome, y de curiosa
pasó la vista a empeñada,
porque es cosa muy notoria
nacer de amor los empeños
de las vistas licenciosas,
pues si los ojos se aplican,
luego el corazón se postra.
Clarindo aplicó los suyos,
quizá porque halló tan pronta
curiosidad en los míos,
donde sacando forzosa
consecuencia de admitido,
tal vez de aquesta lisonja
llevado, al siguiente día
acudió a las mismas horas
al puesto, a que no falté,
porque ya de la misma forma
nuestros deseos estaban,
y esto el deseo ocasiona
repetir las diligencias
por si la suerte se logra.
Repitiéronse las vistas,
repetición tan dañosa
a mi libertad, que luego
la vi perdida, y no es corta
la pérdida, Dorotea,
que cuando el mundo pregona

power, which had always before been a steadfast rock, free from and careful with Cupid's arrows. With little resistance, my freedom found itself the captive of Clarindo's eyes. Listen now to how it all happened.

In St Anthony's Church,[6] where I almost always go to Mass by myself, – as I'm a devotee of that saint and our house is in the neighborhood – I saw him, and he saw me, and those glances changed from curious to committed, because it's well known that commitments to love are born from licentious looks, for once eyes enter the picture, the heart soon weakens. Clarindo fixed his eyes upon me, perhaps because he saw the curiosity in my own eyes, and encouraged by that flattery, once admitted there, he seized power and returned the next day at the same time. As our desires were so similar, I also returned to that place, for desire leads us to take such steps just in case we achieve good fortune. All that gazing at one another was repeated in a way that proved dangerous to my freedom, which I soon realized was lost, and loss is not short-lived, Dorotea, for while the world announces and

6 St Anthony's Church, built on the site of the saint's birthplace and family home, is in the Alfama district of Lisbon near the cathedral. A chapel was first constructed on the spot in the fifteenth century. Anthony became a traveling missionary and later lived and died in Padua, so both the Portuguese and the Italian cities claim him as their patron saint.

y la experiencia publica
que lo perdido se cobra
por Antonio, en San Antonio
quedase yo perdida sola.
Un papel, que alcé del suelo,
que por industria ingeniosa
dejó Clarindo caer
pasando por mí a la hora
que iba ya de San Antonio,
saliendo la gente toda,
fue el sello con que el amor
hizo mi prisión notoria.
'Si las vistas no se engañan'
– decía el papel – , 'señora,
y con los ojos del alma
los del cuerpo se conforman,
que amor a los dos obliga,
sospecha quien os adora,
por lo que respuesta aguarda
de su razón sospechosa'.
Respondí con el deseo
y siendo así no se ignora
cuál sería la respuesta;
'sí', respondí deseosa.
De la noche, pues, siguiente
entre las confusas sombras,
le di punto a que me hablase,
dando por seña amorosa
un 'ay', a que acudiría,
bajando a esa reja angosta
más vecina de la calle
a las doce, hora más propia
de amor para la cautela,
y por dar a su persona
noticias de nuestra casa,
le advertí de aquesta forma:
que habiendo el papel leído,

experience publicizes that everything lost can be found through Anthony, I alone remain lost in St Anthony's.[7] At the very time everyone was leaving St Anthony's, I plucked from the floor a piece of paper, which through ingenious skill Clarindo had dropped when he passed by me; that paper served as the seal that Love used to imprison me. 'If looks don't deceive, my lady,' said the letter, 'and the eyes of your body correspond to those of your soul, the one who adores you suspects that Love is binding the two of us together and awaits a response to his perhaps-questionable reasoning.' I replied with desire, and so as to make my meaning clear, I said 'yes' with great yearning.

I made a point of ensuring that he would speak to me the following evening among the dark shadows. At midnight, the very best time to be prudent in love, he'd give as an amorous signal the word 'Ay!', and I'd go downstairs to that narrow window grating that's nearest the street so we could talk. And I told him in the following way how to find our house: using the same note he had dropped and I had read, with

---

7 St Anthony is considered the patron saint of lost things, lost souls, and lost causes, which speaks to Jacinta's description of loss.

que yo por industria ardidosa[9]
en el mismo sitio eché
– y Clarindo alzó – con toda
sagacidad me siguiese
– que así[10] un amante se informa – ,
hasta entrarme en casa yo,
para quedarle en memoria.
Sucedió como quería,
llegó la ocasión gustosa,
que juzgué por muy felice
por no poder haber otra
en que habláramos los dos,
porque en la siguiente aurora
se partía con la armada
Clarindo para Saboya.
Descubriéronse los pechos,
aunque con palabras cortas,
porque donde hay veras muchas
suele haber razones pocas.
Diome de quien era parte,
a que era deuda forzosa
darle parte de quien era,
y por acortar la historia,
su lucida cualidad
con sus prendas primorosas
fueron para mi deseo
tan poderosa lisonja
que le acepté la palabra
de ser mío, y de su esposa
se la di también, diciendo
de la fineza por honra
que aunque de aquella jornada
no volviera – ¡oh cuánto llora
el alma este vaticinio! –,
no sería poderosa
segunda elección conmigo,

9 The *DRAE* defines *ardidosa* as an archaic form of *ardid* or *ardida* (1.184).

10 In the source text, *casi,* which makes little sense in the context and does not fit the meter.

cunning skill I tossed it (and Clarindo picked it up) in the very same spot, indicating that my lover would thus learn by shrewdly following me till I entered my house – that way, it would stick in his memory. It turned out as I had hoped: the delicious moment arrived, and I judged it a happy encounter, since there wouldn't be another time in which the two of us would be able to talk, as the following morning, Clarindo was leaving at dawn with the armada bound for Savoy.

We opened our hearts to one another in few words, because where there is much truth, there are usually few arguments. He spoke of his background, which then led me to tell him mine. To cut a long story short, his demonstrable quality, as well as his exquisite virtues, so powerfully flattered my desire that I accepted his word that he was mine and also promised that I'd be his wife, saying as a point of honor that if he didn't return from his journey (oh, how my soul weeps at this prediction!), I wouldn't marry anyone

que es de amor sabida cosa
que no se aficiona más
aquél, que más se aficiona.
Con esto nos despedimos,
si él *saudoso*, yo más *saudosa*,
que es cierto que a quien se queda
más las *saudades* ahogan.
No repares en la frase,
que de ausencia este síntoma
solamente se declara
cuando en portugués se nombra.
¿Quién dijera, Dorotea,
que la fortuna envidiosa
malograra tan aprisa
de mi esperanza la gloria?
Mas siendo de amor, no es mucho
que así fuese venturosa,
que de amor las esperanzas
brevemente se malogran.
Malográronse las mías,[11]
que al recogerse la flota,
cuando esperaba el deseo
de sus ansias las mejoras,
mintióme la confïanza,
que las que amor ocasiona
nunca han sido verdaderas,
siempre fueron mentirosas.
Presagio de mi desdicha
fue un sueño en que me transforma
la fantasía a Clarindo,
dando a una espada traidora
la vida, envuelto en su sangre.
No fue ilusión, sino sombra
de mi trágica fortuna,
porque luego se pregona
de su muerte la noticia,
sin saberse hasta aquí otra

11 'Las mías' refers to Jacinta's hopes (*esperanzas*).

else, since it's well known that with love, the one who loves the most will never love another again. With that, we bade farewell, with him *saudoso*, filled with longing for me, and me even more *saudosa* of him, since it's true that *saudades*[8] can suffocate the one left behind – but pay no attention to my phrasing, since this symptom of absence can only be expressed in Portuguese. Dorotea, who could have predicted that jealous Fate would overturn the glory of my hope so quickly? But since they were hopes of love, it's not surprising that I was happy only briefly, as hopes of that sort are ruined in an instant. My hopes were indeed dashed, for as the fleet gathered, when desire hoped to see things get better, faith lied to me, for in love such perfections have never been real; they were always lies. Foretelling my misfortune was a dream in which fantasy transformed Clarindo for me, as he gives his life to a treasonous sword covered with his blood. It was no illusion, but rather a shadow of my tragic fate, because his death was announced without any further news except that

8 A Portuguese term describing the feeling of longing, melancholy, or nostalgia you have when contemplating someone or something that is now absent and may never return.

circunstancia que decirse
que de una herida alevosa
murió, sin que el homicida
se sepa, porque suponga
que fue la desdicha mía
quien tuvo la culpa toda.
Por culpada mi desgracia
en tal caso se conozca,
pues nunca la culpa falta
donde la desgracia sobra.
Ésta es, Dorotea amiga,
lo que pasa, mira ahora
– si has conocido las veras
de una pasión amorosa –
si a Clarindo quise bien,
si aun sus memorias adora
el alma, si le perdí,
y si he de poner por obra
la fineza prometida
– en que amor me hace deudora –
de no admitir otro dueño,
¿cómo es posible que ponga
de parte esta obligación,
si del alma no se borran
de amor empeños primeros?
Eso no, no se acomoda
mi inclinación con aquesto;
morir sí, que en tal congoja
no es tan penosa la muerte,
como es la vida penosa.

Dorotea: Cuando admirada me dejas,
me dejas más admirada
de que, siendo tu crïada,
no sepa hasta aquí tus quejas.
Es verdad que tu primor
no puede en esto culparse,
que de nadie han de fïarse
secretos que son de amor.

he died as the result of a treacherous wound. No one knows who murdered him, because it might be assumed that my bad luck assumed all the blame. In this case, let it be known that my misfortune is at fault, for blame is never lacking where there's bad luck to spare. This, my friend Dorotea, is what happened; see (since you now know the true story of such an amorous passion) that I loved Clarindo well, that my soul adores even the memory of him, that I lost him. And if I have to do as I promised (in which Love makes me its debtor) by not admitting any other man into my heart, how can I possibly set aside this obligation, if my first pledges to love haven't been erased from my soul? Not that; my will can't adjust; dying, yes, for in such anguish, death isn't as painful as a life filled with pain.

Dorotea: When you amaze me, you *really* amaze me that as your maid, I didn't know until this moment about your love complaints. I don't blame you, though, because nobody trusts another with secrets about love. I don't blame you for feeling guilty

No culpo tu sentimiento
de tu malogrado amor;
antes siento tu dolor
y tus *dissabores* siento.[12]
Mas parece sin razón,
si no remedias el daño,
irse tras el desengaño
de esa tu resolución.
El primer amor, no hay duda
que es del alma impresión fuerte,
pero mudada la suerte,
también el amor se muda.
De tu constante firmeza
ya quedas desobligada,
porque la vida acabada,
acábase la fineza.
No, pues, ese amor te impida
otro amor, y si olvidarlo
quieres, procura trocarlo,
que amor con amor se olvida,
y no teniendo poder
amor para te inclinar,
lo que no haces por amar,
hazlo por agradecer.
Agradece de un amante
las veras con que te adora,
pues te merece, señora.

Jacinta: Ten, no pases adelante
si en don Álvaro has de hablar
de Gamboa, porque es hombre,
que hasta la voz de su nombre
me llega, amiga, a enfadar.
Su porfía de amor, ciega,
prolija, importuna y vana
me enfada, que es cosa llana

12 The Portuguese word *dissabor* means 'disgust,' 'displeasure,' 'chagrin,' or 'annoyance.' On the other hand, the Spanish word *desabor* and the Portuguese *dessabor* mean 'insipidity' or 'unsavoriness.'

about your ill-fated love; I feel your pain and distress. But if you can't fix the damage done, it doesn't make sense for you to resolve to follow heartbreak. There's no doubt that first love makes a strong impression on one's soul, but when our fate changes, so can love. You're no longer responsible for your faithfulness, for once a life has ended, so ends that kind gesture towards another. That love shouldn't stop you from finding another person to adore, and if you want to forget him, try to exchange him for another, for an old love is forgotten when a new one enters. And if that new love isn't powerful enough to win you over, what you're doing for the sake of love, do for the sake of gratitude. Thank your lover for the sincerity with which he adores you, for he deserves you, my lady.

Jacinta: Stop, don't take another step, my friend, if you're going to talk about Don Álvaro de Gamboa, because even the sound of his name fills me with anger. His obstinate persistence in love – blind, tedious, annoying, and shallow – instills rage,

que siempre enfada quien ruega.
Sé que le llego a deber
un desvelo peregrino;
pero si amor es destino,
¿qué le debo agradecer?
Bien es que se satisfagan
deudas que el amor publica,
mas si el natural replica,
deudas de amor no se pagan.

Dorotea: Según eso, ¿recibir
una carta que me ha dado
no querrás?

Jacinta: Mal has andado,
Dorotea, en la admitir,
mas ya que lo has hecho así,
cortesía será el vella.[13]
Veamos lo que dice en ella.

Toma la carta.

Yo la abro, pues, dice aquí:

(Lee.) Si puede dar pésames en la causa de un sentimiento quien participa el sentimiento por la misma causa, bien puedo manifestarle a vuestra merced el que me cabe en la muerte de Clarindo, en cuya pérdida nos ha hecho a los dos iguales la desdicha, pues a un tiempo le faltó a mi afecto tan grande amigo, como a su belleza amante. Y aunque debiera quejarme de que hallase su amor tanto agasajo donde el mío siempre esquivez, quedará mi queja con cabal satisfacción, cuando permitiéndome la dicha, que sucediendo en su lugar, merezca tener por dueño a quien me ofrezco por esclavo, cuya persona el cielo me guarde como quiero.

– Don Álvaro de Gamboa

---

13 In the Middle Ages and into the early modern period, it was not uncommon for writers to represent the grapheme <r> as <l> at the end of the infinitive before adding an object pronoun. This is an example of the process known as full assimilation. See Robert McColl Millar, *Trask's Historical Linguistics* (London: Hodder Arnold, 2007), pp. 66-67. In modern Spanish, *vella* is rare to non-existent in favor of the form *verla.* In this *redondilla, vella* rhymes with *ella.*

for men who beg often engender wrath. I know I owe him something for his outlandish efforts, but if love is destiny, what should I be thanking him for? It's good to satisfy debts that love makes known, but if human nature objects, debts of love don't need to be paid.

Dorotea: If that's the case, would you prefer I not give you a letter he wrote?

Jacinta: Dorotea, it wasn't a good idea to accept it, but since you did, it would be discourteous not to take a look. Let's see what it says. *She takes the letter.* I'll open it; it says:

She reads: If one who shares feelings for the same reason can express condolences regarding those feelings, I can well show Your Grace how Clarindo's death also affects me, for his loss has made the two of us equal in unhappiness, since in the same moment, I lost a great friend and you a lover. And although I should complain that you offered his love a magnificent welcome while mine gets nothing but scorn, my complaint will be satisfied in every respect when, if good fortune permits it, I take his place and merit having as my mistress the woman to whom I offer myself as a slave, whose person I ask Heaven to keep for me.

– Don Álvaro de Gamboa

Si hasta aquí con desagrado
he mirado su persona,
este papel me ocasiona
más fastidio y más enfado.
Excusada cortesía,
su osadía lo inspiró,
pues así se resolvió
a tan grande demasía.
Notable facilidad,
y confïanza es la suya,
de que es fuerza que se arguya
su indiscreta vanidad.
¿Y quién le habrá dicho a él,
que era Clarindo mi amante,
para escribirme ignorante
un semejante papel?
¡Ay, que no sé, Dorotea,
qué el corazón imagina,
que mil veces adivina
lo que puede ser que sea!
Don Álvaro fue sin duda
de Clarindo el homicida.
Dorotea: ¡Ay, señora, por tu vida
de tal pensamiento muda!
Y ¿de qué inferirlo puedes?
Jacinta: Mira si tengo razón
en ésta mi presunción,
para que advertida quedes:
don Álvaro se pregona
amigo particular
de Clarindo y alcanzar
podría de su persona
nuestro amor que aunque consigo
quedar debía el secreto,
el que es amigo perfecto
nada esconde de su amigo.
Don Álvaro viendo, pues,
Clarindo favorecido

If up till now I've looked at him with displeasure, his note fills me with even greater disgust and anger. Don Álvaro's sheer audacity inspired this letter, which is nothing more than superfluous, excessive, and over-abundant politeness. Excess and confidence may come easily to him, but they argue even more for his vanity and indiscretion. And who might have told him that Clarindo was my lover, for him to write me such uninformed drivel in this letter? Oh, Dorotea, I don't know what my heart is thinking, as it's guessing a thousand times over what must be true! Don Álvaro was without a doubt Clarindo's murderer.

Dorotea: Oh, my lady, don't speak such thoughts aloud, on your life! And what leads you to say so?

Jacinta: So you're forewarned, see if my assumptions are correct: Don Álvaro is announcing everywhere that he was Clarindo's close friend, which enabled him to learn of our love, for although my beloved should have kept the secret to himself, a perfect friend hides nothing from his greatest ally. Don Álvaro saw Clarindo favored in love and he saw himself loathed,

de amor, y él aborrecido,
que insufrible dolor es,
¿quién duda que de su enojo
por acabar mi esperanza,
queriendo tomar venganza,
fuese su vida el despojo?

Dorotea: ¿Entre amigos tal maldad?
Eso era ser alevoso.

Jacinta: Quien de amor está quejoso
no respeta la amistad,
y no será, no, el primero
que una novela ha leído,
en que el caso ha sucedido
a un amante caballero.

Dorotea: Señora, eso es fingimiento.

Jacinta: Su ejemplo muestra el fingir
y para esto presumir
ya tengo este fundamento.
Yo, pues, intento apurar
quien fue autor de aquesta muerte.

Dorotea: ¿Apurar? ¿Y de qué suerte?

Jacinta: La respuesta has de llevar,
que una experiencia ha de ser
de lo que pensando estoy.
Anda, que a escribirla voy. *(Vase.)*

Dorotea: ¿Qué intenta Jacinta hacer?
Yo apuesto que en hora y media
nadie – según lo imagino –
ha de dar en el camino
que lleva aquesta comedia. *(Vase.)*

Sale Lisarda, vestida de hombre, y Papagayo.

Papagayo: Ya en Lisboa estás y aqueste
el terrero es de Palacio,[14]
tropiezo hermoso de Tetis,
rica adoración del Tajo.

Lisarda: ¡Gallarda plaza por cierto!

14 In this passage, the word *terrero* (or *terreiro* in Portuguese) means 'plaza.'

which is an unbearable sorrow. Wanting to take revenge by destroying my hopes, who can doubt that his anger would deprive Clarindo of his life?

Dorotea: Such evil between friends? That's heinous.

Jacinta: People who are unhappy in love don't respect friendship. And he certainly won't be the first person who has read a novel where the same thing happened to a noble lover.

Dorotea: My lady, that's fiction.

Jacinta: Álvaro's example shows that he can create fictions, and I already have grounds for thinking that. So I intend to put pressure on the person who authored this death.

Dorotea: Put pressure on him? And how will you pull it off?

Jacinta: You'll have to deliver the answer to that, for I'm planning quite an experiment. Come on; I'm going to write it all down in my letter back to Don Álvaro. *She exits.*

Dorotea: What is Jacinta trying to do? I'll bet that in an hour and a half no one will be able to figure out what direction this play is headed (or at least that's how I imagine it). *She exits.*

Lisarda, dressed as a man, enters, as does Papagayo.[9]

Papagayo: You're in Lisbon now and this is the Palace Plaza,[10] a rich monument to the Tagus, where the deity Thetis stumbled at the river's edge.[11]

Lisarda: Truly a striking plaza!

---

9 '*Papagayo*' ('parrot') is a perfect comic name for a *gracioso*, due to the parrot's showy, multicolored feathers and ability to mimic human speech without understanding its meaning (See 'Hablar como el papagayo,' in *Diccionario de Autoridades* 3.112). As exotic examples of the worlds that Portugal once explored and ruled (especially Indonesia and Brazil), parrots were brought back to Portugal by travelers to those lands, and were quite popular.

10 Papagayo refers to the Terreiro do Paço, a square that is known today as the Praça do Comércio, although the metro station there is still called 'Terreiro do Paço.' Named for its location on the bank of the Tagus River, the *paço* was the Ribeira (Riverbank) Palace, which served as the main royal residence from 1502 to 1755, when the Lisbon earthquake destroyed it.

11 In *The Lusiads* by Camões, the Greek sea goddess Thetis (or Thetys) is portrayed as the consort of Vasco da Gama on the Island of Love. She prophesies the coming greatness of the Portuguese empire and shows da Gama the cosmos, which is represented in Ptolemy's armillary sphere, one of the most repeated symbols of Portugal.

Papagayo: Todo en Lisboa es gallardo,
pues no ha visto cosa *boa*,
según lo afirma el adagio,
el que no ha visto Lisboa.[15]

Lisarda: Por la crueldad de los hados
bien a mi pesar la veo,
pues la muerte de mi hermano,
cuyas noticias la vida
a mi padre le quitaron,
me obliga a pisar sus calles.

Papagayo: Mejor – si bien lo he pensado –
dijeras que de curiosa
lo has hecho, porque yo no alcanzo
cómo por aquesta causa
hayas, señora, trocado
a Lamego por la Corte.

Lisarda: No te he dicho, Papagayo,
que me voy tras el deseo
de saber quién fue el tirano
homicida de Clarindo,
pues hasta aquí no han llegado
de su muerte otras noticias
que las que hasta aquí llegaron,
diciéndose, que en la Armada
de Saboya le mataron,
sin saberse quién ha sido
el traidor, el vil, el falso
que de mi hermano en la vida
la de mi padre ha quitado;
yo, pues, que de este disgusto
quedé con vida, no en vano
has de imaginar qué ha sido
sino para que el espacio
de todo el orbe examine,
hasta que de aqueste agravio
pueda encontrar el autor.

15 Papagayo cites the adage, which puns on the name of the city *Lisboa* and the word *boa* ('good'). In Portuguese, the saying goes, 'Quem não tem visto Lisboa, não tem visto coisa boa.'

Papagayo: Everything in Lisbon is striking, for as the old adage affirms, those who haven't seen *Lisboa* haven't seen anything *boa*: 'those who haven't in Lisbon stood truly haven't seen anything good.'[12]

Lisarda: Due to the cruelty of the Fates I'm seeing Lisbon quite well, to my great suffering. My brother's death and the news of which then killed my father compel me to tread the streets of this city.

Papagayo: You might just as well have said that you're doing it out of curiosity, because I can't figure out how that led you to trade our town of Lamego[13] for the royal Court.

Lisarda: I haven't told you, Papagayo, that I'm trying to discover the identity of Clarindo's murdering tormenter; till now no other news of his death has arrived, except for the report from here, saying that he was killed in the Savoyard Armada. They say they don't know the name of the traitor, that vile, lying man who, in taking my brother's life, also took the life of my father. Since I'm the only one left alive in this repugnant situation, you can imagine that I have good cause to search the globe to find the author of such an injustice.

---

12 Wordplay with *Lisboa* and *boa* ('good') in Portuguese.

13 A town in the northern part of Portugal, to the east of Porto. Azevedo, like her character Lisarda, may have been born in Lamego.

Papagayo: Te expones a un gran trabajo,
que será tiempo perdido
averiguar este caso.
Quien busca a quien no conoce,
señora, ¿cómo ha de hallarlo?
¿Sin nombre ni señas quieres
buscar [a] un hombre?[16] ¿Hay tal paso?
Eso vendrá a ser lo mismo
que ha sucedido a un villano
entrando en cierto convento
de frailes[17] que preguntando
por uno, de cuyo nombre
se había el tal olvidado,
dijo, 'Padres, solamente
me acuerdo – si no me engaño –
que el nombre empezaba en Fray'.
'Lindas señas, mentecato',
le respondieron, 'no hay duda
que así podréis informaros,
como si un fray sólo hubiera
en el convento'. Otro tanto
digo por ti, ¿cómo quieres
sin indicio bueno o malo
buscar [a] un hombre, señora,
que a otro la vida ha quitado,
como si hubiera en el mundo
sólo un matador? Buen chasco.

Lisarda: Desatino es del enojo,
no hay duda, mas no hay reparo
en el enojo, que es ciego.
Bien que de una luz me valgo
ya para el intento mío,
pues según me han informado,
desta corte un caballero

16 Unlike Spanish, Portuguese does not use the personal *a* before human direct objects.

17 In Spanish and Portuguese, the words *convento* and *monasterio/mosteiro* are generally used interchangeably without regard for the gender of their residents. *Frailes* (friars) differ from monks, in that monks are cloistered and friars can come and go from their monasteries.

Papagayo: You're taking on a huge task; frankly, you're wasting your time trying to solve the case. Looking for someone you don't even know, my lady, how will you find him? Do you think you can search for a man without his name or address? Is that the way to do it? This is going to turn out like it did to a guy who entered a monastery asking for one of the monks but added that he'd forgotten the man's name. He said, 'Fathers, if I'm not mistaken, all I remember is that his name began with "Friar."' 'Well, that's useful information, fool,' they replied. 'No doubt that'll help you find the person you're looking for,' as if there were only one friar in the monastery. I'll say the same to you, my lady: how, without a single clue – good or bad –, do you plan to find a man who has taken the life of another, as if there were only one killer in the world? That'd be a good trick.

Lisarda: No doubt it's the folly of my fury, but my anger can't see a better solution because it's blind. One small ray of hope can help me accomplish my goal: I've been informed that a nobleman at court was my brother's friend on this journey,

camarada de mi hermano
en esta jornada ha sido,
y dél podré ver si acaso
como amigo que era suyo
algunas noticias hallo.
Bien que del nombre me olvido
que me han dicho, mas del barrio
me acuerdo en que vive.

Papagayo: Bueno
para Lisboa, excusado
es el barrio sin saberse
la calle, porque es tan largo
y tantas calles encierra
un barrio, que por ser tantos
los vecinos ni ellos mismos
las saben, pero veamos,
¿qué barrio es ése?, señora.

Lisarda: San Pablo me han apuntado.

Papagayo: Allá se va por aquí,
que aun me acuerdo destos pasos
de otra vez que acá he venido,
pero para *preguntarmos*[18]
por un hombre amigo de otro
disparate es; pero vamos,
si el nombre fue con San Pedro,
vaya el hombre con San Pablo.[19]
Y de camino quisiera
saber, hallando este hidalgo
– que yo quiero suponerlo –
cuando él no supiere darnos
de aquesta muerte noticias
– que no será gran milagro

18 This is a use of the Portuguese personal infinitive, a construction which does not exist in Spanish. In Spanish the phrase means, 'pero es disparate que preguntemos por un hombre amigo de otro.'

19 In these two lines, Papagayo uses parallel structure and puns on the words *nombre* and *hombre,* which are also an interior rhyme. Lisarda has forgotten his *nombre* (name) – it may have gone to heaven with St Peter or this may be a reference to the saint forgetting or denying Christ three times (Matt. 26: 69–75), but the *hombre* (man) can be found in St Paul's parish.

and I'll see if maybe as his friend he can give me some information. I can't recall his name, but I do remember the name of the parish he lives in.

Papagayo: In Lisbon, knowing the neighborhood won't help if you don't know the street. The neighborhoods are so extensive and have so many streets that many of the neighbors don't even know for sure, but let's see: what neighborhood is it, ma'am?

Lisarda: They indicated it was Saint Paul's parish.

Papagayo: You get there through here; I remember these steps from another time I was here. It's nonsense to ask about a man who's a friend of another one, but let's go. If his name went to heaven with St Peter, let the man himself go with St Paul. And while we're on the way, I'd like to know: after we find this nobleman (for I want to believe we'll find him), what'll we do when he can't give us any news of your brother's death (and that won't be a great miracle, since it's rare

porque es muy raro el amigo,
si no fuere amigo raro,
que en los peligros y riesgos
se halla de su amigo al lado – ,
¿qué haremos?

Lisarda: Ir determino
a hablar al rey a palacio,
y requerirle un decreto,
en que doce mil ducados
prometa a quien descubriere
quién dio la muerte a mi hermano,
que tantos y aun más daré,
amigo, por alcanzarlo,
pues no me faltan dineros
como sabes, y si acaso
este interés me consigue
del matador el hallazgo,
que el interés muchas veces
tiene poder, Papagayo,
para allanar imposibles,
y así por más que este caso
solicite la fortuna
por mi desdicha ocultarlo,
la diligencia del oro
que sabe muchos atajos,
puede tal vez descubrirlo.
Si este logro, pues, alcanzo,
no pienses que por justicia,
Papagayo, he de llevarlo,
aguardando a que el verdugo
deje en su muerte vengado
a mi enojo, porque yo misma,
cogiéndole con mis brazos,
le he de hacer víctima horrible
para ejemplo de tiranos.

Papagayo: ¡Notable crueldad! ¿Tú misma
intentas ser el *carrasco*?,[20]

20 Papagayo plays with the word *carrasco* in referring to both an executioner and trees.

for a friend to find himself at his comrade's side in every single dangerous and risky situation, unless he's a really rare friend)?

Lisarda: I've decided to go to the palace and talk to the king. I want to request a decree from him in which he promises twelve thousand ducats to the person who discovers who murdered my brother. I'll pay all that and much more to catch him, my friend; as you know I have plenty of money. And all that cash may help me find the killer, since interest often wields great power to overcome impossibilities. Therefore, even if Fortune, due to my misfortune, tries to hide the facts of this case, gold, which knows a great many speedy short-cuts, might be able to uncover the truth. If I can accomplish that, Papagayo, don't think for a minute that I'll be turning him in to the law, waiting for the executioner to avenge my anger with his death, because I'll grab him myself and make him my horrible victim as an example for despots everywhere.

Papagayo: What remarkable cruelty! You intend to be the strong and

mas no me espanto, señora,
porque dicen que es probado
que entre los árboles todos
así hay hembras como hay machos,
y así carrascas se encuentran
como se encuentran carrascos.
Y no es mucho que verduga[21]
te ostentes, por lo gallardo
de tu hermosura, que aquesta
la ha hecho el niño vendado
de los hombres matador.

Lisarda: ¿Te burlas y me das chasco?
No me hables en hermosuras,
sino en coriscos, en rayos,
en fierezas, en rencores,
en pasiones, en enfados,
en pesadumbres, en iras,
en furores, en estragos,
que la cólera mi pecho
hizo un incendio en que ardo.

Papagayo: Así lo enseña tu nombre,
señora, que te has mudado.
Si ardo, es de Lisardo el eco;
¿qué mucho, en tu nombre hablando,
que arda Lisarda también?

Lisarda: Aquese nombre he dejado,
y mira, no te equivoques,
que has de llamarme Lisardo.

Papagayo: Cuando Lisarda te llame,
no será el error muy craso,
ni ocasión daré con eso
a que el disfraz que has tomado
de hombre quede conocido
y a todos conste a lo claro

In Portuguese, but not in Spanish, *carrasco* can mean 'executioner' after Belchior Nunes Carrasco, who performed that job in Lisbon in the fifteenth century (see Bluteau 2.160).

21 Papagayo plays with the gender of the word *verdugo*. The grammatical gender of the word is masculine, but Lisarda will be a female executioner.

thorny oak, the executioner? Well, that's not surprising, my lady, because they say it's been proven that among trees, there are female trees as well as male ones.[14] So it's no great leap for you to present yourself as a female executioner due to the nature of your beauty, for Cupid, the blindfolded child,[15] has made you a man-killer.

Lisarda: Are you mocking me, playing some kind of trick? Don't speak of me in terms of beauty; instead, use words like sparks, lightning, fierceness, bitterness, passions, choler, grief, wrath, fury, rage, and ruin, for the anger in my breast created a huge conflagration in which I'm burning.

Papagayo: Even your name shows that you've changed. If I'm burning, *ardo*, I'm *ardent*, echoing Lis-*ardo*, so it's no surprise that you might refer to yourself as *ardent* as well, since you're a blazing fire, Lis-*arda*.

Lisarda: I've abandoned that name, and take care not to make a mistake: you must now call me Lisardo.

Papagayo: Even if I do call you Lisarda, the error won't be serious; it won't expose your disguise as a man and reveal that you're

14 A few species of trees and bushes are called both *carrascos* and *carrascas* in Spanish and Portuguese, allowing Papagayo to play with gender in language as he rambles on about Lisarda's cross-dressing.

15 Cupid is often portrayed with a blindfold, because Love is blind and he is not careful about whom he shoots with his arrows.

que eres mujer. No está el punto
en el nombre. Yo me declaro:
no hace el nombre macho o hembra,
pues entre los papagayos
hay papagayas también,
y en las golondrinas damos
con golondrinos,[22] y vemos
que éstos son apellidados
con el nombre femenino,
y aquéllas también nombramos
con la masculina voz.
Lo mismo en ti estoy pensando,
que aunque mi voz te apellide
Lisarda, ¿quién te ha quitado
el ser Lisardo, señora?,
porque hay mujeres Lisardos
y hay también Lisardas hombres.

Lisarda: De aqueste traje me valgo
para la venganza mía,
con más libertad buscando
de mi hermano el homicida.

Dentro ruido de cuchilladas.

Mas oye, si no me engaño,
que en aquesta casa suenan
cuchilladas.

Papagayo: Está dando
algún maestro de esgrima
sin duda lección.

Lisarda: Subamos,
pues, que la puerta está abierta,
a ver lo que es.

Papagayo: No me allano
a aprehender en esta escuela.

Alberto: *(Dentro.)* ¡Reparad!

22 The grammatical gender of the word *papagayo* (parrot) is masculine, but the *gracioso* jokes that there are also female parrots. The opposite is true of *golondrinas* (swallows); their grammatical gender is feminine, but there are male swallows as well.

really a woman. The point isn't in the name. I'm just saying: a name doesn't make someone male or female, for there are *papagayas* among *papagayos* and with swallows, there are *golindrinos* among *golondrinas*; masculine last names can go with feminine first names, and feminine surnames are often used with men. I'm thinking the same thing about you, for if I call you Lisarda, how does that affect you being Lisardo, since there are female Lisardos and male Lisardas?

Lisarda: I'll use this male outfit to exact my revenge, so I can search for my brother's murderer more freely. *Off stage: the sounds of a swordfight.* But listen: if I'm not mistaken, you can hear swords in that house.

Papagayo: A fencing master must be giving a lesson.

Lisarda: Since the door is open, let's go in and see what it is.

Papagayo: I don't agree to study in this school!

Alberto: *Off stage.* Parry that!

Don Álvaro: *(Dentro.)* Ya no hay reparo
si no es el de los aceros.
Alberto: *[Dentro.]* La confïanza.
Don Álvaro: *[Dentro.]* Es sagrado
el honor.
Alberto: *[Dentro.]* Pues cuando hubiera
escrúpulo, con la mano
de esposo satisfacía.
Don Álvaro: *[Dentro.]* De eso no me satisfago.
Don Álvaro de Gamboa
no satisface su agravio
sino con darte la muerte,
o morir.

Riñen dentro.

Lisarda: ¿No has escuchado
aquel nombre? Pues me acuerdo
que es del hombre que buscamos,
de que me he olvidado, el mismo.
Papagayo: Puede ser, mas ¿no hace al caso
que habrá muchos deste nombre?[23]
Lisarda: Por si es, a saberlo vamos.
Entra conmigo. *[Vase.]*
Papagayo: ¡Ea! Entremos,
aunque harto estoy recelando,
que entrando de uñas arriba,
me salga de uñas abajo. *(Vase.)*

Salen don Álvaro y Alberto, riñiendo.

Don Álvaro: Desta suerte de mi honor
vengar las injurias trato.
Alberto: No el honor así se venga,
que es ofenderlo apurarlo,
y más si son las sospechas
procedidas de un engaño.

23 In the source text, this is a statement.

Don Álvaro: *Off stage.* There's no defense except the kind that comes from steel.

Alberto: *Off stage.* Trust.

Don Álvaro: *Off stage.* Honor is sacred.

Alberto: *Off stage.* If you had any suspicions about my intentions, I was trying to satisfy them with my hand in marriage.

Don Álvaro: *Off stage.* That doesn't satisfy me. Don Álvaro de Gamboa doesn't answer such insults except by killing you or by dying. *They duel off stage.*

Lisarda: Did you hear that name? That's the very name I had forgotten – I remember now that he's the man we're looking for.

Papagayo: It could be, but don't a lot of men have that name?

Lisarda: Let's go see if he's the one. Come with me. *She exits.*

Papagayo: Let's enter, then, though I really fear that a sword fight might end with my death. *He exits.*

Don Álvaro and Alberto enter, dueling.

Don Álvaro. This is how I'll avenge the insults to my honor.

Alberto: Honor isn't avenged like this, since trying to hurry revenge further offends it, and more so if your suspicions are based on a mistake.

Don Álvaro: ¿Qué engaño, aleve?[24] Mi acero
te hará el desengaño claro.
Alberto: Ved primero…
Don Álvaro: Ya lo he visto.

Salen Papagayo y Lisarda metiéndose en medio.

Lisarda: Caballeros, reportaos,
y de los aceros vuestros
reprimid los golpes bravos.
Papagayo: No puedo sacar el mío,
que está mal acostumbrado,
y por ser poco devoto,
nunca hasta aquí le contaron
de Coimbra en la procesión
de los desnudos.
Don Álvaro: Dejadnos.
¿Qué os obligó, caballero,
a entraros acá?
Papagayo: El diablo,
que no fue santo ni santa.
Lisarda: Ea, no haya más, hidalgos.
Alberto: A muy buen tiempo ha venido
este hombre, para excusarnos
a los dos una desdicha,
y así, pues lugar me ha dado,
yo me retiro.
Don Álvaro: Cobarde,
¿huyes? ¡Espera!
Lisarda: Mi brazo *[A don Álvaro]*
os detendrá.
Alberto: Nos veremos
a solas los dos. *(Vase.)*
Papagayo: En salvo
se pone este amigo; acierta.

24 In the source text, this is a run-on sentence: 'Que engaño, aleve, mi azero te harà el desengaño claro.'

Don Álvaro: What mistake, you traitor? My sword will inform you.
Alberto: First, look…
Don Álvaro: I already have.

Papagayo and Lisarda enter, putting themselves between the two.

Lisarda: Gentlemen, restrain yourselves, and contain your swords' savage blows.
Papagayo: I can't unsheathe my own sword, because it's not accustomed to such action, and since it's also not devout, no one's ever mentioned it in Coimbra's Procession of the Naked.[16]
Don Álvaro: Leave us alone. Who asked you, sir, to enter here?
Papagayo: The Devil, who was neither a male nor female saint.
Lisarda: Come on, noble gentlemen, enough of this.
Alberto: This man has arrived at a propitious moment to keep the two of us from further misfortune. Consequently, since he has given me an opening, I'll withdraw.
Don Álvaro: Coward, are you fleeing? Wait!
Lisarda: *To Don Álvaro.* My arm will stop you.
Alberto: The two of us will meet alone at some future time. *He exits.*
Papagayo: He has the right idea: this friend has saved himself.

---

16 A popular nineteenth-century travelers' handbook describes the origins of the procession: beginning in 1423, when Coimbra was hit by the plague, Vicente Martins proclaimed that if, through the intercession the five martyrs of Morocco, whose holy relics were housed in the Santa Cruz Convent, he and his five sons could be spared, they would show their devotion each year by marching in a procession through the streets to the convent, naked above the waist. The procession became quite popular as other penitents later joined the processions, and they continued virtually every year on January 16 until they were finally banned in the 18th century. John Murray [Firm], *A Handbook for Travellers in Portugal* (London: John Murray, 1864), pp. 109-10. See also António Henrique R. de Oliveira Marques, *Daily Life in Portugal in the Late Middle Ages*, trans. S. Wyatt (Madison: U of Wisconsin P, 1981), p. 220).

Don Álvaro: Pues que me habéis estorbado
mi venganza, contra vos
se han de volver mis enfados.
Lisarda: Sinrazón es, que mi acero
sabrá rebatir.
Papagayo: Remalo.
¿Con mi amo es la pendencia?
¿Qué harás en aqueste caso,
Papagayo? Ya se ve,
por si acaso algún cristiano
va por la calle, que acuda [a]
decir de los Papagayos,
siguiendo el común estilo,
'¿quién pasa?, ¿quién pasa?'

Cáese la espada a don Álvaro.

Don Álvaro: ¡Raro
valor! Tened, que la espada
se me ha caído.
Papagayo: ¡Oh bizarro
Lisardillo, que hecho hombre
de espadas ganó la mano!

Dále Lisarda la espada [a don Álvaro].

Lisarda: Tomad y a reñir volved.
Don Álvaro: Eso no, mas las volvamos
a las vainas, y os suplico
– que ya me veo aficionado
a vuestros bríos – , quién sois
me digáis.[25]
Lisarda: A mí, Lisardo
me llaman. Soy forastero
y vengo por un despacho
de servicios a la corte.
Papagayo: Y servicios harto malos.
Lisarda: Calla, bobo.

25 This is a question in the source text.

Don Álvaro: Since you've stood in the way of my revenge, I'll now turn my anger on you.

Lisarda: That would be unwise, for my sword will know how to repel you.

Papagayo: This is really bad. The quarrel's now with my master? Papagayo, what are you going to do in this situation? It's obvious: in case some Christian might be walking down the street, Papagayos come to mind, since following the normal style of all parrots, they squawk, 'Who's passing by? Who's passing by?'[17]

Don Álvaro drops his sword.

Don Álvaro: What rare bravery! Hold on: you've disarmed me.

Papagayo: Oh, valiant little Lisardillo: by becoming a swordsman you won the hand!

Lisarda gives Don Álvaro a sword.

Lisarda: Take it and continue our duel.

Don Álvaro: No, not that; let's sheathe our swords, and I beg you, for I admire your spirit, to tell me your name.

Lisarda: They call me Lisardo. I'm a stranger to this area, and I'm bearing a communiqué of services to the court.

Papagayo: And a lot of them are really bad services.

Lisarda: Be quiet, fool.

---

17 As Doménech notes, '*¿quien pasa, quien pasa?*' is the set phrase in Spanish, similar to '*Polly wanna cracker?* in English, that pet owners teach their parrots (*La margarita*, 223).

Papagayo: Sí, señor,
y voy siguïendo a mi amo
también a la forastera.[26]
Lisarda: ¿Quieres callar, mentecato?
Papagayo: No, porque no son de estima
los papagayos callados,
que se quieren habladores.
Al fin, como voy contando,
paseándonos los dos
por esta calle, escuchamos
cuchilladas acá dentro,
y la puerta abierta hallando,
por esa escalera arriba
subimos. Este es el caso.
Don Álvaro: ¿Y dónde es vuestra posada?
Papagayo: Un mesón de los dïablos
que está a las puertas del mar,
que el mar contra nos airado
nos tiene echado por puertas.
Don Álvaro: Pues, sírvase vuestro agrado
desta casa, que es ya vuestra,
señor Lisardo.
Papagayo: Mil años
vivas, poco más o menos,
pues que tu primor honrado
nos saca de un purgatorio,
cual es un mesón. Me parto
a conducir las maletas.
Lisarda: Eso no. Aunque obligado
quedo a vuestra cortesía,
señor, no quisiera daros
tanta molestia.
Don Álvaro: Lisonja
me hacéis grande, y así pagaos
deste deseo.

26 Papagayo's wordplay with *forastero/forastera* would indicate to a Spanish-speaking audience that he is playing with gender roles. In addition, *forastero* also alludes not only to being new to a place but also strangeness or alienation.

Papagayo: Yes, sir, and just like my master, I'm behaving like a broad from abroad.

Lisarda: Will you shut up, idiot?!

Papagayo: No, because no one likes quiet parrots; everybody prefers talking ones. So, as I was saying, while we were walking down this street, we heard the sounds of a swordfight inside, and, finding the door open, we went up the stairs. That's the story.

Don Álvaro: And where are you lodging?

Papagayo: In a devils' inn near the sea, where the stormy water threw us through the doors.

Don Álvaro: Well, I hope this house pleases you, for consider it yours, Sir Lisardo.

Papagayo: May you live a thousand years, more or less, as your honorable self has pulled us out of that purgatory of an inn. I'll go get our suitcases.

Lisarda: Not yet. Although I'm indebted to your courtesy, sir, I don't want to inconvenience you.

Don Álvaro: You flatter me greatly; please accept my offer, for those are my wishes.

Lisarda: Los míos
ya a vuestro servicio allano.
Ve por las maletas, pues,
Papagayo.
Papagayo: Voy de un salto. *(Vase)*
Don Álvaro: Yo hago luego disponer
a vuestra persona un cuarto. *(Vase)*
Lisarda: De la urbanidad deste hombre
mi afecto está muy pagado.
Don Álvaro: *(Dentro.)* Beatriz, Hipólita, hermana.
Lisarda: ¡Oh, si así como agasajo
encuentro en él, mi fortuna
me hubiera aquí deparado
noticias de lo que busco!
¿Si es éste el mismo don Álvaro?

Sale don Álvaro.

Don Álvaro: Sin duda alguna los cielos
hoy quieren de mis desgracias,
Lisardo, haceros testigo,
que os ha traído a mi casa
la suerte a tiempo que yo
pretendía con mi espada
tomar en mi primo Alberto
de mis ofensas venganza.
Pues dándole el parentesco
confianzas temerarias
para llegar atrevido
a hablar con Beatriz mi hermana,
con ella hablando le hallé
y la vida le quitara,
a no entrar en este tiempo
vuestra persona en la sala
a meterse de por medio,
porque él de mí se escapara.
Y agora que adentro fui,
para que se diera traza
a disponer el aseo

Lisarda: My wishes are satisfied by serving you. Go for the suitcases, then, Papagayo.

Papagayo: I'll get right to it. *He exits.*

Don Álvaro: I'll make sure your room is made ready. *He exits.*

Lisarda: I really like this man's urbanity.

Don Álvaro: *Off stage*. Beatriz, Hipólita, sister…

Lisarda: Oh, if he's the treasure I think he is, my fortune may truly have brought me the information I've been seeking! Could this gentleman be the same Don Álvaro?

Don Álvaro enters.

Don Álvaro: Beyond a shadow of a doubt, Lisardo, the heavens want to make you a witness of my misfortunes today. Fate has brought you to my house at the very moment I was trying to take revenge on my cousin Alberto for his offenses against me. Our kinship had given him the reckless confidence he needed to dare come here and speak to my sister Beatriz, for I discovered him talking to her. I would have taken his life if you hadn't entered the room just then and put yourself between us so he could escape. And now, when I went inside to make sure that everything was clean and ready to give you a grand welcome, I found that Beatriz and her maid

	– ¡Quién jamás lo imaginara! –	
	para el agasajo vuestro,	
	hallo que con la criada	
	falta mi hermana Beatriz,	
	que por una puerta falsa	
	– ¡oh falsa puerta a mi honor! –	
	se han salido, dando causa	
	con esta ausencia a que crea	
	que es ya mi deshonra clara,	
	pues nunca hubiera salido	
	a no estar Beatriz culpada.	
	¿Qué haré, pues, con mis afrentas?	
	¿Qué he de hacer con mis desgracias?	
Lisarda:	Señor, en trances de honor	
	las quejas son excusadas,	
	y quien más las disimula,	
	menos a su honor ultraja.	
	De ausentarle esa señora	
	es presunción temeraria	
	inferirse en ella culpa,	
	pues el recelo obligada	
	de los escrúpulos vuestros,	
	temiendo alguna venganza	
	que de la inocencia suya	
	en esta ocasión tomara	
	vuestra presunción celosa,	
	de alguna vecina a casa	
	se acogería.	

Sale Dorotea.

Dorotea:	Esta carta	
	traigo, señor, para vos.	
Don Álvaro:	¿Para mí?	
Dorotea:	¿Quién tal dudara?	
	Pues, ¿para quién, si a vos dice?	
Lisarda:	(Billete de alguna dama	*Aparte*
	es, que a don Álvaro quiere,	
	que lo merece su gala.)	

are missing (Who would ever have thought it?!). They left through a false door (oh deceitful doorway to my honor!). Their absence only further leads me to believe that my dishonor is now clear, for Beatriz would never have left if she weren't guilty. What shall I do with these affronts to my honor? What shall I do with my misfortunes?

Lisarda: Sir, resentments don't help in difficult situations involving honor, and the one who pardons them the most offends his honor the least. It's rash to assume that just because the lady left, you should infer that she's guilty. If she feared that your jealous suppositions would lead you to take revenge on her innocence, caution might force her to seek refuge in a neighbor's house.

Dorotea enters.

Dorotea: Sir, here's a letter for you.

Don Álvaro: A letter for me?

Dorotea: What's there to doubt? Who else could it be for, if it has your name on it?

Lisarda: *Aside*. (It must be a note from a lady who fancies Don Álvaro, for his sophistication merits such things.)

Don Álvaro: Veamos lo que dice aquí.

Abre y lee para sí. [Dorotea ve a Lisarda.]

Dorotea: No le falta aquí a mi ama
en que escoger, y el mancebo,
que así con tan poca barba
también sus años apoca,
bien de mancebo en la gracia
acaba con los deseos,
porque si mancebo acaba
en cebo, es cebo de amor
para cautivar las almas.[27]

Lisarda: ¿Qué es esto? Amor,[28] ¿tú me tiras,
sin que hasta aquí de tus armas
los tiros conozca? ¡Ay Dios,
que conquista tan extraña!
En celos amor comienza,
¡quién de su ardid tal pensara!
¿De envidiosa emulación
posible es que mi amor nazca?[29]
Sí, que es don Álvaro airoso,
y alguna dama prendada
se ve de su gallardía,
y esta consideración basta[30]
para mover mi afición,
que amor sigue las pisadas
de otro amor y en competencias
sus incendios se señalan.

Don Álvaro: Dorotea, deste amigo
la asistencia cortesana
me hace dejar por ahora
la respuesta reservada.
Yo responderé, y por porte

---

27 Dorotea puns on the words *mancebo* (young man) and *cebo* (bait).

28 Amor is another name for Cupid.

29 An exclamation in the source text. This is an example of Girardian mimetic desire, in which Lisarda falls for Álvaro because she believes that Jacinta loves him.

30 This line contains an extra syllable, nine rather than eight.

Don Álvaro: Let's see what it says. *He opens the letter and reads it in silence. Dorotea notices Lisarda.*

Dorotea: *Aside.* (My mistress certainly doesn't lack men to choose from, and with a sparse beard making him appear even younger, this lad's charm can easily end in her desire. After all, if 'jail bait' ends in 'bait,' it must be because he's Cupid's lure to capture hearts and souls.)

Lisarda: *Aside.* (What's happening? Cupid, are you shooting arrows at me when I haven't felt the shots of your weapons before? Oh, Lord, what a strange conquest! Love can spring from jealousy; who would have believed it?! Is it possible, then, that my affection might be born of green-eyed rivalry? Yes: Don Álvaro is refined and gracious, and some captivated woman might imagine herself basking in his gallantry. It's enough to set my own passion in motion, for one love follows in the footsteps of another love, and their fires are signposts of competition.)

Don Álvaro: Dorotea, because my friend is here with me, I must postpone for now my response to the note. I will respond, and for

de carta tan estimada
de mi afecto, por mi vida
desta sortija te paga.

Dorotea: (Ésta sí que es la respuesta *Aparte*
para mí más necesaria,
que la otra no me importa.)
Besa tus pies esta esclava. *(Vase.)*

Don Álvaro: No puedo ya mis empeños,
Lisardo, encubriros nada,
y pues de mi honor el duelo
sabéis, ved también la causa
de mi amor en un papel,
que cuando gustoso agrada
al alma, entre sus renglones
se mira asustada el alma.

Lee en voz alta. Obligada del amor de vuestra cortesía, y persuadida de la cortesía de vuestro amor, bien quisiera luego premiar vuestra voluntad con las gratitudes, que debo a su inclinación, a no impedirme la deuda de una fineza – pues he hecho un voto de no admitir de hombre alguno la mano mientras Clarindo estuviere vivo – que esta constancia me merecía su afición. Y aunque hasta aquí han corrido noticias de su muerte, como no las hay de quien se las dio, no se da mi desengaño por satisfecho, sin que vos, así como me dais los pésames de esta falta, me deis también sin ella – si lo habéis sabido – del homicida parte, que sólo desta suerte acabaréis con los deseos de vuestra pretensión, como yo con la pretensión de mis deseos.[31] Dios os guarde.

– Jacinta.

Lisarda: (Si éste es mi hermano Clarindo *Aparte*
buen camino me prepara
la suerte para mi intento,
yendo esta dama empeñada
por amor, que le ha tenido,

31 Jacinta uses inverted parallel structure in her letter to pun on the words *deseos* (desires) and *pretensión* ('aspiration' or 'aim'). She sets the terms that Álvaro must meet to end up with his aspiration's desires, and at the same time, she will also end up with her desires' aim.

transporting a letter so esteemed by my affections, let this ring repay you for my life.

Dorotea: *Aside.* (This really is the best way to thank me, since any other expression of gratitude doesn't matter a bit.) This slave kisses your feet. *She exits.*

Don Álvaro: Lisardo, I can't conceal my problems from you anymore, and since you now know about the duel over my honor, you may as well see the circumstances of my love, for as much as the words in this letter please the soul, what's between the lines fills my soul with dread.

He reads aloud. Forced by the love of your courtesy, and persuaded by the courtesy of your love, I'd like to reward your desire with the gratitude that I owe your affection, if only I weren't prevented from doing so by my obligation to another's kindness. I made a vow not to give my hand to any other man while Clarindo was alive – and his affection merited my faithfulness. And though accounts of his death have been circulating, since there's no information on who's spreading the news, my questions haven't been answered, unless, since you're offering me condolences, you can tell me beyond a doubt who killed him, if you know. That's the only way you'll end up with the desires to which you aspire, as I will with mine. May God keep you.

– Jacinta

Lisarda: *Aside.* (If this refers to my brother Clarindo, Fate is paving the way for me and my intentions quite well now that this lady, obligated by the love she had for him, is involved in the

en el lance. Sólo falta
que don Álvaro aquí sepa
la noticia para darla.)

Don Álvaro: La carta que habéis oído,
Lisardo, es tan buena y mala,
que apuntándome una dicha,
me recuerda una desgracia:
dicha, porque me convida
a poseer la esperanza
la mano de una mujer
que tanto el alma idolatra;
desgracia, porque me arguye
de la culpa más extraña
que a hombre alguno ha sucedido.
Oídla en cuatro palabras:
De Lamego un caballero
en la ocasión de la Armada
de Turín vino a la corte
que Clarindo se llamaba,
y embarcándonos los dos,
le tuve por camarada,
de quien fui íntimo amigo
por sus prendas, que eran raras,
y siendo su amigo estrecho
– ¡oh amistad tan mal lograda! – ,
bien puedo decir que fui
amigo suyo *usque ad aras*,[32]
pues su vida sacrificio
fue de mi traición villana.
El caso fue que por veces
de Jacinta, que yo adoraba,
me repetía favores,
con que mi celosa rabia,
viendo encontrarle cariños
donde yo hallaba *esquivanças*,[33]

32 The Latin phrase *amicus usque ad aras* means a friend all the way up to the altar (that is, the grave or death).

33 Here Azevedo uses the Portuguese word, necessary to maintain the assonant rhyme. The

situation. All that's lacking is for Don Álvaro to know the information to give her.)

Don Álvaro: The letter you heard me read, Lisardo, is so good *and* bad that in pointing me toward joy, it also recalls misfortune: joy because it invites me to hope for the hand of a woman my soul idolizes; misfortune because it refers to the most extraordinary guilt that has ever befallen any man. Hear of it briefly: On the occasion of the Turin[18] Armada, a gentleman from Lamego named Clarindo came to Court, and by the time the two of us embarked, due to his rare qualities, I considered him not merely a comrade, but an intimate friend. Being so close (oh badly won friendship!), I can honestly say that I was his friend till death, since his life was sacrificed to my villainous betrayal. He'd often tell me of the favors that Jacinta, whom I adored, was granting him. It got to the point that, seeing him find affection where I only saw scorn

18 An often-contested city in early modern times, in 1563 Turin was named the capital of the Duchy of Savoy.

pues siempre Jacinta hermosa
conmigo había sido ingrata,
se enfureció de tal suerte,
que cuando Clarindo estaba
viniendo en mayor descuido,
con dos fuertes puñaladas
de mis celos en su vida
satisfice la venganza.
Por el ejército todo
su muerte fue divulgada,
sin saberse el homicida
hasta aquí, porque tal traza
supo tener mi cautela
en esta muerte tirana
que el cielo y yo solamente
lo sabemos, y lo alcanza
agora vuestra persona,
a quien por la confïanza
que ya promete de darme
en la lid más empeñada
de mi fortuna, salida
de amor a mis esperanzas,
he fïado este secreto.
Y pues no se desengaña
de la muerte de Clarindo
hasta que noticias claras
del homicida Jacinta
llegue a saber – circunstancia
para que goce dichoso
de su mano soberana – ,
de hacer por mí una fineza
me habéis de dar la palabra.

Lisarda: (¿Ésta es realidad o sueño? *Aparte*
¿Qué es esto que por mí pasa?
¿Que encuentre yo a mi enemigo
a tiempo que amor me embarga

Spanish words, *esquivezas* or *esquiveces*, would not fit. Azevedo apparently knew the word *esquivez*; it appears in Don Álvaro's letter to Jacinta.

from the beautiful Jacinta, my jealous anger became so enraged that when Clarindo was distracted, I avenged my jealousy with two strong knife thrusts that ended his life. News of his death spread through the entire military, without anyone knowing the name of the killer till now, because my cunning and skill were such that only Heaven and I know what happened in this despotic murder. Now you also know: you are the person to whom I've entrusted this secret, in the confidence that, in the bitterest battle of my fate you'll promise to help me secure the results I've hoped for in love. And since Jacinta won't see the truth about Clarindo's death till she learns the name of his murderer (a circumstance that should let me happily win her sovereign hand), I need your word that you'll grant me a favor.

Lisarda: *Aside.* (Is this reality or a dream? What's happening to me? Have I found my enemy at the same time Love restrains me

vengarme? ¿Pues la fortuna
en este hombre me depara
mi ofensor cuando me tiene
ya su amor aficionada?
Mi amor con mi agravio miro,
¿quién vio cosas más contrarias?
¿Qué haré en lance tan terrible?
¿Qué haré en empresa tan brava?
Ea, amor, deja el empeño;
no quieras a quien me agravia.
Ea, agravio, las pasiones
de amor venzan tus audacias.)

Don Álvaro: Parece que divertido
me oísteis, pues me dilata
vuestra atención la respuesta
que mi petición aguarda.

Lisarda: Divertida no, suspensa
se mira y perpleja el alma,
viendo que a un amigo vuestro
disteis muerte tan osada.

Don Álvaro: No hay amigo, siendo amante.

Lisarda: (En mí hay experiencia contraria, *Aparte*
pues con amor no hay enemigo,
cuando luego no te sacan
tu vida aquí mis furores.)

Don Álvaro: Si a lo hecho pues no se halla
remedio, resta que sólo
le queráis dar a mis ansias,
que en la fineza consiste
que os he pedido.

Lisarda: (¿Empeñada *Aparte*
mi palabra a una fineza?
¿Qué puede ser? Pero vaya,
que el amor por él me obliga
a que mil finezas haga.)

Don Álvaro: ¿Qué decís?

Lisarda: Si está en mi mano,
palabra os doy.

from exacting revenge? Does Fate offer me my offender in the person of this man, when Love has already made me his? I see my love united with the wrong done to me: who ever saw such opposites stand side by side? What shall I do in such a terrible predicament? What shall I do in such a tempestuous enterprise? Come now, Love: don't take this any further; don't let me fall for the one who's offending me. Come now, Offense: Love's passions will conquer your audacity.)

Don Álvaro: It appears that my story amuses you, since you're taking so long to respond to my request.

Lisarda: Amused, no: my soul is left lifeless and stunned, seeing how you gave such an outrageous death to a friend.

Don Álvaro: There's no such thing as a friend when he's also a lover.

Lisarda: *Aside.* (In me, the experience is the opposite, for with love, there are no enemies – unless my rage leads me to take your life.)

Don Álvaro: If there's no remedy for what was done, then all that remains is that you remedy my distress, for courtesy demands that you respond if I ask.

Lisarda: *Aside.* (Is my word indebted to an act of courtesy? What act can it be? But enough: for his sake, love forces me to pay him a thousand courtesies.)

Don Álvaro: What do you say?

Lisarda: If it's within my power, I give you my word.

Don Álvaro: Pues pagada
está de mi amor Jacinta,
y para premiarle, basta
saber quién mató a Clarindo
– que aun con su vida se engaña. –
Confesando que fui yo,
aunque su amor fue la causa,
como le ha querido bien
cosa es bien averiguada
que enojada contra mí,
perderé dicha tan alta.
Vos me habéis de dar licencia
y permitir que me valga
de una mentira, diciendo
que esta muerte fue obrada
por vos, consintiendo en esto
porque con mi logro salga,
y cuando de aquí os suceda
alguna fortuna mala,
me obligo yo a deshacerla.

Lisarda: (Sólo aquesto me faltaba, *Aparte*
ser yo mi enemigo mismo
¡y en amores de otra dama!,
mas ya palabra le di,
veamos en qué esto para,
que cuando Jacinta quiera
darle la mano, estorbarla
pienso con otra mentira,
que haré que sea informada
de que él a otra dama quiere,
y si no valieren trazas
para impedirle este logro
y mis celos no se acaban,
sabrá entonces en su vida
tomar venganza mi espada.
En tanto agravio, paciencia,
que por ahora os embargan
los celos la ejecución,

Don Álvaro: I've paid Jacinta with my love, and to reward her, it'll be sufficient to learn who killed Clarindo (for she's still deceived about what happened to him). If I confess that I was the culprit, even though her love for him was the cause, she'll be so angry with me that I'll lose my beloved forever. I'm asking you to let me make use of a lie by saying that you committed this murder, for if you consent, it'll help me achieve my goal. And from here on out, whenever misfortune befalls you, I commit myself to make things right.

Lisarda: *Aside.* (This is all I needed: to become my own worst enemy – and in his love affair with another woman! But I already gave him my word. Let's see how this turns out; if Jacinta decides to give him her hand in marriage, I can get in the way with another lie. I'll make sure she learns that he loves another woman, and if I'm not skilled enough to stop him and I'm still jealous, then my sword will know how to take revenge. With so many grievances, patience; for now, jealousy is hindering the performance, so there'll be

para que agravios no haya
donde hay celos, si otras veces
agravios celos apartan.)
Don Álvaro: ¿Qué me respondéis, Lisardo?
Lisarda: Que aunque es cosa temeraria
tomar sobre mí una culpa,
es nuestra amistad ya tanta,
que haré por vos este exceso.
Don Álvaro: A vuestra nobleza hidalga
mi amor y mi vida debo.
Lisarda: (Y sin duda no te engañas *Aparte*
cuando Lisarda te quiere
y por eso no te mata.)
Don Álvaro: Y pues de mi amor el pleito
tiene ya salida, falta
que la tenga el de mi honor,
y así pues Beatriz mi hermana
no [a]parece y fue el motivo
Alberto, es fuerza que vaya
luego a quitarle la vida,
si así un honor se restaura.
Quedaos, Lisardo, que ya vuelvo.
Lisarda: Tened, porque aquesa llaga
no se cura así.
Don Álvaro: A lo menos
con su sangre así se lava. *(Vase.)*
Lisarda: Tras él voy para impedirle
de su enojo esta desgracia. *(Vase.)*

Salen doña Beatriz e Hipólita.

Hipólita: Señora, imprudente arrojo
fue el de tu resolución.
Doña Beatriz: Diome, Hipólita, ocasión
el recelo de un enojo,
pues pudiera ser despojo
del enfado de mi hermano

no grievances where there is jealousy, even if at other times grievances can move jealousy out of the way.)

Don Álvaro: What's your answer, Lisardo?

Lisarda: That although it's reckless for me to take the blame, our friendship is such that I'll do you this tremendous favor.

Don Álvaro: I owe my love and my life to your noble generosity.

Lisarda: *Aside.* (And don't fool yourself: the only reason Lisarda doesn't kill you is that she loves you.)

Don Álvaro: And since the dispute regarding my love complaint has now been resolved, I need to do the same thing for the problem of my honor. Since my sister Beatriz still hasn't appeared and Alberto is the reason why, I must kill him and thus restore lost honor. Stay here, Lisardo; I'll be right back.

Lisarda: Wait; that's not the way you heal the wound.

Don Álvaro: At least the wound will be washed with his blood. *He exits.*

Lisarda: I must follow him and keep him doing something shameful out of anger. *She exits.*

Doña Beatriz and Hipólita enter.

Hipólita: My lady, your single-minded boldness was imprudent.

Doña Beatriz: Hipólita, I was left in a terrible spot, for even though we conducted ourselves according to the rules of propriety, my life would have been the spoils of my brother's anger

mi vida – que es deshumano
un antojo si lo advierto –
hallándome con Alberto,
aunque en modo cortesano.

Hipólita: Nunca de ti liviandad
llegaría a presumir,
que aqueso era desmentir
tu sangre y tu calidad.
Ninguna facilidad
en la nobleza es censura
de su reputación pura,
pues solamente se advierte
que en quien es de baja suerte
no hay reputación segura.

Doña Beatriz: Una condición celosa,
cual en mi hermano se ve,
sin porqué ni para qué,
siempre ha sido escrupulosa.
Yo pues, como soy medrosa,
de cualquier acción me asusto
y contra el temor injusto
desta suerte me prevengo,
y así, como has visto, vengo
huyendo de su disgusto.

Hipólita: Su disgusto solamente
contra tu primo habrá sido
por haberse introducido
en su casa.

Doña Beatriz: Aqueso siente,
por amarle tiernamente
el alma con más razón.
Sin duda su indignación
le habrá quitado la vida,
Hipólita, que esta herida
adivina el corazón.

Hipólita: Si con tu hermano reñía
Alberto de mano a mano,

(because on impulse he can be cold-hearted) once he found me with Alberto.

Hipólita: I'd never begin to presume you'd be indecent, for that would go against your blood and high rank. It's difficult to censure the pure character of the nobility; those of the lower classes are less secure in their reputations.

Doña Beatriz: You can see that my brother suffers – and with no rhyme or reason – from a jealous disposition; he's always been overly rigorous. I get frightened by everything, so I keep myself from those anxieties by fleeing from his displeasure, as you've seen.

Hipólita: His displeasure with your cousin must only be due to Alberto's presence in your house.

Doña Beatriz: My soul agrees, and with even greater reason, since I love him tenderly. Without a doubt, my brother's anger will cost Alberto his life, Hipólita; that's what my heart predicts.

Hipólita: If Alberto was dueling with your brother in hand-to-hand

también, señora, tu hermano
el mismo riesgo corría,
mas dime por vida mía,
¿de cuál más pena tuvieras?
Doña Beatriz: Si es que amor bien consideras,
en vana pregunta das,
porque siempre obligan más
que la sangre amantes veras.
Hipólita: Más que prima de vihuela
en la de amor eres fina,
mas ¿adónde te encamina,
sin que amor de ti se duela?,
pues conmigo te desvela
a pisar las calles, di.
Doña Beatriz: ¿No se va bien por aquí
de Jacinta a casa?
Hipólita: Bien.
Doña Beatriz: Pues siendo mi amiga, ¿quién
me valdrá mejor a mí?
Su casa me ha de valer
en tal trance.
Hipólita: En eso asiento,
que pensaba que a un convento
te querías acoger,
que monja no quiero ser,
que nunca he sido inclinada
a la vida de encerrada.
Doña Beatriz: Ven, pues, mis pasos siguiendo.
Hipólita: Vamos, que aquí, a lo que entiendo,
se da fin a la jornada. *[Vanse.]*

combat, my lady, your brother ran the same risk. But tell me, on my life, which death would make you suffer the most?

Doña Beatriz: If you think carefully about the nature of love, you wouldn't ask, because true love is even stronger than blood.

Hipólita: You're finer than a *vihuela*'s cousin[19] is at being true to Love, but, do tell, where does this lead you if Love isn't true to you, for it keeps you up at night, spending your time walking up and down the streets with me.

Doña Beatriz: Isn't this the way to get to Jacinta's house?

Hipólita: Yes, right through here.

Doña Beatriz: Well, since she's my friend, who could help me better? In a difficult moment, her house may prove useful.

Hipólita: I agree, since I figured you were going to seek shelter in a convent. I don't want to be a nun, since I've never felt inclined to live all cooped up.

Doña Beatriz: Come on then and follow me.

Hipólita: Let's go, since here, as I understand it, is where the act ends.

They exit.

---

19 Most likely this refers to the guitar, since both were popular stringed instruments from the same family. Both the *vihuela* and the guitar were used to accompany love songs, often played outside a beloved's house. *Vihuelas*, which were popular in Renaissance Spain and Portugal, were played with a bow or plucked.

JORNADA SEGUNDA

[Fuera del méson.] Sale Papagayo con unas maletas como huyendo de Clarindo, que le va siguiendo.

Papagayo: Sombra, fantasma o ilusión,
no me persigas, supuesto
que tengo el ánimo flaco
para semejantes duelos.
¿Que siempre quien es cobarde
tope de aquestos encuentros?
Parece que aquestas cosas
suele deparar el miedo.
¡Jesús! ¿Qué santo *advogado*[34]
se hallará contra los muertos?
Si eres sombra de Clarindo,
como en tu presencia veo,
y vienes a pedir misas,
déjame, que te prometo
de buscar un sacerdote
en la materia más diestro
que el mismo Amaro de Lage,
que por tu ánima luego
se ponga a decir mañana
media docena a lo menos.

Clarindo: Harás como buen cristiano,
Papagayo, que con eso
saldré de mi purgatorio,
que le tengo en este puesto.

Papagayo: ¿Purgatorio? Poco has dicho.
Mejor dijeras infierno,
porque es desesperación
un mesón de los dineros.
Mas, ¿por qué en este lugar
penando estás?

34 In the source text, this word is spelled in Portuguese. The Spanish spelling (in Covarrubias's dictionary and today) is *abogado.*

ACT 2

Outside the inn. Papagayo enters, carrying suitcases, as if he were fleeing from Clarindo, who is following him.

Papagayo: Shadow, ghost, or illusion, don't pursue me; my soul is too scrawny for such grief. Why is the coward the guy who always finds himself having such encounters? It seems like fear tends to produce things like this. Jesus! What holy protector against the dead will we find? If you're Clarindo's ghost, as your presence here attests, and you're coming to ask that masses be said for your soul, leave me alone and I promise you I'll find a priest who's more skilled than Amarus of Lage[20] was in the subject, and tomorrow he'll proceed to say at least half a dozen masses for you.

Clarindo: You'll do it as a good Christian, Papagayo, which will allow me to leave my Purgatory, for this place is one.

Papagayo: Purgatory? That's not so bad. You might as well have said Hell, because an inn leads to despair over lost money. But why are you suffering here?

---

20 Several towns named Lage may be found in Portugal, with the best known located in the northern part of the country. Saint Amaro (or Amarus the Pilgrim), often identified with Galicia in Spain, was said to have made a long sea journey to find the Earthly Paradise. According to legend, he discovered a beautiful castle that he was not permitted to enter, although he was able to glimpse its wonders, including the Tree of Life and the Virgin Mary, through a keyhole. See C[arlos] A[lberto] Vega, *Hagiografía y literatura: La vida de San Amaro* (Madrid: El Crotalón, 1987).

Clarindo: En él peno
de cuentas por un engaño.
Papagayo: ¿Engañaste al mesonero?
Clarindo: Engañé.
Papagayo: ¡Quién tal pensara!
¡Lo que son juicios del cielo!
Desde niño me arrullaron
con aquel vulgar proverbio
que quien esta gente engaña
al cielo se va derecho.
Clarindo: Pero entre mis penas, ¿sabes
cuál es mi mayor tormento?
Papagayo: ¿Cuál es?
Clarindo: El olvido, amigo,
de mis amigos y deudos,
que con sufragios de mí
no se acuerdan.
Papagayo: Mal es viejo
que se hace un hombre olvidado
en poniendo tierra en medio.
Clarindo: Sin duda no me han tenido
con certidumbre por muerto.
Papagayo: ¿Cómo no? Todos lo saben
también como yo lo creo,
pues han corrido noticias
de que en la armada te han muerto.
Clarindo: ¿Y el homicida se sabe?
Papagayo: No es posible, aunque se han hecho
diligencias en el caso.
Clarindo: (El quedará descubierto *Aparte*
a manos de mi venganza;
en tanto disimulemos,
celos, hasta averiguaros,
que aunque dicen que primero
son que celos los agravios,
primero ahora son celos.)
¿Y qué se ha hecho mi padre?

Clarindo: It's due to a deception involving my tab.

Papagayo: Did you swindle the innkeeper?

Clarindo: Yes, I tricked him.

Papagayo: Who would have thought it! Oh, how great is Heaven's justice! When I was a child, I was rocked to sleep with that popular proverb 'Those who trick dishonest people will go straight to Heaven.'

Clarindo: But of all my suffering, do you know what torments me the most?

Papagayo: What?

Clarindo: Being forgotten, my friend, by all my friends and relations, who don't remember to pray for me.

Papagayo: It's an old evil truth that when a man is dead and buried six feet under, others will forget him.

Clarindo: Surely they haven't considered me dead with any degree of certainty.

Papagayo: Why not? Everybody also knows what I believe, for there's news all over that you were killed in the Armada.

Clarindo: And is the name of the murderer known?

Papagayo: No, though the investigation of the case is moving forward.

Clarindo: *Aside.* (He'll be unveiled by my avenging hands. Meanwhile, Jealousy, let's stay hidden till you know for sure, for although they say that affronts to one's honor and life come before jealousy, right now, jealousy comes first.) And what has become of my father?

Papagayo: Tomó las de Villa Diego[35]
su vida con este enojo.
Clarindo: ¿Murió?
Papagayo: De una vez el viejo.
¿No le has por allá encontrado
por el final hemisferio?
Clarindo: ¿Y mi hermana?
Papagayo: (Aquí está el punto, *Aparte*
pues si la verdad le cuento,
aunque por su causa hizo
Lisarda tan grande exceso,
será la pena doblarle,
sabiendo su arrojo fiero.
Viva, pues, el secretillo
y quédese en el silencio,
que ni aún de los difuntos
se ha de fïar un secreto.
Mas no sé qué he de decirle,
que no puedo hablar de miedo.)
Tu hermana se metió fraile.
Clarindo: ¿Fraile?
Papagayo: Monja decir quiero,
que esto de frailes y monjas
todo viene a ser lo mesmo,[36]
pues tienen hábitos todos
y viven en monasterios.
Clarindo: Y tú, dime…

[Clarindo se acerca a Papagayo.]

Papagayo: Quita allá,
¿no puedes hablar de lejos?
Clarindo: ¿Quién te ha traído a la corte?
Papagayo: Yo sirvo a un vecino nuestro,
treinta casas más arriba,

---

35 As Soufas notes, 'tomar las de Villa Diego' means to flee (*Women's Acts* 316). Clarindo's father has fled this life.

36 The *DRAE* defines *mesmo* as an archaic form of *mismo* (2.1362). The source text uses both forms, but prefers *mismo*. The assonant rhyme scheme requires *mesmo* in this case.

Papagayo: His wrath led him to flee this life.
Clarindo: He died?
Papagayo: The old gentleman died suddenly. Haven't you by chance run into him out there in the great beyond?
Clarindo: And my sister?
Papagayo: *Aside.* (Here's the point: if I tell him the truth, even though Lisarda did all she did because of him, it'll double his suffering when he finds out about her bold actions. Let's let the teensy little secret live by keeping quiet about it, since even dead guys can't be trusted with secrets. But I don't know what to say; I'm so scared I can't even speak.) Your sister became a monk.
Clarindo: A monk?
Papagayo: I mean nun, 'cuz this stuff with monks and nuns is all the same to me, since they all wear habits and live in monasteries.[21]
Clarindo: *Clarindo approaches Papagayo.* You, tell me…
Papagayo: Move back; can't you talk from further away?
Clarindo: And who brought you to the royal Court?
Papagayo: I serve a neighbor of ours, thirty houses up the hill, and I'm

---

21 In Spanish and Portuguese, the terms for 'convents' and 'monasteries' are generally used reciprocally and more likely point to the size of the building, rather than the gender of those who reside there.

y a la corte con él vengo
a proveernos de bulas,
para venderlas al pueblo;
y la mala vecindad
de chinches deste aposento
me hace mudar a otra parte
aquestos trastes que llevo.
(No hay poeta, vive Dios, *Aparte*
que mienta como yo miento.)
Clarindo: Y dime, ven acá.
Papagayo: Tate,[37]
no te avecines, que tengo
una poquita de sarna
y pegártela recelo.
Clarindo: Aqueso no temas tú.
Papagayo: Pues esotro es lo que temo.
Clarindo: Dime.
Papagayo: Oh, ¡cuánto 'dime'! Aguarda *[Aparte]*
(désta[38] me escapo) que ya vuelvo. *(Vase.)*
Clarindo: Fuese y el miedo que ha tenido
le hace de mí ir huyendo,
que por muerto me ha juzgado.
Sin duda un común concepto
se ha formado de mi muerte,
y el fin sólo de mi intento
consiste en disimularlo,[39]
y ánimo me da para ello
el juicio de Papagayo,
que quedó de pavor lleno
en viéndome en la posada,
del cual, cauteloso, viendo
que el susto me confirmaba
la opinión en que estoy puesto,
fui con él disimulando,

37 *Tate*, probably from the imperative form of the verb *estar*: *estate*. According to the *DRAE*, it means *cuidado* or *poco a poco* (2.1945).

38 Here *désta* may stand for *de esta manera.*

39 In the source text, *dissimulallo.*

coming with him to buy some papal bulls[22] to sell to other people. And the rotten community of bedbugs that live in this inn has forced me to pack my things and move somewhere else. *Aside.* (My God, there's no poet in the world who lies like I lie.[23])

Clarindo: Come here and tell me more.

Papagayo: Be careful; don't get too close 'cuz I have a slight case of scabies and I'm worried that I'll give it to you.

Clarindo: Don't be afraid of that.

Papagayo: Well, that's not what I'm afraid of.

Clarindo: Tell me.

Papagayo: Oh, hold on to all your 'tell me's' till I return. *Aside.* (That way I can escape.) *He exits.*

Clarindo: He's gone, and his fear is what made him flee from me, since he believes I'm dead. Without a doubt everybody now considers my death an established fact, so to achieve my goal, I need only pretend that it's so. Papagayo's opinion of the matter encourages me to go forward, for when he saw me in the inn, he was terrified, and his fright confirmed how people must view me now, so I kept on pretending and

---

22 Dispensations to shorten the time people must spend in Purgatory.

23 The audience will know that Papagayo is referring to a dramatic poet, the early modern term for 'dramatist.' In a metadramatic move, Azevedo is playing with the theater – and with truth and lies – inside her play.

figura de muerto haciendo.
¡Cosas suceden extrañas!
¿Quién dijera que viniendo
a dar en aquesta casa,
donde el huésped, que es arriero,
me ha traído de Madrid,
camino por donde vuelvo
desde Nisa, do[40] he quedado
en casa de un caballero,
herido de un falso amigo,
de que sucedió que luego
– según me informé – se tuvo
– por morir en aquel tiempo
un soldado de mi nombre –
mi muerte por caso cierto,
había de hallar aquí
Papagayo? ¡Extraño encuentro!
¿Qué querrá aquesto decir?
Que como él no es verdadero
y del miedo el sobresalto
le dejó de juicio ajeno,
no me fío en sus razones.
Bien que pesaroso advierto
que en lo que toca a mi padre,
ninguna duda le puedo
poner, que una nueva mala
tiene aqueste privilegio.
Sea lo que fuere al fin,
que yo no he de ir a Lamego,
sin primero una venganza
satisfacer y unos celos,
venganza contra un ingrato
que la amistad ofendiendo,
me quiso sacar la vida
– ¡oh traidor, falso y grosero! – ,
envidioso de Jacinta

40 The *DRAE* defines *do* as an archaic form of *donde* (1.768).

assumed the figure of a dead man. Strange things really do happen!

Who would have thought that I'd wind up in this house, where my host, a muleteer, brought me from Madrid? It's all part of my long journey home from Nice,[24] where I'd been staying in a gentleman's home after being wounded by a false friend. Who would have thought that because a soldier with the same name died about that time, my death would be treated as fact and that I'd find Papagayo here? What a strange encounter with him! What does all this mean? Since he's not telling the truth and his fear and shock have left him bereft of his senses, I don't trust his judgment. But sadly, I can tell that with regard to my father, I cannot doubt him, for bad news takes precedence. However it turns out in the end, I won't go home to Lamego without first avenging my honor and my jealousy. I'll take revenge against the ingrate who, offending friendship, tried to take my life (oh false and scurrilous traitor!) because he envied the fact that Jacinta was the mistress of my feelings.

---

24 A city on the Mediterranean coast of Savoy, located in France today.

ser de mis sentidos dueño,[41]
celos de aquesta hermosura,
porque de sus ojos bellos
cuando me aparté, me dijo,
que aunque los hados siniestros
no me dejasen con vida
llegar de Lisboa al puerto,
siempre de mí la memoria
tendría tanto en el pecho,
que ya más pudiese inclinarse
de amor a otro alguno empleo.
Desta, pues, promesa suya,
experiencia hacer queriendo
con muerto disimularme,
saber agora pretendo
– pues ya sé que está Jacinta
por casar – si los deseos
de don Álvaro conquistan
la belleza porque muero,
y si Jacinta rebate
sus amantes galanteos
con la constancia debida
que de su fineza espero.
Bien cuesta a la ofensa mía
el disimulo que apresto,
que a don Álvaro tomara
quitarle la vida luego,
mas de mi amante cuidado
quedo ahora, por consejo,
muerto para mi venganza
y vivo para mis celos.[42]
Y muerto disimulado,

41 The word *ser* in this phrase is a use of the Portuguese personal infinitive. In Spanish the phrase means, 'envidioso que Jacinta fuera dueño de mis sentidos.'

42 In standard Spanish syntax, this hyperbaton might read, 'El disimulo que apresto cuesta bien a la ofensa mía, que tomara quitarle la vida a don Álvaro luego, mas quedo ahora, por consejo de mi amante cuidado, muerto para mi venganza y vivo para mis celos.' In Spanish, the adverb *luego* means 'later,' but in Portuguese, *logo* signifies 'right now' or 'at this instant,' which is more likely the meaning in this passage.

Jealous of that beauty and of the loveliness of her eyes when I said goodbye, for she claimed that although the sinister Fates might keep me from returning to the port of Lisbon alive, she'd carry the memory of me so deeply in her heart that she'd never again love another.

I've been wanting to find out about this promise of hers by experimenting with feigning death so as to discover – since I know that Jacinta is about to get married – if Don Álvaro's desires have conquered the beauty I've been dying for and if she has rejected his courtship with the constancy I expect of one so refined. The dissembling I'm planning will cost me a great deal, for I'd love to take his life right now, but I've taken counsel from my love for her and will remain dead for my revenge and alive for my jealousy. As someone who's presumed dead, I'll save for another day

mejor ocasión reservo
para el desagravio mío,
que con el disfraz, que observo,
cuando esté más descuidado
y seguro, presumiendo
mi enemigo que no vivo,
tendrá con su muerte encuentros.
A tal disimulación,
amante celoso, apelo
para adquirir desengaños
de lo que a Jacinta debo,
mas para hacer más exacta
esta experiencia que emprendo
de su firmeza y confianza,
¿qué traza hallaré? ¿Qué medio?
Si amor tiene de enseñarme,
vamos a estudiar, Ingenio,
para dar en la salida
de mi amante desempeño.

Vase y sale[n] Hipólita y Dorotea.

Dorotea: Vea usted cómo ha de ser,
¿cómo tengo de decillo?[43]
Sin más detención mi anillo
al punto me ha de volver,
que estaba en mi cofrecillo.
Hipólita: Es usted muy confïada
cuando tanto se arrojó,
que mal de mí presumió,
que esto en mujer tan honrada
no sucede como yo.
Dorotea: Oh, pues, si a la honra va,
que en su merced resplandece,
cosa es que no se encarece.
Usted muy honrada será,
mas mi anillo no [a]parece.

43 In modern Spanish, *decillo* would be *decirlo*. In this *quintilla, decillo* rhymes with *anillo* and *cofrecillo*.

my response to the offenses committed against me. This disguise will help: when my enemy's not paying attention and thinks he's safe because he believes I'm dead, he'll meet his own death. As a jealous lover, I'll resort to such a masquerade so I can learn the truth about what loyalty I owe to Jacinta, but to perfect this experiment that tests her firm character and trustworthiness, what skills will I use? What means? If Love has something to teach me, my Wit, we will study ways to resolve the predicament with my beloved.

He exits and Hipólita and Dorotea enter.

Dorotea: You see how it has to be: how else can I say it? My ring, which was in my jewelry box, must be returned to me this second, and not a second later.

Hipólita: You're mighty sure of yourself, presuming that I did something so horrid; these things don't happen to an honorable woman like me.

Dorotea: Well, then, if we're talking about Your Grace's resplendent honor, that's something that no one else praises. You may be quite honorable, but my ring hasn't appeared. It's not the

No tiene ella culpa. ¿Sabe
quién esta culpa ha tenido?
Mi ama, que no ha advertido
que en ninguna casa cabe
quien no ha en su casa cabido,
y gente así deste talle
nunca ha sido de provecho.
A tal gente, de ver hecho,
que se ha de enseñar la calle,
pues no entra con pie derecho.

Hipólita: Hable bien, que si salimos
de nuestra casa, en verdad
que no ha sido liviandad,
porque solamente huimos
temiendo una adversidad.

Dorotea: Liviandad, no, a fe; inquietud
no tome usted, ni se asombre;
al tener en casa un hombre,
dale nombre de virtud.
Diga, mi reina, ¿a qué nombre?

Hipólita: De un primo, que en casa entró,
¿qué culpa puede formarse?
¿puede en eso repararse?

Dorotea: No, señora, y ¿que sé yo,
si el primo llegó a llamarse?
Y aun diciendo está su cara,
que tendrá usted buena treta
para de amor estafeta.

Hipólita: Cuando usted me lo enseñara,
fuera entonces alcahueta.

Dorotea: No soy mujer que de un vicio
tan afrentoso me venza,
que soy mujer de vergüenza.

Hipólita: Este interés del oficio
apunta su desvergüenza.

Enséñale el anillo.

ring's fault. Do you know who's to blame? My mistress, since she hasn't noticed that there's no room in any house for someone who doesn't fit in her own: people like that are never honest. When the truth comes out, you need to show them the street; they never enter on the right foot.

Hipólita: Be nice, for we were forced to leave our own home and we certainly didn't do so frivolously, because we were fleeing, fearing danger and adversity.

Dorotea: Frivolous, you? No, by my faith. Don't you worry; don't be frightened because you had a man in your house; make it sound virtuous. Tell me, my Queen, what was his name?

Hipólita: He was a cousin who entered the house. How can she be blamed for that? Does anyone even take notice?

Dorotea: No, ma'am, and what do I know if he was called a cousin? Your face shows that you'll be a good courier for lovers.

Hipólita: If I learned from you, I could become a procuress.

Dorotea: I'm not a woman who can be conquered by such an outrageous vice; I'm a woman of dignity, with a sense of shame.

Hipólita: This interest in the 'profession' signals how shameless you are. *She shows Dorotea the ring.*

Dorotea: (Miren la traza en que ha dado *[Aparte]*
para hacer la confesión
del hurto; buena razón,
y piensa que ha disfrazado
así su mala opinión.)

Hipólita: Pues diga, ¿puede negar,
que ha sido de mi señor
este anillo, que de amor
por anuncio usted le dar,[44]
se le daría en favor?

Dorotea: Yo con intento sencillo
le he llegado a recibir.

Hipólita: Así lo llego a advertir;
sin duda obispo de anillo
la quiso constituir.
Es usted muy linda joya
y ¡qué bella es la criatura!
Es una inocencia pura;
para hacer una tramoya
no vi más linda figura.

Dorotea: Con sus términos villanos
por lo menos no convengo.

Hipólita: Es una, pero no tengo
boca.

Dorotea: Pues yo tengo manos
con que de infames me vengo.

Dale.

Hipólita: Acudan, que una traidora,
mis señoras, me maltrata.

Dorotea: El anillo suelta, ingrata,
o te he de matar agora.

Hipólita: Acúdanme, que me mata.

Salen Jacinta y doña Beatriz.

---

44 The placement of the indirect object pronoun in this question follows a Portuguese pattern. In Spanish syntax, the pronoun would follow and be attached to the verb. The question would read, '¿puede negar que se le daría en favor por darle anuncio de amor?'

Dorotea: *Aside.* (Look at the trick she fell for to make her confess the theft. And great thinking: she believes this means she has disguised her bad judgment.)

Hipólita: Tell me, then: do you deny that this ring belongs to my master and that he's given it to you to announce his love?

Dorotea: I received it out of purely innocent intentions.

Hipólita: So noted. No doubt he wanted to turn it into a bishop's ring.[25] You're a fetching jewel, and your young mistress is so attractive! She's a pure innocent; there's no one lovelier for pulling off a scheme.

Dorotea: At least I don't use your villainous words.

Hipólita: It's actually only one word, but I have no mouth to say it aloud.

Dorotea: Well, I have hands to take revenge on despicable people. *She hits her.*

Hipólita: Come rescue me, my ladies: a traitor is beating me up!

Dorotea: Let go of the ring, you ungrateful fool, or I'll kill you right now!

Jacinta and Doña Beatriz enter.

---

25 A new Catholic bishop is consecrated by and receives a ring from his superior, a cardinal. The bishop's ring signifies his faithfulness to the Church; here, Hipólita mocks Dorotea, ironically insinuating that she is unfaithful.

Jacinta: ¿Qué es aquesto, Dorotea?
Doña Beatriz: Hipólita, ¿qué es aquesto?
Jacinta: Vuestro rumor manifiesto, …
Doña Beatriz: Vuestra impensada pelea, …
Jacinta: … ¿qué ha sido?
Doña Beatriz: … decidlo presto.
Hipólita: Señora, esta su crïada
osada me descompuso
y en mí, cruel, sus manos puso.
Dorotea: Si estoy, señora, culpada,
el castigo no rehúso,
mas tengo tanta razón,
que un anillo le pedí
que me ha tomado, y así
por no hacer restitución
contra ella me enfurecí.
Doña Beatriz: ¿Cómo a tal desenvoltura,
Hipólita, te atreviste,
que a Dorotea ofendiste?
Dime, ¿aquesa travesura
en mi casa la aprendiste?
Hipólita: Yo, como el anillo hallé
haber sido de tu hermano,
a restaurarlo me allano,
y por eso le tomé,
para volverlo a su mano.
Dorotea: Él me lo dio, por mi vida,
por más que he instado con él,
por corresponder fïel
con su urbanidad crecida,
como porte de un papel.
Jacinta: (A saber que no le quiero, *Aparte*
no tuviera ese primor.)
Doña Beatriz: (Si Jacinta tiene amor *Aparte*
a mi hermano, en ella espero
iris[45] contra su rigor.)

45 The *DRAE* defines 'iris de paz': 'persona que logra apaciguar graves discordias' or 'acontecimiento que influye para la terminación de algún disturbio' (2.1189).

Jacinta: What's this, Dorotea?

Doña Beatriz: Hipólita, what's going on?

Jacinta: Your loud voices, …

Doña Beatriz: Your poorly considered fighting, …

Jacinta: …what happened?

Doña Beatriz: …explain it quickly.

Hipólita: My lady, this brazen maid of hers annoyed me and laid her hands on me most cruelly.

Dorotea: If I'm to blame, my lady, I'll take my punishment, but I'm on the side of right. I asked her for a ring she took from me, and when she failed to make restitution, I flew into a rage against her.

Doña Beatriz: Hipólita, how dare you insult Dorotea so brazenly? Tell me, did you learn this type of mischief in my house?

Hipólita: When I found that the ring belonged to your brother, I stole it back so I could restore it to him, and that's why I took it, to return it to his hand.

Dorotea: On my life, no matter how much I insisted otherwise, in keeping with his great gentility he gave it to me because I bore him a letter.

Jacinta: *Aside.* (If he knew I don't love him, he wouldn't be so genteel.)

Doña Beatriz: *Aside.* (If Jacinta's in love with my brother, I hope she'll serve as a peacemaker against his cruelty.)

Jacinta: Pudieras disimular
más, Dorotea, tu queja,
que de urbanidad se aleja
con los huéspedes quebrar.
Doña Beatriz: Aquesa porfía deja,
Hipólita, y la sortija
da a Dorotea, que es suya.
Hipólita: Mi voluntad es la tuya.
Tome, hermana, y no se aflija,
ni de villana me arguya.

Va a darle el anillo.

Jacinta: Muestra este anillo. (Parece *Aparte*
que es el que a Clarindo di.
contra don Álvaro aquí
ya más mi sospecha crece.
¿Aquí mi anillo? ¡Ay de mí!)
En verdad que es pieza hermosa.
De mí le puedes fïar,
que ya te lo volveré a dar,
muestra a ver.
Dorotea: No hay que dudar;[46]
de ti fïaré la cosa
mejor que se puede hallar.
Doña Beatriz: Hagan las dos abrazadas
paces.
Dorotea: Basta que lo digas.

Abrázanse.

Hipólita: ¿Somos amigas?
Dorotea: Amigas,
que sólo son las crïadas
de sus amas enemigas.

Sale don Rodrigo.

46 Azevedo adds a sixth line to this *quintilla*.

Jacinta: Dorotea, you could do a better job of concealing your complaint; one can always politely walk away from ruining things with one's guests.

Doña Beatriz: Put an end to this stubbornness, Hipólita, and give the ring to Dorotea; it's hers.

Hipólita: Your wish is my command. Sister, take this and don't lament, or reproach me for being a villain. *She gives her the ring.*

Jacinta: Show me the ring. *Aside.* (It looks like the one I gave Clarindo. My suspicions against Don Álvaro are growing. My ring, here? Woe is me!) It truly is a beautiful piece of jewelry. You can trust me to give it back to you; let me see it.

Dorotea: I don't doubt that: I trust you more than anybody else with it.

Doña Beatriz: Embrace one another as a sign of peace between you.

Dorotea: You have only to ask. *They embrace.*

Hipólita: Are we friends?

Dorotea: Friends, for maids are only enemies of their mistresses.

Don Rodrigo enters.

Don Rodrigo: Ya, señora, me informé
y tengo claras noticias
del lance de vuestro hermano
con vuestro primo; con vida
están los dos.
Doña Beatriz: Dios os guarde,
señor, pues tanto me alivia
esa nueva que me dais
cuanto el corazón temía
que entre los dos sucediera
alguna grande desdicha.
Don Rodrigo: Lo que agora importa es
que en este caso se elija
el más prudente consejo,
para que aquí se consiga
contra tan penoso *abalo*,[47]
la bonanza más tranquila.
Doña Beatriz: ¿Qué consejo más prudente
puede deparar la dicha
en aflicción semejante
que el que mis desgracias fían
de esas venerables canas,
que la esperanza me animan
para en mis tribulaciones
hallar remedio o salida?
Don Rodrigo: Pues yo con vuestra licencia
voy buscar a toda prisa
vuestro hermano[48] y darle parte
de cómo en la casa mía
se queda vuestra persona,
con que viendo que mi hija
tiene tan grande amistad,
aunque la pena es precisa

47 *Abalo* is a Portuguese word meaning 'earthquake.'

48 This clause looks like a Portuguese construction; in Spanish the *ir* + infinitive construction requires an '*a*' and the phrase also requires a 'personal *a*' to mark the direct object. In standard Spanish, the phrase would read, 'Pues yo con vuestra licencia voy a buscar a toda prisa a vuestro hermano…'

Don Rodrigo: My lady, I've learned all the details regarding the incident between your brother and your cousin; they're both alive.

Doña Beatriz: May God keep you, sir, for this piece of news relieves me greatly; how my heart feared that a great misfortune had befallen the two of them.

Don Rodrigo: What matters now is that the most prudent advice be followed for this situation, so that we can experience the calm after the storm.

Doña Beatriz: What more prudent advice can bring me happiness in such an affliction than that provided by the wisdom of your years, which my misfortunes trust? You encourage my hope that you'll find a resolution to all my problems.

Don Rodrigo: With your permission, then, I'll hurry and look for your brother and inform him how you came to stay at my house. I'll say that even though your absence might cause him pain, seeing as how my daughter is such a dear friend, you'll be

que le dará vuestra ausencia,
quedará más divertida,
descansando su cuidado
– si hay descanso que se admita
en los cuidados de honor – ,
rogándole que permita
que deis a Alberto la mano,
pues no pierde su hidalguía
en esto por ser de Alberto
la nobleza bien sabida,
que mire las circunstancias
de la ocasión que le obliga
a aquesta resolución,
que de otra suerte peligra
la honra, que el qué dirán
pone mancha en la más limpia.
Y porque más se compongan
estas cosas, determina,
señora, mi voluntad,
cuando de aquesta se sirva,
ofrecerle – lo que a muchos
puede ser causa de envidia –
a mi hija por esposa,
que aunque es cierto que Jacinta
no se inclina a aqueste estado,
viendo como vuestra amiga
que hay conveniencia aquí vuestra
– pues vuestro hermano cumplida
la pretensión que aspiraba
de ser yerno mío ha días,
según lo que me ha constado
por señas que me lo indican,
con este gusto quizá
que vendrá en lo que le pidan,
olvidando pesadumbres,
que experiencias nos avisan
que a veces con un cuidado
otro cuidado se olvida –

better entertained by taking a break from your worries (if rest is really possible in worries concerning honor). I'll beg him to let you give Alberto your hand in marriage: no one's noble status will be affected by doing it this way since Alberto's nobility is well known. I'll tell him to look carefully at the circumstances of the situation, which force him to accept this resolution; any other approach places his honor in danger, for idle gossip will leave a stain on even the purest honor. And to make sure things are set right, my lady, when it's the right time, my will has determined to offer him something that many men would envy: my daughter as his wife. Indeed, based on signs he has given over the last few days, I'm quite sure your brother has been hoping to become my son-in-law, so maybe it'll make him so happy that he'll do what's asked of him and forget all his sorrows. After all, experience teaches us that at times one concern helps us forget another one. Although it's true that Jacinta isn't leaning towards getting married, when she sees that she'd be helping you, her friend, further your interests, my daughter will agree that

no dejará de inclinarse
a aqueste interés mi hija.
(En buena ocasión mi intento *Aparte*
repite aquesta conquista,
que es de su mano don Álvaro,
por cierto, persona digna.)

Doña Beatriz: (Plegue al cielo, que así sea.) *Aparte*

Jacinta: (Antes perderé mil vidas.) *Aparte*

Don Rodrigo: En tanto, de aquesta casa,
como vuestra casa misma,
servíos, señora, y tened
buen ánimo, que un buen día
espero en Dios que ha de darnos.
Ea, trata de divertirla. *(Vase.)*

Hipólita: Ya de amigas nuestras amas
pasarán a cuñaditas.

Dorotea: Y de amigas pasarán,
que amiga y cuñada implica.[49]

Clarindo: *(Dentro.)* ¿Quién quiere algo de la tienda?,
que traigo cosas muy lindas
de Génova, de Venecia,
de Alemania y de las Indias.

Llega Dorotea al paño.

Dorotea: Señora, va por la calle
vendiendo una caloyita[50]
muchas cosas tan airosa
que su gracia certifica

---

49 As Doménech explains, *implicar* used to mean 'to be opposite' of something (*La margarita*, 255). In his *Vocabulario portuguez e latino,* Bluteau defines *implicar*: 'Ser contrario. Ser huma cousa opposta a outra' (4.72).

50 The word *caloyita* likely comes from *caloyo,* a 'lamb' or 'kid.' Soufas suggests that the word may derive from *caló,* a Romany dialect spoken in Portugal, Spain, and France (*Women's Acts* 316). Doménech believes the word may be spelled with a cedilla: *çaloyita,* from the Portuguese word *saloio* (in Bluteau, also spelled *saloyo* and *çaloio*) (*La margarita*, 255). In the Midddle ages, *saloio* referred to a particular group of Moors who lived on the outskirts of Lisbon north of the Tagus river. S*aloios* came into Lisbon to sell their farm products. As a slang term, the word has come to mean 'peasant,' 'rustic,' or 'bumpkin' (Bluteau 7.450).

it's in her own interest as well. *Aside.* (That way, my plan produces a second victory when she gives Don Álvaro her hand in marriage; he's clearly worthy of it.)

Doña Beatriz: *Aside.* (I pray to Heaven that it be so.)

Jacinta: *Aside.* (I'll die a thousand times before that happens.)

Don Rodrigo: Meanwhile, consider this house your own, and be of good spirit, for I hope that God will grant us a good day. Come, try to amuse her. *He exits.*

Hipólita: Our mistresses will soon move from being girlfriends to sisters-in-law.

Dorotea: And they'll move beyond being friends, for 'friend' is the opposite of 'sister-in-law.'

Clarindo: *Off stage.* Who wants something from my little store? I'm bringing you lovely things from Genoa, from Venice, Germany, and the Indies.

Dorotea: *She goes to the screen at the side of the stage as if looking out a window.* Ma'am, a little lamb is coming down the street, selling things so happily that her grace guarantees that

que las vende muy baratas,
porque es de caras envidia
su cara.

Hipólita: Desas villanas
hay algunas muy bonitas.

Dorotea: ¿Llamémosla para *vermos*?[51]

Jacinta: Llámala si es que se inclina
doña Beatriz mi señora
a ver alguna cosita.

Doña Beatriz: Esto de curiosidades
gusto a los deseos brindan;
me holgaré de ver.

Dorotea: Mi reina,
llegue usted, suba acá arriba.

Hipólita: ¡El cielo influya en mi ama
comprarme algo,[52] que tenía
para prender el cabello
necesidad de unas cintas!

Sale Clarindo en hábito de mujer con una canastilla en la cabeza.

Clarindo: Dios guarde a vuesas mercedes.
(¡Qué bella es la compañía *Aparte*
que aquí con Jacinta está!,
bien que si a la luz se mira
de sus hermosos luceros,
toda belleza se eclipsa.)

Doña Beatriz: ¡Qué hermosa que es la muchacha!

Hipólita: De pascua es una carita.[53]

Jacinta: (¡Válgate Dios por mozuela! *Aparte*
No sé qué en su rostro miran
mis memorias, pues parece
de Clarindo copia viva.)

---

51 This is a use of the Portuguese personal infinitive, a construction which does not exist in Spanish. In Spanish the question means, '¿Llamémosla para que veamos?'

52 This clause looks like a Portuguese construction; in Spanish a preposition would be added: 'El cielo influya en mi ama para (*or* a) comprarme algo.'

53 The *DRAE* defines 'cara de pascua': 'cara apacible, risueña y placentera' (1.404).

her products must cost very little, because her countenance counts: the beauty of her face cheapens the facades of all others. Face it.

Hipólita: Some of those country lasses are truly fine-looking.

Dorotea: Shall we ask her in so we can see for ourselves?

Jacinta: Indeed, ask her in, as long as my lady Doña Beatriz would enjoy seeing her trinkets.

Doña Beatriz: I'd love to see novelties that bring pleasure.

Dorotea: *[Calling off stage.]* My Queen, come on up.

Hipólita: I hope heaven influences my mistress to buy me something, since I need some ribbons to tie back my hair.

Clarindo enters in women's clothing, with a basket on top of his head.

Clarindo: May the Lord keep Your Graces. *Aside.* (What attractive company Jacinta is keeping here, although when her lovely eyes sparkle with light, they eclipse all other beauty.)

Doña Beatriz: How beautiful the girl is!

Hipólita: What a pleasant face she has.

Jacinta: *Aside. (*My goodness, what an attractive girl! I don't know what in her face is triggering my memories, but she looks like a living copy of Clarindo.)

Clarindo: (Ya Jacinta cuidadosa *Aparte*
en mí repara. Amor, rija
bien mis disimulaciones,
a que en tal traje me anima
mi edad, que aun le faltan señas
por do el hombre se divisa.)
Dorotea: Veamos, pues, lo que aquí trae;
ponga usted la canastilla.
Jacinta: Y, ¿cómo se llama?
Clarindo: Clara. *Aparte*
(Aqueste nombre me sirva
de disfraz.)
Jacinta: (¡Aun semejanzas *Aparte*
– ¡ay, tristes memorias mías![54] –
tiene en parte de aquel nombre
por quien el alma suspira!)
Doña Beatriz: Bien es que Clara se llame
quien con tal donaire brilla.
Clarindo: No se burle, mi señora,
porque tengo de entendida
solamente el conocerme.
Hipólita: Descubra usted sus droguitas.[55]

Va enseñando.

Clarindo: Aquí tengo ricos guantes,
obra en verdad peregrina
de Milán, que dan de mano
a los de mayor estima.
De cristal claros espejos,
tan verdaderos, que avivan
a las feas desengaños,
si a las hermosas animan.

---

54 Here and in the first lines of Act 3, Azevedo alludes to Garcilaso de la Vega's 'Soneto X', 'Oh dulces prendas', which ends with the lines: 'sospecharé que me pusistes / en tantos bienes porque deseastes / verme morir entre *memorias tristes*' (emphasis ours).

55 The *DRAE* defines 'droga': 'Sustancia mineral, vegetal o animal, que se emplea en la medicina, en la industria o en las bellas artes' (1.779). In this context, *droguitas* refers to the cosmetics, potions, and trinkets 'Clara' might be selling.

Clarindo: *Aside.* (Jacinta is examining me carefully. Love, guide me as I disguise myself, since in this outfit my youth encourages me: you can't tell that I'm a man.)

Dorotea: Let's see what you've brought; put your basket here.

Jacinta: And what's your name?

Clarindo: Clara. *Aside.* (Let this name serve as my disguise.)

Jacinta: *Aside.* (Oh, sad memories – she even shares similarities in the name of the one who makes my soul sigh!)

Doña Beatriz: It's good that a person who sparkles with such elegance be named Clara.

Clarindo: Don't make fun, my lady, because I know little except myself.

Hipólita: Show us your cosmetics, potions, and trinkets.

Clarindo: *Showing each item and putting some on.*[26] Here are some luxurious gloves, exotic works from Milan, which bring esteem to the hands of those who wear them. Mirrors made of glass so true that they heighten the disappointment of ugly women and encourage beautiful ones. I bring rare rings of

26 'Clara's' descriptions of her wares are filled with jokes and wordplay.

De piedras inestimables
traigo aquí raras sortijas,
que no hay que poner el dedo
en más noble gallardía.
Medias de precio estimadas,
con quien las medias más finas
se llevan el lustre a medias,
que en éstas es sin medida.
Abanicos primorosos
que por su gala excesiva
del aire de su donaire,
aire el mismo aire mendiga.
Bolsillos de tanto precio
que cada dobla metida
en ellos dobla el valor
en más corriente valía.
Al fin, cintas, tan hermosa
traza del arte que afirma
que jamás hasta aquí se puso[56]
para parto igual en cinta.[57]

Jacinta: Bien sabe vender sus cosas.
Doña Beatriz: Cierto que es encarecida.
Hipólita: Maña tiene su lisonja.
Dorotea: El vender todo es mentira.
Hipólita: ¿Una docena de varas
cuánto destas cintas, diga,
me ha de costar?
Clarindo: Mil reales,
que las vendo baratillas.
Hipólita: ¿No más? ¿Viose tan barato?
Clarindo: Soy una mujer perdida.
Bien muestro que ha poco tiempo
aqueste oficio ejercita
quien tan mal sabe vender.

---

56 This line contains an extra syllable, nine rather than eight.

57 'Clara' plays with double meanings throughout this speech. For example, 'she' puns on the words *medias* (stockings), *a medias* (halfway), and *sin medida* (beyond measure); the word *donaire* (grace) and two meanings of the word *aire* (air and style); and *cintas* (ribbons), *parto* (birth), and *en cinta* (a play on the word *encinta,* which means pregnant).

precious stones that make one's fingers look especially fine. Priceless stockings; they'll bring you pleasure; the finest hose till now are but half the treasure, for the splendor of these is beyond measure. Exquisite fans, which due to the great splendor they share, dare to bear the grace that begs air from air itself.[27] Purses of such value that each doubloon put inside them doubles the amount of its current value. Finally, ribbons of such beautiful design that Art affirms that never before has anyone spawned superior strips of beribboned substance.

Jacinta: She certainly knows how to sell her wares.

Doña Beatriz: It's true: she can really urge people to spend their money.

Hipólita: She has the knack of knowing how to flatter people.

Dorotea: Salesmanship is all about telling lies.

Hipólita: Tell me, how much will a dozen yards of these ribbons cost me?

Clarindo: A thousand *reales*;[28] I'm selling them cheap.

Hipólita: Not more? Have you ever seen anything cost so little?

Clarindo: I'm a lost woman, and it's easy to see that someone who doesn't know how to sell has only been practicing this trade for just a little while.

---

27 Mujica offers a persuasive translation: 'Lovely fans, so breathtaking that they make the air itself gasp for breath' (244).

28 A *real* is a Spanish coin used between the fourteenth and eighteenth centuries.

Hipólita: ¿Cuánto tiene desta vida?
Clarindo: Algunos piensan que es muerte.
No tengo un mes todavía.
Jacinta: Dígame, ¿cuál es su patria?
Clarindo: Hay de aquí allá muchas millas.
Jacinta: ¿Cuál es?
Clarindo: Yo soy saboyana;
nací en la ciudad de Nisa.
Jacinta: ¿Qué la ha traído a Lisboa?

Clarindo: Palabras de hombres fingidas
que engañan a las mujeres.
Pues en la ocasión lucida
de la armada en que Lisboa
dejó la tierra turina
de admiración de su gala
tan llena, que aun hoy se admira, …
Jacinta: (Verdugo es esa memoria *Aparte*
para un alma tan sentida.)
Clarindo: …cierto galán desta corte,
por amistad que tenía
con mi padre, tuvo entrada
– confianza mal permitida –
en su casa, y tantas veces
me habló que la cortesía
se hizo amor, que estas dos cosas
siempre fueron muy vecinas.
Con promesa al fin de esposo
– ¡oh promesa fementida! – ,
me robó amante la joya
que en el mundo más se estima.
Con la armada en fin partióse,
diciendo a la despedida
que iba a disponer sus cosas
y que entonces volvería
para ponerse en efecto
la palabra prometida.
Viendo, pues, que de la vuelta

Hipólita:	How long have you lived this life?
Clarindo:	Some people think it's not life, but death. Not quite a month.
Jacinta:	Tell me, where are you from?
Clarindo:	It's many miles from here to there.
Jacinta:	What is it?
Clarindo:	I'm from Savoy; I was born in the city of Nice.
Jacinta:	What has brought you to Lisbon?
Clarindo:	Feigned words of men, who deceive women. On the magnificent occasion of the armada in which so many from Turin were filled with admiration for Lisbon's elegance and pomp that even today they still admire…
Jacinta:	*Aside*. (That memory torments my sensitive soul.)
Clarindo:	…a certain gallant of this court, due to the friendship he had with my father, was given entry to his house (what ill-advised permission!). He spoke to me so often that the courtesy turned into love, for these two things live near one another. Finally, with the promise that he'd marry me – oh, false promise! – my lover robbed me of the most esteemed jewel in the entire world. He finally left with the armada, saying as he departed that he'd make arrangements and would then return to fulfill his promise to marry me. Later, seeing that the time he had

el plazo pasado había
que me dio, por engañada
me di luego en su malicia,
y hurtando a mi padre joyas
y dineros, ofendida
y mujer – dos circunstancias
que un arrojo facilitan – ,
de hombre el hábito tomando
y alquilando a toda prisa
una mula, que ligera
de Belerefonte hacía
olvidado el bruto alado,
conmigo en la Corte Villa[58]
di, y con igual brevedad
en aquesta esclarecida
ciudad, y por este ingrato
haciendo varias pesquisas,
no he sabido parte dél,
con que pienso fue mentira
y que me supuso el nombre,
pues por él no hallo noticias.
Y viendo que una mujer
de aqueste trato tenía
libertad para correr
las calles y desta guisa
entrarse en cualquiera casa,
me ha animado a que le siga
por si topo su persona
ingrata y desconocida.

Jacinta: ¡Caso extraño! Desa suerte
también puede ser fingida
su patria y no ser Lisboa.

Clarindo: Tal mi desgracia sería,
pero como aquesta corte
es una feria continua,
a que acude tanta gente,
no será gran maravilla
toparle.

58 As Doménech indicates, the *Villa y Corte* is another name for Madrid (*La margarita*, 261).

given me for his return had passed, I considered myself deceived by his malice, and stealing jewels and money from my father, as one offended and as a woman (two circumstances that facilitate an act of daring), wearing male clothing and renting a mule even lighter than Bellerophon's Pegasus,[29] I found myself in Madrid, and shortly thereafter I arrived here in this illustrious city.[30] I began making various inquiries about the backstabber, but I haven't heard any reports of him, which leads me to think it was all a lie and he was using an assumed name with me. And seeing that a woman who's selling things is free to go up and down the streets and as such, can enter any house she chooses, I've been motivated to keep on going in case I run into this ungrateful person.

Jacinta: How strange! It may also be the case that he didn't tell the truth about where he's from and if he's really from Lisbon.

Clarindo: That would be a disaster for me, but since this court is a continuous festival that draws people from all over, it'll be more than possible to run into him.

29 Pegasus, the winged horse, traveled swiftly because he could fly.

30 Early modern Lisbon was probably the most cosmopolitan city in Europe; it was filled with foreign embassies and merchants who could arrive with ease at the port on the Tagus River.

Jacinta: ¿Y cómo era el nombre,
que ese galán se ponía?
Clarindo: Muy bien la mentira entablo. *Aparte*
Se llamaba…
Alberto: *(Dentro.)* Me permita,
don Rodrigo, mi señor,
licencia vueseñoría
para besarle la mano.
Hipólita: Señora, esta voz se indica
de tu primo.
Doña Beatriz: ¿Cómo es esto?
Hipólita: Como el amor adivina,
habrá sabido sin duda
que aquí estás.
Doña Beatriz: Si mi salida
ha sido tan impensada,
no es posible.
Jacinta: Él se visita
con mi padre muchas veces,
y así aquesta su venida
será por ese respecto.
Dorotea: ¿Hay más de que se despida?
Pues mi señor no está en casa.
Doña Beatriz: Dorotea se lo diga.
Hipólita: No, que licencia dará
para cuatro palabritas
Jacinta.
Jacinta: Yo le doy lugar.
Quita esos trastes, Clarilla,
y recojámonos todas.
Doña Beatriz: Eso no. Sin que me asista
tu persona, no he de hablarle.
Jacinta: Yo no tengo de ser vista.
Clarindo: (Aqueso es lo que me agrada.) *Aparte*
Doña Beatriz: Queda tú en mi compañía,
Hipólita.
Hipólita: Abierta está
la puerta.

Jacinta: And what name did this gallant use?

Clarindo: *Aside.* (I'm doing a good job establishing the lie.) His name was…

Alberto: *Off stage.* My lord Don Rodrigo, I request license from your Excellence to kiss your hand.

Hipólita: My lady, that sounds like your cousin's voice.

Doña Beatriz: How can that be?

Hipólita: Because Love is so good at deducing things, he undoubtedly will have figured out that you're here.

Doña Beatriz: That's impossible, since my departure was so unplanned.

Jacinta: He often visits my father, so he must have come for that reason.

Dorotea: Shall I show him out? My master isn't home.

Doña Beatriz: Dorotea can tell him.

Hipólita: No; that'll give Jacinta permission to say 'just four little words'.

Jacinta: I'll leave, then. Clarilla, take off all your trinkets, and let's gather up our things.

Doña Beatriz: Not that. If you're not here to help me, I'm not talking to him.

Jacinta: I don't have to be seen.

Clarindo: *Aside.* (That's what I like to hear.)

Doña Beatriz: Stay here with me, Hipólita.

Hipólita: The door's open.

Vanse las tres[59] *y se quedan Beatriz e Hipólita.*

Doña Beatriz: Y mi alma afirma
que abiertas están las suyas.
Hipólita: Entre quien es; suba arriba.

Sale Alberto.

Alberto: Beatriz mía, ¿qué ventura
es la que Amor me depara,
pues aquí – ¡quién tal pensara! –
me encuentro con tu hermosura?
Ausente de tu luz pura,
cuando el alma le anochece,
¿ya la aurora le aparece?
¿Son del deseo esto antojos,[60]
pues la estrella de tus ojos
por milagro me amanece?
¿Qué milagro es este, amores?
¿Qué novedad, prima mía?
Dime, mi bien, ¿por qué vía
debo a Amor estos favores?
Hipólita: Esto fueran *dissabores*
que de mi señor temió,
y así tanto que le vio
de espadas contigo hacerse,
temió en el juego perderse,
con que afuera se salió.
Doña Beatriz: Dirás que fue demasía
y arrojo en una doncella,
pero por todo atropella
de un temor la cobardía,
y como es amiga mía
Jacinta, a su casa apelo,
asaltada del recelo

59 'Las tres' refers here to the three women, including 'Clara' (Clarindo) as one of the women.

60 In standard Spanish syntax, this hyperbaton might read '¿Esto [the "miracle" of Alberto finding Beatriz at Rodrigo's house] son antojos del deseo…' A similar case occurs in line 1879, 'Esto *dissabores* fueran que…'

The three women [Jacinta, 'Clara,' and Dorotea] exit, and Beatriz and Hipólita remain.

Doña Beatriz: And my soul affirms that theirs are open, too.

Hipólita: Enter, whoever you are; come on upstairs.

Alberto: *Enters*. My Beatriz, what good fortune Love has offered me, for I find myself here with your beauty (Who would have thought it possible?). Your pure light is absent when nightfall darkens the soul; does Dawn now appear? Are these the cravings of desire, since the star of your eyes dawns as a miracle for me? What miracle is this, Love? What liberation, my cousin? Tell me, dear one, how is it that I owe Love for these favors?

Hipólita: Maybe they were the disfavors that she feared from my master. And so, when she saw your cousin dueling with you, fearing she'd be killed in the process, she left.

Doña Beatriz: You could say it was all intemperance and daring in a young woman, but the cowardice of fear tramples all else. And since Jacinta is my friend, I appealed to her house to protect

del peligro de los dos,
aunque más, primo, por vos
se empeñaba mi desvelo.
¿Pero qué milagro, primo,
es el que hace a mi deseo
aquí el amor? Pues que veo
sin esperar lo que estimo.

Alberto: A don Rodrigo me animo
de amor en este accidente
mi amigo a pedir que intente
a don Álvaro ablandar
su prudencia, que acabar
suele un gran pleito un prudente.[61]

Hipólita: Los dos que estaban parece
hablados, que a mi señor
ya fue del viejo el primor
hablar en lo que se ofrece.[62]
Mucho en el mundo acontece;
vino el suceso pintado.

Doña Beatriz: Don Rodrigo es tan honrado
que esto tomó por su cuenta,
y lo que mi hermano intenta
presto verá mi cuidado.

Alberto: ¿Y qué hombres – pregunto yo –
serían, Beatriz, aquellos
que subieron y uno de ellos
a los dos nos apartó?

Hipólita: ¿Quién sabe acá quién entró?
¿Viene celos a pedir?
Sólo aqueso por venir
falta ahora a mi señora.

---

61 In Spanish, this hyperbaton requires another preposition; standard syntax would read: 'En este accidente de amor, a don Rodrigo, mi amigo, me animo a pedir que intente su prudencia [a] ablandar a don Álvaro, que un prudente suele acabar un gran pleito.'

62 This clause is another example of the Portuguese *ir* + infinitive construction. In standard Spanish, the phrase requires an '*a*' and would read, 'el primor del viejo ya fue [a] hablar a mi señor en lo que se ofrece.'

me, as I'm assaulted by the suspicion of danger from the two of you, although you, cousin, are the source of most of my sleepless nights. But what miracle, cousin, is Love giving my desire, for I see the one I cherish without having to wait any longer?

Alberto: In this accident of love, I'm encouraged to ask of my friend Don Rodrigo that his prudence try to assuage Don Álvaro, for a prudent man can often resolve a great dispute.

Hipólita: It seems the two have spoken, because the skillful old man already went to talk to my master about the various possibilities offered. A lot can happen in the world; he presented the case in detail.

Doña Beatriz: Don Rodrigo is so honorable to step in of his own accord. I'll soon learn whatever my brother is planning.

Alberto: And I've been wondering, Beatriz, who were the men who climbed the stairs and separated the two of us?

Hipólita: Who knows? Are you going to act all jealous? That's all my lady needs now.

Alberto: Celos no, porque la adora
mi alma sin los admitir.

Doña Beatriz: Yo de aqueso no sé nada,
que por otra puerta fui
así que[63] a mi hermano[64] vi
sacar contra ti la espada,
quedando de ansias cercada,
presumiendo un mal extraño,
hasta que de aqueste daño
me aseguré, que a mi ruego,
me dio, informándose luego
don Rodrigo el desengaño.

Hipólita: No se hable en aqueso más;
a lo hecho no hay remedio.
Lo que importa es ver si es medio
el viejo de aquesta paz.

Alberto: Y si no fuere eficaz,
¿qué haremos, amor?

Doña Beatriz: Sufrir,
penar, callar y sentir.

Alberto: Eso es la vida acabar.

Hipólita: Pues yo os tengo de ayudar
a los dos a bien morir.
No se anticipe la pena
y póngase ahora pausa
a la ternura, que causa
escrúpulo en casa ajena.

Alberto: Hasta ver, pues, lo que ordena
en este de amor vaivén
la fortuna, adiós,[65] mi bien.

Doña Beatriz: Adiós, que tendré memoria
de avisarte.

Hipólita: Y después gloria
por siempre jamás, amén. *(Vanse.)*

---

63 In Spanish, the adverbial phrase *así que* means 'thus.' In Portuguese, *assim que* means 'as soon as,' which seems to be the sense here.

64 In the source text, *hermana.*

65 In the source text, this word always appears as *a Dios.*

Alberto: Jealous? No, because my soul adores her and won't let jealousy enter.

Doña Beatriz: I don't know anything about that since I left by another door as soon as I saw my brother draw his sword against you; I was surrounded by my anxieties, believing that some awful thing was going to happen. I finally reassured myself about that danger: Don Rodrigo later filled me in on what had happened.

Hipólita: Don't talk about it anymore; what's done is done. What matters is to learn if the old man is able to achieve this peace.

Alberto: And if he isn't successful, what will we do, my love?

Doña Beatriz: Suffer, live in torment, say nothing, and lament.

Alberto: That's death.

Hipólita: Well, I'm here to help you both have a good death. Don't anticipate your suffering nor put a halt to your tenderness, for that can cause problems for others.

Alberto: Until I see what Fortune ordains in this seesaw of love, good-bye, darling.

Doña Beatriz: Good-bye; I'll keep you apprised of what's going on.

Hipólita: And after that, glory forever and ever, amen. *They exit.*

Salen don Rodrigo y don Álvaro.

Don Álvaro: Si acaso, señor mío,
de honor en las adversas ocasiones
puede un dolor impío
algunas permitir satisfacciones,
con la nueva mi pecho
que me dais queda en parte satisfecho.
Si amparado se hubiera
en la desatención en que ha caído,
de alguna que no fuera
vuestra casa, Beatriz, que le ha valido,
por este arrojo osado
no pasara, mas fuese a lo sagrado.
Que mucho me costara,
de su recato en tal descompostura
que a otra parte llegara
de un tan grande desaire la censura,
mas en vuestra nobleza
ha tomado buen puerto su flaqueza.
Y así, pues no se suelda
la menor quiebra – que es un *vidro*[66] fino –
del honor, que una celda
de un convento la oculte determino.
Por vos, pues, si la muerte
no le doy, la sepulto de esta suerte.

Don Rodrigo: Eso es dar ocasión,
para que de Beatriz, contra el decoro,
alguna presunción
se atreva a concebir algún desdoro
y de honra las materias
piden unas consultas mucho serias.[67]
Lo que bien me parece,

66 In the source text, this word is spelled in Portuguese. The Spanish spelling (in Covarrubias and today) is *vidrio.*

67 This looks like a Portuguese construction; the adverb *muito* can modify nouns, adjectives and other adverbs. In Spanish, the adverb *mucho* modifies nouns and *muy* modifies adjectives and adverbs. In standard Spanish this clause would read, 'las materias de honra piden unas consultas *muy* serias.'

Don Rodrigo and Don Álvaro enter.

Don Álvaro: My lord, if a terrible pain in the adversities of honor can allow some measure of satisfaction, the news you've given me has helped satisfy my heart. If Beatriz had sought shelter and protection from the disregard into which she has fallen in any house other than yours, she wouldn't have gotten through this dangerous mess. In such an insult to her modesty, it would have cost me dearly had she gone and been censured elsewhere, but her weakness has found a safe haven in your nobility. And so, since the smallest failure of honor, as fragile as fine glass, can't be patched up, I've determined to hide her in a convent cell. Because of you, I won't kill her, but I'll bury her this way.

Don Rodrigo: Against all decency, that will produce suspicions of dishonor against Beatriz, and matters of honor should be taken very seriously. What seems good to me, since Alberto is your

pues Alberto es su deudo y caballero,
que su mano merece,
que se case con él.

Don Álvaro: Yo considero,
que por aqueste modo
se hace la presunción cierta de todo.
Pues viéndose que Alberto
es tan pobre y Beatriz tan bien dotada,
el escrúpulo advierto
del vulgo, si con él la ve casada.

Don Rodrigo: No hace desigualdad
la pobreza, en la sangre y calidad.[68]
Si Alberto y Beatriz, pues,
son iguales, no puede esto extrañarse,
y cuando digan que es
efecto que de amor pudo causarse,
no se agravian primores
de honor, que muchos casan por amores.
Y si así se mejora,
don Álvaro, de honor aqueste susto,
no saldrá esta señora
de mi casa sin darme aqueste gusto.
Y cabal porque sea,
ya vengo en lo que vuestro amor desea,
que a Jacinta bien sé
pagáis – nada se esconde – ha muchos días
– que a porfías se ve
de paseos – de amor idolatrías.

Don Álvaro: El alma a esa señora
nunca puede negar cuanto la adora,
mas tan poca privanza
mi amor con su agasajo ha merecido,
que ni aún confianza
de poderla mirar he conseguido.

Don Rodrigo: Su recato excesivo
jamás verse ha dejado de hombre vivo.

---

68 In the source text, *qualidad.* The two words *calidad* and *cualidad* both existed since the Middle Ages and were sometimes used interchangeably.

relative and a gentleman who merits her hand, is that she marries him.

Don Álvaro: I believe that if they follow that path, the suspicions about them will ring true. Since Alberto is so poor and Beatriz has such a big dowry, I'll notice the misgivings of the masses if they see her married to him.

Don Rodrigo: Poverty doesn't create inequality in a person's blood and quality. If Alberto and Beatriz are equal in rank, then it can't seem too strange, and if people say that the effects of love are what led them to get married, the delicate nature of honor isn't offended, as many people marry for love. And so, Don Álvaro, if this resolves your anxieties regarding honor, the lady will not leave my home without giving me the pleasure of arranging her marriage. And because that marriage is perfectly proper, with regard to what your love desires, I know (for you can't hide anything from me) that you've been worshipping Jacinta for quite a while.

Don Álvaro: My soul can never deny how much I love that woman, but she has paid me so little attention that I haven't even had the confidence to look at her.

Don Rodrigo: Her extreme discretion has never allowed any living man to see her.

Don Álvaro: Y si muerto algún hombre
pudiera ser testigo, lo afirmara.
Don Rodrigo: ¿Qué decís?
Don Álvaro: No os asombre;
mi amor con esta carta se declara.

Dale un papel, y lee para sí don Rodrigo.

También curiosidades
hubo allá, si hubo acá facilidades.
(Para que don Rodrigo *Aparte*
sepa, si a Beatriz fácil amor pinta,
que en la carta testigo
halla de que lo fue también Jacinta,
y no sola mi hermana
se quede con la nota de liviana.)
Aunque yo sí muy bien creo
– porque todo Clarindo me decía –
que en el honesto aseo
de Jacinta, no ha habido demasía,
sino honesta afición,
cual de Beatriz me enseña la opinión.
Don Rodrigo: Admirado me deja,
don Álvaro, esta carta, pues juzgaba
de Jacinta mi queja,
viendo como a casar no se inclinaba,
que en el mundo no hubiera
hombre alguno que bien le pareciera.
¿Hay caso como aquesto?
No hay formar de mujeres pareceres;
engaño es manifiesto
fïar en condiciones de mujeres.
Don Álvaro: No, pues, aqueste antojo
os venga a ocasionar algún enojo,
que yo desde aquí me ofrezco,
no sólo por esposo, mas crïado
ya ser suyo apetezco.
Y pues por su constancia – que he estimado –
que ya el alma la imagina,

Don Álvaro: And if a dead man were a witness, he'd affirm it, too.
Don Rodrigo: What are you saying?
Don Álvaro: Don't be shocked; this letter testifies to my love.

He gives him a letter, and Don Rodrigo reads it in silence.

Don Álvaro: *Aside.* (The letter reveals both indiscretions and opportunities. Don Rodrigo now knows that although Beatriz is portrayed as a bit wayward in matters of love, the letter describes Jacinta's behavior as well: my sister isn't the only one who'll look capricious. I certainly believe – since Clarindo explained everything – that there was nothing improper in Jacinta's honorable behavior, only virtuous affection, which offers me a similar perspective regarding Beatriz.

Don Rodrigo: Don Álvaro, your letter surprises me, for I'd been judging Jacinta harshly, complaining that the reason she was rejecting marriage was because there wasn't a man alive who seemed good enough for her. Have you ever heard of something like this? We should form no opinions concerning women; it's clearly a mistake to trust their character.

Don Álvaro: Don't let what you suggest annoy you; from here on out, I not only offer myself as Jacinta's husband, but I'd also be honored to serve you. And because she was so faithful to

como con otro fue, conmigo fina
no tiene de admitirme,
sin que sepa quién dio a Clarindo muerte
Jacinta, he de servirme
de vos en la respuesta desta suerte,
que está tan admitida
de mí aquesta su cláusula advertida,
que cuando ella quisiere,
el homicida tengo de mostrarle.

Don Rodrigo: Adiós, pues, que Dios quiere
sin duda a mi vejez buen yerno darle. *(Vase.)*

Don Álvaro:[69] A Lisardo debiendo
la traza estoy que cauteloso emprendo,
y con qué agradecerle
la fineza no tengo en cuanto valgo.
¿Do estará para hacerle
presente lo que pasa aqueste hidalgo?
Para darle le espero
cuenta como a un amigo verdadero. *(Vase.)*

Sale Clarindo.

Clarindo: Ya la celosa invención
e industriosa estratagema,
que hallé para de Jacinta
entrar en la casa mesma,
he visto tan bien[70] lograda,
que a mí Jacinta me ruega
a que me quede en su casa,
obligándome a que venga
buscar a aquesta posada[71]
mis ropas que aquí se albergan,
y haga a su casa mudar
mis trastes con diligencia.
Que como ha considerado

69 Identified as *D. Alb[erto]* in the source text.

70 In the source text, *tambien.*

71 This clause looks like a Portuguese construction; in Spanish a preposition would be added: 'obligándome a que venga a buscar a aquesta posada mis ropas.'

another man, which I do believe is true, Jacinta won't accept me until she finds out who killed Clarindo. I must use your help in responding, for she won't be mine till this condition is met: when she wants me to do so, I have to show her the murderer.

Don Rodrigo: Go with God, then, for God doubtless wants to give me a good son-in-law in my old age. *He exits.*

Don Álvaro: I owe Lisardo a great deal for this plan that I'm so cautiously undertaking, and I don't know how I can ever repay him. Where can he be? I need to let him know what this noble old man is up to. I want to tell him all about it, since he's such a true friend. *He exits.*

Clarindo enters.

Clarindo: I've now also succeeded in my scheme to enter Jacinta's home, for she's begging me to stay there, which means I need to get the clothes and trinkets I left at the inn and move them to her house. From my hints and descriptions of that gallant

por las *inculcas*[72] y señas
que le di de aquel galán
que he dicho me supusiera
el nombre para engañarme,
– y a la verdad bien lo piensa
en cuanto a la ofensa mía –
que es don Álvaro, y desea
su padre con él casarla,
con pie de que se concierta
así de Beatriz su hermana
el alboroto, pues ella
de su casa se ha valido,
tomando ya por su cuenta
de don Álvaro aplacar
el rencor de tal manera
que con Alberto, su primo,
que case su hermana quiera.
Viendo que en esto vendrá,
pues le dan en recompensa
de su pesadumbre un gusto,
pues ha mucho tiempo anhela
de Jacinta ser esposo,
y como ella le desprecia,
así por poco inclinada
como por tener sospecha
– según lo que me ha advertido –
que de mi muerte – supuesta –
fue el actor, quiere que yo
acompañándole *este[j]a*[73]
para conmigo embargar
la ejecución que se espera,
diciendo que no se casa
con quien dio a otra doncella
su palabra. Hasta aquí miro
constancia en Jacinta bella,

72 *Inculca* is a Portuguese noun, which in this context means ‘suggestion’ or ‘hint.’

73 In the source text, *estea,* a combination of letters that does not exist as a word in Spanish or Portguese. The Spanish form *esté* does not fit the rhyme scheme, but the Portuguese *esteja* does.

who feigned his name to deceive me (and she's right that he committed an offense against me in deceiving me), she has concluded that the villain is Don Álvaro; her father wants to marry Jacinta to him as soon as he arranges an agreement about all the uproar with Beatriz, who has also taken shelter in their house. Don Rodrigo has taken on the task of calming Don Álvaro's wrath to such an extent that he'll let his sister marry her cousin Alberto. Seeing that it's all coming together, in recompense they're giving him some pleasure to balance his grief, since he has long hoped to become Jacinta's husband. And (as I've been informed), since she despises him and refuses to marry him because she suspects he was the actor behind my (supposed) death, Jacinta wants me to join her in taking control of the performance she expects to pull off and stop the marriage by saying that she can't marry someone who gave his word to another. Up to now my lovely

de aquí adelante veremos
como en ella persevera,
porque no he [de] descubrirme
hasta apurar la fineza.

Sale[n] Lisarda y Papagayo.

Lisarda: ¿Aquí dices que le has visto?
Papagayo: Aquí – aun el alma me tiembla –
con mis ojos pecadores

le vi, mas ésta tu tema
me admira, que es desatino
procurar que te aparezca
un muerto.
Lisarda: Está en mi cuidado,
Papagayo, tan impresa
la memoria de Clarindo,
que aun muerto el alma quisiera
visitarle.
Papagayo: Pues supón
que la fortuna reserva
ese encuentro para mí,
porque de nosotros tenga
cada uno su aventura.
Porque tú – según me cuentas –
encontraste al matador
cuando conmigo se encuentra
el muerto, mas yo reparo
en que hasta aquí tu cautela
no me ha dicho quién ha sido.
Lisarda: (No le he dicho por vergüenza *Aparte*
de ver que el amor me embarga
la venganza de mi ofensa.)
Aun lo sabrás, Papagayo.
Mira, ¿qué fregona es ésta?
¿Será acaso del mesón?

Jacinta has been faithful, so we'll see how it goes from here on out, because I won't reveal myself till it's time.

Lisarda and Papagayo enter, speaking to one another.

Lisarda: Did you say this is where you've seen him?

Papagayo: Here's where I saw him with my own sinful eyes (even my soul is trembling), but the whole subject overwhelms me, since it's folly to try to raise a dead man.

Lisarda: Papagayo, Clarindo's memory is so imprinted in my brain that even though he's dead, my soul would like to visit him.

Papagayo: Well, suppose Fate has reserved this encounter for me, so each one of us can have our own adventure. You're telling me you found the killer when the dead man found me, but I have some qualms about the fact that up till now you've been careful not to reveal who it is.

Lisarda: *Aside.* (I haven't told you because I'm ashamed that Love is keeping me from avenging the offense against me.) You'll know soon, Papagayo. Look, what kitchen maid is that? Do you think she might be the one from the inn?

Papagayo: Será, que en las mesoneras
como hacen las cuentas caras,
hay caras de mucha cuenta.[74]

Lisarda: Cierto que la moza es bella.

Clarindo: (Papagayo es él que miro *[Aparte]*
y éste que con él se acerca,
su amo será sin duda,
con quien dijo que viniera
de Lamego. Pero dudo
que de aquella ciudad sea,
que galán de aqueste talle
jamás le he visto en mi tierra.
Gentilhombre es en verdad
y si así como fue hembra
mi hermana, fuera varón,
y fuera viva,[75] dijera
que era la misma.)

Lisarda: ¿No miras *[A Papagayo]*
lo mucho que se asemeja
con el semblante a Clarindo?
¡Ay, si mi hermano[76] viviera
y así como fue varón
fuera mujer, con firmeza
afirmara que era él mismo!

Papagayo: Yo no, que aun me representa
el miedo aquí su persona
y hallo mucha diferencia
de aquesta cara que mata
para aquella cara muerta,[77]
si no es que en cuerpo le he visto

---

74 Papagayo puns on the double meanings of the words *caras* and *cuentas.* The 'cuentas caras' are bills that cost a lot. Papagayo suggests here that table maids add extra charges to a customer's bill. The 'caras de mucha cuenta' are faces that really count (beautiful faces).

75 Clarindo might consider his sister '*muerta al mundo'* (dead to the world), because he believes she has entered a convent to become a nun.

76 In the source text, *hermana.*

77 Papagayo puns on the phrases *aquesta cara que mata* (this face that kills, i.e., with its beauty) and *aquella cara muerta* (that dead face).

Papagayo: She must be, for innkeepers' *charges* are quite *dear*, so it makes sense that the *dear, dear* girls who work there would *charge* quite a lot.

Lisarda: The girl certainly is lovely.

Clarindo: *Aside.* (I see Papagayo, and the one near him is doubtless his master, with whom he said he came from Lamego. But I don't think he's from there; I've never seen any gallant in my land who resembles him. He's truly a noble *man*, and if my sister wasn't dead to the world in a convent and was instead a man, I'd declare he was she.)

Lisarda: *To Papagayo.* Don't you see how much that person's face resembles Clarindo's? Oh, if my brother was alive and was a woman instead of a man, I'd insist she was he!

Papagayo: Not me, since that body still scares me. I see a lot of difference between this gorgeous *killer face* and that *dead face* unless what I saw before was his walking corpse, and

y será su alma aquesta
Clarinda, porque en el nombre
todas las almas son hembras.
Lisarda: Apropinquémonos más.[78]
Clarindo: (Retírome, que se acercan *[Aparte]*
y entiendo que en mí reparan.)
Lisarda: Aguarde usted.
Clarindo: ¿Qué me ordenan?
Papagayo: No ordenamos, que no somos
obispos,[79] si es que lo piensa.[80]
Lisarda: ¿Es cierto que por aquí,
diga, una sombra se muestra
que dicen ser de un Clarindo,
si es de casa?
Clarindo: (Aquesta nueva *Aparte*
manifestó Papagayo.)
De casa soy yo y de veras
por aquí esa sombra anduvo
y ha días que no se encuentra.
Lisarda: ¿Y usted le ha visto también?
Clarindo: También y de la manera
que ustedes viéndome están,
pero en casa más enteras
noticias le pueden dar,
que yo soy criada y la mesa
a un huésped voy a poner.
Papagayo: Añada dos servilletas
para los dos, que aquí estamos.
Clarindo: El dinero hace la cuenta. *(Vase.)*
Papagayo: ¿Quieres aun de mi verdad
más clara y evidente prueba?
El buen Clarindo sin duda
de misas alguna deuda
tenía, y así voló [en] tanto

78 *Apropincuarse,* an infrequently used verb in Spanish, means *acercarse*.
79 Papagayo puns on the word *ordenar,* which means both 'order' and 'ordain.'
80 In the source text, a question.

this Clarinda[31] is his soul, which I say because everyone knows that the word for soul is feminine.

Lisarda: Let's get a little closer.

Clarindo: I'd better leave, since they're approaching and I can tell that they've noticed me.

Lisarda: Wait.

Clarindo: What are you ordering me to do?

Papagayo: We're not ordering or even ordaining, because we're not bishops in holy orders, in case you might think so.

Lisarda: Tell me, is it true that the spirit of someone named Clarindo is showing itself around here?

Clarindo: *Aside.* (Papagayo is the one who reported that bit of information.) I live here, and the spirit really did walk around, and we haven't come across him in days.

Lisarda: And you've also seen him?

Clarindo: Yes, I have, and looking just like you see me now, but they can give you more details inside, since I'm a maid and need to set the table for a guest.

Papagayo: Add napkins for two, because the two of us are here.

Clarindo: The money pays the bills. *He exits.*

Papagayo: Do you want me to offer you an even clearer and more obvious explanation? Good Clarindo no doubt was in need of some masses, and his soul flew away as soon as I promised to pay

31 There is no character in the play named 'Clarinda.' Papagayo believes that Clarindo is dead, but he changes his name to the feminine because the word and concept for 'soul' in Spanish are feminine.

que[81] dellas le hice promesa.
Y así vámonos de aquí
y dejemos la contienda,
que ya es hora de comer,
y estamos en casa ajena.
No demos con la demora
a don Álvaro molestia,
que por nosotros aguarda
y yo, bien sabes, que en ausencia
de la hermana y la crïada,
le sirvo de cocinera.[82]
Y para comer los dos
medio mi nombre me cuesta,
porque yo os dispongo la papa
y sólo el gayo me queda,[83]
que éstas hoy de un papagayo
son en la corte las medras.

Lisarda: Vamos, pues, que el corazón
más viva la pena lleva
de la muerte de mi hermano,
porque aquesta mesonera,
tan vivo traslado suyo,
sus memorias me recuerda.

Vanse y salen don Rodrigo y Jacinta.

---

81 The Spanish adverbial phrase *tanto que* means 'so much so' or 'so much that.' *En tanto que* can mean 'as soon as,' which is the sense in this passage. The comparable Portuguese phrase would be *assim que* or *logo que.*

82 Papagayo is playing with gender here. Hipólita served as the *cocinera,* and he has taken her place. He might call himself a *cocinero,* but genders the noun as feminine, again calling attention to the play with physical gender in the text.

83 Papagayo puns on the two halves of his name, *papa* and *gayo*. He has to give up half his name, the *papa* ('potato' or 'bland soup'), to feed Álvaro and Lisarda. He is left with the *gayo,* or its homonym *gallo* (rooster). This may be a reference to the aphorism, 'Iránse los huéspedes, y comeremos el gallo' (The guests will leave, and we will have to eat the rooster). *Autoridades* explains the saying, 'se le dilata, o difiere el castigo que merece a alguno, por atención a los que están presentes, hasta que se vayan' (the punishment that someone deserves is postponed or deferred, out of courtesy to those present, until they leave) (2.14). In this case, to *comer gallo* is a punishment and the *gracioso* complains that he is left with the unpleasant half of his name.

for them. But let's move on and stop squabbling: it's time to eat, and we're far from home. We don't want to annoy Don Álvaro with the delay, since he's waiting for us, and, as you well know, I've been serving him as his cook in the absence of his sister and her maid. So if you're going to eat, it'll cost me half my name, for I'll prepare the *Papa* for you and I'll stick with the *Gayo* for me – those are the perks of being a parrot at Court.[32]

Lisarda: Let's go, then; my heart still carries the vivid pain of my brother's death, because that kitchen maid who looks so much like him brings back memories.

They exit and Don Rodrigo and Jacinta enter.

---

32 Papagayo is complaining that the soup goes to everyone but him and he is left eating rooster, which renders ironic his comment about receiving the perks of being a parrot at Court.

Don Rodrigo: ¿Es posible, Jacinta,
que tanto disimulas
de un amor el cuidado
que de un padre le ocultas?
¿Aquesta la exención
era porque rehúsas
tan constante el estado
que mi elección te inculca?
¿Quién de ti tal pensara?
¿Quién presumiera de una
modestia tan altiva,
como entendí la tuya,
Jacinta, aqueste lance?
Mas pues ya no se excusa
aquello que ha pasado
y tienes la disculpa
en que de amor la fuerza
tal vez viene de alguna
influencia de estrella
o simpatía mucha
que inclina los sujetos,
y así entre ti, sin duda,
y aquel de quien observas
aun memorias difuntas,
lo mismo considero.
No hay aquí que te arguya,
y agora sólo apruebo
la elección que procura
en Álvaro tu suerte,
el cual – pues que así apuras
tu amante desengaño –
la cláusula que apuntas
acepta y pronto está
para que te descubra
quién dio a Clarindo muerte.
La respuesta ésta es suya.

Jacinta: De doncella el recato,
padre y señor, disculpa

Rodrigo: Is it possible, Jacinta, that you'd hide your problems with love to such an extent that you'd conceal them even from your own father? Was the freedom you constantly insisted on merely an excuse to resist my suggestion that you get married? Who would have thought that of you? Who would imagine such a predicament for someone so proudly circumspect, as I understood was true of you, Jacinta? But at this point you can't undo what happened, and you have the excuse that Love's power may come from the influence of the stars that govern their subjects. I consider this true of the situation between you and the man who now only lives in your memories. There's no arguing about it, and now I'll approve only the choice your fate finds in Álvaro, who accepts the condition you placed on marrying him and will soon reveal who killed Clarindo. This is your answer.

Jacinta: My father and lord, a young woman's circumspection

no haberte dado parte
de mi amante fortuna,
y así pues que confiesas
como discreto y juzgas
que es un destino amor
que corazones junta,
no debes extrañar
la afición lisa y pura
que entre dos corazones
plantó de amor la industria.
Clarindo viome y vile
y como se divulgan
por los ojos del pecho
las pasiones ocultas,
ajustados quedamos
y así cada uno jura
de no admitir empleo,
más que el que Amor le apunta.
En la armada le han muerto
y algunas conjeturas
tengo de que don Álvaro
fue de mi suerte obscura
el autor y queriendo
experiencia en mis dudas
hacer, le he puesto, padre,
la condición que apuntas,
que como el sí de esposa
con diligencias muchas
de mí pretende – ha días –
porque el deseo cumpla
– como en nada repara
quien de un deseo busca
el logro – , si él la tiene,
confesará la culpa.

Don Rodrigo: ¡Caso extraño! Y, ¿qué intentas
cuando él no te la encubra
y en sí mesmo te diere
del homicida *inculca*?[84]

84 Here the Portuguese noun *inculca* denotes 'information' or 'indication.'

excuses me for not informing you about my beloved. And now that you're showing discretion by judging that love is a fate that joins hearts together, you shouldn't see anything strange in the plain, pure affection that love's diligence sowed between two hearts. Clarindo saw me and I saw him, and since the heart reveals secret passions through the eyes, we grew closer, with each of us swearing not to let anyone else into our hearts, except for the one whom Love suggests. He was killed in the armada, and I believe that Don Álvaro was the author of my dark fate. Wanting to appease my doubts, father, I gave him the condition you're alluding to. For days, he's been diligently working to get me to agree to be his wife and thereby achieve his desire (for those who seek success in reaching such a goal will do all they can to can to keep things going smoothly). If he's guilty, he'll confess it.

Don Rodrigo: What a strange situation! And what do you intend to do if he doesn't hide it from you and then names himself as the killer?

Jacinta: De mi amor con su muerte
vengar la extraña injuria.
Don Rodrigo: ¡Terrible estás! ¿No miras
que adquieres la censura
de negar tu palabra
– que en nobles no se excusa – ,
hallando en ti por premio
su confesión tal furia?
Jacinta: A palabra cualquiera
no se extraña que huya
un ánimo quejoso.
Don Rodrigo: Y a las sospechas tuyas,
¿si él diere el desengaño
y con claridad pura
muestre que el homicida
otro fue?
Jacinta: Porque acuda
entonces de su hermana
a la causa – si juzga
tu parecer que así
las pasiones se excusan –
le admitiré, con tanto
que a doncella ninguna
haya palabra dado.
Don Rodrigo: ¿Palabra? ¿Y pues tú dudas
sobre el dar su palabra?
Jacinta: A aquesa tu pregunta
en casa tengo yo
quien responda.
Don Rodrigo: ¿Qué lucha
es ésta de embarazos?
¿Y quién?
Jacinta: Esa disputa
ha de ser la postrera,
que primero procuran
mis pretensiones ver
cómo a cumplir se ajusta
la promesa don Álvaro.

Jacinta: His singular insult to my love will be avenged with his death.

Don Rodrigo: You're horrible! Don't you see that you'll be attacked for going back on your word (which is never excused among nobles) and reveal your fury as a prize for his confession?

Jacinta: It's not surprising that such an annoying soul would flee from any word whatsoever.

Don Rodrigo: And as for your suspicions, what if he were to prove that the killer was someone else?

Jacinta: Because he might then turn to his sister's situation (assuming it's still your opinion that love can excuse a great deal), I'll accept him as my suitor as long as he hasn't given his word to marry anyone else.

Don Rodrigo: His word? So you doubt his ability to keep his word?

Jacinta: I have someone right in this house who can answer your question.

Don Rodrigo: What battle of obstacles is this? And who are you talking about?

Jacinta: That fight will have to be left for later; first, I intend to see how Don Álvaro will resolve to keep his promise.

Don Rodrigo: Yo le aviso. ¡Importunas
confusiones, salgamos
de aquesta lid confusa!
¡Salgamos y los cielos
por mis quejas acudan! *(Vanse.)*

Don Rodrigo: I'm going to warn him. Chaotic commotion, let's leave this confusing battle! Let's depart, and may the heavens hear my complaints! *They exit.*

JORNADA TERCERA

[Dentro de la casa de Jacinta.] Salen Jacinta y Clarindo cada uno por su parte, sin verse.

Jacinta: Cuando, tristes memorias,
que apuntando me estáis perdidas glorias...
Clarindo: Cuando, dulces deseos,
que echándome estáis ricos empleos...
Jacinta: ...que apenas convidando,
del corazón la vida van quitando, ...
Clarindo: ...que gustos ofreciendo,
al corazón lisonjas van haciendo, ...
Jacinta: ... ¿tendrán con mis pasiones
vuestras riguridades compasiones?
Clarindo: ... ¿tendrán en mis desvelos
el deseado fin vuestros recelos?
Jacinta: Acabe ya una vida,
que su esperanza toda ve perdida.
Clarindo: El disfraz ya se acabe,
que cuesta mucho a un pecho que amor sabe.
Jacinta: Si a Clarindo he perdido,
poco siento hasta aquí, pues que he vivido.
Clarindo: Si a Jacinta a ver llego,
encubrirme mucho es, que amor es ciego.
Jacinta: Ea, pues, pena impía,
muramos, que ya allá va la vida mía, ...
Clarindo: Industria, pues, celosa,
declarémonos ya, que sois penosa, ...
Jacinta: ...mas tened, que en mi daño
habéis de ver de todo el desengaño.
Clarindo: ...mas dejad, que en la empresa
de Jacinta apuramos la firmeza.
Jacinta: ¡Clara!
Clarindo: ¡Jacinta bella!
Jacinta: ¿Aquí estás?
Clarindo: Aquí estoy, que era querella
del amor, mi señora,

ACT 3

Inside Jacinta's house. Jacinta and Clarindo enter, each from a different direction, without seeing the other.

Jacinta: When, sad memories that signal lost glories, …
Clarindo: When, sweet desires that engage me, …
Jacinta: …that briefly inviting life to enter my heart, then take it away, …
Clarindo: …that offering pleasures flatter the heart, …
Jacinta: …will your cruelty show my passions compassion?
Clarindo: …will your suspicion find its desired goal in my sleepless nights?
Jacinta: Let this life come to an end, for all its hope is lost.
Clarindo: Let the disguise come to an end, for it's too hard on a heart that knows what love is.
Jacinta: Although I've lost Clarindo, I have few regrets because I've truly lived.
Clarindo: If I run into Jacinta, all I need to do is conceal my feelings, for Love is blind.
Jacinta: Come, then, ungodly suffering, let us die, for my life departs, …
Clarindo: Jealous ingenuity, let's declare our love then, for you're distressing, …
Jacinta: …but wait, for in my suffering, you'll see the entire heartbreaking disappointment.
Clarindo: …but stop, for in this matter, we're only encouraging Jacinta's firm resolve.
Jacinta: Clara!
Clarindo: Lovely Jacinta!
Jacinta: You're here?
Clarindo: I am indeed, my lady, for a love complaint has kept me from

dejar de estar contigo en cualquier hora
quien tu casa ha tenido
por puerto contra el hado desabrido,
y por tantos favores,
deben siempre asistirte mis primores.

Jacinta: No favores se indica
lo que mis conveniencias certifica,
que ve el alma, imagina
en ti, lo que ya no ve por mi mohína;[85]
y aun por esto me ordena
tu vista darme gloria cuando pena,
porque del bien pasado
tormento viene a ser ver el traslado,
bien que quien se recrea,
como yo, ya en su pena la desea,
con que por retratarme,
Clara, a Clarindo, puedes recrearme.

Clarindo: Huélgome y juntamente
me pesa de que en mí se represente
su copia, pues tormento
te doy cuando te llego a dar contento.

Jacinta: Y tu tienda, ¿qué la has hecho?[86]

Clarindo: Ya della, mi señora, me he deshecho,
que ya nada vender quiero,
que a comprar sólo aspiro lo que quiero.

Jacinta: ¿Y están acá tus *trastes*?

Clarindo: Sí, que la suerte a mí me dio contrastes.[87]

---

85 In standard syntax, this hyperbaton might read, 'No se indica lo que certifica mis conveniencias favores, que el alma ve, imagina en ti, lo que por mi mohína ya no ve.'

86 This line contains an extra syllable, eight rather than seven.

87 The Portuguese word *trastes* means hoarded 'stuff,' 'junk,' 'gear,' or 'things,' which seems to be the meaning indicated in this passage, and the Portuguese spelling also rhymes with *contrastes*. The Spanish word *trastos* communicates the same idea. Clarindo puns on the sound of the word *contrastes,* which spoken on stage would also sound like *con trastes,* so the cross-dressed lover is either saying that Fate has opposed him in his love pursuits or that fate has tossed him into a pile of his own hoarded stuff. Throughout this exchange between Jacinta and Clarindo about the location of his things, the lovers are talking at cross purposes; Jacinta refers to 'Clara's' belongings, and in the double meaning of Clarindo's replies, he laments the current circumstances of his relationship with Jacinta. This conversation is tied up with Azevedo's exploration of linguistic differences, the slippery borders between

you – you, who has offered her home as a safe port against harsh Fate, and because of the many favors you've bestowed on me, my attention should always be focused on serving you.

Jacinta: What works to my advantage shouldn't be called a favor, for my soul sees, imagines in you, what, to my displeasure, it doesn't see. And even so, the very sight of you also brings me glory in suffering, because I can now see a copy of my long-past torment. As someone whose amusement in her own suffering leads her to desire it, so, Clara, your strong resemblance to Clarindo entertains me.

Clarindo: It would be my pleasure, but at the same time, it weighs on me that I look so much like him, for I'm torturing you when I'm here to make you happy.

Jacinta: And your little shop, what you have done with it?

Clarindo: My lady, I've undone it and destroyed it; I don't want to sell anything anymore, since the only thing I really aspire to do is buy the thing I most love.

Jacinta: Have you brought your things here?

Clarindo: Yes, since Fate has given me the opposite of what I wanted.

Jacinta: Habla en tu lengua, Clara,
porque yo della noticia tengo clara.
Clarindo: De mi dicha la mengua
aun olvidarme ha hecho de mi lengua.
Por eso me he inclinado
a la española.
Jacinta: En breve la has tomado.
Clarindo: La lengua castellana,
que es buena de tomar, es cosa llana,
mas vamos otra vez
a lo que dices dese portugués,
¿que a él soy semejante?
Jacinta: Me parece tenerle aquí delante.
Clarindo: Así es, que ya me decía
mi padre que con él me parecía,
que con él se trataba
y como a un hijo suyo le estimaba,
y aun por eso muy fuerte
sentimiento he tenido de su muerte.
Jacinta: Y dime, ¿nunca – ¡ay triste! –
quién haya sido su homicida oíste?
Clarindo: No, mas puede saberse,
que sin saberse nada llega a hacerse.
Jacinta: Pues yo – aquí me consumo –
has de saber, Clarilla, que presumo
– no sin causa lo digo –
que de las dos hay sólo un enemigo
y que es quien te engañó
el mismo que a Clarindo muerte dio.
Clarindo: No yerras el camino,
que así también, Jacinta, lo imagino.
Jacinta: Que don Álvaro fue
de quien te quejas, Clara, bien se ve,
pues fuera de las señas
que tú de su persona ya me enseñas,
bien se confirma aquesto
con el nombre que dicho me has supuesto,

---

discourse and meaning, and efforts to communicate meaning.

Jacinta: Speak in your native tongue, Clara, for I understand it well.

Clarindo: I've been so unhappy that I've even forgotten my language. That's why I tend to speak Castilian.

Jacinta: You've acquired it quickly.

Clarindo: It's a good thing the Spanish language is easy. But let's return to what you're saying about this Portuguese man – do I really resemble him that much?

Jacinta: It seems as if I have him here in front of me.

Clarindo: It must be him; my father used to tell me that I looked just like him; they socialized with one another and Father valued him as his own son. Because of that I've been greatly affected by his death.

Jacinta: And tell me (oh, I'm so sad!): you've never heard a word about who his murderer might be?

Clarindo: No, but the truth can be discovered, for until we know, nothing can be done about it.

Jacinta: Well, you should know, Clarilla, (this is driving me mad) that I believe (and not without cause) that there's only one enemy for the two of us: the person who tricked you is the same one who murdered Clarindo.

Clarindo: You're headed down the right path, Jacinta; I believe the same thing.

Jacinta: Don Álvaro was the man who insulted you, that's clear, for apart from the description of him you provided, his name

porque, si bien lo advierto,
es 'Urbano de Lago Amado' cierto
y cabal anagrama
de don Álvaro, porque así se llama,
de Gamboa, este hombre,
que las letras contiene de aquel nombre,
que su industria, sin duda,
por engañarse el nombre así se muda.

Clarindo: (No lo fue sino mía,[88] *Aparte*
que este nombre trazó mi fantasía.)
¡Oh, que diste en la treta;
nadie puede quitarte el ser discreta!
Como el nombre lo pinta,
este mismo mi ingrato fue, Jacinta.

Jacinta: Pues que fue de mis daños
el autor, fuera de otros desengaños,
este anillo lo muestra,

Enséñale un anillo.

que a Clarindo – ¡ay de mi suerte siniestra! –
le di de amor por prenda,
que a la mano me vino, porque entienda
que de su infame arrojo
ha sacado esta prenda por despojo.

Clarindo: (Este anillo al partirme *Aparte*
me dio Jacinta que después de herirme
y dejarme el traidor
por muerto, me robó, que fue el rigor
que sentí más severo
por ser prenda del alma que venero.
¿Por qué ardid, por qué arte
vino a dar el anillo en esta parte?
Con él para prendada
ser del traidor, Jacinta mal pagada
dél está,[89] ni él debía

---

88 'Mía' refers to Clarindo's ingenuity (*industria*).

89 In standard Spanish syntax, this hyperbaton might read, 'Para ser prendada del traidor con él, Jacinta está mal pagada de él…'

confirms it. 'Urbano de Lago Amado' is a true and exact anagram of Don Álvaro, for that's his name, Don Álvaro de Gamboa. It contains the very same letters, and his ingenuity in deceiving others with this alias doubtless allows him to shed his old identity.

Clarindo: *Aside.* (That ingenuity was nothing more than my own, for my imagination concocted it.) Oh, you hit on the trick; you're so wise! Since the name defines him, this man was indeed, Jacinta, my egotistical backstabber.

Jacinta: Well, as he was the author of all my injuries, in addition to other deceptions, this ring will also prove it – *She shows him the ring* – for I gave it to Clarindo as a pledge of my love (oh, sinister fate!). It fell into my hands because in his loathsome boldness he stole this promise of my love as his plunder.

Clarindo: *Aside.* (When I left, Jacinta gave me this ring, and after wounding me and leaving me for dead, he robbed me, which hurt me even more, since this token was the pledge of the soul I worship. Through what ruse, by what art did the ring come to be here? If the traitor gave it to her as a love token, Jacinta was badly paid. He must not have done so, for if that

dárselo, porque entonces descubría
su alevosa traición.)
Jacinta: ¿Qué piensas?
Clarindo: Aprobando tu razón
conmigo estoy, que yo,
cuando Urbano de mí se despidió,
le vi con este anillo.
Jacinta: Con eso acabo, pues, ya de inferillo,[90]
bien claro ver se deja
que es un mismo el autor de nuestra queja,
y sólo por tu causa
a mi venganza puedo poner pausa,
que yo bien quisiera darle
la muerte, pero aqueso era quitarle,
Clara, el logro a tu amor.
Clarindo: No por eso suspendas el rigor;
satisface tu agravio,
porque ése viene a ser mi desagravio,
que en tus enojos ya
el desempeño mío todo está,
que yo no busco a este ingrato
por amor, que ofendida sólo trato
con su muerte venganza
tomar de su malévola *esquivança*,
y si dicen que aparta
la *esquivança* el amor, mi amor se encarta[91]
ya en odio y así intenta
con su sangre mi honor lavar su afrenta.
Pero si a quien me ofende
– por ser grata con él que te pretende –
de amor darle la paga
quieres, y desta suerte así se apaga
el enfado que tiene
contra su hermana y él con esto viene

90 In modern Spanish, *inferillo* would be *inferirlo.* In this *pareado, inferillo* rhymes with *anillo.*

91 *Encartar* means to exile someone by affixing a notice in public places (Bluteau 3.86). The sense here is that 'Clara's' love for Álvaro has been banished (turned into hatred).

was the case, his mistake would allow her to discover his treacherous betrayal.

Jacinta: What do you think?

Clarindo: I agree with your reasoning, for when Urbano bade me farewell, I saw him with this ring.

Jacinta: Though I inferred it before, it's now clear that the man behind our suffering is one and the same person. For your sake alone, I'll put my revenge on hold, as I want to kill him, but that, Clara, would keep you from attaining your love.

Clarindo: Don't rein in your cruelty for that reason. Satisfy your grievance, for this will become a way for me to punish him; all I want to do is support you in your anger. I'm not searching for this lowlife because I'm in love; as one he has offended, I'm only trying to avenge his malevolent *esquivança*, his coldness, with his death, since they say that coldness pushes love away. My love has been banished and turned into hatred, and so my honor intends to wash away his affront to it by spilling his blood. But if you want to repay the man who offends me by returning his love (and expressing gratitude to the man who seeks your hand) and thus extinguishing his anger towards his sister, which will let her marry her cousin

– como me has referido
que, Jacinta, tu padre ha presumido –
en dejarla casar
con su primo, me quiero acomodar
con mi injuria excesiva,
y así muera mi ofensa y su amor viva.

Jacinta: Eso no. Dese modo
yo a pagarlo venía entonces todo,
que es, Clara, cosa cierta,
que antes me moriré. ¿Me quieres muerta?
Si yo muriendo al disgusto
acudo de Beatriz, de morir gusto,
mas no desa manera.

Clarindo: Don Álvaro, pues, muera.

Jacinta: Muera.

Clarindo: Muera.

Salen don Rodrigo, doña Beatriz, Hipólita y Dorotea.

Don Rodrigo: Suspended, Beatriz señora,
por vida vuestra el intento,
hasta que de aqueste lance
se tome el último acuerdo.

Doña Beatriz: Del corazón – que adivina –
está temiendo el recelo,
que no consienta mi hermano,
que sea mi esposo Alberto.
Y aunque yo pudiera casarme
sin este consentimiento,
a su gusto quiero tanto
que sin su gusto no quiero.
Y así, pues, que este *abalo*
dispuso el hado siniestro,
y no he de volverme a casa
viendo mi peligro cierto,
que aunque mi hermano conoce
que agravio al honor no he hecho,
honor es escrupuloso
y corre mi vida riesgo.

– as you've told me, Jacinta, your father had assumed – I'll come to terms with my own injury, letting my offense die and her love live.

Jacinta: Absolutely not. I'd be the one paying for everything; that, Clara, is for certain, and before that happens I'll die. Do you want to see me dead? If my dying takes care of Beatriz's troubles, I'm happy to die, but not that way.

Clarindo: Then Don Álvaro must die.

Jacinta: Let him die.

Clarindo: Let him die.

Don Rodrigo, Beatriz, Hipólita, and Dorotea enter.

Don Rodrigo: Beatriz, put a hold on your plan until we've settled the final resolution of this affair.

Doña Beatriz: My heart fears that my brother won't let me marry Alberto. And although I could marry without this consent, I want to please Álvaro so much that if I can't win his support, I don't want to get married at all. So, since malicious Fate ordered this calamity, I can't go home given the danger I'm in. Although my brother knows I haven't done anything to offend his honor, honor is fragile, and my life is at risk. Sir,

¿Qué queréis, señor, que haga
metida en tan grande aprieto?
No quiero enfadaros más.
Voy meterme[92] en un convento.
Adiós, Jacinta, adiós Clara,
Dorotea, adiós. Aquesto
ha de ser, y tú, mis pasos
ven, Hipólita, siguiendo.

Hipólita: Ese parecer no sigo,
que en esta casa experimento[93]
mucho agasajo y no es justo
que della nos ausentemos.

Dorotea: Señora doña Beatriz,
aunque dice allá el proverbio
que el día en que se despide
el huésped es el más bueno
para una casa,[94] en verdad
que hoy por ésta no lo entiendo,
pues le tendremos muy malo
cuando sin usted quedemos.

Jacinta: Así lo confiesa el alma,
porque es un apartamiento
verdugo de corazones
cuando es el amor perfecto.
Y de Beatriz como amiga
tan de veras me confieso,
siento que quedo sin mí
cuando sin ella me quedo.

Doña Beatriz: Decir que sin vos quedáis
más justifica mi afecto,
pues cuando de vos me aparto,
Jacinta, en el alma os llevo.

Clarindo: Bien viene aquí la cuestión

---

92 This sentence is another example of the Portuguese *ir* + infinitive construction. In standard Spanish, the sentence would read, ‘Voy [a] meterme en un convento.’

93 This line contains an extra syllable, nine rather than eight.

94 Several Spanish proverbs or aphorisms refer to house guests. Dorotea may have this one in mind: ‘El huésped dos alegrías da, cuando viene y cuando se va.’

I'm in such deep trouble; what do you want me to do? I don't want to anger you anymore. I'm going to enter a convent. Goodbye, Jacinta; goodbye, Clara; Dorotea, farewell. This has to be; Hipólita, follow me.

Hipólita: I certainly don't agree with your view of things, for I've been well entertained in this house, and it's not fair that we have to leave.

Dorotea: Lady Doña Beatriz, although the old proverb says that the day a guest says goodbye is the best day for a house, I don't understand how it's true today, because things won't be good without you.

Jacinta: That's what my soul confesses, too, because when love is perfect, separation becomes the hangman of hearts. And I confess that I'm such a true friend of Beatriz that I feel as if I'm not myself when I'm not with her.

Doña Beatriz: To say that you're not yourself justifies my affection for you even more. When I leave, Jacinta, I'll carry you with me in my heart.

Clarindo: This raises the question that has long been disputed and has

que se alterca ha mucho tiempo
y en problema se ha quedado
que hasta aquí no se ha resuelto.
Viene a ser que de una ausencia,
¿quién más siente el golpe fiero,
quien se queda o quien se va?

Hipólita: Ea, vaya de conceptos
y a Beatriz divirtamos.

Doña Beatriz: Nunca del mal me divierto.

Don Rodrigo: Entretenedla, muchachas.

Jacinta: Tu parecer sobre esto
di, Clara, pues has tocado
el asunto.

Clarindo: Asunto es viejo,
pero sobre viejo asunto
decir se puede algo nuevo.

Jacinta: Pues, ¿cuál es tu parecer?

Clarindo: El tuyo, señora, espero.

Jacinta: Sólo por oírte a ti
he de decir lo que entiendo.
Quien se queda – a mi sentir –
padece mayor tormento
de ausencia que quien se va.

Clarindo: Yo digo que siente menos.

Jacinta: Yo digo que siente más
y en una octava lo pruebo.

Clarindo: Venga, porque siendo tuya
por maravilla la tengo.

Jacinta: La memoria que deja el bien ausente
es verdugo crüel de un pecho amante,
y el puesto adonde estuvo no consiente
divertirla a quien queda ni un instante,
y si el dolor es fuerza que se aumente,[95]
si fuere la memoria más constante,
quien se queda, no hay duda – así lo siento –
que llega a padecer mayor tormento.

95 In the source text, *augmente.* The infinitive is now spelled *aumentar* in both Spanish and Portuguese, but Bluteau's dictionary spelled it *augmentar* (1.670).

remained unresolved until now. It's this: in an absence, who feels the blow more strongly: the one who stays or the one who leaves?

Hipólita: Come on, enough conceits; let's entertain Beatriz.

Doña Beatriz: I'm never entertained by what's bad or evil.

Don Rodrigo: Girls, amuse her.

Jacinta: Clara, tell us your opinion on this, since you brought up the subject.

Clarindo: It's an old topic, but one can always say something new about old topics.

Jacinta: So, what's your position?

Clarindo: I'm waiting to hear yours, my lady.

Jacinta: I'll say what I believe, then, if only to hear you. I feel that the person who stays behind suffers more torture from absence than the one who leaves.

Clarindo: I say that person suffers less.

Jacinta: I say more, and I'll prove it in a poetic octave.

Clarindo: Show me, because if the poem comes from you, I already consider it a marvel.

Jacinta:
The mem'ry left by a good man gives vent
To cruelly torture his loved one's breast,
And the place that heart lay will not consent,
To please the abandoned one so distressed
And if that horrible pain must augment,
And the mem'ry's constancy were expressed,
The girl left behind – no doubt, for I know –
Will surely suffer the very most woe.

Don Rodrigo: Tiene razón.
Dorotea: Bien ha dicho
mi señora.
Clarindo: Así lo creo,
mas yo la opinión contraria
sigo en aqueste soneto:

La mudanza de amor en la fortuna
es tirano martirio del cuidado
y entonces el martirio es duplicado
si la mudanza fuere más que una.
La suerte a quien se va tanto importuna
que deja el bien y el puesto deseado,
donde el mismo bien suyo se ha quedado
que a quien queda alivio es sin duda alguna.
Apartarme del puesto en que tenía
el bien e irme del bien que más venero,
duplicada mudanza se valía,[96]
pues ausente no vivo con quien quiero
y dejo de asistir donde quería,
con que es de quien se va el mal más fiero.

Doña Beatriz: ¡Buen juicio!
Hipólita: ¡Lindo!
Dorotea: ¡Gallardo!
Don Rodrigo: Discreta es Clara por cierto.
Jacinta: (También con Clarindo Clara *Aparte*
se parece en el ingenio.)

Sale Papagayo.

Papagayo: Buena está la compañía,
y en buenas cuentas el viejo,
que es destas Ave Marías
me parece el Padrenuestro.

96 In the source text, *avalia.* Soufas maintains the source text's spelling in her edition (*Women's Acts,* 119), but *avalia* does not rhyme with *tenía* and *quería*. Doménech places a written accent over the 'i' (*avalía*) (*La margarita*, 291), but in the imperfect tense the third-person singular conjugation of the archaic verb *avaliar* would be *avaliaba. Avaliar* and *valer* (the verb I have chosen) are near-synonyms.

Don Rodrigo: She's right.
Dorotea: My lady has said it well.
Clarindo: I believe it, but I'll offer the opposite opinion in this sonnet:

In the fortunes of love, change is unkind,
a cruel torment of worry and care,
and the torment is doubled then and there
when the change is of more than one kind.
Hostile fate follows the one reassigned:
leaving his love and his home, he'll despair;
all that remains is the good he'll forswear,
which brings relief to the one left behind.
Bidding farewell to the place where I loved
and to all the good, devotion I'd give,
counting as double the changes thereof,
absent, I go not where I loved to live,
nor do I live with the one that I loved;
absent, such suff'ring cannot be outlived.

Doña Beatriz: Great wit!
Hipólita: Beautiful!
Dorotea: How elegant!
Don Rodrigo: Clara is truly intelligent.
Jacinta: *Aside*. (Clarindo resembles Clara in wit, as well.)

Papagayo enters.

Papagayo: The group seems in good spirits, and the old man's in good stead, for he's the Our Father of all these Ave Marías.[33]

33 Papagayo refers to the two most traditional of Catholic prayers, which come from the New Testament (Matt. 6:5–13 and Luke 1:28, 42).

Perdonen haberme entrado
acá sin llamar primero,
porque como soy de casa,
no he hecho reparo en eso.
Don Rodrigo: ¿De casa sois? ¿Qué decís?
Papagayo: Un pájaro soy doméstico,
que Papagayo se llama.
¿Ve usted como soy casero?[97]
Clarindo: (¿Papagayo? ¿cómo aquí?) *[Aparte]*
Jacinta: Este hombre ha perdido el seso.
Dorotea: ¿Qué casta de papagayo
es ésta?
Doña Beatriz: ¿Hubo tal gracejo?
¿Hay tan suelta confianza?
Hipólita: Si es papagayo, esté preso.
Papagayo: ¿Cuál es aquí la señora
doña Beatriz? Que deseo
agradecerla una gracia.
Doña Beatriz: ¿Qué gracia?
Hipólita: El chasco está bueno.
Papagayo: De haber dejado su casa,
y su moza, por respectos
que no importa que se digan,
para que por cocinero
yo sirva agora a su hermano,
porque él y otro caballero
que conmigo allí ha aportado,
comamos.[98]
Doña Beatriz: ¿Y qué hacen ellos
en esa casa?
Papagayo: Acudimos
de una grave riña al pleito
que usted debe de saber,
si es que autora ha sido. El celo
quiso el hombre, pues, pagarnos

97 Azevedo puns on the words *soy de casa* ('I belong to the house' or 'I am part of the family') and *casero* ('domestic' or 'homemade').
98 In the source text, marked as a question.

Excuse me for having entered without first announcing myself, but since I live in this house, I have no qualms about doing so.

Don Rodrigo: This is your house? What are you saying?

Papagayo: I'm a domesticated bird who belongs to this house, and Parrot is my name. Don't you see how that makes me a domestic?

Clarindo: *Aside.* (What's Papagayo doing here?)

Jacinta: This man has lost his senses.

Dorotea: What breed of Parrot is this one?

Doña Beatriz: Was there ever such wit? Isn't he acting a bit familiar in taking such liberties?

Hipólita: If he's a parrot, arrest him.

Papagayo: Which one of you here is the lady Doña Beatriz? I'd like to thank her for a favor.

Doña Beatriz: What favor?

Hipólita: This'll be a good one.

Papagayo: She and her maid leaving this house, for reasons that don't really need mentioning, so now I can serve her brother as cook, and he and the other gentleman who arrived there with me can eat.

Doña Beatriz: And what are the people in that house doing?

Papagayo: Dealing with a serious duel over the dispute that you happen to know all about, since you were behind it. The man wanted

y así nos ofreció luego
su casa, que esto en Lisboa
y para dos forasteros,
como los dos que a un negocio
y de bien poco provecho
a la corte hemos venido,
importa mucho dinero.
Clarindo: ¿Y es buen cocinero, diga?
Papagayo: No será con tanto aseo
como usted.
Clarindo: Deso sé poco.
Papagayo: Yo – si bïen me acuerdo –
la he visto a usted en parte
donde pudiera saberlo.[99]
¿No es mesonera?
Clarindo: (Acordado *Aparte*
se ha del mesón.) Ya no tengo
ese oficio, que aquí vivo.
Papagayo: Muy buena mudanza ha hecho.
Mas volviendo a la cocina
que es mi oficio a que me vuelvo,
con tanto primor lo hago
que al más melindroso enfermo
puedo guisar la comida.
Hipólita: ¿Que es en aquesto tan diestro?
Papagayo: ¡Qué mal me conoce! ¿Sabe
que una cátedra me he opuesto
y no hay en la universidad
quien más entienda los textos?
Hipólita: ¿Y hay también en los estudios
esta escuela?
Papagayo: Antes no vemos
que sin ella estudios haya.
¿No prueban los cocineros?
Pues aquesto de probar
anda siempre en argumentos.
Hipólita: Grandes sujetos habrá.

99 In the source text, marked as a question.

to repay us for our daring by offering to let us stay at his place, which, in Lisbon and for two strangers who've come to court to attend to some business with very few funds, amounts to a lot of money.

Clarindo: And you're a good cook, you say?

Papagayo: I don't have as much garnish as you do.

Clarindo: I don't know much about that.

Papagayo: If I remember well, I've seen you in a place where you'd know all about it. Aren't you a kitchen maid?

Clarindo: *Aside*. (He has indeed remembered the inn.) I don't have that job any more, since I live here.

Papagayo: You've come up in the world. But returning to the kitchen, which is the job I'm returning to, I'm so skillful that I can cook up a meal that'll please the most finicky sick person.

Hipólita: You're that competent?

Papagayo: How little you know of me! Don't you know that I've taken my opposition exams to win a chaired position, and no one in the university understands cookbooks better than I do?

Hipólita: Are there classes on that to study?

Papagayo: There can't be classes without 'em. Don't cooks taste things to examine them and prove if they're good to eat? Well, examining and finding proofs are always a part of many subjects.

Hipólita: They must be important subjects.

Papagayo: Hay sujetos a lo menos
que la corte tiene grandes,
la universidad sujetos.[100]
Hipólita: Mucho deben de saber.
Papagayo: Según tiene el condimento,
es que cada uno sabe
cuál es dulce, cuál es tierno,
cuál es duro, cuál es agrio,
cuál salado, y cuál advierto
con tan poca sal que el hombre
que estuviere más hambriento
no puede tal vez tragarlo.
Dorotea: Gracia tiene el majadero.
Hipólita: ¿Quién hoy por hombre mayor
se tiene allá?
Papagayo: Con exceso
se aventaja San Cristóbal
en la procesión del pueblo;
éste es el mayor de todos.
Y si fuere al más pequeño,
el enano del obispo,
de todos se lleva el premio.
Don Rodrigo: El hombre es entretenido.
Papagayo: A mucha gente entretengo,
como Papagayo soy.
Don Rodrigo: Excusad de *entreternos*[101]
más y decid, ¿qué queréis?
Papagayo: Acabe, porque muriendo
estaba ya por decirlo,
pero nunca a hablar me atrevo,
señor, sin que me pregunten
para parecer discreto.
Mas yo traigo comisión

---

100 Papagayo's remarks in this scene are part of an extended metphor filled with wordplay; for example, he puns on the various meanings of the words *probar* ('to test' and 'to taste') and *sujetos* ('individuals' – as in royal subjects – and 'courses of study').

101 In this passage, the source text includes the Spanish words *entretenido* and *entretengo*, and then the Portuguese word *entreternos*. The Spanish word would be *entretenernos*.

Papagayo: There are subjects that at least in the royal court are considered grandees, [and] university subjects.

Hipólita: The students there must know a lot.

Papagayo: Each one knows, depending on the condiment, what's sweet, what's fresh, what's hard, what's bitter, what's salty, and what has so little salt that the hungriest man in the world can't swallow it.

Dorotea: The idiot has flair.

Hipólita: Who does everyone think is the greatest?

Papagayo: St Christopher has the clear advantage in size according to most people; he's the greatest one of all. And if the honor goes to the littlest guy, the bishop's dwarf would win the prize over everybody else.[34]

Don Rodrigo: The man is entertaining.

Papagayo: I entertain many people since I'm Papagayo, the Parrot.

Don Rodrigo: You're excused from entertaining us anymore. Tell us: what do you want?

Papagayo: I've been dying to tell you, but I never dare speak, sir, without being asked, so as to appear modest. I've been assigned the

34 Papagayo appears not to understand (or, as *graciosos* often do, is playing with) the women's insults, which results in this non sequitur. St Christopher is iconographically represented as a giant. It is possible that Azevedo is also commenting on the connections between art and physicality by comparing the tall saint with the bishop's dwarf, which calls to mind Velázquez's *Las meninas*, among his other paintings of similar subjects. See also Doménech (*La margarita* 296).

para decirlo a los viejos
y no a las mozas.
Don Rodrigo: ¿Conmigo
viene a ser el pleito luego?
Ea, pues, dennos lugar.
Jacinta: Todas, pues, lugar le[s] demos. *(Vanse.)*
Papagayo: Eso sí, porque esta gente
no es mucho para secretos.
Don Rodrigo: Decid, que solos estamos.
Papagayo: Digo, pues, que está dispuesto
don Álvaro de Gamboa
para dar el cumplimiento
a aquello que le ha advertido,
señor, el aviso vuestro,
que os agradece el aviso,
mas que él estaba previendo
la cautela que importaba
observar para este efecto.
Que cuando él tuviera culpa
(sí, la tiene el majadero, *Aparte*
mas no quiere confesarla,
que aunque amigo suyo es el viejo
al fin de Jacinta es padre),
en tal caso del silencio
no saldría porque el logro
suyo no tuviese riesgo.
Y entonces buscara un hombre,
que en la fe de defenderlo,
se confesara el culpado,
que todo lo hace el dinero,
pero que sin este ardid
tiene en casa un caballero
que el autor del caso ha sido,
que con él se ha descubierto
por amistad que se tienen,
el cual se obliga a su ruego
por no hacer a su amor daño,
en presencia del objeto

task of speaking to the older gentlemen and not to the young women.

Don Rodrigo: Then the dispute relates to me? Say, then, give us some room to talk.

Jacinta: Let us women give him space. *They exit.*

Papagayo: Good idea, because these people aren't much for keeping secrets.

Don Rodrigo: Speak, then, now that we're now alone.

Papagayo: What I have to say is that Don Álvaro de Gamboa is willing to do what you've advised, sir, and he thanks you for that advice. He was anticipating the need for caution that should be observed in this situation in case he was guilty (*Aside*. Yes, the fool is guilty, but he doesn't want to confess it; although the old man's his friend, when all is said and done he is Jacinta's father). In that case, he'd keep quiet so he wouldn't risk achieving his goal. And then he might look for a man who, thinking he was helping him, would confess for him, since money takes care of everything. But then, without even having to use this ruse, it turns out that there's a gentleman in his house who's actually the one to blame in the incident, and the gentleman has revealed himself to him because of the friendship they have for one another. This other man feels obligated by his friend's entreaties not to cause further harm to his love, and when he's in the presence

que amante pretende hacer
confesión de lo que ha hecho,
con seguro que le ha dado
de quedar por esto expuesto
a defender su persona
y que aqueste desempeño
le digáis cuándo se hará.

Don Rodrigo: Muy bien. Mañana le espero,
y que me he holgado mucho,
le decid, deste suceso.

Papagayo: Pues con esto, a Dios quedad. *(Vase.)*

Don Rodrigo: Id con Dios. Mucho me hüelgo
que otro, y don Álvaro no,
fuese el matador, que a serlo,
no hay duda que de Jacinta
fuera el aborrecimiento
estorbo de que llegaran
a cumplirse mis deseos
que se fundan en tener
a don Álvaro por yerno.
Pues como Jacinta quiso
bien a Clarindo, sabiendo
que él la muerte le había dado,
le rehusara por dueño.
Pues vi en ella deste agravio
el odio tan manifiesto
y por eso le he avisado
que se encubriese, atendiendo
a ser de Jacinta traza
y experiencia que su intento
hizo con él, sospechosa
de que él a Clarindo ha muerto.
Pero como ha sido otro,
según me avisa, tenemos
la dificultad vencida,
con que solamente veo
por vencer la de haber dado
su palabra a otro sujeto.

of that love object, he intends to confess what he did, even though this will surely leave him exposed and needing to defend himself. He requests that you tell him when this whole thing will take place.

Don Rodrigo: Very well. I'll expect him tomorrow, and tell him that I'm pleased with this outcome.

Papagayo: With that, then, may God keep you. *Papagayo exits.*

Don Rodrigo: Go with God. I'm really pleased that someone else, and not Don Álvaro, was the killer, since if it was him, he'd no doubt be the object of Jacinta's loathing and an obstacle to what I hope to accomplish, which is founded on having Don Álvaro as my son-in-law. Since Jacinta truly loved Clarindo, if she knew that Álvaro had murdered him, she'd reject him as her husband. I saw such manifest hate in her regarding this grievance that I advised him to conceal himself, taking heed of Jacinta's plan and experience, which guide her intentions in this regard, as she suspects that he killed Clarindo. But since I now know that it was someone else, we have the problem all but conquered: all that's keeping us from winning the battle is that she gave her word to marry someone else.

Mas como Jacinta ha dicho
que está de puertas adentro
quien puede servir de embargo
a este logro, yo no siento
quien pueda ser sino Clara,
esta moza que su afecto
por su belleza y su gracia
le robó con tal extremo
que siempre en su compañía
la tiene, pero yo no tengo
por parte esta tan forzosa
que sirva de impedimento
a don Álvaro si está
su amor en Jacinta puesto,
pues siendo mujer común
– porque hasta aquí no sabemos
que sea de calidad – ,[102]
con dote para un convento
acomodarse podrá.
Y juntamente veremos
si se compone la causa
de doña Beatriz y Alberto,
pues que tomé como honrado
ya por mi cuenta este pleito.
Yo, como de Alberto amigo,
mucho en verdad lo deseo
y así en ello he de empeñarme.
Lo demás, hágalo el cielo. *[Vase.]*

Sale Lisarda.

Lisarda: Accidentes tan notables,
sucesos tan peregrinos
como los que me suceden,
¿a quién habrán sucedido?
¡Que venga yo tras mi agravio
y, topando a mi enemigo,
me embargue el amor que tome

102 In the source text, *qualidad.*

Still, Jacinta has said that someone on the inside can put a stop to that, and I don't see who else it could be but Clara, the young girl whose beauty and grace have stolen her feelings to such an extreme that Jacinta always has her by her side. But I don't consider her an inevitable impediment to Don Álvaro if he truly loves Jacinta, since Clara's a commoner – we don't even know if she's a woman of quality. With a dowry she could be quite comfortable in a convent. And at the same time, we'll see if Doña Beatriz and Alberto's cause can be set to rights, since as an honorable person I took on that quarrel on my own. As Alberto's friend, I truly care for him, and so I have to get involved. As for everything else, let Heaven take care of it. *He exits.*

Lisarda enters.

Lisarda: Who else would experience such remarkable and strange coincidences as the ones that are happening to me? Chasing after the wrong done to me, and running into my enemy, who would imagine that Love would stop me from avenging

satisfacción del delito!
¡Y que a pesar de mis celos
lo tengo yo prometido
de hacerme misma el culpado,
porque él logre sus designios!
¡Que en paga desta fineza
por mostrarse grato amigo
de mi persona, y por odio
que tiene a Alberto su primo,
que de mi esposa la mano
don Álvaro haya querido
me dé su hermana, pensando
que soy yo él que me finjo!
¿Vieronse lances más raros?
¿En qué comedia se han visto
más extrañas novedades,
ni enredos más excesivos?
El amor quiera sacarme
ya de aqueste laberinto
de confusiones, que aquesto
hace perder los sentidos.

Quédase [Lisarda] a un lado hablando consigo. Sale don Álvaro.

Don Álvaro: ¿Qué duelos más portentosos,
qué más pasmosos prodigios
por hombre alguno han pasado
que los que pasan conmigo?[103]
¡Que hallase luego mi hermana
doña Beatriz por abrigo
del temor de mis enfados
la casa del dueño mío!
¡Y que por esta ocasión
me llegue a mí don Rodrigo
a ofrecerme de Jacinta
la mano que amante aspiro!
¡Y que este logro que anhelo

103 In the source text, marked as an exclamation.

the crime! And in spite of my jealousy, I've promised to transform myself into the guilty party so he can carry out his plans! To show that he's my grateful friend, and because of the hatred he has for his cousin Alberto, Don Álvaro has offered me his sister's hand in payment for this kindness, thinking I'm who I'm pretending to be! Have you ever seen more unusual difficulties? In what play have you witnessed more unbelievable happenings, or a more unconscionable mess? May Love lead me out of this labyrinth of confusions, for it's enough to make me lose my senses.

She moves to one side, talking to herself. Don Álvaro enters.

Don Álvaro: What more extraordinary suffering, what more amazing wonders have happened to any man other than those that are happening to me?! Due to her fear of my anger, I find my sister Doña Beatriz seeking shelter in my master's house! And as a result, Don Rodrigo is giving me Jacinta's hand – the hand that I've aspired to have as her lover! And

me lo ofrezca por partido
de consentir que mi hermana
dé la mano al que abomino!
¡Que se llegue con mi intento
a conformar el aviso
de don Rodrigo, pues tengo
dispuesto lo que me ha dicho!
Que si me advierte que traza
de Jacinta fue el arbitrio
de poner por condición
porque yo logre sus cariños
declararle quién ha hecho
de Clarindo el homicidio,
que sin este desengaño
no he de ser della admitido,
por ver – como ya sospechas
de que el homicida he sido
tiene – si por tal respecto
homicida me publico,
para en vez de me pagar
lo mucho que la he adquirido,
sabiendo que hice esta muerte,
probar su desdén esquivo.
Lo anteví yo, y al primor
de Lisardo he recorrido,
para que fingiendo ser
el homicida, el camino
me deje franco a mi amor,
pues habiendo yo cumplido
la condición de mostrarle
quien dio la muerte a Clarindo,
viendo su sospecha vana,
ya no puede haber desvío.
¿Quién tal confusión ha visto?
Pero Lisardo aquí está.
Mucho me obliga este amigo;
mucho debo a su amistad.
¿Lisardo?

this result that I've longed for is offered if I consent to my sister giving her hand to the man I loathe. And the way to accomplish my plan is to do what Don Rodrigo advises, for I've done everything else he's told me to do! He tells me that the suggestion of revealing who murdered Clarindo so I can win Jacinta was actually her ruse, and that unless I agree, she'll never let me into her heart.

But, since she already suspects that I'm the murderer, if she sees me announce publicly that I did it, instead of repaying me for everything I've done for her, once she knows I committed this murder, I'll receive nothing but her scornful disdain. I saw it coming, and I've appealed to Lisardo's skill: by pretending to be the murderer, which fulfills the condition of showing Jacinta who killed Clarindo, I'll have a clear path to my love, and when she sees her suspicion proven groundless, there won't be any more detours. Ah, Lisardo's here. This friend binds me to him; I owe a great deal to his friendship. Lisardo?

Lisarda: ¿Qué hay del servicio
vuestro, don Álvaro?
Don Álvaro: Vio,
Lisardo, en vuestro capricho
mi afecto tan empeñado
con vos que sólo pediros
debo que de mí os sirváis.
Y tanto el deseo mío
se mira a vuestra amistad,
Lisardo amigo, rendido
que igualmente, como soy
de Jacinta amante fino,
vuestro amigo soy de veras.
Y aun – dejadme así decirlo –
a dejar de ser Lisardo
– por vida mía os afirmo –
y otra (muy bien lo encarezco) *[Aparte]*
Jacinta fuérades, digo,
que por vuestro amor dejara
a quien ahora me inclino.
Lisarda: ¡Grande extremo de amistad!
¿Y ese imposible vencido,
cuando Jacinta no fuera
(muy bien su amor averiguo) *Aparte*
y fuera otra dama yo,
¿fuera lo mismo?
Don Álvaro: Lo mismo.
Lisarda: (No me suena mal aquesto.) *Aparte*
Grande amistad apercibo
en vos.
Don Álvaro: Y aun por eso quiero,
para *sermos*[104] más que amigos,
que nos hagamos hermanos,
buscando en vos un marido
para Beatriz de mi gusto.

---

104 This is another use of the Portuguese personal infinitive. In Spanish the phrase means, 'para que seamos más que amigos.'

Lisarda: How might I be of service to you, Don Álvaro?

Don Álvaro: Lisardo, my affection towards you just saw in your good humor that all I have to do is ask and I owe you for serving me. And my desire, Lisardo my friend, also sees itself devoted to your friendship in the same way: just as I'm Jacinta's good lover, I am your true friend. And even if you stopped being Lisardo and were another Jacinta, I swear on my life I would leave the woman I love for the sake of your devotion.

Lisarda: *Aside. (*That's the height of friendship!) And if that impossibility was really true and Jacinta wasn't the person you thought she was – although I know her love for you is real – and if I was a woman, would it be the same?

Don Álvaro: The same.

Lisarda: *Aside*. (That doesn't sound bad to me.) I feel great friendship for you.

Don Álvaro: And that's why, to be even more than friends, I'd like us to become brothers. You're my idea of a perfect husband for Beatriz.

Lisarda: Esa honra mucho estimo,
mas eso fuera de Alberto
para el amor caso impío.
Don Álvaro: Si eso es tener presunción
de que hay en el honor limpio
de Beatriz la menor nota,
por el cielo cristalino,
que cuando yo tal pensara,
a ella y al fementido
Alberto hiciera despojos
de mi enojo vengativo.
Lisarda: No lo digo yo por tanto,
porque otra opinión concibo
de las doncellas de sangre,
en que no hay de honor peligros.
Dígolo por no robarle,
señor, el logro debido
al empleo de los dos,
que no puede haber más digno
sujeto de tal ventura
que Alberto.

Sale Papagayo.

Papagayo: Si no me libro
con cuatro vuelos, voló
el dicho Papagüillo.
¡Arre allá[105] con tal encuentro!
Lisarda: ¿Qué fue?
Don Álvaro: ¿Qué te ha sucedido?
Papagayo: No es nada, no. Aquel Alberto
o dïablo, que es tu primo,
con quien, señor, peleabas
cuando a la riña acudimos,
al pasar por esa calle
se llegó a mí, y me dijo:

---

105 The *DRAE* includes *arre allá* as an archaic colloquial interjection, meaning 'manifiesta desprecio o enfado [que] se emplea para rechazar a alguien' (1.195). Bluteau says that *arre* derives from Arabic and is the term used to prod cattle (1.550).

Lisarda: I value that honor a great deal, but it would be terrible for Alberto's cause in courting her.

Don Álvaro: If it were based on even the slightest mark against Beatriz's pure honor, by the crystalline sky, when I even consider such a thing, I'd turn her and that perfidious Alberto into the rubble of my vengeful anger.

Lisarda: I'm not saying that's the case, since I have a different opinion regarding young women of noble blood, in which no dangers are based on questions of honor. I mention it only so as not to rob him, sir, of achieving the success owed to those who work hard for it, for there can't be anyone more worthy of such good fortune than Alberto.

Papagayo enters.

Papagayo: As the old adage says, Papaguillo flew the coop. Be off with you; I need to escape from that damned confrontation!

Lisarda: What was it?

Don Álvaro: What happened to you?

Papagayo: It's nothing. Your cousin Alberto, or devil, the one you were fighting with when we happened upon the duel, came up to me as we passed on the street and asked, 'Aren't you the servant

'¿No sois vos del caballero
que en casa se ha recogido
de don Álvaro crïado?'
Que el propio era, le he dicho.
Y él volvióme, 'pues yo tengo
de su estada presumido
que mi primo con su hermana
quiere casarle, y así os digo
que le digáis que conozca
que Beatriz es dueño mío,
y que no ha de ser su esposa,
porque es mi amor tan altivo
y mis celos tan brïosos
que deste acero a los filos
llegará su vida a ser
de mi enojo sacrificio.
Y para que en la memoria
mejor os quede este aviso,
tomad', y alzando la mano,
cuanto yo no me retiro,
tanto me imprime en el rostro
él sus mandamientos cinco.
Mis narices y mis barbas
libraron de un gran conflicto,
pues sin duda me quedara,
cuando me acertara el tiro,
con una cara más mala
que la que tengo, que afirmo,
según tan mala la tengo,
que harto le he encarecido.[106]

Don Álvaro: ¿Hay término tan bellaco?
¿Viose mayor desatino?
Mirad, Lisardo, por quien
se empeña vuestro capricho,
patrocinando un aleve,
que a no tener tal padrino,
ya hubiera muerto a mis manos,

106 Azevedo puns on the words *cara* (face) and *encarecido* (praised).

of the nobleman who's now living in Don Álvaro's house?' 'I am indeed,' I told him. And he then declared, 'Well, based on Lisardo staying in your house, I assume that my cousin wants to marry that nobleman to Beatriz, and therefore I'm telling you to inform him as follows: 'Beatriz is my beloved and she will not be his wife, because my love is so superior and my jealousy so proud that the sharp edges of this sword will cause his life to be sacrificed to my rage. And so that the memory of this warning stays with you, take that!' And raising his hand, since I'm not backing up, he leaves such an impression on my face that you can see a commandment for each of his five fingers. My nose and my beard then escaped a great struggle, for without a doubt if he had hit the mark, I'd be left with a face even worse than the one I have, which, I avow, is already such a mess that it's hard to praise.

Don Álvaro: Can there be such a scoundrel? Have you ever seen greater folly? Lisardo, look how your crazy notions make you blind to this person; you're supporting someone treacherous, someone I'd kill with my own hands if he didn't already

pues habiendo yo querido
darle la muerte, dos veces
me lo habéis vos impedido.
¿Y quién le dijo al infame
que yo, Lisardo, determino
daros Beatriz por esposa?

Papagayo: (Y lleva muy buen marido.) *Aparte*
Será brujo o hechicero
el bueno del Albertillo.

Lisarda: Donde hay amor siempre hay celos,
y donde hay celos hay juicios,
y así de Beatriz amante,
viendo Alberto como asisto
en vuestra casa, juzgando
que somos grandes amigos,
sin duda por consecuencia
de aquí sacar ha podido
que para mí reserváis
el logro de los cariños
de Beatriz.

Don Álvaro: Bien inferido
lo ha, pero quedaráse
con sus celosos arbitrios
y mi hermana con la suerte
de un esposo tan lucido
como en vos le tengo hallado.

Lisarda: En el alma os gratifico,
don Álvaro, honra tan alta,
mas no quiero ser motivo
de eclipsar inclinaciones,
que eso viene a ser martirio
para Alberto y pesadumbre
para Beatriz, que en su primo
puesto el amor ya tendrá.

Don Álvaro: En esto está el gusto mío,
en que seamos cuñados.

Lisarda: (A grado mayor aspiro.) *Aparte*

have you as his godfather. You've stopped me from killing him twice already. And, Lisardo, who told the villain that I've decided to give you Beatriz as your wife?

Papagayo: *Aside*. (And he'll make a fine husband.) The good Albertillo must be some kind of a sorcerer or enchanter.

Lisarda: Where there's love, there's jealousy, and where there's jealousy, there are judgments. Therefore, because he loves Beatriz, when Alberto sees me in your house and judges us to be great friends, as a consequence he doubtless concludes that you're reserving Beatriz's love for me.

Don Álvaro: You seem to have deduced it, but he can keep his jealous judgments and my sister will have the good luck of gaining a husband as splendid as the person I've found in you.

Lisarda: Don Álvaro, I thank you from the bottom of my soul for this high honor, but I don't want to be the reason for eclipsing their intentions, for that would result in martyrdom for Alberto and sorrow for Beatriz, who has surely already fallen in love with her cousin.

Don Álvaro: It would give me great pleasure if we were brothers-in-law.

Lisarda: *Aside.* (*I* aspire to a higher position.)

Don Álvaro: Que en Beatriz no hay gusto propio;
esto ha de ser pues.
Lisarda: Yo os pido
que elijáis mejor acuerdo.
Don Álvaro: Sólo aqueste acuerdo elijo
y hablemos en otra cosa.
¿Qué te ha dicho don Rodrigo?
Papagayo: Que mañana por ti aguarda
para el desempeño dicho.
Don Álvaro: Bien está. Mañana espero
ver mis intentos cumplidos,
Lisardo, con la palabra
que me habéis dado en fingiros
el que a Clarindo dio muerte.
Papagayo: (Será dos veces fingido.) *Aparte*
Lisarda: (Otros mis intentos son, *Aparte*
y tengo de conseguirlos
esperanza, pues pagado
que está de mí tengo visto,
diciendo que a ser yo dama,
hiciera su amor retiro
de Jacinta para mí;
y con esto más le obligo,
confesándome el culpado,
porque él logre su designio;
y cuando quiera lograrse,
saldré entonces a impedirlo,
diciendo que en casa tiene
otra dama a quien debido
ha su afición que soy yo,
descubriéndome.)
Don Álvaro: Imagino
que estáis, pues suspenso os veo,
ya, Lisardo, arrepentido
de darme aquella palabra.
Lisarda: No me arrepiento, mas miro
el aprieto en que me pongo
por vos, porque conocido

Don Álvaro: Beatriz's pleasure is not an issue; that's how it is.

Lisarda: I'd like to ask you to choose a better agreement.

Don Álvaro: This is the only agreement I choose. Let's talk about something else. What has Don Rodrigo told you?

Papagayo: That tomorrow he'll await you to carry out the terms of the agreement.

Don Álvaro: Excellent. Tomorrow I hope to see my intentions accomplished, Lisardo, with the promise you gave me to pretend to be Clarindo's murderer.

Papagayo: *Aside.* (That's double the pretending.)

Lisarda: *Aside.* (Those aren't my goals, and I have to achieve them, Hope, for when I reveal that I'm a woman and he's repaid, I envision him replacing his love for Jacinta with love for me. I'll tie him to me 'so he can carry out his plan' by confessing that I'm the guilty party. Then, when he wants to put it all into action, I'll put a stop to it, saying that he has another woman in his home to whom he owes his affection and that I'm that woman. Then I reveal myself.)

Don Álvaro: Lisardo, since you're looking so baffled, I can imagine you're sorry you gave me your word.

Lisarda: I'm not sorry, but I see the predicament I've put myself in for

por homicida, me arriesgo
con evidencia al peligro
que amenaza a un delincuente.
Don Álvaro: Entonces a ese conflicto
acudiré yo, mostrando
que soy el que ha delinquido.
Lisarda: Ea, pues, estamos conformes.
Papagayo: No toméis, señores míos,
enfados, que aquí estoy yo
que haré cierto el dicho antiguo
de pagar el inocente
por el que lo ha merecido,[107]
pues que ya sin merecerlo,
quería Alberto conmigo
hacer el proverbio cierto.
Con que, siendo Dios servido,
será otro día mañana,
y pues ya la noche avisos
nos da de horas de cenar,
agora a los dos convido
a que conmigo cenéis,
que pues la comida os guiso,
soy desta casa el patrón.
Vamos, pues.
Don Álvaro: Vamos. El tiro[108]
logrará mi amor mañana. *(Vase.)*
Lisarda: Para mañana remito
de mi afición el avance
o de mi agravio el castigo. *(Vase.)*
Papagayo: No es cosita de cuidado, *[Al público]*
señores, el enredillo.
Ven ustedes a Lisarda
amante de su enemigo

107 A Portuguese proverb states, 'O justo paga pelo pecador.' Spanish has some similar sayings, for example: 'Pagan justos por pecadores' and 'Pagar justo por pecador, no es lo mejor.' In Rojas's *Tragicomedia de Calixto y Melibea,* Celestina reverses the adage, when she tells Melibea 'No paguen justos por pecadores' (Act 4).
108 The *tiro* is the shot of Cupid's arrow.

you, because once I'm known as a murderer, the evidence will mean that I risk the dangers that threaten a criminal.

Don Álvaro: Then I'll reach out in that conflict, showing that I'm the one who committed the crime.

Lisarda: Well, then, we're agreed.

Papagayo: Don't get mad, my lords, but I'm here to prove the old adage about the innocent person paying for what someone else deserves, since without me deserving it, Alberto wanted to prove the proverb with me. Still, God be served, tomorrow's another day, and since tonight we need to eat, I now invite the two of you to dine with me, for since I cook the food, I'm the boss of this house. Come along, then.

Don Álvaro: Let's go. Through the shot of Cupid's arrow, my love will be in reach tomorrow. *He exits.*

Lisarda: I'll postpone my love's progress or my grievance's punishment till tomorrow. *She exits.*

Papagayo: *To the audience*. Ladies and gentlemen, this tangled little love affair is no small thing. You see Lisarda, in love with

y homicida disfrazado,
lisonjeando su apetito,
y de don Álvaro, esposo
de su hermana pretendido.
¿Qué dïablo de poeta
maquinó tantos delirios?
¡Parece cosa de sueño!
¿Han ustedes esto visto?
¿En qué ha de parar aqueste
de confusiones abismo?
Mucho tengo que contar
si désta[109] bien nos salimos.

Vase y sale Alberto.

Alberto: Esperanzas y recelos
en mi corazón *concorren*,[110]
haciendo que titubee
entre amantes confusiones,
recelos de que Beatriz
trueque mis afectos nobles
por otros, que a mi cuidado
ya mis celos me suponen.
Pues de Lisardo mi primo
como amigo se conoce,
que casa y mesa le ha dado.
Tengo bastantes razones
para que celoso infiera
que para esposo le escoge
de Beatriz para vengarse
de mi amor con sus rigores.
Con cuya suerte sin duda
me asisten ya presunciones
– que nunca a un celoso faltan –
de que Beatriz se acomode,

109 *Désta* refers to *confusión*.
110 In the source text, *concurren*. The word means to 'compete' or 'coincide.' The Spanish form *concurren* does not fit the rhyme scheme, but the Portuguese *concorren* does. If Azevedo wrote *concurren* here, it would be the only time she missed a rhyme in the entire play.

her enemy, disguised as a male murderer, delighting in her own desire, and courting Don Álvaro's sister. What the devil kind of dramatic poet plotted so much nonsense? It seems like something from a dream! Have you ever seen such a thing? How will this abyss of confusions end? I'll have a lot to tell if we come out on the other side of this chaos.

He exits and Alberto enters.

Alberto: Hopes and misgivings converge in my heart, making it vacillate between a lover's confusions, misgivings that Beatriz may be exchanging my noble affections for another's, for my jealousy already imagines this concern. Everybody knows that my cousin, as Lisardo's friend, has given him his house and table. I have plenty of jealous reasons to infer that he's chosen him as Beatriz's husband to take revenge on my love with his cruelty. In addition to that misfortune, I suspect (for suspicions are never absent in a jealous man) that Beatriz agrees, since up till now she appears to have

pues quedando de avisarme
de lo que pasa olvidóse
hasta aquí, grande argumento
para que mis celos formen
este concepto. Esperanzas
por otra parte me ponen
de su amor en confïanza,
pues don Rodrigo avisóme
de que me hallase mañana
en su casa, que ocasiones
se ofrecen que puede ser
que a mi amor mucho le importen.
¡No sé lo que aquesto inculca,
ni lo que de aquesto note,
o si alguna buena nueva
me esperara en mis amores!
¿Estará mi primo acaso
ya con mi intento conforme?
Que sí, responde el deseo;
que no, el recelo responde.
¡Oh día, apresura el paso
si vienes porque yo mejore!
¡Vuela, noche, si eres plazo
de que por dicha se logren
mis amorosos cuidados!
¡Llega día, vuela noche! *(Vase.)*

Sale Jacinta.

Jacinta: El plazo, sospechas mías,
de vuestras dudas llegóse,
que presto habemos de ver
del desengaño a las voces
quién el autor fue del daño,
que es bien que mis ojos lloren
sin tasa, que ésta es la deuda
que a mi afición corresponde.
Ea, desengaños míos,
en breve espero que os conste

forgotten to let me know what's going on, which argues for my jealousy. On the other hand, hope gives me faith in her love, because Don Rodrigo suggested that I come to his house tomorrow since events are taking place that may be of great import to my love. I don't know what that indicates, or what to make of it, or if some good news regarding my love is awaiting me! Could my cousin perhaps be satisfied with my plan? Yes, my desire replies; no, my misgivings answer. Oh, daylight, if you're coming so I can soon feel better, please hurry. Fly away, night, if you're what's keeping me from happily attaining my love! Come, day; fly away, night! *He exits.*

Jacinta enters.

Jacinta: My Suspicions, it's time to assuage your doubts, for soon we'll be able to tell from the emotion of everyone's voices the person who was behind all the pain. It's good for my eyes to cry without stopping, for my tears reflect my feelings. Come now, my Disappointment, I'll expect shortly to give

de quien penas a mi pecho
ocasionó tan atroces.
Apercibid la venganza
contra aquel ánimo doble,
que dos vidas ha sacado
de su crueldad con un golpe.
Haced, iras, vuestro ensayo
para el que os espera choque,
sin que mujeril piedad
el desempeño os estorbe.
Mas si don Álvaro está
inocente y a mis dolores
otro fuere quien ha dado
las infaustas ocasiones,
si le he dado la palabra
de agradecerle el informe
con el premio de mi mano,
tiro de sus pretensiones
que es el gusto de mi padre,
para que así se conforme
con permitir que Beatriz
con Alberto se despose,
cuando afuera de Clarindo
aborrezco todo el hombre,
que solamente se inclina
una vez un pecho noble,
obligándome mi padre
a que su elección otorgue
con don Álvaro, ¿qué haré?
¿Sujetarme a los rigores
de casar contra mi gusto?
Eso no, mas que me corten
el cuello con un cuchillo,
mi vida aquí me perdone.

Pónese a un lado hablando a solas. Sale doña Beatriz [también hablando a solas].

you the details of who caused my heart such horrid pain. Note the double revenge against that spirit, whose cruelty has taken two lives with one blow. Anger, take on the one who's expecting your blow, without womanly pity getting in the way. But if Don Álvaro is innocent and someone else is behind my suffering, although I've given my word to thank him for the information with the prize of my hand in marriage, I'll shoot down his intentions, which are my father's pleasure, so he'll let Beatriz marry Alberto. What shall I do with my father forcing me to agree to his choice of Don Álvaro when – aside from Clarindo – I hate all men, for a noble breast falls in love only once? Must I subject myself to the rigors of marriage against my will? Not that; better that they slit my throat with a knife, may my life here forgive me.

She moves to one side, talking to herself. Doña Beatriz enters, also talking to herself in an aside.

Doña Beatriz: (En una balanza puesta *[Aparte]*
llega mi amor a advertir
su esperanza sin saber
lo que ha pesado hasta aquí.
Ya pende para una parte,
ya para otra parte, y así
se queda en duda el cuidado
sin que le pueda medir
el peso. Piensa[111] el deseo
que se inclina para mí,
pero la desconfïanza
no se puede persuadir
a que ella para mí pese,
diciendo que para sí
es que se inclina el pesar.
Miente sin poder mentir.
No miente, porque mi suerte,
como es tan poco feliz,
es fuerza que a mi pesar[112]
el logro me ha de impedir.
Miente que como no espero
bien que me pueda venir,
viene a ser de mi esperanza
todo el pesar para mí.
Pero Jacinta aquí está
y aguarda sin duda aquí
a que le venga mi hermano
poner a sus dudas fin,[113]
que esta es, poco más o menos,
la hora que oí decir
se ajustó para apuntarle
el que llegó a delinquir
en la muerte de su amante,

---

111 In the source text, *piense.*

112 Beatriz puns on two meanings of the word *pesar* ('to weigh' and 'grief' or 'sorrow') and on the phrase *a mi pesar* ('in spite of me').

113 This clause looks like a Portuguese construction; in Spanish a preposition would be added: 'aguarda sin duda aquí a que le venga mi hermano *a* poner a sus dudas fin.'

Doña Beatriz: *Aside.* (Its hope placed on a scales, my love approaches without knowing till now how much it weighs. First the balance hangs down on one side, and then the other, and thus the problem remains in doubt until its weight can be measured. Desire hopes that it's leaning towards me, but Distrust can't be persuaded that I'm the one who tips the scales, saying instead that it's tipping in its own direction, that the weight of sorrow tells lies without being able to lie. It doesn't lie, because my unhappy fate constrains me from attaining my sorrow. It does lie since, as I don't expect that anything good can come to me, my hope turns into my suffering. But Jacinta is here and is no doubt waiting till my brother comes to put an end to her doubts. This is the agreed-upon hour for him to let her know who killed her

que para ella le admitir
por esposo.[114] Aqueste pacto
ha hecho y de aquesta lid
no sé que sepa mi hermano,
mas como pretende al fin
a Jacinta por esposa,
le daría amor ardid
para saber lo que amor
sabe enseñar trazas mil,
para que imposibles llegue
un amante a conseguir.
Pensativa debe estar,
pues no ha llegado a sentir
mis pasos. Yo llego.) Amiga, *[A Jacinta]*
señora, ¿en qué os divertís?

Jacinta: Como es grande mi cuidado
no se puede divertir.

Doña Beatriz: ¿Será del amor pasado?

Jacinta: Cuidado dese amor, sí,
pasado, no, que no pasa
cuando se llega a advertir
fino el amor, que se llega
en las almas a imprimir,
y a mi amor, como carácter,
nunca, Beatriz, le perdí.

Doña Beatriz: Ya con el estado nuevo[115]
se olvidará.

Jacinta: No, Beatriz,
que los primeros cuidados
no se pueden omitir.

Hablan las dos a solas. Don Rodrigo y Alberto al paño.

114 The word *admitir* in this phrase is another use of the Portuguese personal infinitive. In Spanish the phrase means, 'para que ella le admita por esposo.'

115 Beatriz refers to Jacinta's *estado civil* (marital status). She suggests that when Jacinta is married to Álvaro, she will forget Clarindo.

lover, so she can accept him as her husband. She made this pact, and I don't know what my brother knows about the dispute. But, as he's ultimately seeking Jacinta as his wife, Love must give him the cunning to know that it can teach him a thousand skills, so that as a lover, he can accomplish the impossible. She must be absorbed in her thoughts, since she hasn't noticed me. Let me approach.) *To Jacinta.* My lady, my friend, how are you amusing yourself?

Jacinta: Since my worries are many, I can't be amused.

Doña Beatriz: Might those worries concern past love?

Jacinta: Worries about love, yes; past love, no. Love doesn't end when it's remembered; rather it's the kind of love that becomes imprinted on your soul, and the essence of my love, Beatriz, I never lost.

Doña Beatriz: Perhaps when you marry, it'll be forgotten.

Jacinta: No, Beatriz, for first loves can't be set aside.

The two talk quietly to each other. Don Rodrigo and Alberto enter; they are concealed from the other characters by a screen.

Don Rodrigo: No habéis de pasar agora,
señor Alberto, de aquí
hasta ver en lo que para
de aquesta ocasión el fin.
Alberto: Mi obediencia es vuestro gusto;
aquí estoy para cumplir
las disposiciones vuestras.
Don Rodrigo: Entonces podéis salir
cuando os llegue a llamar yo.
Alberto: Bien está.
Don Rodrigo: Jacinta, allí
viene don Álvaro. Aquesto,
hija, te vengo a decir,
para que tú estés de acuerdo.
Y vos, señora Beatriz,
retiraos. No conviene
que agora aquí estéis. Salid
cuando os llegue yo a llamar.
Doña Beatriz: Hago lo que me advertís,
señor mío.

Retírase [Beatriz] a otra parte.

Don Rodrigo: Pues yo llego
a la puerta a recibir
a don Álvaro. Ea, entrad;
la casa es vuestra. Subid,
señor.
Jacinta: Ea, corazón,
ya el plazo quiso venir
de morir o de matar.
El valor apercibid,
o para matar a quien
mi dicha quiso impedir,
dando la muerte a mi bien,
o cuando no sea así,
para morir si mi padre
me obliga a casar a mí
con don Álvaro, que tomo
por más süave el morir.

Don Rodrigo: You mustn't leave here, Alberto, till you see how this situation turns out.

Alberto: Your pleasure is my will; I'm here at your command.

Don Rodrigo: Then you can enter when I call for you.

Alberto: That's fine.

Don Rodrigo: Jacinta, Don Álvaro is arriving. I've come to tell you, daughter, so you'll act accordingly. And you, Beatriz, may leave. It's not good for you to be here. You may return when I call for you.

Doña Beatriz: I'll do as you ask, my lord.

She retires to a different part of the stage.

Don Rodrigo: I'll go to the door to greet Don Álvaro. Enter; my home is yours. Come on upstairs, sir.

Jacinta: Now, my heart, the time has come to die or to kill. Prepare your courage, either to kill the one who destroyed my happiness by killing the love of my life, or if that's not the case, to die if my father forces me to marry Don Álvaro, for I consider death the sweetest option.

Salen don Álvaro, Lisarda y Papagayo con unas ropas debajo de la capa.

Lisarda: ¿Has traído, Papagayo, *[Aparte a Papagayo]*
aquello que te advertí?
Papagayo: El vestido de mujer *[Aparte a Lisarda]*
aquí le traigo.
Lisarda: Servir
me puede; escóndele agora. *[Aparte a Papagayo]*
Don Álvaro: Llegó, señora, el abril
para un deseo, que invierno
ha llegado a presumir
el tïempo en que no ha visto
esa rica flor de lis,
y así agora que la suerte
me llegó la dicha a abrir,
viendo a quien más deseaba,
ya la primavera vi,
que hasta aquí mi amor lloró,
mas ya se puede reír.
Jacinta: Unos ríen y otros lloran,
y en tan contrapuesta lid,
si la risa es para vos,
será el llanto para mí.
Lisarda: (Dama es Jacinta gallarda *Aparte*
y esto me da que sentir,
que hace grande oposición
a mi esperanza.)

Al paño Clarindo.

Clarindo: Advertir *[Aparte]*
de aquí puedo lo que pasa.
Álvaro: Llanto para vos decís.
Eso es enturbiarme el gusto
de veros yo. Despedid
ya, señora, las memorias
de amor pasado y admitid
de mi corazón las veras,
pues ya para os disuadir
de la duda que en vos hay

Don Álvaro, Lisarda, and Papagayo enter (the latter with clothing under his cape).

Lisarda: *Aside to Papagayo.* (Papagayo, did you bring what I asked?)
Papagayo: *Aside to Lisarda.* (I've brought a woman's dress.)
Lisarda: *Aside to Papagayo.* (It will serve me; for now, hide it.)
Don Álvaro: My lady, the April of my desire has arrived, for winter only flirts with the time since we last saw the lovely *fleur de lis*.[35] And now that Fate has arrived to grant me happiness, as I see the one I love most, I have glimpsed springtime, for till this moment my love wept but now it can laugh out loud.
Jacinta: Some laugh and others cry, and in such a conflicting controversy, if you laugh, I'll be the one who's weeping.
Lisarda: *Aside.* (Jacinta is a lovely woman, and I regret that she offers opposition to my hope.)

Clarindo from a side screen.

Clarindo: *Aside.* (I can see what's happening from here.)
Don Álvaro: You say that you're the one who's weeping? That mars the pleasure I had in seeing you. Bid farewell now, my lady, to the memories of past love and welcome the true ones from my heart. To dispel your doubts regarding Clarindo's

35 A springtime flower representing renewal and, by extension, Álvaro's renewed hope for his relationship with Jacinta.

de aquella muerte infeliz
de Clarindo, aqueste hidalgo
quiso conmigo venir,
debajo de la palabra
que de asegurarle di
su persona. Esta fineza
por mí ha querido cumplir,
confesando la verdad
que él, señora, ha sido al fin
el delincuente.

Clarindo: Ah, traidor,
no ha de valerte el ardid
de buscar quien por ti haga
un papel que es tan ruin.
¡Que de Papagayo el amo
por él se llegue a fingir
homicida! ¡Qué hombre es éste
que en tan grande frenesí
ha dado! Grande interés
le pudo a esto *impelir*,[116]
que de un interés la fuerza
a un arrojo tan civil
sólo obligar puede a un hombre.

Jacinta: ¿Vos (mejor talle no vi *Aparte*
de hombre y con Clarindo, ¡ay Dios!,
algo su talle gentil
se parece) el delincuente
habéis sido?

Lisarda: Permitir
lo quiso así mi desgracia,
siendo los dos – ¡ay de mí! –
tan amigos que de hermanos
nos tratábamos.

Jacinta: Decid,
¿qué ocasión os dio?

---

116 The source text uses the Portuguese word *impelir*, necessary to maintain the assonant rhyme in the *romance*. In Spanish the word is *impeler*.

unfortunate death, this nobleman has come with me, under my promise that I'd keep him safe. He intends to repay this kindness by confessing the truth: that he, my lady, is the criminal.

Clarindo: Oh, traitor, you won't be helped by seeking someone to play a part for you in this hoax; it's contemptible that Papagayo's master would pretend to be a murderer! What kind of man would create such chaos! Great personal interest must drive him, for only the power of profit can force a man to act with such daring in public.

Jacinta: *Aside*. (I've never seen a more handsome man, and, oh Lord, he really resembles Clarindo.) *You* were the criminal?

Lisarda: My misfortune willed it; the two of us (oh, Lord!) were such good friends that we treated each other like brothers.

Jacinta: Tell me, what was your motive?

Lisarda: De juego
fue una porfía.
Jacinta: (¿Es así, *Aparte*
presunción mía? Diréis
que no, porque descubrís
en el anillo otra cosa.)

Saca el anillo.

¿Por dónde os llegó a venir *[A Álvaro]*
esta sortija a la mano
que a Dorotea pedí?
Don Álvaro: (¡Oh, que inadvertido anduve, *Aparte*
que he dado sin advertir
de Clarindo a Dorotea
el anillo!) Recibí
de Clarindo aquesta prenda.
Jacinta: ¿Os la ha dado? ¿Qué decís?
Don Álvaro: Me la dio por amistad.
Clarindo: (Ya no puedo más sufrir.) *[Aparte]*

Sale [Clarindo de detrás del paño].

¡Decid que se la robastes![117]
Don Álvaro: (Cielos, ¿qué mujer aquí *Aparte*
desmentir a mí me puede?
¡No sé lo que a discurrir
la imaginación me enseña,
que en aquesta moza vi
a Clarindo retratado!)
¿Quién sois que me desmentís?
Jacinta: Sin duda él es de quien Clara
se queja, a quien descubrir
llegó tal vez por amante
este secreto.
Clarindo: A decir
quien soy, pues no lo sabéis,
ya llego. Aguardad. *(Éntrase.)*
Don Álvaro: ¿Qué oí?

117 In the source text, a statement.

Lisarda: It was a gambling dispute.

Jacinta: *Aside*. (Is that it, my suspicion? You'll say it's not, because the ring reveals something else.) *She takes out the ring and then addresses Álvaro.* How did this ring, which I asked Dorotea to give me, manage to fall into your hands?

Don Álvaro: *Aside*. (Oh, how inattentive I was: without even noticing, I gave Clarindo's ring to Dorotea.) I received this memento from Clarindo.

Jacinta: He gave it to you? What are you saying?

Don Álvaro: He gave it to me out of friendship.

Clarindo: *Aside.* (I can't take any more of this.) *He enters from behind the screen.* Say you stole it!

Don Álvaro: *Aside*. (Heavens, what woman is this who's able to give the lie to everything I say? I don't know what she's revealing or what to think, for I swear I saw a portrait of Clarindo in that girl!) Who are you and why are you contradicting me?

Jacinta: No doubt he's the one Clara's been complaining about, perhaps the lover who came to reveal this secret.

Clarindo: Since you don't know, I'm going to tell all of you who I am. Wait for me. *S/He exits*.

Don Álvaro: What did I just hear?

Jacinta: No os turbéis. Esta doncella
a quien quisisteis mentir,
engañándola, parece
que desto sabe.
Don Álvaro: ¿Yo mentí
a esta dama? Es falsedad.
Jacinta: Falsedad es, señor, sí,
lo de aquel nombre supuesto
con que el engaño cubrís.
Don Álvaro: ¿Qué nombre?
Jacinta: Urbano de Lago
Amado, que incluye en sí
las mismas letras que tiene
vuestro nombre.

Don Álvaro: ¿Yo proferí
tal nombre?
Jacinta: Ella lo dirá
que fue para conferir
la verdad alguna seña,
según de ella lo entendí,
a buscar.
Don Rodrigo: ¿Qué es esto, cielos,
que veo?[118] ¿En qué ha de venir
a parar esto?
Lisarda: ¿No es ésta *[A Papagayo]*
la mesonera que vi
contigo?
Papagayo: La misma es
o algún duende que aquí urdir
nos quiere alguna tramoya.

Sale Dorotea.

Dorotea: Señora, algún frenesí
ha dado sin duda a Clara
que agora la vi vestir
de hombre.

118 In the source text, an exclamation.

Jacinta: Don't get so upset. This young woman you tried to lie to and deceive appears to know all about it.

Don Álvaro: I lied to this lady? That's false.

Jacinta: What is false, sir, is the fabricated name you used to cover up the deception.

Don Álvaro: What name?

Jacinta: Urbano de Lago Amado, which includes the very letters found in your name.

Don Álvaro: I proffered such a name?

Jacinta: She'll tell all about it: what I understood from her was that the name was some sign intended to speak the truth of what she was seeking.

Don Rodrigo: Heavens, what's this I see? How's it all going to end?

Lisarda: *To Papagayo.* Isn't that the kitchen maid I saw you with?

Papagayo: Yes, indeed, or a spirit that wants to weave some intrigue around us.

Dorotea enters.

Dorotea: My lady, a delirium seems to have struck Clara, for I just saw her get dressed as a man.

Jacinta: ¿Qué? ¿Qué es lo que dices?

Dorotea: Que agora con ella di
en su aposento, quitando
el hábito mujeril,
y de hombre tomando el traje;
y ella es la que viene allí.

Sale Clarindo de hombre.

Clarindo: Nadie se admire de verme
en este traje, pensando
que es ajeno, que este es mío,
porque el otro era prestado.
Yo soy Clarindo, que algunos
por muerto hasta aquí juzgaron,
viviendo yo, que hasta aquí
fui muerto disimulado.
Por la maldad de un amigo
– si es amigo aquel que es falso –
de la armada en la ocasión,
que no sólo a saboyanos,
mas a todas las naciones
sirvió de envidioso pasmo,
quedé en la ciudad de Nisa,
herido de su vil mano,
que me quiso dar la muerte,
dejándome atravesado
de dos puñaladas fuertes
una noche por engaño,
obligándome a salir
a coger el aire al campo
sin armas, que su fin todo
era hallarme desarmado.
Después de conversación
que entre los dos de ordinario
se movía sobre ser
yo quien más era estimado
de Jacinta, que hallé en ella

Jacinta: What? What are you saying?

Dorotea: I just ran into her in her room, taking off her women's clothing and putting on a man's garb; and look over there: she's here.

Clarindo enters, dressed as a man.

Clarindo: Don't marvel at seeing me in this clothing, thinking it belongs to someone else, for this is mine and my old clothing was borrowed. I'm Clarindo, who some of you have judged as dead until now; I'm alive, and up to this moment, I was presumed dead. Because of the wicked actions of a friend (if someone who is false can be called a friend), on the occasion of the Armada that served as a source of jealous amazement not only to the Savoyards but to people of all nations, I remained in the city of Nice. One night, I was wounded through deceit by the vile hand that tried to murder me, leaving me pierced by two deep stab wounds, which forced me to leave the city, seeking the country air without my weapons, for his aim was to disarm me. We had been having a conversation we often had about which of us Jacinta esteemed the most, for she had given me a warm and

un amoroso agasajo,
imprudencia de mi amor
– que amor de prudencia es falto –
hacer aquesta jactancia
con quien estaba agraviado
como don Álvaro, pues
siempre fueron despreciados
sus afectos de Jacinta.
Un puñal – ¡quién tal agravio
de un amigo presumiera! –
celoso y crüel sacando,
me lo envainó por el pecho
dos veces, que a resguardado
no estar de un fuerte coleto,
me diera el mortal letargo.
Yo, viendo que por celoso
fue conmigo tan tirano,
disimulándome muerto,
me dejé caer postrado,
por ver si con esta industria
quedaba en el desengaño
don Álvaro de mi muerte,
para que habiendo librado,
después hiciese experiencia
con amoroso cuidado
de la fe de mi Jacinta,
y si don Álvaro acaso
la pretendía o si ella
le admitía, que empeñado
su amante primor me había
de no hacer de otro amor caso,
aunque en la armada muriese.
Sucedió así: que pensando
que me quitara la vida
don Álvaro, que un gallardo
anillo, por hacer prueba
de mi muerte, me ha quitado
del dedo, que consentí,

amorous reception; I showed a lack of prudence regarding my love (for prudent love is indeed lacking) by boasting of it with someone who was as aggrieved as much as Don Álvaro, for his affections towards Jacinta had always been spurned. Jealous and cruel, he pulled out a dagger (who would imagine such an affront from a friend!) and plunged it into my chest two times, and if my breast weren't sheltered by a strong leather jerkin,[36] the blade would have given me my mortal slumber.

When I saw how his jealousy had treated me so harshly, I feigned my death, letting myself fall to the ground to see if it would lead Don Álvaro to think I had died, so that once I freed myself, I could test my Jacinta's faith with loving care. I needed to see if Don Álvaro by chance was courting her or if she was allowing it, when she had pledged not to pay attention to any other love, even though I might die in the Armada. It happened just like that: thinking that he had taken my life, Don Álvaro took an elegant ring from my finger to prove I had died, which I allowed him to do to fake my

---

36 A part of sixteenth- and seventeenth-century male attire, a jerkin was a tight-fitting, sleeveless jacket or vest, usually made of leather.

sabe amor con qué trabajo,
por ser de Jacinta prenda,
mi muerte disimulando.
Fuese y dejóme por muerto,
y yo de un caballero honrado
buscando el abrigo y puesto
en manos de cirujanos,
aunque no eran peligrosas
ni a mí me daban cuidado
las heridas, del coleto
que digo por el resguardo.
Empero[119] con una fiebre
que me sobrevino, he estado
siete meses en un lecho,
mas ya estaba casi sano
cuando la armada a Lisboa
se recogió, y un soldado
que se llamaba Clarindo
como yo, que de un fracaso
de unas heridas murió
en esta sazón, ha dado
motivo a que se tuviese
de mi muerte – pues pensaron
que yo era – aquesta opinión.
Viéndome, pues, mejorado,
me partí para Lisboa
por tierra, adonde buscando
traza para entrar en casa
de Jacinta, haciendo exacto
examen de su fineza,
y probar si en su cuidado
conservaba mis memorias,
fingíme mujer de trato,[120]

119 The *DRAE* includes *empero* as a learned adverb, meaning 'but' or 'nevertheless' (1.811).

120 In Spanish, *trato* refers generally to dealings, negotiations, or treatment, but in Portuguese, Bluteau defines *trato* specifically as business dealings, buying, and selling (8.259).

death; Love knows how hard that was, as it was a token of Jacinta's love.

He left and left me for dead, and I was helped by an honorable nobleman while seeking shelter and placed in the hands of surgeons, although my wounds weren't dangerous and didn't concern me, because of the jerkin that had kept them relatively safe. However, a fever came over me, and I spent seven months in bed. I was almost healthy when the armada bound for Lisbon began to assemble, and a soldier also named Clarindo, who had died of his wounds at that time, confirmed public opinion about my death (since everyone already considered me dead).

Judging my health improved, I left for Lisbon by land, where, seeking a way to enter Jacinta's house, testing her refinement, and proving if she was keeping memories of

yendo a su casa a vender,
que el amor, como es vendado,
sabe vender.[121] Admitida
della fui, suerte que alcanzo,
con la que formé mentira,
diciéndole que un ingrato
galán buscaba que a mí
me había palabra dado
de esposo en nombre supuesto,
que Urbano de Lago Amado
se decía. Y ella advirtiendo
deste nombre, que forjaron
con otras que le di señas,
los ardides de mi agravio
y de mis celos, las letras
de que es el nombre formado
de su amante y mi enemigo.
Como quería casarlo
su padre con ella, a quien
su afecto no era inclinado,
afuera de que sospechas
tenía de que el tirano
me había dado la muerte,
quedarme dejó a su lado
para que a su casamiento
saliese con el embargo
de haberme el honor debido.
Y así, pues, ya que informado
de la constante fineza
de Jacinta – que es milagro
de las finezas tener
de un muerto amante cuidado –
estoy, y presente está
quien con deseo villano
me ha muerto, bien es que pruebe
para ejemplo de los falsos
amigos de aqueste acero
el castigo.

121 Azevedo puns on the words *vendado* (blindfolded) and *vender* (to sell).

me in her care, I pretended to be a female vendor, going to her house to sell things, for Cupid, who contends with his blindfold, knows more than anyone just how he must vend. I was fortunate that she allowed me to enter her home, and that good fortune led me to invent a lie, saying that I was looking for the ungrateful man who had given his word to marry me, but who had used an assumed name, for he called himself Urbano de Lago Amado. And taking note of this name, along with the ruses tied to my grievance and jealousy and other signs I gave her, she saw that the letters forming the name were those of her lover and my enemy. Although she felt no affection for him, her father wanted to marry her to Don Álvaro, and with her suspicions that the tyrant had murdered me, she let me stay at her side so she could escape marriage, since she owed me that honor.

And so, now that I'm here and know of Jacinta's constant devotion (for it's a miracle of devotion to care so much for a dead lover), and the person who murdered me with villainous desire is present, it's time for this steel to confer punishment as an example to false friends. *He draws his sword.*

Saca [Clarindo] la espada.

Lisarda: Aqueste brazo
su reparo sea.

Saca Lisarda la espada.

Clarindo: ¿Quién
sois, que le hacéis reparo?
Lisarda: Con palabra que me deis
de suspender un rato,[122]
os lo diré.
Clarindo: Me suspendo;
decid.
Lisarda: Llega, Papagayo,
al tope de la escalera
conmigo.
Papagayo: (Ya estoy en el caso; *[Aparte a Lisarda]*
quieres mudar de vestido.)

Entra[n]se Papagayo y Lisarda.

Doña Beatriz: (¿Hubo suceso más raro? *[Aparte]*
¿Quién dijera que era Clara
Clarindo y que así mi hermano
se hubiese con él?)
Jacinta: (¿Es sueño *Aparte*
esto, cielos soberanos?
¿Clarindo vive y no muero
de contento? ¡Ea animaos,
corazón! Que si hasta aquí
con el dolor inhumano
de su concebida muerte
pudisteis, más alentaros
habéis menester ahora,
que más arriesga a un desmayo
un gusto que una tristeza.)
Don Álvaro: (¿Esto es cierto o estoy soñando? *Aparte*
No puedo hablar de confuso.)

122 This line lacks one syllable; it contains seven rather than eight.

Lisarda: May my arm come to his defense. *Lisarda draws her sword.*

Clarindo: Who are you to defend him?

Lisarda: If you give me your word to stop dueling for a bit, I'll tell you everything.

Clarindo: I'll stop; tell me.

Lisarda: Papagayo needs to come to the top of the stairs with me.

Papagayo: *Aside to Lisarda.* (I understand the situation; you want to change your clothes.)

Papagayo and Lisarda exit.

Doña Beatriz: *Aside*. (Have you ever seen anything more bizarre? Who would have said that Clara was Clarindo and that my brother had done away with him?)

Jacinta: *Aside*. (Sovereign heavens, is this a dream? Clarindo is alive, and I'm not dying from happiness? Come, my heart, come back to life, for you've been able to keep on beating till now, even with the inhuman pain of his imagined death! But you truly need to take heart now, for more than sadness, pleasure puts you at risk of fainting.)

Don Álvaro: *Aside*. (Is this real or am I dreaming? I'm so confused I can't speak.)

Don Rodrigo: (¿Quién vio caso más extraño?)[123] *[Aparte]*
Clarindo: (Pasmados a todos veo, *[Aparte]*
y no es mucho que pasmados
estén con caso tan nuevo.)

Sale Hipólita.

Hipólita: Señores, ¿hay más encantos, *[Al publico]*
que los que hay en esta casa?
¿Hay más confuso palacio?
¿En qué más metamorfóseos[124]
los dioses se transformaron?
¿Una mujer se hizo hombre
y agora – ¡quién ha pensado
tal cosa! – un hombre mujer
se ha hecho?
Jacinta: ¿Qué es?
Hipólita: Que un hidalgo
que agora de aquí se ha ido
en traje se está mudando
de mujer.
Jacinta: ¿Cómo es aqueso?
Hipólita: Como él viene a declararlo.

Sale[n] Lisarda de mujer y Papagayo.

Papagayo: Plaza, plaza,[125] que aquí viene
vuelto Lisarda Lisardo.
Clarindo: (¡Cielos, mi hermana es aquésta!) *[Aparte]*
Don Álvaro: (¡Lisardo en mujer trocado!) *Aparte*
Alberto: (Si es mujer como parece, *[Aparte]*
mis celos han sido vanos.)
Lisarda: No se admire quien conoce
que suelen efectos varios
una afición y una pena

123 All of the questions between lines 3595–3611 were marked as exclamations in the source text.

124 In the source text, *Methamorfosios*. The *DRAE* defines *metamorfóseos* as an archaic form of *metamorfosis* (2.1364). As Doménech mentions, this is a reference to Ovid's classic book (*La margarita*, 327).

125 Papagayo is using the expression 'haced plaza,' but the *haced* is understood.

Don Rodrigo: *Aside.* (Who has ever seen such a strange situation?)

Clarindo: *Aside.* (Everyone is astounded, and that's not surprising, considering that they're dumbfounded by such a novel situation.)

Hipólita enters.

Hipólita: *To the audience.* Ladies and gentlemen, are there any more magic spells other than those already here in this house? Is there some other palace that's more confusing than this one? In what additional metamorphoses did the gods transform themselves? A woman turned into a man and now (who would have thought such a thing!) a man has become a woman?

Jacinta: What's happening?

Hipólita: A nobleman who up till now has been wearing male clothing is turning into a woman.

Jacinta: How could that be?

Hipólita: It could be just as he's coming to tell us.

Lisarda, dressed as a woman, and Papagayo enter.

Papagayo: Make way, make way! Here comes Lisardo, transformed into Lisarda.

Clarindo: *Aside.* Heavens, it's my sister!

Don Álvaro: *Aside.* Lisardo changed into a woman!

Alberto: *Aside.* If she's a woman, as she appears, all my jealousy was for nothing.

Lisarda: Those who know that affection and heartbreak tend to cause a

causar en un pecho humano
de lo que me ha sucedido
siendo mujer, porque es claro,
siendo más flaco este sexo,
que siempre es más arrojado.
De la imaginada muerte
de Clarindo, que llegando
de mi padre a las orejas,
viéndose de un hijo falto
que por ser único, fue
de su amor tan estimado,
quitóle el dolor la vida,
y con dolor duplicado,
viéndome sola, conmigo
ha podido tanto el bravo
enojo desta desdicha
que no teniendo otro hermano
ni deudo que solicite
desta ofensa el desagravio,
buscando por todo el mundo
de su homicida tirano
noticias, porque ningunas
de quien fuese se alcanzaron,
enojada y resoluta,
mi hacienda y casa dejando
a un vecino que en mi ausencia
tuviese desto cuidado,
en traje de hombre partíme
sola con este crïado
para esta corte por ver
si descubría algún rastro
de mi intento, que en Lamego
ya me habían informado
que un don Álvaro había sido
su camarada, y pensando
que él me daría noticias
del traidor para buscarlo
y darle la muerte, oí,

variety of reactions in the human breast shouldn't be amazed. This has happened to me, a woman, because it's clear that the weaker sex is always the most reckless. When my father heard of Clarindo's supposed death and saw himself without his dear only son, the pain of his loss took his life. With my own pain multiplied by two and seeing myself alone, the fierce anger of this misfortune possessed me so that without another brother or other relative to make amends for this insult, I've traveled the world seeking news of his tyrannical murderer, since no other news had come to light. Angry and resolute, leaving my home and estate to a neighbor who has cared for them in my absence, alone except for this servant, I left wearing male clothing, bound for the Court to see if I could discover any scent of him.

In Lamego they'd told me that a certain Don Álvaro had been Clarindo's friend, and thinking that he might give me news of the traitor so I could seek him out and kill him, when

de don Álvaro llegando
a la puerta, en casa riña
y por su nombre nombrarlo,
y hallando la puerta abierta
me fui tras el nombre entrando,
donde le hallé con un primo
riñendo. Pude apartarlos,
donde quedó de mis bríos
don Álvaro tan pagado,
que su casa me ofreció,
adonde estuve por Lisardo[126]
hasta aquí, y como amor
cuando menos se ha pensado
suele cautivar un pecho,
conmigo ha podido tanto
que en don Álvaro topé
el mismo autor de mi agravio,
pues se descubrió conmigo,
y cuando para matarlo
me impelía la pasión,
la de amor no sólo embargos
me puso, mas aun por él
este arrojo temerario
hice de hacerme homicida,
porque él su amor deseado
con Jacinta, a quien quería,
lograra, porque era pacto
de Jacinta el no admitir
de don Álvaro la mano
sin darle parte primero
del autor de aqueste caso
por confirmar de la muerte
de Clarindo el desengaño,
porque si por homicida
se descubría don Álvaro,
del logro de sus intentos
temía quedar privado,

126 This line contains an extra syllable, nine rather than eight.

I arrived at Don Álvaro's door, I heard a duel being fought inside, and I heard his name called out. Finding the door open, I followed the sound of that name and entered, where I found him dueling with his cousin. I managed to separate them, and my bravery left Don Álvaro so well paid that he offered me his house, where I pretended to be Lisardo until now.

And as Love often captivates one's heart when least expected, it has taken hold of mine. In Don Álvaro I came across the very author of my offense, for he revealed his crime to me, and when passion impelled me to kill him, the passion of love not only stopped me from doing it, but for his sake I even took on this foolhardy act of daring, of making myself the murderer so he could win Jacinta's love, for he loves her deeply. It was Jacinta's condition that she wouldn't agree to marry him until he told her the murderer's name and thereby confirmed the heartbreak of Clarindo's death; if Don Álvaro was revealed as the killer, I was afraid to keep the attainment of his intentions private: it would enrage Jacinta

que a Jacinta enojaría,
viéndole autor de sus daños.
No fue mi intento que al logro
don Álvaro del amado
objeto de sus amores
llegase, que amor avaro
es de aquello que se quiere
sin querer participarlo,
y así sólo para mí
es que a don Álvaro guardo.
Lo hice sólo por fineza,
para más lisonjearlo,
fingiéndome delincuente
por quien sólo es el culpado.
Y cuando llegase a punto
de quererle sus cuidados
premiar Jacinta, tenía
intención yo de estorbarlo,
diciendo que otra mujer
tenía en casa a su lado
que era yo y ponerme entonces
del traje en que agora salgo,
que para aquesta ocasión
lo traía Papagayo.
Y así hermano, pues que vives
y he por tu repecto obrado
este exceso, y pues amor,
por destino o por acaso,
en don Álvaro me quiso
de mi amoroso cuidado
dar el dueño, cuando él quiera
serlo, le perdona.

Don Álvaro: Esclavo
suyo a sus pies me confieso,

Híncase de rodillas.

pidiendo humilde y postrado
perdón de la culpa mía,

to see him as the author of all her pain. It was never my intention that Don Álvaro would succeed in becoming the beloved object of her love, for love is miserly and does not want to share what it wants to keep for itself, and therefore I'm keeping Don Álvaro for myself alone. I did it only to show him my love, to flatter him even more, pretending to be a criminal for the sake of the sole person who's guilty. And when things got to the point that Jacinta wanted to reward his attentions, I had planned to get in the way, saying that he had another woman at his side at home, and that it was me; then I'd put on the clothing I'm wearing now, which Papagayo brought for this occasion.

And so, brother, since you're alive and I've worked out this extravagant plan out of respect for you, due to fate or to chance, Love gave me Don Álvaro as the master of my affections; whenever he decides to accept this role, pardon him.

Don Álvaro: I am your slave and throw myself at your feet. (*He falls to his knees.*) Humble and prostrate, I ask your forgiveness for my

que envidias de amor causaron
en amistad tan estrecha
este arrojo.

Clarindo: Levantaos,
que si amor así lo quiere,
quiero constante mostraros
que soy para vos amigo,
y vos para mí cuñado.

Don Álvaro: Cuñado en mí no tendréis,
mas un verdadero hermano,
pues Lisarda mi señora
me hace tan feliz.

Clarindo: Las manos
os dad, pues.

Don Álvaro: Con el deseo.

Lisarda: Con igual afecto lo hago.

Danse las manos.

Clarindo: Y a vos, Jacinta, querida,
llegó el tiempo de pagaros
el amor que os he debido
con el que os tengo, otorgando
vuestro padre y mi señor
estos deseos.

Don Rodrigo: Mi agrado
y mi gusto apruebo.

Jacinta: Aplaudo
con el alma solamente
mi ventura, pues no alcanzo
con las voces mi contento.

Clarindo: Tuyo soy, mi bien.

Jacinta: Me alabo
de ser tuya.

Danse las manos.

Don Rodrigo: Para ser
este gusto bien logrado,
señor don Álvaro, hacedme

culpability, for envy in love caused this imprudence in what was such a strong friendship.

Clarindo: Stand up, for if Love wants it this way, I want to show you that I am your friend and you are my brother-in-law.

Don Álvaro: You won't have a brother-in-law in me, but a true brother, for my lady Lisarda makes me so happy.

Clarindo: Take each other's hand, then.

Don Álvaro: Gladly.

Lisarda: I'll do so with equal affection.

They each take the other's hand.

Clarindo: And, dear Jacinta, the time has come to pay the love I've owed you with the love I have for you, if your father and my lord grants these desires.

Don Rodrigo: I consent with approval and pleasure.

Jacinta: I can only applaud my good fortune with my soul, since I can't express my happiness in words.

Clarindo: I'm yours, my love.

Jacinta: I'm proud to be yours.

They each take the other's hand.

Don Rodrigo: Don Álvaro, to make this pleasure complete, grant me a

una merced de barato,[127]
pues la suerte me impidió
el haber en vos logrado
el yerno que deseé.

Don Álvaro: Siempre soy vuestro crïado
y en todo he de obedeceros.

Don Rodrigo: Pues salid de aquese cuarto,
señor Alberto. Salid,
señora Beatriz. Tomado
he por mi cuenta este empeño
y vos habéis de otorgarlo.
Este casamiento es mío.

Salen Alberto y Beatriz.

Don Álvaro: En día tan celebrado
no ha de haber ningún disgusto.
Dense en buen[a] hora las manos.

Alberto: La mía es ésta y la vida.

Doña Beatriz: Con ésta, primo, te pago.

Danse las manos.

Papagayo: Agora, pues, de los primos
pasemos a los crïados.
¿Cuál de aquestas dos mozuelas
se aficiona a este lacayo?

Dorotea: Yo no, que con mi señor
he de quedar siempre al lado.

Hipólita: Pues yo sí, que siempre amiga
he sido de papagayos.

Papagayo: Real respuesta, real,
de aquí Portugal te llamo.[128]
Dame esa tu mano y sea
jaula de aquesta mi mano.

---

127 The *DRAE* defines *de barato* as a rarely used adverbial phrase, meaning 'freely' (1.263).

128 The expression 'Papagayo real, para Portugal' or 'Papagaio real, rei de Portugal' comes from Portuguese-language ballads. People sometimes teach the phrase to their pet parrots.

mercy of your own free will, for Fate kept me from having found the son-in-law I desired in you.

Don Álvaro: I will always be your servant and will obey you in every way.

Don Rodrigo: Come on out of that room, then, Alberto. Come, Beatriz. I have taken on this commitment as my responsibility, and you must agree to it. You owe your marriage to me.

Alberto and Beatriz enter.

Don Álvaro: On such a celebrated day as this, there'll be no arguments. Congratulations; take each other's hand.

Alberto: This is my hand and my life.

Doña Beatriz: I repay you, cousin, with this hand.

They each take the other's hand.

Papagayo: Now then: let's move from the cousins to the servants. Which of you two girls likes this lackey?

Dorotea: Not me, for I'll always stay at my master's side.

Hipólita: Well, I do, since I've always been a friend of parrots.

Papagayo: That's a real royal response. I'm calling you 'Royal Portugal' from here on out. Give me your hand and let my hand be its birdcage.

Clarindo: Y aquí tiene fin dichoso
El muerto disimulado.
Papagayo: Tal caso no ha sucedido,
pero como casos raros
suceden, también supongo
que ha sucedido este caso.

LAUS DEO.

Clarindo: And now *Presumed Dead* has its happy ending.

Papagayo: Such an affair didn't really happen, but since strange things do occur, I suppose that this one did, too.

PRAISE BE TO GOD.